DATE DUE	

Sanjo

Evelyn Wilde Mayerson

Sanjo

J. B. Lippincott Company
Philadelphia and New York

U.S. Library of Congress Cataloging in Publication Data

Mayerson, Evelyn Wilde, birth date
Sanjo.

I. Title.
PZ4.M4694San   [PS3563.A9554]   813'.5'4   78-27300
ISBN-0-397-01348-5

To my mother, Charlotte, who knew all about caring

Sanjo

1

School was over for the year. Students and teachers began the long summer vacation that was originally intended to allow farm children in an agrarian society to attend to critical summer chores and that many contemporary teachers consider the only worthwhile feature of their jobs. The children returned to the block, roving back and forth across the streets like swallows rediscovering Capistrano, reclaimed to the neighborhood for a few weeks until their parents sent them off to camp. After their parents spent hours putting name tapes on shorts, shirts, socks, and equipment, they would be led to buses and trains, deposited in the care of counselors not much older than themselves, and sent overnight or by day to camps with Indian names where they would get tan, play ball, get homesick, short-sheet each other's bedding, get stoned, and conduct homosexual and heterosexual experiments. Their parents, relieved of all responsibility for a summer, would use the time to improve their tennis or golf, be grateful for a postcard that asked for more money, and forget about them, confident that they were better off at camp. Now, while their parents were still in the clothes-labeling stage, the children crisscrossed the street with their skateboards and their energy, quick-sketching infrared traceries of heat.

Sanjo sat on the porch steps with her father, Morris, and a

[9]

man who wore yellow slacks, white shoes, and a white belt to match. His name was Ralph and he sold insurance. Although he was a young man by Morris's reckoning, under forty, his chest had already slipped down to his stomach, so that, in his yellow summer slacks and yellow and pale-blue shirt, he looked like a toy of Sanjo's called Toby Tippy with a low center of gravity that threatened to tip over and never did.

"You think I need more insurance?"

Ralph shook his head. "When is enough ever enough?" He often answered questions with questions.

"How much would another fifty cost me?"

"I'll have to give you a ballpark figure. I don't have my rate book with me."

"Just give me an idea, Ralph. I won't hold you to it."

Ralph screwed up his mouth. They all said that and they all did.

"Sanjo, stay on the porch."

Sanjo hauled herself to her feet and waved to Toby Wright, fourteen years old, wearing green and yellow Adidas SL-76 and a T-shirt that said *Mothers of Invention*. A brachial development from jerking two hundred pounds of barbells nightly put his arms and shoulders in a permanent state of flexion so that he held them out like a coat hanger. Toby gave Sanjo comics, mostly old Bugs Bunnies. He walked on the other side of the street with a girl.

Toby was in love with Judy Haskell. At fourteen she was gifted with newfound power. All she had to do was slip off her Maidenform bra and walk downtown with the bra stuffed in the pocket of her jeans. The sight of her unbound breasts under her madras shirt made older men, born under a different dress code, have trouble with their short-term memory. Toby, whose perceptions evolved during an entirely different epoch, did not notice Sanjo. He sprinted from one side of Judy to the other, as if he were spinning a cocoon.

Ralph unscrewed his mouth long enough to twirl his pen in it. "At eight dollars per hundred . . . mmm . . . four–five thousand, probably."

[10]

"Why so much?"

"Morris, you're not a young man. Let's face it, you're seventy-one," explained the agent—patiently, as if the idea never occurred to Morris, and loudly, in case his hearing, like that of so many of his aging clients, was deficient. "You're not a candidate for cheaper rates."

"I'm not running for election. I just want to get a little more insurance. I should have listened to that other fellow. What was his name?"

Ralph hated it when they couldn't remember things. The other fellow was the previous insurance agent, Ralph's predecessor, a statistic of his own actuarial tables and of a thick coating of cholesterol, dead at fifty-seven of advanced coronary disease. He tried to be helpful. "What did it begin with?"

Morris struggled with memory cells that slipped in and out of his grasp like goose-fat wrestlers. It was hard to get one to stay still.

Ralph cupped his hands. "Short name?" It was gone from his head; Morris sighed and gave up the search. Ralph changed the subject. "Look, every year you live decreases your chances."

That did it. Morris stopped and stared at the agent. "My chances for what?"

"Your chances of living."

Now Morris was worried that something was really happening to his mind. Maybe he missed something. He had been making mistakes lately. Not serious ones, but little ones like last week when Florence gave him old clothes to deposit in the Goodwill receptacle and he stuffed them in the ice machine instead. The only reason he found out what he had done was that the concessionaire called to repair a broken ice machine found the clothes. An old library card stuffed in a pair of pants led him to the Bernatskys' front porch, where he deposited the frozen bundle and a bill for $47.00. If his mind was going, it was all over.

"We have to go by the actuarial tables," explained Ralph.

"Actuarial tables don't have my troubles."

"I know, Morris, believe me, I know."

They both looked at Sanjo. She was trying to buckle her sandals. It was hard to slip the metal pin into the hole. Her stubby fingers, the middle one on each hand shorter than the others, wouldn't cooperate, and she struggled to complete the task in spite of them.

"Look, I could arrange for you to borrow on your insurance."

"For what?"

"Well, for liquidity."

"I don't need cash. I got enough to get by on. I need more insurance. What's the next step?"

"Well, we'll have to work something out," Ralph said, although what he meant was he didn't know. With an answer for everything, or at least a question, he had none for this. Trained, schooled, coached, and lectured to, subjected to intense workshops, simulations, and videotaped instruction which prepared him for every contingency and for which he received achievement awards, the agent had no remedy.

"Poppy, help." Sanjo lifted her foot to her father. Using his arms as levers, he raised himself out of his chair with some difficulty, then lowered himself on the step next to his daughter to buckle her sandals. His eyesight was bad and he had to hold her foot out in order to see. After some trial and error, the pin slid home. He tried to stand, but without the catapulting action of the chair arms he had more difficulty getting off the step than he had getting on it. Ralph stood up to help him and almost tipped over; then Poppy sank into his porch chair and sighed a deep expulsion of air that emptied his lungs. He ran his freckled hand over his scalp.

"The doctor says—can you imagine this?" Poppy began to whisper. "He says I should be grateful"—he looked up—"forgive me, God—I should be grateful that she is living toward middle age; they used to die before twenty just a few years ago. I never had a middle age. I went from a young man to an old man. I can't go on forever, and then what's going to happen?"

Ralph still had no answer.

[12]

Poppy looked at Sanjo in the way he looked at a scab on his elbow that never healed. Not in anger, not in annoyance, just in grim acceptance of a condition over which he had no control. When Sanjo was born thirty-four years ago, the doctor took Morris Bernatsky aside in the fathers' waiting room. When the doctor put his arm around his shoulder, Morris knew it was trouble. He told him something about Down's syndrome. Later that night, Morris went to his younger brother, Jerry, who was a druggist and therefore educated. "What does it mean, Jerry?"

"It means mongolian idiot."

Jerry and his wife, Mickey, talked Home. "You owe it to yourself, Morris. You and Florence have a life."

Morris was in agreement. There was an agency that would take such children. Jerry found out about it. Morris went to talk to the administrator, a remarkably understanding woman who looked as if she would rather cradle his head against her bony chest than escort him through the fetid-smelling wards lined with oversized cribs. Everything was set. The only thing they didn't reckon with was Florence. When she heard Home, she screamed and the nurses had to come and close the door.

"You mean put away? Like a dog? Babies you don't put away." Her eyes took on a soft glow.

"You don't understand, Flo. It won't be like other babies." He could not give it a gender. It would be months before he could even say Sandra Joanne. Flo would not listen. At thirty-six, nothing on this earth could have persuaded her to give up her first and only child.

The defense of her baby became a full-time occupation. She even tied a red ribbon on the carriage to ward off the evil eye, though her sister-in-law, Mickey, said it was too late.

Morris went into mourning just as deep and sorrowful as when his parents died. He awakened each morning with a nagging pain that, on full consciousness, turned into a sandbag on his sternum. He couldn't sleep, he didn't care about his custom-built dinettes, and he was constipated, which seemed a final insult since he had been constipated to begin with.

He even wanted to take his own life, but this he never told anyone. The idea bogged down when he couldn't decide on a suitable method. Everything hurt, or took too long, or was dangerous to someone else. The gas-in-the-garage idea was good, but that would probably mean the death of his wife or the family cat, not to mention the child. Actually, he would not have minded killing the cat, an insufferable animal named Bigboy that used its litter pan as home base. Whenever Morris tried to put it out, it would squat over its litter, safe!

He did save pills. It was a sort of precautionary hobby. If he ever decided to go that way, he wanted to be sure to have enough. By his last count he had 1,835, a pharmacological galaxy. As other people counted stamps or coins or glass animals, Morris counted his pills.

Morris's only comfort had been Runi Bindlehouse, unmarried and ten years older than he. Runi had been a socialist in her youth, was one of the organizers of the International Ladies' Garment Workers Union, and believed in unlicensed cohabitation. Until the stroke that left her with a dangling left arm and an aphasia that made her call everything a table, Runi was everything a man could ask for. She wanted nothing, honored him with her flanks, poured him a little tea, and didn't have any children. Now she sometimes called on the telephone on the afternoons Ma went to the hairdresser, which was always Friday. "Table." "Not today, Runi." How do you tell an eighty-one-year-old woman you are not in love with her anymore?

"Excuse me," said Poppy. An enlarged prostate the size of an Idaho potato caused him to urinate with frequency. He could figure on two hours, that was about it, and he regulated his day around convenient toilet stops. Like someone with emphysema who must plan puffing stations in advance—places where he can stop and breathe—Morris Bernatsky planned in advance when and where he would go to the bathroom. "I'll be right back." He went into the house.

The agent looked at Sanjo. "How ya doin', Sanjo? How's my girl?" The agent crossed his legs.

His girl waited and watched. Her eyes blinked like a lizard's.

The agent recrossed his legs and addressed his remarks to a couple of show-off cardinals, reeling in tandem as they marked off their air rights in the summer sky. He couldn't bear to look at Sanjo's face as long as her nose was running. "Atta girl, *Sanjo*." He sounded like a cheerleader. A lot of people sounded like that when they spoke to Sanjo. "You want some gum?" He offered the gum at his side, blindly, confident that she would get it. Sanjo took the gum in her mouth.

"Good gum, huh, Sanjo?"

"Pretty good," said Sanjo. It was one of the rare times she used an adjective, a tribute to this particular combination of gum base, corn syrup, dextrose, and mint.

A dark-blue Volkswagen drove up to the house next door. For a few minutes nothing happened. Then three people got out, a man, a woman, and a little girl. They stood on the sidewalk for a while facing the house and looking like people about to sing the national anthem. The little girl was four years old and her name was Penny. This was her first house. Before, they had lived in an apartment in the city, close to the university where her father was a physics instructor. They bought the house for Penny because they wanted her to be able to go to kindergarten in the suburban school system, although they told their city friends they wanted her to have a place to run. The first thing her mother told her when she got out of the car was not to run.

There was no baby brother or sister, nor would there be for a long while. Penny's parents were into spacing, both personally and in a global sense. They felt a strong responsibility to Malthus and a firm commitment to their obligation to keep the world population and the world supply of food at compatible levels.

Sanjo watched the little girl follow her parents. She had pale blond hair the color of lemon sherbet and she spun up the walk as if she were distributing thistles, as lightly and freely as a dandelion puff. The little girl disappeared into the house.

Sanjo clung to the railing to watch the door, at that moment a spiritual sister to the paleolithic person who discovered fire.

Maybe the little girl would come out again. She walked down the steps.

The insurance man recognized trouble. "Morris." He stood up.

Sanjo went one step at a time. She held on to the rail and paused once to point at the house. "Little girl goes in." Sanjo's words slid into one another and stuck together. The agent could not pull them apart.

"Now wait a minute, listen, your father definitely wants you to stay on the porch. I think you should come back, Sanjo." He pulled out another piece of gum and pointed it at her like a pistol. *Another step.* "Look, Sanjo, gum." *Another step.* "Seriously, he's going to be very annoyed." *Another.* "Please come back!" *Down.* The voice of reason changed in an instant to the wail of a little boy whose mother was leaving him in the dark. "Morris!"

Sanjo planted herself on the sidewalk to begin her vigil, as stolid and immobile as the lamp post on the corner. Children on skateboards, with too much vital business of their own, swirled around her.

The agent bounced down the steps, waving his arms before Sanjo like a praying mantis. Sanjo smiled at him and waved her arms in awkward parody, matching him movement for movement, until, from the waist up, they began to execute a faithful, if not skillful, pas de deux.

"What's the matter, Ralph?" Ma had heard his cries and was at the front door. She sized up the situation instantly. She rolled her eyes, trying to tuck them under her brows, adjusted the collar of her Lane Bryant half-size green-and-pink print, and cleared her throat. "Sanjo, get back up here right away." Sanjo held. She did that from time to time with a surprising resistance that made her parents say, when other parents talked of their children's accomplishments, like medical school, or marriage, or a new baby, "She has a mind of her own, that one." It wasn't much of a trade but at least it put them in the running.

"Little girl there."

"What little girl? Where? What is she talking about?"

Ralph remembered his other calls. "I don't know. She keeps pointing to the house next door."

"Bring her back, would you please?"

He tried to make tactile connection to Sanjo but couldn't. His hands had lost their usefulness. They flopped beside him, hypotonic appendages that had lost their will. It was like the only time he had been with a prostitute. He couldn't touch her either. He had just closed his eyes and pretended he was masturbating.

Ma shook her head. She went down the steps and, with consummate tact born of years of experience, took Sanjo's arm. She said, "The sidewalk's not for you," pivoted, and returned to the safety of the porch while Ralph was still wondering what had happened to his hands.

Poppy, meanwhile, had forgotten that Ralph was waiting for him and was in the locked bathroom, counting his pill collection.

The afternoon sun, especially vigorous even for the end of June, scorched the grass, turned the flowers into seed heads, and baked the sidewalk and the asphalt street, sending shivers of heat to radiate like wires. It was as effective as the threat of nuclear attack. Everyone was off the streets. The grown-ups had gone indoors. The animals had scurried to their hiding places. Insects went into shadows and became shadows themselves, birds left the skies to wait it out on tree branches, dogs crawled under porches to hang out their tongues and perspire with greater efficiency, cats lounged under bushes, and rats and mice skittered into tiny covey places, so secret that not even other rodents knew where they were. Only a pair of vibrating butterflies, so eager to copulate they didn't mind the heat, arched to meet each other on a maple leaf. The sun had even depleted the energies of the children, who retired to swimming pools or to air-conditioned movies, draping their feet over seats and harassing pimply ushers who vowed never to see another movie as long as they lived.

Poppy had gone into his bedroom to take a nap. He was already fast asleep, his belt loosened over his stomach, his head flung back, and his adenoids fanning the air past his pharynx into a staccato rattle. Ma was in the bathroom soaking her degenerating hip sockets in a hot lemon Vitabath tub. If she squinted her eyes and got enough suds going, she could blur the pendulosities and varicosities into the body of a forty-year-old.

Sanjo sat by herself in the dining room. Actually, it was not a room but the base of an L, the place for a dining table, chairs with pagodas on the finials, and a giant red credenza with dragons on the doors. The style of the furniture was once referred to as Chinese Modern.

Sanjo sat at the table bolstered by two cushions. She worked at a felt pad with a pair of blunted scissors, surrounded by strips of newspapers and magazines. Sanjo's tongue was pushed against her nose. Her breathing grew labored, and tiny beads of sweat dotted her forehead. She was looking for pictures of cats. Ever since Bigboy had died of a lingering feline ailment that destroyed his mind and made him run after dogs, she cut out every cat in sight and pinned the pictures on the bulletin board in her room. Sanjo concentrated. It was hard to find cats, and when she did, she had to work very carefully. The newspapers had nothing, but one of the magazines had a cat-food ad showing a white spray-starched and blow-dried Persian that looked as if it were being electrocuted. Sanjo cut around the cat, snipped off an ear and an eye, and wobbled off the cushions to pin it on her board.

The telephone rang. Sanjo was allowed to answer the telephone. It was the doorbell that she couldn't answer by herself, ever since she let in the Jehovah's Witness while Ma was in the basement doing the laundry. He had stayed an hour, a clean-cut young man in a jacket and tie, who asked nothing of Sanjo except that she listen to his stories of the Apocalypse to come, of life cleansing, and of revelations. They were good stories, and Sanjo was a willing and polite listener. She didn't say a word. The Jehovah's Witness had some like this, people who quickly saw the light and heard the word in a divine rush of understanding. He gave her a copy of *Watchtower*. When Ma came upstairs, he was sitting on the couch, his jacket off, his tie loosened, explaining to a rapt and smiling Sanjo, who was putting cat pictures in her suitcase, that they were gathering in the Arizona desert the next month to await the coming. Ma came into the living room at the precise moment he was describing the buses that would take them there. She threw him out and tossed the *Watchtower* after him. "And don't come back here again with your *mishegas.*" Sanjo wished she could go to the desert too. Although she didn't know what it was, it sounded nice and she liked bus rides. She cried after he left and Poppy had to go out for chocolate-swirl ice cream. It was the only thing that would stop her deep, choking sobs.

The telephone rang for the fourth time. Sanjo picked it up. "Hullo." She listened. "Table, table, table," she answered.

The voice on the other end grew louder and more shrill. "Table, table!"

"Table, table," replied Sanjo.

The voice on the other end added a new note of despair. "Table." The line went dead. Sanjo recognized the voice. It belonged to a nice lady she met on the street with Poppy named Runi. The lady always gave her candy.

Sanjo went to the dining table to cut out more cats. She couldn't find any. She decided to look out the window to see if the little girl came out. A mail truck went slowly past the house. Sanjo could see it from the window. She tried to be quiet and not wake Poppy. It was hard to do. She lumbered quietly out the front door, her tongue teasing her cracked lips with moisture which would only make them crack more, and made her way slowly and carefully down the steps. The postal truck backed up.

Mr. Niemeyer was the postman. He had a son in the army and he had a kind round face with pale pink lips and cheeks and light blue eyes. He often mopped his face with a handkerchief and sometimes put extra stamps on packages and letters that didn't have enough postage. He liked the people he served and he liked his job. He really believed that his duty was to deliver mail, no matter what, and once he even drove his truck with a strangulating hernia. The only house he wouldn't serve was the Ryans' and that was only because their dog, a Yorkshire terrier named Skippy, had bitten him on the leg. The Ryans had to go to the post office to get their mail, and Mrs. Ryan had to buy Mr. Niemeyer a new pair of pants for $32.50. Mr. Niemeyer refused to give them a second chance. That was his policy. A dog would never get another opportunity to bite him.

Mr. Niemeyer crooked his finger and parked his truck in the heavily shrubbed driveway of the Stebbins house. The Stebbinses had gone away for the summer and their untrimmed bushes sprouted crazily. "Sanjo, I got a special delivery for you." Sanjo made her way to the truck. She loved special delivery. He had to help her on by pulling one arm. Sanjo made it into the truck after banging her shins on the step. "Good girl, Sanjo. Wanta make a special delivery?" Sanjo nodded. Mr. Niemeyer cast a practiced look about the neighborhood. In the back of the truck were boxes of mail that had incorrect addresses or no zip codes. Mr. Niemeyer considered them fair game. Alongside them were stamp pads. Sanjo crawled over the packages. She knew exactly what to do. She had done this many times before. She took a stamp pad in her hand and began to stamp the packages. ADDRESS UNKNOWN. RETURN TO SENDER. INCOMPLETE POSTAGE.

Mr. Niemeyer cast another look around and, confident that she was out of the line of sight and that no one had seen her getting into the truck, bent down and hooked his thumbs into the elastic of her pants. "That's a girl, Sanjo. Stay just like that. Want another stamp?"

No. Sanjo was fine. SPECIAL DELIVERY. AIR MAIL.

Mr. Niemeyer tried again, this time with success. He held on to Sanjo's hips and made a few thrusts through the blue serge pants that Mrs. Ryan had bought. When he was finished, he pulled her pants up for her, since he knew she had trouble doing that for herself, and straightened out his own. "Here's a letter, Sanjo. Take it to your mother . . . Oh." An afterthought. "Here's an Almond Joy for you. I couldn't get a Hershey." Mr. Niemeyer was very good to Sanjo. He never hurt her, talked nice to her, always made sure she was properly dressed when she left the truck, gave her candy, and sometimes, like today, gave her a letter.

Sanjo waved at the mail truck and started walking home. Somewhere someone was using a saw. It sounded asthmatic. Mr. Niemeyer backed his truck out of the Stebbinses' driveway, glanced around, and sped away. Skippy snarled. Mrs. Ryan would remark to her husband that night that Skippy always seemed to know when Mr. Niemeyer's truck was around.

The saw was at the Cervitanos'. Spig Cervitano was slicing down an old tree trunk as neatly and easily as a salami. Two of his three brothers, Sally and Bruno, were advising their mother on her lawn, pointing excitedly to the bright green glass ball and the yellow plaster duck and ducklings nestled in the grass.

Descendants of Etruscans, cross-pollinated by Huns and Ghibellines, with eyelids tinged as blue-black as their hair, the Cervitano brothers numbered among those men who, in the opinion of women, were the most handsome on earth. They knew this, of course, but were charming and unassuming in the face of it. They lived within blocks with their own families but always spent time on the weekend with their mother. It was not that they did not love their wives. They were devoted family men. It was just that the pull to their mother was too strong. It had nothing to do with Oedipus, an idea of the Greeks long before Freud got hold of it. It had to do with an environment that produced a maternal adulation.

The only reason Richard was not there with his brothers was that one of his most important clients, the garbage collectors' union, was threatening a walkout in the face of an injunction which the city filed for and obtained only hours ago. He was at this moment trying to convince an enraged assemblage that dumping additional garbage in the city streets was not in their best interest.

"Ma, no more stuff on the lawn. You have enough."

"I didn't ask you, Salvatore. I expressed the wish to have a rock garden." She was a tiny woman with the face of a valentine. In her youth she had been exquisite; even with a mustache, everyone had said she looked like Merle Oberon. Today she looked like any other aging madonna. When she married, her husband's people, of stout Calabrian stock, despaired. No child would ever navigate with success that narrow pelvic girdle. She fooled everyone and had, with ease, four.

Bruno, at twenty-eight, was the baby. "Sally's right. There just isn't enough room. Why not the backyard? You've got plenty of room in the backyard."

Mrs. Cervitano clucked her tongue. It was a conditioned response. Her attention had been diverted to the sight of a sweating Sanjo. Mrs. Cervitano hugged Sanjo whenever she saw her, called her *poveridra,* gave her cannoli to eat, and let her pet the ducklings. Unlike the other women on the block, she never discussed her own four handsome grown sons in business for themselves with Sanjo's mother.

"Where have you been, *poveridra?*" She did not wait for an answer. She took her hand and passed it over Sanjo's broad forehead to wipe away the perspiration. "Sanjo, what's the matter? You want a drink of lemonade? Nice and cold." The question was rhetorical. Mrs. Cervitano even knew what glass she would pour it in.

Sally Cervitano smiled at Sanjo. The irises and pupils of his eyes were indistinguishable, giving them, through their fusion, the quality of pansies. "Hello, Sanjo."

They were the same age. Mrs. Cervitano and Ma had pushed the two of them side by side in identical blue sailcloth strollers around the block over and over again as if they were winding a bobbin. The development of their speech separated the babies forever. Sally talked at fourteen months. His first word had been *mama* and his second was *'noli.* Sanjo didn't speak until four and no one knew for sure what her first word had been. There was a lot of speculation, the biggest odds being given to *cat.*

Although he had studied Mendel and his peas in school, Sally didn't know exactly what made people like Sanjo come to be. His mother said it was because she got hit in the head with a swing when she was two, but Sally had his doubts. He was just grateful that a benevolent God had spared his five children.

"Sally pretty." Sanjo laid her head on his chest, a repository for countless women who had said the same thing, although perhaps in other words. She rubbed his back. Sally suffered this affection with grace. He was used to women making a fuss over him.

"Come in for lemonade." Mrs. Cervitano turned a heart-shaped face to her sons. "Dig."

The interior of the Cervitano house smelled like a sacristy and looked like one. The dark mahogany furnishings, covered in plums and deep greens, were protected by plastic jackets that promised to preserve them with the same fidelity with which Amenhotep was preserved in Thebes. All available wall space had been converted into built-ins. Before he died, there was not an evening Mr. Cervitano did not spend hammering and planing the wood he shaped into places to put things. While he was a highly skilled carpenter, although he was never admitted into the union, he actually earned his living as the foreman of a road gang. Whenever she passed his photograph, which stood on one of his own shelves, Mrs. Cervitano sighed.

The lemonade had little seeds floating with the pulp. Sanjo poked at the seeds with her fingers and managed to get one out before she tipped the glass back and drank in long, satisfying gulps while Mrs. Cervitano watched for signs of choking. Although it burned her lips and tongue, it soothed her throat. Mrs. Cervitano wiped her mouth with a napkin. Sanjo was offended. "Sanjo do that."

"Little sweetheart, tell your mama I said hello."

Sanjo walked by herself the distance of the next two houses. Her leg was wet and she wiped it with the envelope. A few feet away, a squirrel was holding a hazelnut in his paws. He looked like the squirrel hero of an animated movie that Poppy took her to two weeks ago when Ma went to have her hair done. The squirrel talked and his name was Poco. Through his friendship with a little boy, he saved a city from the destruction of an earthquake. Poppy watched until the part when the first subterranean rumble alerted all the animals and then fell asleep. He didn't have to worry about Sanjo. Although her attention span was limited, she was not restless like the children and did not have to run up and down the aisles for candy or water, although she did have to go to the bathroom once. Poppy did, too.

The squirrel seemed to be offering a present. His breakneck metabolism caused him to make movements with the nut so rapid they sometimes blurred. Sanjo stopped and turned in a slow pivot. "Poco." The wall-eyed squirrel, first making some furtive and hesitant movements, slipped a tooth expertly into the preformed groove of the nut and cracked it. He looked up at Sanjo, alert for signs of trouble, and continued his deft and hasty maneuvers, which consisted of stripping away the shell, daintily stuffing his mouth, and discarding what he considered inappropriate. The coordination of these actions required concentration and precision, both qualities which were the squirrel's for the asking. "Come here." Sanjo plodded over to the squirrel. He looked from side to side, decided on his escape route, and scampered up a pine tree. Sanjo went to the base of the tree and shouted up. "Come down, Poco!" The squirrel, with all the evidence of trouble he needed, was now ready for his final feat. With body flat, legs spread as wide as possible, and fluffy tail bushed to catch the uprushing air, he launched himself into midair, made connection with the neighboring pine, and vanished into limbs and needles. "Hey," said Sanjo. "Why you go away?" Patchwork sunlight filtered through the treetops. Her neck began to hurt. She waited. There was no answer.

The house next door had been newly painted, although it was a botched job, done in haste by the previous owners eager to sell. The wall behind the missing black shutters was simply painted black, a *trompe l'oeil* effect, visible only on close inspection. Although Sanjo's head was down, she saw them right away. The

[24]

little girl's mother, a serious young woman in rimless glasses with a grim and determined expression that would prevent anyone from ever telling her a joke, was hurrying down her walk. Behind her skipped the little girl, spinning out her thistles. Sanjo stood still, envelope in one hand, Almond Joy in the other. The little girl's mother saw Sanjo right away. She was a social worker and, having had some experience with birth anomalies, understood everything there was to know about Sanjo the minute she saw her. She also was imbued with ideas of social consciousness, born one night ten years before when, as one of four dozen college students who had camped overnight in the provost's office, she had made violent love under the provost's kneehole desk with a Weatherman. Ever since then she felt an obligation to like and respect everyone, no matter what.

Sanjo walked up to the little girl, who stopped at the sight of the smiling fat lady with the squinty eyes. She put out a stubby hand and touched the child's hair. "Hullo." Both of them had milk-white skin, but Sanjo's was peeling. The little girl pushed away Sanjo's hand.

"Don't." Her mother was quick to intercede. "Penny, this must be our new neighbor," which statement was prejudicial since Sanjo could have been the Avon lady. She smiled and offered her hand to Sanjo's truncated fingers. "I'm Lillian Lowen, and this is Penny." Sanjo dropped the candy bar and grabbed the hand, shaking it as if she were priming a pump, smiling all the while. Lillian Lowen's eyelids and brow retracted to display a widened sclera, a look reminiscent of the train porter in movies of the thirties who says, "Feet, get moving." She eased her hand from Sanjo's grip, put it on Penny's shoulder, and pushed her forward, a hostage to social consciousness.

The little girl unconsciously sized Sanjo up, an activity she was learning to do to all human beings she encountered. The person before her was as tall as a grown-up but was not one herself. Something set her apart, probably the fact that she did not bend over Penny and act silly. In fact, this person said nothing at all about her but just stared. Penny made a summary decision.

"How old are you?" asked Penny. "I'm this many." She held up four fingers.

Sanjo wasn't sure. She offered the next best thing. "Sanjo." Lillian Lowen swung around for the source of this unexpected sound, seemingly pitched from the belly of a three-hundred-pound basso-profundo acromegalic.

"That's not how old you are, that's your name. How old are you? How many?" Penny showed her fingers, spread them out like a fan, and wiggled them.

Sanjo held up her fingers, the end ones curved, and, just like Penny, wiggled them, too.

Lillian Lowen knew how to rescue. "Where do you live?" she asked. Sanjo stabbed a finger in the direction of her house, which was next door. "Poppy and Ma home." She reached out to touch Penny's hair again.

"Don't," protested the little girl as she swung her head free. "I don't like that."

"Please don't touch her head, Sanjo. Penny doesn't like her head touched."

"Put your tongue back in your mouth," said Penny. Sanjo tried to push her tongue in with a forefinger but stabbed her gums instead. They bled.

Lillian Lowen interceded again. "We have to leave now, Sanjo, but when we come back we would like it if you came over to our house." They slipped into the blue Volkswagen and were gone. Sanjo watched them go and then, when the car turned the corner, walked across the grass to her own house. The squirrel, which had been watching all the while, darted across the walk, snatched up the fallen candy bar, and raced back to the safety of the trees.

Sanjo lugged herself up the steps, one at a time. When she got to the top, she turned around for one last look, but the car was still gone. She opened the screen door and went inside.

Ma's face was covered with an avocado pack that tightened her folds, pouches, and lines into a slick and shining facade, a heroic testimonial to the astringent quality of the preparation.

Her mouth was stretched by the mask into the smile of someone who died in her sleep. "What have you got in your hand?" she asked, although what came out was "at ah u ot in ur an?"

They had been with each other a long time and Sanjo understood. She handed the letter over. "Special 'livery." Ma took the letter and went into the kitchen to get her glasses. Sanjo followed.

When Ma first became presbyopic, she took the news hard. That was because she had lost most of her upper teeth and was forced to wear partial dentures that slipped whenever she said "sister." Believing that the world was ordered on a principle of fairness, she figured that she had paid her dues to old age by having to keep some of her teeth in a glass. The loss of her sight first came to her attention when the print in the telephone book began to get ridiculously small. She mentioned that to Poppy, who laughed and said her eyes were going bad. At first she outright refused to wear glasses. She still had many options left. These included standing farther away from things or holding them out at a distance. When this began to fail, she stopped reading. She got her information from the radio and from television and from Mrs. Cervitano. She was further able to compensate by memorizing menus at her favored restaurants, and that worked for a while, but when she got into her sixties, she began to forget what she had memorized. Finally, she went to the eye doctor and wound up with pearlized harlequins which she wore around her neck on a chain.

"What is this? This isn't Special Delivery. And what's this on the envelope?" She pulled open the envelope and studied the contents. Sanjo hugged her. "I don't believe this." Ma walked into the bedroom, Sanjo still draped around her waist like a sarong. "Morris, wake up and read this."

Poppy roused himself slowly. He was not an efficient riser. He groaned and stretched. "What?" It took a while.

"This invitation. Listen, it's from a group called the Handy-Caps. They're having a party the week after next."

Poppy was still calling his senses to attention, trying to turn himself on organ by organ like a series of electric lights. His reticular activating system, responsible for rousing him into consciousness, was ill inclined to do so. "What party?"

"Poppy," said Sanjo. She began to snore in perfect imitation. Her enlarged adenoids helped.

"A get-together for Sanjo," Ma replied.

"Sanjo and who?"

"Sanjo and people who are disabled."

"What have they got to get together for?" Poppy remembered his pants were open.

"What does anybody get together for?"

"You talk crazy," Poppy said. "Other people go to talk, shoot the breeze a little, fool around. Where did they get her name?"

"Well, apparently this is a new group. All the people who used to go to the special school."

Poppy remembered the special school. Sanjo went there for seven years. In that time she learned how to tie her laces, go to the toilet by herself, feed herself, put Kotex on a belt (forget Tampax), have three meals a day and lots of water, wear clothes, know several colors, say her address (if you listened closely), leave a building on fire (run and yell), cross the street (turn your head both ways), and love a teacher called Miss Furlowe, who single-handedly did it all, beyond reason. The special school had been incorporated into the township's school system only during Sanjo's last two years as a student. For the first five years it cost Poppy $2,000 yearly. It was a sizable hunk out of his income, but he managed. The township did not see its duty clear until the parents, led by Joey Binko's father, with Richard Cervitano as attorney, brought a class-action suit against the school board.

Before the parents resorted to legal remedy, the school board first deferred, then tabled the matter. It said it needed time to consider the motion because of the impending teachers' strike. Once it even lost the papers. The thing that really put it over was that the Supreme Court of the United States had decided that school segregation on the basis of race was an inappropriate way to educate the nation's young. Joey Binko's father was able

[28]

to convince the school board that mental retardation, like race, was not a viable criterion for segregation, although in this case segregation was not so much the issue as negation.

"What do they want? She doesn't need to go to school anymore."

"They don't want her to go to school. They just want her to know about the HandyCaps. I'm going to answer this. You want to go to a party, Sanjo?"

"Yes." Sanjo banged her fists together. The joyful feeling.

"Count me out."

"You have to drive us, Morris."

"Poppy come too." Sanjo undraped herself from her mother's waist and attached herself to her father like a snail to the side of a fish tank. Morris was too weak to fight. She went to parties infrequently. They were usually family occasions: the birth of a baby, an anniversary, a birthday party for one of the children, or a funeral. That counted as a party too, since there was always food supplied by the grieving family. She liked parties very much.

When Poppy entered the living room with Sanjo still attached, Ma was already on the telephone with her sister-in-law, Mickey, telling her about Sanjo's invitation. Mickey said she would come over next week to help plan what Sanjo would wear to the party. Poppy only wanted to stop feeling dizzy. He was saved by Toby, who loomed suddenly at the front screen door, a coat hanger carrying Spider-man, shading his eyes to look into the house. Seen from the inside, the visitor cast a grotesque shadow.

Sanjo recognized the shadow immediately. Its arms were held away from its body. She broke away from Poppy. "Toby."

"I'm going to read to her, Mr. Bernatsky."

Morris sighed. "You're a good boy, Toby." Thank God for small favors.

Toby and Sanjo sat on the steps. Toby was feeling much better. His mother had stopped hassling him about his barbells, due to his father's intervention. In addition, he had taken a downer that afternoon at the suggestion of his friend Larry, after he complained that the greenies were freaking him out. He was mellow now. The 'lude, which purported to cool him down, lived up to its claims. He stretched his long and growing limbs the length of the porch steps. Sanjo sat at his side, her chin resting in her cupped hands. "Read."

Toby flipped the first page. "I couldn't get you my newest Bugs, Sanjo. My brother packed it in his camp trunk. I got Spider-man. See here? That's Spider-man."

"Where?"

"Here, this guy with the red arms and red head. See, his boots are red, too. Over here is Night-crawler. He's a bad man. He wants to get rid of Spider-man."

Sanjo studied the pictures, then banged a hand on Night-crawler. "Bad man."

"That's right, Sanjo, you got it. He's b-a-d. Bad." Having set the scene, Toby now leaned back to read.

" 'What brings you to this neck of the woods, Night-crawler? I thought you were doing time.' 'No thanks to you. But as you see, Spider-man, I'm free. Free to settle old accounts.' *Thwickt!*"

Movement returned to the neighborhood. The afternoon sun was tempered by a few clouds that darted in front of it like fans in front of an old-time stripteaser. The two-o'clock movie was over, and while the ushers were sweeping the aisles and watching the exit doors to prevent a few who had not bought tickets from walking backward into the theater, their earlier patrons were beginning to filter back into the neighborhood. The animals came out of hiding, slowly at first, then with confidence as the word passed that the baking heat was over. The rush of traffic increased as people raced home to get ready for the evening. Near Toby's feet, an earthworm, blind and deaf, flexed its segmented body as it sucked in earth through its mouth, pulverized it in its craw, and then expelled the digested earth through its anus. Sanjo listened as Spider-man was planning how to get Night-crawler put away for Murder One, while Night-crawler was planning how to choke him with his own web.

2

The next morning Sanjo was waiting for Ma and Poppy, sitting on the front steps like a good girl, her feet planted on the steps below, her skirt covering her stubby legs, and her hair combed. She had done that just a few minutes earlier, carefully running her comb slowly down the straight sparse brown hair cut to her ears. It was one of the things she did best.

Sanjo watched the cars. An ant crawled over her foot. It was a front-runner, a scout looking for water for its nest mates, and it traced a half-crazed path of zigzagged urgency upon the cement walk. Sanjo wished she could make nice-nice.

She had discovered nice-nice by accident one night in bed when she was in an explorative mood. It was a happy surprise, nicer than chocolate-swirl ice cream, nicer than Hersheys, nicer than Uncle Jerry's mustache, and nicer than making bubbles in a pipe, but she learned you couldn't do nice-nice except in the bathtub or in bed. The way she learned this was at Opportunity Sabbath. Ma had bought her a yellow dress. Sanjo sat on the pulpit with a lot of others. The rabbi, a dapper man with blond hair that he wore parted at his ears and wrapped around his forehead like a turban, was talking. From time to time he turned to Sanjo and the others and pointed or smiled.

"This is a special occasion, a very special occasion. On the pulpit today are young people who are part of our Opportunity Class. Some might say they are unfortunate. There are even those who would say they are handicapped." At that moment Joey Binko, a handsome young man of twenty-two with the black-patent-leather look of the silent movie stars, started to stick his tongue out of his mouth. He looked as if he were trying to catch something. There was nothing, just air. Joey Binko made for the air with expert darts. His yarmulka fell off. "In the sight of God there are no handicapped, because all, in God's eyes, are handicapped in one way or another. Each of us has an imperfection. These young people today, although imperfect, have studied the Torah, my dear friends, the Torah. For their remarkable efforts they are to be awarded certificates."

It was time for nice-nice. It was easy to find the place. There was a stir in the congregation. The stir sounded like a Mixmaster with accelerating speeds. Poppy and Ma were opening and closing their mouths like birds. Ma started to wave, and Poppy clapped his hand to his forehead. The rabbi turned and saw Sanjo making nice-nice.

"Oi." This ancient lament of his fathers escaped uninvited. He deplored its use, since it was the language of the ghetto, and turned once more to face his congregation. He hoped they did not hear. He made a gesture that was probably older than his language, an anguished search for a helping hand that the hidden choir mistook for a signal to begin. They started to sing "God is in his holy temple."

"So when I call their names, you will know that this is an accomplishment." He had to yell to project over the choir. He turned back to Sanjo. She was smiling.

Ma could not stand it any longer and vaulted up on the pulpit. She grabbed Sanjo's hands. "What are you doing? Are you crazy?" Then Ma sat down next to Sanjo with the look of a warrior and faced the congregation.

"From the reverent heart and simple . . ."

The rabbi heard his cue go by. He had intended to turn on the words *and simple* in pointed illustration and face the honorees, but now everything was thrown off.

"Joey Binko. . . ."

The day was hot. A stain began to creep down Sanjo's side from under her arms. She touched the wet and remembered that she forgot to spray under her arms. That was another thing she knew how to do by herself. She knew how to depress the button and not spray anywhere else and how to hold her breath until she was finished. Ma liked it when she didn't forget.

Next door a big truck had pulled up in the driveway. Three big men who alternately laughed and yelled at each other came out of the truck carrying and dropping crates, furniture, and rugs, which they pushed, threw, and dragged into the house next door. Sanjo waved to the men, a kind of tentative half salute, a just-in-case wave made by scratching the air with the first digits of her fingers. The men did not seem to see her.

Two boys came by, weaving back and forth on the sidewalk like the ant that crawled over her foot. Sanjo remembered them. She used to watch them wait for their school bus. It was on the corner, and they chanted, "The bus, the bus, the b-u-s," every morning, rain, shine, snow, or whatever. Sanjo knew it by heart and chanted it with them whenever she heard it. One of the boys, nine years old and already a hero for his wizardry on the skateboard, looked up and saw her, then poked his friend.

"Hello, Sanjo."

The friend looked troubled. He recognized the mocking tone. "You better watch out, she's a grown-up," he said.

"She's no grown-up, she's a dope."

"Get out!"

"No kidding. Watch. Hey, Sanjo!"

Sanjo smiled, showing her pegged small teeth, irregular in the receding reddened gums. She liked it when the children talked to her. "Hullo."

"Hullo, yourself, you big dope. That's what you are, a dope." The boy looked hastily at the house. When he was sure Sanjo had no handy champion, he got bolder. "Say you're a dope, Sanjo."

[33]

Sanjo was so happy, she hugged her knees. She spoke, a low-pitched guttural sound. "Sanjo dope."

Something made the boys fold back like the Red Sea. It was Toby with his eyes fixed on the sidewalk, having had a major hassle with his mother that morning over his barbells. In a tin can buried in an empty lot on the next street was a cache of uppers that would soon make everything right.

Sanjo smiled at Toby. "Where Bugs?"

"I don't have any comics today, Sanjo. I'll bring you Bugs tomorrow." Toby walked like a man with a purpose. The boys fell in beside him, flanking him on either side.

"Hey, Toby." He didn't answer.

"Sanjo, me and Poppy are ready to leave." Ma and Poppy came down the steps. It was hard to tell who supported whom. The boys took one look and sprinted away, this time in a straight line.

Ma had on a white pants suit that covered up the developing hump on her back, which was beginning to make her look like a question mark. A white and pink scarf was wound around her neck, only slightly less tight than might have been twisted by a killer. Her hair was a light pink, and she wore it fluffed out like a small cloud. Poppy had on his usual baggy slacks, a plaid short-sleeve sport shirt, and a pale-green golf hat with a laundry ticket stuck in the band.

Ma gave Sanjo a few practiced flicks with her fingers as if she were erasing her. "Don't get your skirt dirty. You look very nice in it and it's expensive."

Sanjo looked down at her clothing. She was wearing a T-shirt and a skirt that wrapped around her waist. Sanjo learned how to wrap it herself. It was very hard but she finally got it, after draping it around her feet, her shoulders, and her eyes and tripping once. It took a lot of practice and a lot of coaching.

"Sanjo, your left hand, take your left hand . . . this one, this is your left hand." When Sanjo finally got it, she was sweating. She came into the kitchen in her underpants, her stomach flopping over the elastic, carrying the skirt in her hand, while Ma was putting away the groceries on the middle shelf, a place she

[34]

used with greater frequency since it began to be difficult to bend over and reach the lower level. Sanjo smiled and showed her trick. "Lookit," she said.

Ma wore lipstick. It was called Coral Island and had a special ingredient to prevent it from seeping into the grooves over her top lip. It looked very pretty. Sanjo didn't wear lipstick. She didn't wear any makeup. Her mother and father decided that after much deliberation when she was around fifteen. They didn't want her to be too attractive. It was not in her best interest. Clean and neat, yes; attractive, no. Now they didn't have to worry. Her body looked like a wedge. Wide triangular cartilage gave her a flattened saddle nose. Her eyes had a hooded look, the lids with an epicanthic fold which made her look, to some people, Oriental. In fact, some of the neighborhood kids called her Chinko, among other names like Momo or Turkey or Gomer. Chinko, however, was the favorite. Actually, these were not the same kids who first called her Chinko. They had grown up and married and had kids of their own. But there were always new ones who saw her and decided to call her Chinko.

Sanjo walked with Ma to the car in her customary unsteady gait, stooped, her head hanging forward and her feet spread wide apart. Her arms hung straight down from her shoulders with her palms facing behind her.

Poppy got into the car ahead of them. He sat in an automobile that was clearly too high for him. Either that or he was too short. His eyes barely cleared the dashboard. His bald head was freckled. From the outside, it looked as if a speckled cantaloupe were driving the car.

Luckily he was a very slow and careful driver. Other drivers often spun around them in anger, wheels shrieking as they tore away from behind his tedious jurisdiction. But he had a spotless record, never an accident.

"Doesn't she look nice? Look at Sanjo's new skirt."

"Yeah."

"No, really, Morris, take a look, she really looks very nice."

Poppy turned around. "You look nice, Sanjo."

Sanjo grunted.

[35]

"You could take the bus, you know."

"If I was just going to the clinic, okay, but I want to go to Swann's later. Besides, you know what happens on the bus." She arched her brows. "Anyway, it's better for Sanjo to spend some time with you, too."

"Sanjo always spends time with me."

"You're in a mood today, I can tell. Poppy's in a mood," she said, supposedly to Sanjo, but to no one in particular since her eyes were straight ahead. "Did you take your medication?" An indirect hit.

Poppy grunted.

"What does that mean? Did you take it or didn't you?"

"I took my medicine, yes."

"Medication, it makes you sound stupid when you say medicine."

"What's the difference, either it cleans my blood up or it doesn't," said Poppy.

The hospital was only a few minutes away. Sanjo recognized it as soon as they turned the corner. It had granite steps that hurt her shins. Sanjo took the steps one at a time, planting both feet solidly together before reaching for the next step. Beads of perspiration blossomed on her upper lip and carved her bangs on her forehead in the same striations that a plasterer might make on a ceiling.

Soon they would pass over the beam of light that was programmed to snap the plate glass doors open at the approach of any object over forty inches tall, which prevented stray cats and dogs from springing in and out of the hospital. Sanjo was afraid of the door. She had not made the connection between her steps and the door's opening, and it seemed to her as threatening and unpredictable as a jack-in-the-box she once had that had hit her on the nose. She hung back. "Sanjo, walk," Ma urged.

Sanjo smiled. "Poppy go." Abraham offering Isaac.

Ma would never allow Sanjo to go any place last. "No, Sanjo, you go."

Poppy was more to the point. "Move." He put a hand on

[36]

Sanjo's shoulder. Because he was shorter than she was, he had to reach.

Sanjo faced the door. Fear made her heart thud against her broad, undeveloped chest. She pulled away.

Ma and Poppy, two experienced corner backs, dropped sideways for the play, expertly grabbed, each one, an arm, and propelled Sanjo through the door. Their combined breadth forced Poppy off center and he grazed a finger on the plate glass door. It began to bleed. He sucked it like a mongoose sucking an egg. "It's always got to be something," he said.

Sanjo looked back at the doors, now demurely closing behind them. "Bad boy," she said.

Sanjo liked the hospital. She smiled at the walls and the people and stuck her tongue toward the smells, some sharp that made her wrinkle her nose, like when Ma cleaned the toilets, and some sweet and compelling, like Mrs. Cervitano's rose-bushes. There were chimes, voices on the intercom, and bells, and people in green and white clothes looped and threaded with stethoscopes and tubing chasing up and down the corridors in packs. The packs tore around people in wheelchairs, narrowly avoided an old man leaning on a walker, and once collided with a trolley whose occupant lay with an I.V. stuck in his hand that connected to a bottle swinging over his head. The collision made the bottle swing wildly and the liquid in it foamed up the sides.

Poppy led them to the elevators by walking a few feet in front of them and pointing out directional shifts.

A pinch-faced operator wearing a little lace collar and white gloves herded them all into the cab, jammed it to where no one could move their arms, then asked everyone for their floors. A woman, anxious to breathe, backed up into Sanjo and stepped on her toes. Sanjo pushed her. "Go away," she said. The woman turned around, started to say something, saw Sanjo and her mother, and, instead, molded herself into the wheelchair in front of her, deciding that it was the lesser of two evils. A tall black man pressing a tray full of vials and bottles to his chest leaned against the far wall. Sanjo saw the syringe sticking out. "No shot," she warned. The man with the tray scarcely glanced at her. Everyone cringed when he approached. He was used to it.

Their waiting room was at the far end of a long speckled-vinyl corridor flanked with painted arrows that darted into recesses and around corners. In the middle of the waiting room at the top of an arrow was a desk. A woman sat behind it watching the people in the waiting room like a proctor on the lookout for cheaters. Her blue eyes were set like marbles in her round, doughy face. She rolled the marbles toward Ma.

"I have an appointment with Dr. Perry," said Ma.

The woman checked this information against her book, a huge ledger color-coded for efficiency. She found the entry at once. Although she had seen Ma every other month for over two years, she gave no indication that she recognized her. "Take a seat. We'll call you," she said.

Poppy pointed them to their seats, taking the first one for himself. His Corfam shoes barely cleared the floor, and he concentrated on stretching his legs to their fullest extension. Ma gave her scarf an extra tug to hold her neck folds closer together.

A man with a wad of cotton at his neck sat opposite them. He was very thin, and he tugged at the hole at the center of the cotton from time to time, touching the rubber which rimmed it and then looking at his fingers as if he expected to see its imprint. A woman next to him was pretending to read the *Reader's Digest*. At the far wall a man in a paper gown sat waiting huddled for X-ray. He looked like a piece of loosely wrapped fruit. The gown barely covered his thighs, and he clutched at its strings as if trying to stem a flood tide.

Sanjo surveyed the lot. She was scanning lips and eyes, trying to find a smile. Sometimes if she smiled first, the person she was looking at would smile back. It was risky. She tried the man with the cotton around his neck. He kept poking his finger in the hole in his neck. The woman next to him caught Sanjo's eye and began to flip the pages of her magazine looking for the most unforgettable character she ever met. The man on the bench in the paper gown was too occupied with covering his jockey shorts.

Sanjo heard him before she saw him. Sounds musical and muted, like water running over rocks, came from the next aisle. Sanjo turned her head like a turtle coming out of its shell. The source was a baby who toddled from one side of the aisle to the other. His mother watched him, never taking her eyes from him, while the baby lurched like a drunk toward Sanjo. Sanjo's mouth stretched back wide and full, showing her pegged teeth. Her eyes crinkled almost shut. She clapped her hands together. The baby moved toward her surely and purposefully, although unsteadily, like a nuclear sub without a gyroscope. When it reached her, it swayed against her knees in one final lurch.

"Baby," she said.

The baby threw his head back, spread his dimpled hands on Sanjo's knees, and hurled his call: "Laaa," a musical note, a greeting, an announcement.

"Laaa," replied Sanjo.

The baby's mother, watching all the time, was over in one faultless move that began as a low leap and ended as a dip at Sanjo's feet. She grabbed her baby and swung him in a long easy arc to safety, as simply as tossing a head of lettuce into a pickup truck.

Sanjo watched the baby, now back in his own aisle. "Baby, Ma."

"Yes, that's a baby."

Poppy, the family's early warning system, was alert. "Forget the baby," he said.

"Baby say Laaa."

"Yes, that's right," said Ma, "the baby said La. Look how she notices everything."

Poppy wiped a hand across his forehead, an air traffic controller who was losing contact with his plane. "Forget the baby," he said.

Sanjo stood up.

Everyone in the waiting room stopped what they were doing. All movement was suspended, including the woman at the desk, her blue marbles fixed and staring; the man with the rubber hole with his finger at his neck, a mastodon of the twentieth century, forever captured in his disbelief; the man waiting for X-ray, clutching his paper gown; and the mother standing in front of her baby, a goalie ready for the next strike.

The woman at the desk was the one who broke the spell. "Mrs. Bernatsky, the doctor can see you now."

Ma stood up and grabbed Sanjo in a half nelson. "She's better off with me," she said. Poppy didn't argue.

"No shot," said Sanjo.

"Don't worry. It's for me."

Inside the cubicle Ma took off her pants-suit jacket and her scarf and hung them up behind the door. She sat in her bra with her black patent purse clutched in her lap. Sanjo sat beside her, keeping an eye on the hypodermic needles. The doctor walked in carrying a chart. He was twenty-eight years old with freckles on his nose, sparse blond hair that was beginning to lose itself to pattern baldness, and rimless glasses. He looked very serious.

"Well, Mrs. Bernatsky. How are you feeling lately?"

"I'm feeling pretty good," she said.

They all said that. The doctor pursued his quarry. "Have you had any problems since I've seen you last?" He thumped her back.

"No."

"Any chest pains?" He tapped her front and back with his stethoscope like a priest with a miter.

"No."

"Any shortness of breath?"

Sanjo took out a Q-tip.

"No."

He placed two fingers against her neck, first one side and then the other. "Ringing in your ears?"

"No."

"Any numbness, weakness, trouble talking?" He slipped a cuff on her arm.

"No."

"Sit where you are. Dizziness?"

"I'm a little light-headed."

He arched one brow. "When you sit and watch TV?"

"Who has time to watch TV? Sanjo, stop that. Don't stick that in your ear. You'll go deaf."

"Stand, please. When do you feel light-headed?"

"When I go to the bathroom."

"What does it feel like?"

"Well, it's more like being clogged up, being full in the head."

The doctor looked discouraged. Sanjo smiled at him but he continued to frown. "I think your problem needs to be investigated further."

"What do you mean?" asked Ma.

"I would like to hospitalize you."

"Why?"

"I can't treat you on an outpatient basis. There are too many things I need to find out."

Ma shook her head patiently. "It's out of the question. I have too many responsibilities."

The doctor twisted his lips as if closing a jar. "Listen, you're having signs that tell me to worry about you. I honestly feel as if you should go into the hospital. Who's going to take care of your responsibilities if something happens to you?"

Ma never heard the last sentence. She reached for her jacket.

"At your age we can't take any chances."

She knew she shouldn't have taken off the scarf. She wound it around her neck.

"Just a few days and I'll have an answer for you."

"I already know the answer and it's not good," she said.

The doctor knew when he was finished. He made a few notes in his chart and pointed his pen toward Sanjo. "How's she doing?" he asked.

"She's fine," said Ma. "Ask her yourself."

The doctor smiled as if acknowledging a joke and walked out. Ma poked some fat under her bra, put on her jacket, grabbed Sanjo's hand, and followed him out. She handed a piece of paper to the woman at the desk and collected Poppy.

"Well?" asked Poppy.

"I'm fine," said Ma.

They had some trouble finding their car. Poppy forgot where he parked it. After trudging back and forth, they finally saw the pink pompom waving from the antenna.

"Now where?" asked Poppy.

"Take us to Swann's. They're having a sale."

"Count me out. I'll drop you off. And take it easy. I'm not a rich man. I'm retired, remember?"

"You don't have to be a genius to remember, Morry."

"What's that supposed to mean?"

Sanjo's heart beat faster. She looked from one to another, alert to this new voice tone that always meant yelling, heavy silences, and sometimes crying. She tugged at Ma's sleeve. "I got pocky." Ma looked straight ahead. "Look, Ma. Pocky." In her lap Sanjo clutched a small handbag. In it was a handkerchief which she never used, her name, age, and address on a piece of paper, and a package of LifeSavers. Ma wanted her to carry this. It made her happy. Sanjo wanted to make her happy.

"You smell, Sanjo." Ma wrinkled her nose. She looked like a rabbit. "Didn't you spray deodorant?" Sanjo shook her head. Ma looked out the window.

At Swann's, Ma held Sanjo's hand very tight. It was the Blast-a-thon sale, and there were hundreds of shoppers pillaging through the aisles, engaging in the same behavior that, if done on the street, would get them arrested. A chime with exquisite clarity cut through the din with secret codes for the employees, such as *dong dong dong,* they're on the first floor, *ding dong ding,* they're heading past notions. Swann's air conditioner wafted gallons of Christian Dior perfume that in a few hours would mysteriously mingle with the Freon to turn back into ambergris.

They got stuck at the escalator when Sanjo couldn't decide which moving step to take. It was a serious problem since they all looked exactly alike. Ma yelled encouragement, like "Now,

Sanjo; jump, Sanjo; now, that one, take that one!" But Sanjo stood immobile.

Some of the people who backed up behind them started to get angry. "There, that's a nice one," said a woman behind Ma.

"Take that one, it's prettier," said a little boy. Sanjo thought so too, and they took it.

They shopped through lunchtime, which made Sanjo very upset. She had learned when she was eleven and attending special classes, at the same time other children of her age were learning about carbohydrates and proteins, that she was supposed to have three meals a day. The purpose was to teach her to take care of herself and the theory was that if it was drummed into her through rote and practice that she was supposed to eat morning, noon, and night, she would have a better chance of survival.

The learning experience was constantly reinforced by family and school, so that now, twenty-three years later, Sanjo behaved like an obsessive compulsive who had to tap his right knee every time he bumped his left. She couldn't not do it. Forget explaining that the calories in brunch were equivalent to breakfast and lunch combined, or that a meal could be skipped. There was too much latitude in such a concept.

It came to a head in lingerie. "Eat, Ma." Ma was comparison-shopping long-line bras whose manufacturer promised that not only would they lift breasts but, fastened properly, would push up faces as well. "Eat, Ma." Sanjo pulled at her sleeve. A small crowd soon gathered.

"Take her and feed her," demanded an irate couple.

They went to the lunch counter in the basement and waited behind two women who took their time and smoked cigarettes. When the women left, Sanjo and Ma claimed the stools. Sanjo couldn't get on and neither could Ma and so they ordered two hot dogs to go. Ma turned to Sanjo. She wanted to make sure this counted, as she didn't think she could go through it again. "That's lunch," she said.

The women's shoe department was especially lively. Shoes of

[43]

all kinds were heaped high on a table. Never a pair, which was easy to shoplift, but single sandals, wedgies, clogs, and pumps. The idea was to get a shoe you liked and ask for the mate. Ma plunged in with one hand, which was pretty good when you considered that her other hand was occupied with holding on to Sanjo. A veteran, she was able to hold her own with the other plungers and finally came up with a brown sandal.

Sanjo and Ma took two adjoining seats, and finally a salesman came. He had a big space between his nose and mouth which he filled with a mustache. His eyes were watery, the look of someone with a perpetual allergy. "What can I do for you ladies?" Ma was girded for battle. She had a standard armamentarium of furrowed brow, clenched jaws, upthrust chin, and a steely gaze so intimidating she convinced an unwilling registrar to enter Sanjo's name on the voting list without an argument. For heavy duty she sometimes added crossed arms. This was not such an occasion.

"This. We want this."

"What size is it?"

"Nine medium."

"We have those in all colors."

"This is the one I want."

"Very well. A terra-cotta bandolino in a nine medium." He walked away and Sanjo started to sing. She had a favorite song about tying a yellow ribbon around a tree upon whose theme she improvised. Sanjo had a deep, if not good, voice.

"Don't sing here."

Sanjo looked into her lap and whispered the words against her chest. The man came back with the sandal's mate. He looked up in question. "For which one of you ladies?" Ma pointed to Sanjo's feet. The salesman grabbed a stool and drew it up to Sanjo. He took her foot to remove the sneaker.

Sanjo looked at him and smiled. She whispered one word to him. "Ribbon."

He liked feet. He made his wife wear toenail polish which he lovingly put on himself, tenderly putting wads of cotton between

[44]

each toe. He got frequent erections from touching and fondling feet. Sometimes a customer got wise, but usually he could handle metatarsals and arches to his heart's content. He was very happy that ankle straps were coming back in vogue. They gave the foot a look no other shoe could.

Sanjo looked at the brown shoe he was putting on her foot. She liked red better. She kicked her foot. "No."

The man looked up. "All right." He was undaunted. Sometimes he had a pile of rejected shoes banked around a particularly discriminating woman like a wall. He was used to women saying no. "Another shoe, perhaps?"

"Sanjo, let the man try the shoe on you."

He got a good look at Sanjo, sized up a situation that had been staring him in the face for fifteen minutes, and hunched backward on his stool until he was resting on his coccyx.

Ma took off the sneaker herself and proffered the reluctant foot. "Put the sandal on."

The man hesitated. "What if she doesn't want?"

"She wants."

It was one of the few times he wished he was in luggage. The commissions weren't as good, but you dealt with some pretty nice people. All happy travelers going to Marrakesh, London, Israel, the Canadian Rockies. None of this.

He gingerly picked up the foot and slid the sandal on. This was one of the rare feet that did nothing to him. He could have been handling his mother's foot. He was so nervous he couldn't get the buckles done. Maybe they wouldn't notice. "Well, now, why don't you walk in it?"

Sanjo got up and decided she didn't mind brown. She stumbled all over the shoe department with the buckles flapping around her ankles, knocking over boxes, looking in every mirror, even bending down once to see one on the floor. When she was satisfied, she came back smiling. Ma charged the shoes.

It was somewhere in Housewares that they got separated. Sanjo was standing beside her mother, who was looking at a crepe pan. Ma had never used one, but Mickey did and talked about it all the time. It looked like a frying pan. Something else caught Sanjo's eye. There was a copper display of pots, pans, and molds. Sanjo walked over and touched the shiny, smooth metal. No one came and said don't touch, so she touched to her heart's content. A few people watched her lovingly caress the copper, rubbing it against her cheek and murmuring to it, but they dismissed it as a publicity stunt and walked away.

A couple in jeans stood to watch. "She's really into those pots," the man said.

"There's something wrong with her," whispered the woman. "Maybe we should tell the saleslady."

"What for?" asked the man. "She's not hurting anyone."

A saleswoman did come. Alert for signs of shoplifting, her eye was arrested by the movement of the peculiar woman rubbing the pan along her cheek. "That's the finest copper you can buy," she said.

"Nice."

"Yes, it really is nice. The beauty of it is in the cooking, of course."

Sanjo touched the copper with her tongue.

"I don't think you should do that," said the saleswoman.

Sanjo smiled. "Good," she said.

The saleswoman turned and ran for the security officer, a robust woman in plainclothes who could deck any man with the bend of a knee and the twist of a wrist. She had just been eluded by a booster she had been trailing for an hour, trying to catch her in the act. Somehow—the officer didn't know how she did it—the merchandise was there one moment and gone the next. It was like watching a magic show. The booster, a tall, stately woman with red hair, apparently had no accomplice. She wasn't trying anything on. She didn't carry a raincoat or a shopping bag, and she wasn't swinging anything under her shirt. The only way the officer knew she was boosting was that she was getting fatter by the minute.

This particular booster's trick was a hook clutched in her palm that dangled from a long piece of elastic attached to her shoulder. When she had something she wanted—and she was particularly discriminating—she placed it on the hook, released the hook from her hand, and the elastic sprang the item up into her capacious blouse.

The security agent, heading toward Sanjo, was still thinking about the booster, whose method had escaped her and who was, at this very minute, robbing the store blind. When she saw Sanjo covered with pots, she knew the job ahead of her wouldn't be easy. "You can't do that here."

Sanjo looked worried. The lady didn't smile at her. She flung the pans aside.

"You don't have to get nasty," the security officer said.

Sanjo started to cry. The saleswoman whispered something to the security officer.

"What's your name?"

"Sanjo."

"Sanjo what?"

"Ma!" Sanjo was crying hard now. Where was Ma? Poppy? She wanted to go home.

The security officer caught on. She raised her speech volume as if she were shouting across a field. "Let's go to my office. It's just across the floor." She took Sanjo's arm. "Come on, honey. Let's not be difficult."

Something happened to Sanjo's struts, and she sank to the asbestos tile. Her world of unpredictable shifts of circumstances that produced peaks of calamities and joys was a puzzle, and Sanjo had none of the pieces. Abandoned and frightened, she sat on the floor, rubbed her fists into her eyes, and cried. So great was her misery that she soiled her pants, something she hardly ever did.

"Ma!" Now she was wailing. The security officer got down on the floor beside her. The saleswoman, who was making a frantic attempt to escape to Gift Wrap, twisted her ankle on a salmon mold and joined them both.

The loudspeaker blared: *We have a missing person—Sandra Joanne Bernatsky. She is wearing a blue shirt and a blue and*

[47]

white skirt. She has on brown sandals and white socks. She is carrying a purse that says Snoopy on it. Miss Bernatsky is thirty-four years old and chubby. Will Sandra's mother please come to the office for her?

Sanjo sat in a small, sparsely furnished room with the two women who had apprehended her and a strange man. The man was young (he had only recently given up "Star Trek"), one of an army of newly trained managers in a university-sponsored internship. He shaved only twice a week but didn't tell anyone. Privately he was worried that he was not producing sufficient testosterone. Publicly, in front of his older brother, he changed his blade daily. He believed in such things as management by objective and participative decision-making and was out to bring new light to the commercial system. He had just given Sanjo a melting Hershey bar that he got out of the machine in the basement. "Have Helen make that announcement again," he said. This was something the MBA program had not prepared him for.

Sanjo wasn't sad anymore. Eating the Hershey was a total hand-eye-mouth involvement, causing her to fingerpaint herself with chocolate in haphazard stripes, a graffiti artist whose spray can was losing pressure. The saleslady, who limped, smelled like a flower. She was close enough to Sanjo that Sanjo could smell her as much as she wanted without even trying. The only problem was to coordinate the Hershey with the smelling. Sometimes it was confusing and once she inhaled the Hershey, choking and flailing her arms. The security officer, trying to avoid the waving chocolate, pounded her on the back with the bob and weave of a prizefighter.

The manager intern wiped Hershey off his fingers. Actually, he felt sorry for Sanjo, but he didn't want the women to mistake compassion for weakness. Instead he said, "My luck—the Blast-a-thon, every booster in the city out there, and we're in here with this."

"Why don't we call a hospital?" suggested the saleslady. Hurt from her fall, she hopped to the desk, where she began to file a workman's compensation claim. Even though she leaned all the way forward in her seat, Sanjo couldn't smell her anymore.

"What hospital?" asked the man.

"Any one."

"You just can't get someone into a hospital. You have to be sick."

"She doesn't even know her last name. If that doesn't qualify her for admission, then I don't know what."

The door flew open. Sanjo's mother fell in, leaned against a desk to steady herself, saw Sanjo, and groaned. "Oh, my God. Don't do this to me, Sanjo. Don't do this to me." Ma turned to the manager. "Where was she?"

"Housewares," he answered.

"What was she doing there?" Sanjo's mother had learned long ago that the best defensive was a good offensive.

"What was she doing . . . ? Now listen, lady, what is she doing here in the first place unescorted? Something serious could happen to her."

Ma drew herself up and almost straightened out the question mark into an exclamation point. "She came with her *mother*, and she has every *right* to be here. *Every* right. She got a little lost, that's all, and if your people had been on the ball, this wouldn't have happened. Come on, Sanjo, we're going home."

Sanjo smiled. "Go home." She was so happy to see Ma.

"Look at your hands. Now we have to wash your hands."

The manager ran to a sink in the corner and wet a towel. "Here, use this." The quicker he got them out of the store, the better.

Ma made another quick assessment of Sanjo's condition but decided not to give the other hostile parties to the scene further satisfaction. They could take care of that when they got home. She wiped Sanjo's hands and face, then took her arm and propelled her out the door but turned for one last sally. "And it wasn't such a sale, either. The merchandise is marked the same as last month. And you got a few bait-and-switches going. I know about that stuff. My husband was in dinette sets."

Poppy's instructions had been explicit. They were to wait on the southeast corner of Market and Eighth next to the pretzel man, not the bootleg pretzel man, who sped from corner to corner defying the police and the corner bosses, but the regular guy, the one who had been there for thirty years with the little awning over his stand. Poppy would come by at exactly four. Not two minutes after, but four. That would mean they could make a getaway before all the offices and stores disgorged their employees, whose escape to their cars would turn the city streets into long parking lots.

The sidewalk was mobbed. Glanced at head on, it looked like a crowded dance floor, except that the dancers were rushing away from their partners. Hustlers, most of them young, waited in doorways to scan the crowd like radar, offering sex, dope, or anything else a connection might have in mind. A group of four black teenagers walking abreast swept through the mob with the efficiency of a Roman phalanx, brushing aside the dancers, who fell away before them like so many Carthaginians. One of them wore a green tam-o'-shanter.

"Nice hat." Sanjo pointed at it.

The youth turned. "What you starin' at?"

Ma pulled Sanjo back against the building. She faced the youth with her total armamentarium, steely gaze, crossed arms, and all. He turned to catch up with the others, switching the air behind his pants in smart and stylish salutes.

Sanjo and Ma stood on the corner waiting for Poppy. Behind them in the window two men were taking the clothes off a dummy. The arm was lying on the ground next to it. One of the men draped the other arm around his shoulder like a fur piece as he bent to unpin the garment from behind the dummy's plastic hips.

A group of pale young people with shaved heads, yellow robes the color of curried rice, and tambourines were dancing up and down singing about Krishna. One of them came up to Ma and asked for a donation. Ma waved the boy away. He reminded her of her brother Manny's grandson, Steve. All she could think of was his mother. That must be some headache.

Poppy eased his gray Dodge sedan into the second lane and stopped traffic. He would have parked in the no parking/no stopping zone to pick up Ma and Sanjo, but that was full. The car behind him honked. The driver leaned out and yelled, then backed up, tapped the bumper of the car behind him, and jerked his car alongside Poppy. He rolled down his window and yelled, "Cocksucker!" Poppy didn't care. He felt the righteous calm of someone with a clear entitlement. Anyone would only have to look to know. Sanjo got into the back seat and Ma reached in and pushed her button down, then slid into the front seat with Poppy. "You wouldn't believe the day I had," she said.

Sanjo was beginning to smell as ripe as a sunbaked farmyard. Ma was grateful that Poppy's sinus condition, in addition to his declining sensory abilities—one of the reasons they had recently installed a safety tap on the gas range—made him unable to smell anything.

Sanjo bent down to inspect her new shoes. They were still flapping. No one had bothered to fix the buckles. The leather smelled good, and Sanjo tried to lift her foot to her nose, but it was hard to do. Poppy and Ma were talking good talk, the tones soft and even and warm. A feeling began to rush through Sanjo, flooding her nerves and muscles with an effervescent flush that threatened to lift her skyward. It began as a prickle on her skin, erected the hairs on her arms and legs, and continued as a flood rising in her chest. She leaned her head back and smiled a big open-mouth smile that showed all her teeth, her tongue, and her uvula; the smile crinkled her eyes, and the epicanthic fold retracted. Sanjo's skin took on a translucent quality. She put all her fingers in her mouth and pulled down her lower jaw, then made fists which she clapped together. Soon she began to rock. "Cockser," she crooned to the window.

3

Jerry and Mickey paid them a visit the next week. They were on their way to the airport, where they would board a TWA 1-1011 to Las Vegas, guests of Big Murray's junket, an all-expense-paid trip to the city in the desert. The reason they were so honored was that Jerry was a high roller. For fifty weeks of the year a white-coated conscientious dispenser of pharmaceuticals, Jerry became for the other two weeks a crazed crapshooter. It was hard to believe that the same man who had apologetically asked the bearer of a prescription reading *Give him all the Seconal he wants whenever he wants it* to have his physician call him would tomorrow be screaming for a hard eight.

Mickey at sixty-two was still pretty, although the nasolabial folds that lined her crafted nose were deeper than they might have been since the supporting cartilage had been whacked away. She used some kind of perfume that made the room smell like the inside of a tangerine. Poppy sat as far away from her as he could for two reasons. Her perfume made him sneeze. In addition, she had told him once at a family dinner that she heard short men were virile. Women sometimes said suggestive things like that to men and it didn't mean a thing. He counted this as serious because when she passed him the brisket she brushed his arm with her breast. Runi Bindlehouse was one thing. His brother's wife was another matter.

Mickey had an opened box before her. Poppy, Ma, and Sanjo were waiting for something to come out of the box. Jerry, with hocks lifted off the edge of his chair and his eyes bouncing wildly like pinballs, had the look of a fugitive. He already knew what was in the box; besides, he was anxious to get to the crap table.

"I knew it was perfect when I saw it. Sandra, dear, it's you." With a ceremonial flourish of her bangled wrists, Mickey lifted from the box a cheongsam, a collarless high-necked garment of deep-blue silk with red lining at the throat and at the slit in the long skirt. Tears glistened in Mickey's eyes.

Sanjo grabbed the box with the cheongsam and hugged it to her.

"What is it?" asked Ma.

"It's a Chinese dress. It's a natural."

Poppy didn't get the point. "What's natural about it?"

Jerry, alert to the possibility that the surprise might be a terrific flop, eased his way out. "I had nothing to do with it."

Ma sat up straight. "I don't get it either."

"Are you kidding?" asked Mickey. "With her eyes?"

"What's the matter with her eyes?"

You had to hand it to Mickey. She was facile. "Look, you don't fight something, you go with it. Jackie Kennedy doesn't fight her body. She's skinny. She makes the most of it. Lauren Hutton *prefers* to be photographed with the space between her teeth. She doesn't fight it. It's her greatest asset."

Poppy knew who Jackie Kennedy was. He never heard of Lauren Hutton. He didn't see the point and began to worry about his mind again.

Mickey went in all the way. "The dress is Oriental, like her eyes." Hiroshima. Ma never saw the cloud. Mickey was too fast for her. "If you think it's easy to get a size fourteen, you're crazy."

Sanjo meanwhile had a full heart. She rocked her head back and forth with a palm on either cheek, humming an improvised melody of limited range but heavy vibrato.

[53]

Mickey was used to more ordinary displays of joy. She wanted to set the record straight. "It's for the party," she said.

"Thank Aunt Mickey," said Ma, in the same conspiratorial tone she might have used to say, "Don't go too wide on the turns."

"Thanks," said Sanjo.

"We have to go." Jerry knew to the minute how long it would take them to park their car, check in at the airport, and find Big Murray. His biorhythm was flawless.

"Wait, Jer, let's see how she looks in it."

Sanjo, with some help from Ma and Mickey, put on the cheongsam. She didn't look bad, although the straight skirt had a hobble effect and it was hard to walk. Spun from the glistening filaments of millions of cultivated worms and dyed the color of a night sea, the imperious fabric dispensed largesse to whoever wore it. The silk scratched on the stubble of hair, growing back on Sanjo's legs, which Ma had shaved two weeks ago. Sanjo learned she could create a rasp by bending her knees. "Stop that," said Ma. "It's giving me shivers."

Ma and Mickey decided that the hem could come up about four inches. The real problem was the thirty-five hooks and matching eyes in the back. Neither Poppy nor Ma, whose responsibilities included buttoning backs, could see well enough to fasten them together. It was further decided that the tailor in the dry cleaners would put in a zipper instead.

"This good dress," said Sanjo, when the dress was back in its box. Sanjo carried it clutched to her chest like a shield.

"I knew she would like it," said Mickey on her way to the car. Jerry's time clock told him that if they wanted to get the car to the airport valet they had to leave in the next twenty seconds.

They all walked together to the red-interiored black Fleetwood. Everyone bobbed and dipped for good-bye kisses. Mickey kissed Poppy's head, made a prophylactic swoop for Ma's cheek, and tried to do the same to Sanjo but missed and kissed the dress box instead. When Jerry gave Ma hers, he whispered, "Make sure Morris takes his pills."

[54]

Ma rolled her eyes up into her head.

"No, I mean it, Flo, it's very important."

"Tell *him* that. He says they make him dizzy."

"Then go back to Dr. Vogel and get him to write a new prescription."

"What's the big conversation?" asked Poppy.

A car came jouncing over the potholes. The foot on the gas pedal was uneven. Toby's mother, who was driving, was working her mouth like an orangutan trying to get the banana off its teeth. Toby sat slumped beside her. Sanjo gave them a half wave, her cupped hand dipping at the level of her eye. They didn't see her.

Mickey and Jerry sped off, and Poppy and Ma supported each other up the steps. Sanjo was right behind them, clinging to the railing and turning on each step to see if the little girl was outside. Ma paused on the top step to catch her breath. "Even Jerry worries about you, Morry. Take your pills."

Poppy pinched her upper arm. It was warm and soft, and its texture vaulted him backwards over fifty years to when he came to take her from the room she shared with all those people. "You think Sanjo'll go to sleep?" he asked.

"Who knows?" replied Ma. It was the closest thing to a yes he had had in years. Poppy tightened his abdominal wall and slammed his liver into his pancreas. At seventy-one he was still in the ball game.

The Oriental theme was carried through by Mr. Tommy. When Ma and Sanjo went to the beauty shop the next day, Ma told the hairdresser about the cheongsam. He swiveled his head around as if meeting the eyes of the wall, engaged the wall in a locked gaze, and swiveled back. "Of course. It's been staring me in the face and I never saw it. Stupid." He pronounced this last as if it were stoopid. Mr. Tommy gave Sanjo a china-doll cut.

The 110-decibel rock that blasted from the Bang and Olufson speakers set the beat. Everyone responded to it, although some were unaware that they were doing so. At the rate of one's own heart or, more elementally, the dimly remembered rate of one's mother's pulse, it was difficult not to. Pelvises, feet, heads, shoulders, and vaginal muscles moved to it like responses in a litany. Even Ma was not left unaffected, although the higher frequencies were lost on her waning hearing abilities.

Everyone in the shop came over to watch. Step, slap, nod. The scissors flew. Thrust, pump, step. So did Sanjo's hair. Rock, swivel, step. The chain he wore around his neck swung like crazy. Sanjo wanted to grab it except she remembered that he got mad the last time.

The result was an approximation of a hairdo that usually went with an obi, which was actually Japanese and didn't belong to any china doll in the first place. Mr. Tommy stepped back. He grabbed his chin with his thumb and forefinger and then moved in quickly for a last attack, a guerilla with the pin in his teeth. "There."

Everyone applauded. A lady under a dryer poked her head out long enough to say to Ma, "They can make somebody out of anybody," and was pushed back under by her operator.

Sanjo saw her haircut reflected back through the mirror that Mr. Tommy passed over her head like a miter. She liked to see herself in the mirror. She banged her knuckles together. "Look," said Mr. Tommy's assistant. "She's applauding too."

It was a good week. Sanjo had a new haircut, Poppy took his pills as he was supposed to, and Ma was looking forward to the party. She found an old photograph taken during the Christmas show when Sanjo was fourteen. It was not hard to find her. Sanjo was draped in a white sheet and had a crown on her head that squeezed her forehead. She was Balthazar. Ma wondered how many of the children who were in the picture with Sanjo would be there. She was especially anxious to see Sanjo's teacher, the one who organized the party. Miss Furlowe stood in the middle of the first row, a proud master of ceremonies surrounded by her cast. Half the children were blurred. It was hard to get everyone to stay still. Joey Binko, who in those years was confined to a stroller, played the Christ child. Even though the nativity did not figure with prominence in their own religious ceremonies, the Binkos and the Bernatskys were satisfied with the Christmas show. Like everyone else, they cried when Mary, played by Margaret Paley, who was unintelligible the year before, asked, "Wanna see my baby?"

Miss Furlowe was proud of them all nonetheless and smiled into the camera, sparking her special brand of robust benevolence like a Roman candle. That was twenty years ago. Ma made a quick calculation and placed the woman's present age at about fifty. Her relationship to others was through relative chronology. She was almost twenty years older. Ma didn't think of herself as old, even though she carried definite proof like her Medicare card. Age was a sort of accident. She somehow slid into it, and before she knew it she was there.

Ma knew many of the mothers. They used to talk together during PTA meetings, never addressing their private sorrows directly but speaking of such things as falls from bassinettes, oxygen deprivation, and forceps that had been too forceful. Never did anyone allow the possibility that in some way, through their own genetic arrangements, some of them bore the onus.

The neighborhood was relatively quiet. All the children except Toby had gone off to camp. Their pets grieved, but they did that in silence, sniffing and rejecting their reconstructed protein while they conducted fruitless searches through backyards and under porches.

The steady heat was still unrelieved by rain. No one had any grass left, and the bared earth was developing crevices like discarded strip mines. Many of the neighbors seeded the scorched spots and covered them with old sheets which they watered relentlessly morning and night. The bandaged block looked shell-shocked. Some of the asphalt in the street had buckled and created potholes which threw wheels out of alignment, tore into mufflers, bottomed out shocks, and sent a few tires to be plugged. There was seldom anyone outside except in the morning and in the evening when they watered their sheets. It was just too hot.

That week Sanjo began her association with Penny. The idea

was completely hers. She walked over by herself in the afternoon when Poppy and Ma were sleeping. She didn't knock or ring the bell. She just stood and waited, as patient and still as a crag on a cliff. Penny's mother came out to get the afternoon paper and walked into her. She only yelled a little, more like a yelp, took a second to recover, then invited her in.

The house had little furniture except beanbag chairs, a door that had been converted into a coffee table, and books heaped all around the corners of the room. Penny had just woken up from a nap. She didn't need a chair next to her bed anymore and was a reliable sleeper who would stay put. She was telling this to her grandmother on the telephone. Her pale blond hair, moistened by the perspiration of sleep, clung to her face like a wilted ruffle. She had the chipmunk cheeks of early childhood that made her irresistible to most adults and after which dolls were modeled. Penny was glad to have someone to play with. She didn't know any children her own age, and her daddy was away for most of the day, more than he was during the school year. He was in school himself this summer to earn his doctorate, a union card that would help him get tenure and a title that would cause strangers to tell him their medical symptoms.

Sanjo and Penny watched television that first time. Their postures were synchronized as they sat on the floor together, the little girl forty inches tall and the stolid woman weighing one hundred and forty pounds, their hands supporting them at their sides and their legs stretched out in front of them. Penny turned on the set just at the time the cookie monster was making his demands. Penny's mother thought he sounded like Sanjo and was afraid that Penny would make that onerous comparison out loud. She didn't. They watched the rest of "Sesame Street" and then the news. Penny turned from time to time like a simultaneous translator to explain to Sanjo what was happening. The announcer said that Pierre, South Dakota, had a reading of 120. "That means that Pierre wins," said Penny. Penny's mother smiled, but mainly in her mind. It was hard for her lips to move in anything but a straight line. She made a mental note to tell that to her husband later that night. She also decided that Sanjo was harmless. When Sanjo left to go home, Penny's mother said, "Next time, Sanjo, knock."

The second time they played together was at Sanjo's house three days before the HandyCaps party. Penny's mother dropped her off. Ma decided that the younger woman was plain, as she would anyone who didn't wear lipstick. At first Ma did not like having responsibility for a four-year-old child even for an afternoon. She was beginning to get tired more frequently and guarded her reserves of strength like someone expecting shortages. The only reason she consented was that Sanjo was beating her knuckles together and showing her uvula. "Sanjo will watch her," Ma said. Penny's mother thought to say something but changed her mind.

At first they stood together in the dinette, one down and one up, like a scale that has been overweighted. Penny gave her first order. "Let's color."

"Okay," said Sanjo.

"Well, get your crayons, silly."

Sanjo didn't mind being called silly. She shuffled into her bedroom with her head down in slow and heavy movements that in someone else would be signs of despondency. Actually, she was happy to get her crayons and her paper, and even would have brought her cat pictures if Penny had asked.

They spent the afternoon at the dining table, Sanjo on two cushions and Penny kneeling on the seat. Ma sat in the kitchen writing a letter to the editor of the newspaper. She wrote about once a month. It was like a homework assignment. Whenever there was a piece of news about which she had a question, or for which she sought the forum of the editorial page, she would write a letter. So far eight of her letters had been printed. She saved them all. Her most eloquent one was a plea for pity for Richard Nixon. "He has enough with a loose blood clot running around in his veins," she argued. When a paper came out with her letter in it, she bought extra copies for Mickey and Jerry and special friends. She found it helped to get published if she varied her signature. Sometimes she signed *Fed Up* or *A Reader* instead of her name. Today she was writing about the young people who threw beer cans from their car windows.

The crayons were fat and easy to get hold of. Penny was expert. She already knew how to shade, how to combine two colors, like blue and yellow to get green, and how to stay within the lines. It was harder for Sanjo. She tried with all her might, her tongue thrust farther out, her breathing labored, but the crayons slipped out of her grasp or nudged color past the line. Sections remained unfilled, and a windmill and a Dutch girl were colored alike. She used only red and yellow, while Penny had created beauty and precision with the full spectrum of Crayola.

Penny was patient. "Stay in the lines," she said.

"Okay," said Sanjo.

"No, like this. Look how I do it." Sanjo watched the tiny hand feather a giraffe in blended ochre. "Now you."

Sanjo took her yellow crayon and obliterated the giraffe.

"That's mean. You did that on purpose!" Penny began to cry.

Ma rushed in from the kitchen. "What's the matter?"

Sanjo was miserable. "She crying."

"I know she's crying, but why?"

Sanjo shrugged. She fixed her eyes on Penny. Penny screwed her face tighter and tighter, corrugating her forehead and nose until all she had left was a mouth. Sanjo tried to do it but only came as close as squeezing her eyes.

"Don't you start," said Ma. Tears gushed from slits that used to be Penny's eyes. Copious and lavish, they bathed her face and her little pink T-shirt with the white balloon.

Sanjo cupped her stumpy hand and clubbed Penny on the back. "Don't cry," she said.

Penny had never been clubbed before. The novelty dried up her tears like a hand on a faucet. It was over. "Don't touch my work again," she said.

"Penny cry," said Sanjo to Ma.

"I need this?" said Ma, and went back into the kitchen to

finish her letter. Maybe she'd sign it *A Concerned Citizen*. She thought that in all fairness they should really charge Penny's mother for baby-sitting.

Sanjo and Penny spent the next hour coloring. A mail truck crawled past the house. Sanjo, intent on staying within the lines, never saw it. Penny had an idea. It illuminated her face. "Start in the middle," she said. Sanjo didn't know what the middle was. Penny poked a tiny finger in the center. "Right here."

It helped a little to start from the middle. Sanjo was able to get closer to the line without going over. Things looked smaller without their full perimeter, but neater. Sanjo was proud. "Look, Ma! Middle!"

Ma came rushing in from the kitchen again, then leaned against the credenza to search for breath like a fish on the sand. As she labored to supply more oxygen for her bloodstream, she thought of her widowed friend Minnie Hightower, whose children had sent her on a cruise around the world and who was at this moment eating her way through Europe. Sanjo was waving a picture of a disproportionate mare and colt, two ghostly apparitions with unfinished exteriors and red-delineated interiors. "That's good work," gasped Ma. Penny didn't need encouragement. She knew she was good. The mail truck went by a second time.

They were on their second book when Poppy came back from the community center. He felt good. A successful match with Lou Green, a retired accountant, showed him that at least in chess there was nothing wrong with his mind.

Lou Green wore a colostomy bag. No one mentioned it. Everyone was sympathetic. It was the next to the ultimate catastrophe. At first they had had a minor disagreement over what constituted a touch move. Lou, a compulsive man who irrigated his stoma for hours, was a stickler for form. He insisted Poppy follow through on a move when Poppy was only straightening the piece. "We're playing touch move now, remember?"

"Who touched it?" asked Poppy.

[61]

"You did," replied Lou. "You just touched it. With your whole hand."

Morris looked around. There was always an audience of other men. They shook their heads in disapproval, a Greek chorus of ancients, there to explain the story, forecast doom, pronounce judgment, and sometimes, when the weather was nice, play a little bocce. Poppy could not bear the stigma of cheater. He pursed his lips, shrugged his shoulders, and made the move.

In the end justice had triumphed. In one of his best traps he let Lou take his bishop. The trap was sprung. Morris took his rook like plucking a feather from a still-living bird and slapped his knee. Only a few more moves to checkmate. Everyone knew it. It was a moment to be proud of.

Now Poppy had on his robe and leaned into the kitchen to make an announcement. Like railroad conductors, Poppy and Ma called out their stops. "I'm going to take a nice rest."

Ma looked up from her letter. "That's a good idea. Sanjo's watching the little girl next door."

"What little girl? The Giddens don't have any children."

"The Giddens moved out. These are new people."

"What do you mean, watching?" asked Poppy. This was not really a question for Ma. It was under his breath.

The child was pretty. Morris tightened his robe. He wasn't sure what to say around small children.

"You're a good girl," he said.

"Is that your grandpa?" asked Penny.

"He's Poppy," replied Sanjo.

"My grandpa takes me on his sailboat," said Penny. "I have to wear a jacket. It's *this* color."

On his way past Sanjo and the little blond child, the telephone rang. Poppy answered it. "What?"

It was Runi. "Table, table."

He knew immediately who it was. "You must have the wrong number."

"Table!"

A woman should know when it's over. He lowered his voice.

"Runi, please, I'm a family man. Don't call anymore."

There was a sob. The phone clicked. Poppy went to bed.

"Is it three o'clock?" asked Penny. That was her time limit.

Sanjo didn't know.

"Can't you tell time?" she asked.

Sanjo scratched her arm.

"I can." Penny slid off the seat. "This is the big hand." She stretched on her toes to point to a clock that was sitting on the credenza.

Sanjo pushed her chair back from the table and stood up. "Big hand," she said.

Penny jumped back a little when she saw the dragons on the doors. She still wasn't sure what time it was since her instructions on time telling up to that point had been confined to which was the big or the little hand. She fled with grace. "My mommy wants me." She ran to the door and stood in front of it. "Open the door, I can't get out."

With some effort and a finger pinched in the slide, Sanjo slid out the chain and opened the door.

Penny bounced down the steps like a ball. Sanjo stood and watched her for a long time, even after she entered the door of her own home. Although Sanjo stood still, her shadow didn't. She would have stayed longer except that Ma came to the door. "Close the screen, Sanjo. All the bugs are coming in." That was a lie. The bugs were waiting for nightfall.

By the end of the week, the summer had taken over as completely as the military junta took over Chile. There was no escape. A temperature inversion laid a blanket of heat over the city, trapping the carbon monoxide and sulfur dioxide beneath to create a pollution count of an unacceptable seven. This qualification by the weatherman who described the situation was gratuitous, since no one had a choice. They had to accept it. Even with his Telstar photos and computer readouts he was helpless and he knew it. To hide his embarrassment he made jokes about isobars, calling them good guys and bad guys. The

[63]

weather had a soporific effect. Everyone was stuporous and slept most of the time. Ma spent as much time as she could indoors. The heat affected her breathing, poking its way into her lungs like fingers. She was beginning to think she should have her chest x-rayed at her next checkup. Even the baby mosquitoes clustered on the surface of the evaporating stagnant water knew it wasn't a time to do anything but float on their egg rafts.

The only time Ma and Poppy could do their supermarket shopping was early in the morning when it first opened. At 8 A.M., except for the stock clerks, meat-cutters, and checkers, they were the only customers in the store. Poppy pushed the cart, Ma threw in what they needed, and Sanjo held on. It was a sophisticated operation. Sanjo provided the necessary ballast to keep the cart from tipping over. It took them about an hour.

On Thursday they had an unpleasant incident in the produce section. The vegetable man complained about Sanjo, who had accidentally drooled over some oranges. Ma was outraged. She accused the vegetable man of defiling the oranges in worse and unspeakable ways with his hands. The vegetable man added counter abuses, which included something about someone letting them out who shouldn't have, and within seconds the affair, which now included the manager and another customer, escalated out of all proportion. Poppy made it simple. "Wipe her mouth and let's go," he said.

It was like the time they were asked to leave the Land of Steak. The headwaiter, a young man wearing a cowboy hat and chaps who provided them with a catalog of grievances, said among other things that the patrons complained that the drooling upset them and they couldn't eat. Poppy and Ma learned to avoid such restaurants. The criteria they selected were (a) restaurants with no seated children, (b) restaurants with headwaiters, and (c) restaurants that did not have their menus posted outside.

On Friday afternoon Ma went to Mr. Tommy's to have her hair spun into cotton candy. It was the one time during the week that she was alone. The commotion in the shop was like the preparation for an evacuation. Everyone ran. Some ran from the waiting room to the shampoo girl, some ran from the shampoo girl to their operator. Some ran the wrong way and had to be rerouted. It was all coordinated through the receptionist, a steely-faced woman of immense determination, who barked out orders like a troop-train marshal. Ma liked the excitement. When she was told to get washed, she moved pretty fast too, even with her arthritic hip sockets, in a sort of side-to-side gait like a crab.

Poppy and Sanjo were alone in the house. Sanjo was keeping a vigil at the window for Penny like a Synge heroine waiting for her sailor son. The only sign of life so far had been Penny's father bringing in some boxes from his car. Poppy had just finished counting his pills. He decided to throw in the rest of his medicine, since it was making him feel dizzy again. That brought the count up to 1,855. He decided to take Sanjo to a movie.

He looked in the newspaper for a suitable picture and found one. It was called *Pussycats on Parade.* He knew that Sanjo was crazy about cats ever since Bigboy, whom she never forgot. The cat picture would occupy her and he could sleep.

"You wanna go to a movie, Sanjo?"

"Movie!" declared Sanjo. She patted her tongue.

"Yeh, a movie, about cats."

She threw her head back and rested it on her vertebrae. "Bigboy."

"This isn't Bigboy. It's just plain cats."

With some difficulty Sanjo got to her feet and, in a gesture of magnanimous affection, smothered her face in Poppy's arm. They walked that way to the car.

The theater was a little farther away than the theater they usually went to. It was located in another part of town pockmarked by signs both formal and informal. The formal ones, carefully lettered on cardboard, were advertisements and said *Adults Only* and *Yes—We Have Layaway* and *Thunderbird 92¢.* The informal ones were written with spray paint on walls and said *Cool Earl* or *Clubhead is the one,* advertisements of people who wanted to leave their marks on the world.

When Poppy and Sanjo got out of the car, a man walked by

with his dished-in lips glued to a bottle in a paper bag. He was edentulous, having long ago lost the need of teeth.

It was a small theater. Poppy paid for two adults since he never argued, and besides there was only one price. Inside the theater was cozy and dark, like someone's living room with the lights turned down low. It smelled of soggy velour and half-eaten Mallomars. A few isolated patrons sat scattered like birdshot, marking off whole rows for themselves. Poppy and Sanjo crawled over a man with a hat in his lap. Sanjo knocked his hat off onto the floor. With elaborate polishing movements, the man smoothed the brim with his sleeve, then put it back in his lap exactly as it had been placed before. They moved to the other end of the aisle.

"Poppy, Hershey."

"I don't believe it. Why didn't you ask me before?"

"Poppy, Hershey."

"I don't want to get up again."

Sanjo had few wants. The ones she had were powerful. "No. Hershey, now." For chocolate she could be a tyrant.

Poppy groaned, eased himself up again, and crawled over the man in the center, but not before the man grabbed his hat and put it on his head for safety.

When he came back with the Hershey, the man was clearly annoyed. "You guys should stop jumping around. This ain't no playground."

Poppy didn't answer him.

The movie began. It showed a delivery man and a housewife talking about the meaning of existence. Poppy sighed. There was not a single cat in the movie. Another loser. Within minutes he fell asleep. The housewife and the delivery man took off their clothes. They did things to each other on the kitchen table. The man in the aisle was doing something under his hat. The house- wife beckoned at the door. Her neighbor came in. She took off her clothes, too. People kept ringing the doorbell and taking off their clothes. Then they combined in an artful mélange to explore each other's orifices with lots of different body parts.

[66]

The camera zoomed in like a flyswatter in case there was any question. At one time a single labia minora was projected over 400 square feet. Sanjo finished the Hershey in the first reel and waited for the cats.

Poppy woke up when the housewife was saying good-bye to her friends. "Did you have enough?" he asked.

"Uh-huh," she replied.

"Let's go."

Sanjo squinted against the full sunlight. Her pupils constricted to tiny pinpoints. "Special 'livery," she said.

At seven o'clock a beanie of heat sat on the city like a cardinal's cap. A few male crickets were tuning up for their cucaracha band, using their long front jumping legs, which they rubbed against one another, for bows. The females, as usual, were quiet. Mrs. Cervitano was watering the sheets spread over her lawn. Ma, Poppy, and Sanjo were inside getting ready for the Handy-Caps party.

Getting dressed all at once always involved a commotion. Tonight they banged into one another like plates of the earth's crust, tectons crashing in hallway and bathroom, in massive and resounding movements. Poppy nicked himself shaving. He didn't want to shave in the first place but Ma insisted. He would have liked to grow a beard like Phil Schussel, whose grandson, also a beard wearer, trimmed it for him. "Why?" asked Ma. "So Swann's could hire you for Santa Claus?" He balked when it came to clothes. He had put on a sport shirt and slacks. The slacks, like all his pants, were baggy and uneven and in some places had enough material for another person, but he liked them. Ma said he would look better if he wore a coat and tie. It was a diversionary tactic. If people looked at his top they wouldn't look at his bottom. Poppy said nothing could get him into a jacket and tie, not even his own funeral. Ma said God forbid. Meanwhile she was having her own problems. Her new long-line bra cut into her middle. She was weighing having uplifted breasts against a pain-free stomach when Sanjo fell.

[67]

Sanjo took the dress out of the box before Ma said she could. She tried to slip it over her head. When that didn't work, she tried stepping into it. She got it as far as her hips, made one hop, and fell to the ground like a stone.

Poppy came in from the bedroom. "What?"

Ma came in clutching her robe. "Who told you to put it on? It's not time yet for you. You're last." They tried rolling her over but failed until Poppy dragged the dress off her feet.

The night-blue silk, as elegant as the dynasties it was designed for, was unscathed. Sanjo was not so lucky. She had banged her mouth in the fall and cut her tongue on her teeth. She began to cry. "Hurts me. Hurts me." Ma scrambled into the bathroom, grabbed a towel, and returned to staunch the wound. Poppy, who was on the floor beside her patting her head, turned away. For the moment his thirty-four-year-old chest pain was back.

When they got the bleeding stopped, the only thing left was to get the dress back on Sanjo. Poppy lifted it over her head. Sanjo, still sniffling, stuck her arms over her head and waited for Poppy to slip the dress on. Ma helped him pull it down to Sanjo's knees, then zipped up the back. Finally, they were ready to leave, Ma, saggy-breasted in a spring-green pants suit, Poppy, freshly shaved, in a sport shirt and slacks, and Sanjo, resplendent in the cheongsam, even with a washcloth held over her tongue. As they were getting into the car, Mrs. Cervitano blew kisses to Sanjo.

The HandyCaps, through their agent Miss Furlowe, had selected the auditorium of the special school as the site of their first get-together. Actually, it was never only the special school but a junior high school of which the special school was just a small part. Sanjo remembered it right away. Although the bleeding had stopped she still carried the bloodied washcloth. "My school." She touched the cloth to the building, daubing the bricks in joyful recognition.

"Look how she knows," said Ma. Poppy walked beside them like someone in a dream.

[68]

Inside, the auditorium, which also doubled as a gymnasium, was all lit up, although it was only the far end that was in use. Green and red balloons and streamers hung from the rafters where they had been stapled by Frank, the janitor, who didn't remember any of these people but who had been paid five dollars by Mr. Binko to do the job. Left over from Christmas, the decorations hung motionless, wafted into flight only when the rotating fan pointed their way.

Folding chairs had been set up along the far walls. Many of these were occupied, although some of the guests were in wheelchairs. One was in a combination chair and table over which his head, jerked into false alarms by damaged neurons, bobbed like an apple in a tub.

The Bernatskys knew the Binkos and made their way to them first. Joey was more handsome than ever. He was dressed in a pale-blue cord suit with a vest. A blue tie with tiny red figures and a perfect knot met at his throat to set off his black-fringed, innocent blue eyes. His black hair had been shaped into an outline which stroked down his well-molded skull, the finishing touch to a young man of exquisite beauty. He had not had to sit in a stroller for fifteen years, due to the efforts of several physical therapists, including one who had strange ideas about teaching him to crawl first. Now he was able to sit, stand, and walk like everyone else. The only thing he had not learned to do was talk. Joey didn't appear to recognize the Bernatskys and was pushed into social response by his parents, who operated him like a pair of puppeteers. "Joey, see Sanjo." They turned Joey in her direction. "And here's Mr. and Mrs. Bernatsky." They turned Joey in the other direction. Joe was patient. They could turn him any way they wanted. He always waited for the next command, still and beautiful, perfectly poised except when he made tongue darts at the air.

"Sanjo, say hello to Joey," said Ma. Sanjo knew Joey. They went to Opportunity Class together and got certificates. She thought he was pretty, like Sally Cervitano, and patted his arm.

"Joey—" Mrs. Binko gasped. She was going to say "Move

away, Joey," but she was too late to save Joey's suit from the washcloth.

Parents, in middle age or later, were reintroducing themselves to one another. A lot of them told each other that they didn't look any different, but of course that was a lie. They did look different. Tissues had dropped, hairlines had receded, and total body bulk had shifted emphasis enough to erode their distinctive features just as the tide changes the look of the sand.

The big surprise was the children. They were now adults in their twenties and thirties. Because of a general inability to grasp an abstraction like development and change, few of them recognized each other, and the parents, who faced another kind of disability, recognized none except their own. For some illogical reason, the parents expected to see the children as they had been, and they were not prepared for these other people, many of whom were taller than they. Those who were not held by anxious family wandered around the periphery of the gathering, slowly and shyly making their way into the center, even a few in wheelchairs, all except Paul Macintyre, who was hyperkinetic and made his way through the maze of unconnected people like a hysterical rat.

In the middle of the auditorium was Miss Furlowe, billowing and bellowing her enthusiasm like a hurricane revolving around its eye. She was the only one who recognized each and every person there. She had not changed. Ma decided it was because when Miss Furlowe was thirty she looked fifty. When she saw Sanjo, she drew her into her arms, which were covered with a Mexican shawl, and hugged her. The fringes tickled Sanjo's nose. Sanjo sneezed.

"My goodness, you're sturdy! Isn't she sturdy?" she asked. Miss Furlowe could find something good about anyone.

Sanjo took the shawl, handcrafted by the citizens of Pueblo, and draped it over her own shoulders. Poppy grabbed it back and offered it to Miss Furlowe, who didn't seem to notice any of the exchange.

"You know who this is?" asked Ma.

Sanjo remembered. It was hard to forget love. "Furlowe." She sank her face into her teacher's arm.

Ma asked about the different children she had remembered and their mothers. Like a guide in an art museum, Miss Furlowe pointed out certain people in the room as the matured so-and-so. Ma remembered an adorable little girl called Cindy with brown curly hair and an elfin face. Miss Furlowe indicated with a wave of her other arm a tall heavy woman with an elfin face and puzzled eyes. Ma asked about Andy Brown. She and Mrs. Brown had taken turns getting the children off to school. Andy was spastic and had to be tied in a chair so he couldn't bite his hands, although he did bite off pieces of his lip. Miss Furlowe looked sorrowful for a moment. Her billowing stopped. Andy had died. So had seven of the other children. Then the sadness passed, and she whirled once more at the center of the gathering, winding the survivors together like ribbons on a Maypole.

Sanjo found her way to the punchbowl and discovered by watching Paul Macintyre that one could get something good to drink by dipping a ladle in the bowl and pouring it into a cup. Sanjo couldn't quite duplicate the movements. She grasped the ladle in her stubby fingers and got it into the punchbowl, but the return route to the cup gave her trouble. It was then that the punch spilled on her dress, leaving a stain that seeped from her right shoulder to her left waist like a royal decoration. Paul was happy to oblige. He was short, hairy, had thick lips, elbows flexed at his side that helped him pour, a big forehead, and a chronic nasal discharge. He also had an immediate attraction to Sanjo and her dress and followed her for the rest of the evening, touching the drying silk and bringing her punch. Poppy spent the evening running interference. "Go over there," he would say, or, "Your mother wants you." Paul was undaunted. Like the Mad Hatter entertaining Alice, it was his tea party, and with frenetic movements he continued to bring Sanjo cups of punch which spilled out most of their contents on the floor and on other people. Once he brought her a streamer. Alice put it on her head.

The former members of the special class continued to make their way through the small gathering like caravans crossing the desert. Sometimes they spoke, sometimes they touched, and sometimes their only communication was a look. At one time things got particularly stressful when Imogene Panelli, colossally fat, who had eaten an entire tray of cookies, began to stamp her tiny feet and scream for more food. Her open turned-down mouth spewed forth her terrible rage. Her tired-looking sister was trying to comfort her but was not succeeding. Imogene's hunger was an awesome thing. She was known to steal food and eat garbage to assuage it. Now everyone trembled in its wake.

"Get some more cookies," someone suggested.

"How could we run out so fast?" asked another.

"She ate them all." This report from Paul Macintyre. No one remembered seeing her do it. It was quite a feat: four packages of Oreos and one box of Boston tea. She was led away by her sister and Miss Furlowe, who quieted her at the rear of the hall.

Since the food was all gone, Miss Furlowe got everyone to sit down. This was the first meeting and they would have a lot to talk over. She called upon Margaret Paley to begin the discussion. Margaret was one of the few who had come alone. She was a neat woman with a tight, shiny face and long brown hair which she wore bound with a twisted rubber band. She did not look as shy as the others. Margaret stood.

"We thought it was a good idea, Miss Furlowe and me, to write to everyone so they should come tonight. Miss Furlowe wrote. I licked the envelopes." The Virgin Mary was all grown up, carried a canvas shoulder bag, and wore a yellow summer dress. Miss Furlowe nodded encouragement. "We should have a club."

"I like a club," said Paul Macintyre, dancing away from Sanjo with his arms flexed and flapping like a mummer's.

"We should meet and talk," continued Margaret. "Things are hard for me. I know that it's harder for lots of you. We should still meet and talk." Miss Furlowe whispered something. Margaret continued. "Miss Furlowe wants me to tell you about my job. I put glass in tissue paper. Like this." She showed them a few movements. "Then I put it in a box. They pay me money. They're nice to me." Margaret Paley sat down. Then got up again quickly. An afterthought. "Maybe some of you could get jobs too."

Everyone applauded. She stole the show again, just as she did twenty years ago in the Christmas play when she had asked, "Wanna see my baby?"

Paul rushed back with his eleventh cup of punch, but Poppy brushed him away like a fly. "Get away with that!" he hissed.

Mr. Binko got up to speak. Miss Furlowe came down on him like a boom just as he was formulating his first word. He had his lips pursed for a "w." "Mr. Binko, please sit down." Mr. Binko, with three hundred employees, at least two hundred and fifty of whom didn't even dare to speak to him, sat and unpursed his lips. "Joey," she asked, "do you want to say anything to the others?"

"Stand up, Joey," said Mrs. Binko. Joey stood up, Apollo ready to be cast. He darted his tongue in the air.

Miss Furlowe said, "Joey isn't ready yet. Maybe another time." She was an incredible optimist. "Would anyone else like to say something?" A few people stepped forward. What they said was largely unrelated, but it didn't matter. Applause followed each one. The meeting was beginning to have the aspects of a revival.

A young man in jeans pushed forward his friend in the tabletop chair. The head of the man in the chair continued to jerk. His hands flailed about him in twisted helpless movements. It was harder to understand him than anyone else. He spoke in groans which approximated speech only through their stresses. Miss Furlowe translated.

"You don't like the name of this club, Mark?"

"Uh-uh."

"Would you like to change it?"

"Uh-huh."

"What do you suggest?"

More groaning and flailing.

"You're suggesting that the club be called Disabled Sons?"

The flailings grew more violent. His friend in the blue jeans spoke from behind the handlebars of the chair. "Mark said Disabled Citizens."

"Oh, citizens," amended the teacher.

"That's a good name," said Margaret Paley. "We should vote."

Miss Furlowe explained to the group. "Mark thinks it would be a good idea to call this club Disabled Citizens instead of HandyCaps. Margaret thinks it's a good idea too. It's time to vote. That means we will count up the number of people who like one name, then we will count up the number who like the other name. We'll see which name wins." They voted. Paul voted twice because he was in a different part of the room during each count. Disabled Citizens won hands down.

Spirits were high. Sanjo wanted to talk too. She shuffled forward with her head hanging down and held up the washcloth like a winning ticket. "I fall down."

Ma noticed the stain that crossed her chest like a banner. "Oh, my God, look at her dress." Poppy didn't hear her. He was busy waiting to brush away Paul.

The applause was sweet. Sanjo was not ready to relinquish the spotlight. She hesitated for a moment, laid her head back on her vertebrae, showed her uvula, and came to her conclusion. "This new dress."

4

Sanjo tried to tell Penny about the HandyCaps but did not have enough words. "Furlowe," she said.

"What?" Penny had to shade her eyes to look up. "I don't know what you mean."

"Sanjo go poddy."

"You have to go potty? Don't make poo-poo in your pants. My mommy won't let you stay."

Sanjo kept trying to explain. The effort forced her tongue out of her mouth.

"Put your tongue back." Penny was tired of looking up. She directed her remarks to Sanjo's stomach. "You wanna make a peep show?"

"Uh-huh."

"Do you know what it is?" Sanjo stared at the figure below her. "Oh, silly, I'll show you."

Penny led her to the backyard with one hand while carrying a piece of plastic and a spoon with the other. "Kneel down," she ordered. Penny dug a little hole in the ground with the spoon and placed the plastic on top. Sanjo tried to dig too but Penny pushed her hand away. "Let me," she said. Penny covered the plastic with grass. "See, now we can have a peep show." She flicked the grass aside with her tiny finger.

Sanjo stared. It was the same hole in the ground.

"We have to put something in the peep show," said Penny. "I'll get something. Wait here." Sanjo sat rooted. Penny returned with a dark green crayon. "I don't like this color," she said. She lifted the plastic and dropped the crayon in the hole.

"Peep," said Sanjo.

"Now *you* get something."

Sanjo didn't move.

Penny articulated slowly, the way she did to her teddy bear. "Go home and get something to put in the peep show."

Sanjo raised herself to her feet. She smiled at Penny and walked home, bent forward at the waist with her head hanging down.

She returned with all her cat pictures. "They're too big," said Penny. "Get something smaller." Sanjo took her cat pictures home and tacked them back on her bulletin board. She went into the bathroom and opened the medicine cabinet. On the no-no shelf was a tube. She took it down.

"That's better," said Penny. She lifted the plastic and dropped the tube inside, then put the plastic back in place. "You can put the grass on." Sanjo heaped grass on top. Penny brushed the blades aside. "Look, Sanjo."

Sanjo looked. Inside the hole was a dark green crayon and a tube from the no-no shelf. "We have a peep show," said Penny. They spent the next hour alternately uncovering and covering the plastic until Penny's mother sent Sanjo home.

Poppy was surprised to see Mr. Niemeyer at the door. The mailman never rang the bell unless he had a package or a Special Delivery. As he handed Poppy a trial laundry softener in a little box and two letters, he seemed to be studying the screen. Stains shaped like scimitar blades underscored his arms. His pink face was flushed roseate and he mopped it with a handkerchief.

"You wanna glass of water?"

"No, thanks, Mr. Bernatsky." The mailman continued to look past him.

Poppy turned around. "You wanna use the bathroom?"

Mr. Niemeyer pointed to the laundry softener. "Some people are taking these out of other people's boxes."

"Yeah?" Poppy turned the laundry softener over in his hand. It was hard to imagine Mrs. Cervitano slipping a hand into his mailbox to steal it.

"How's your family?" asked Mr. Niemeyer.

Poppy was perplexed. He had lived in this house for over thirty years and in that time the only words he had ever heard from this postman or the one before him had been "postage due" or "sign here." "They're okay."

They stood for a moment looking each other over.

"Well, so long." The postman gave one more furtive look through the screen door and left.

Poppy recovered in time to yell to the truck, "How's yours?" Mr. Niemeyer didn't hear him. The mail truck left, jerking its way over the potholes in the street.

Poppy brought in the mail. One of the letters was addressed to Sanjo. No one ever wrote to her except political candidates seeking office who got her name from the voting list, and they didn't count.

Ma came in from the bathroom where she had been scrubbing the dirt from under Sanjo's nails. "Who's writing to you, Sanjo?" she asked. The question was directed to the air. She slipped her finger in the envelope and slit it.

Sanjo followed from the bathroom with water dripping from her fingers. "Mine?" she asked.

"Yes, a letter for you."

"Special 'livery," said Sanjo.

"No, it's not Special Delivery." The envelope was rent asunder. Ma lifted her glasses from her chest and read.

"What does it say? Who's it from?" asked Poppy. The event of Sanjo getting a personalized letter was as noteworthy as if the state department had called her asking what to do with Angola.

"Gimme," said Sanjo.

"Wait, I'll read it to you." The letter was typewritten.

[77]

Dear Miss Bernatsky,

Our meeting two weeks ago was just a beginning. We plan our first club meeting next month and hope you can come. Dues are two dollars a month. I hope that you can make it. If transportation is a problem, call Margaret Paley at 555-5099. If you don't understand this letter, call me in the evening at 555-6789 and my roommate will explain it to you.

Yours truly,
Mark Kinnon,
Secretary
Disabled
Citizens

Poppy took the letter and read it himself. "Crazy. They're making a regular thing out of this. Which one was Mark Kinnon?"

Ma grabbed it away. The letter passed back and forth between them like a basketball. "I'm not sure. There were so many," said Ma.

"Mark in chair," said Sanjo.

"Which one in the chair?" asked Ma. Sanjo bobbed her head up and down many times. "Oh, that one. He wrote this letter?"

Poppy grabbed it back. "He didn't write it. His friend wrote it. The kid who pushed him." The guard jumped for the ball. "Did you understand the letter?" Poppy asked Sanjo. As a guard he was relentless.

"What's the difference, Morry. Here's your letter, Sanjo." She handed the letter over. Sanjo pressed it to her chest and then tucked it in her Snoopy purse and snapped the lid closed.

Poppy was glad to put it out of his mind. He had been traumatized by the adult disabled citizens. They were as seriously handicapped when they were children but somehow it was much worse now that they were full-grown.

"This is for you, Morry," said Ma. "Some lawyer, see, a firm name."

"Now what?" asked Poppy. He opened his letter a little slower than Ma had opened Sanjo's.

Ma stood behind him. She was everybody's censor. "What does it say?"

"Flo, I don't even have it open yet."

Sanjo watched from one to the other.

"Read Poppy letter," she said to Ma.

"Poppy can read it by himself."

"Self," said Sanjo to her chest. Sanjo knew all about reading. People read by looking at paper and talking. She took the letter out of her Snoopy purse and opened it up. Then she spoke. "Sanjo come to club, call Margaret, truly Mark." Said over and over again, it was like an incantation.

Meanwhile, Poppy's reading had an immediate effect. His color drained away from his face as if someone had pulled out plugs in his feet. "Morry, what?" asked Ma.

"I don't know. It's nothing."

"What do you mean, nothing. Is it Mr. Giddens? Is he suing us? Remember he slipped on our sidewalk when he was moving?" Poppy's thoughts swept him away from the moment as effectively as a tsunami washes away whole villages. He was afloat on a banana leaf somewhere in the South Pacific.

The first time he met Runi Bindlehouse she came in to buy a dinette chrome and Formica two-seater, one of his advertised specials. He told her that actually she was better off with a four-seater, but Runi replied that the two-seater would do fine since she lived alone. Something about the woman appealed to him. Morris tried to remember what it was. Maybe it was her independence and the way she couldn't be switched to a number she didn't need. Maybe it was her eyes, which promised to give all and ask nothing in return.

"What does a lawyer want with you?" He was off the banana leaf and in the water. A flash of inspiration, the kind that came to him from time to time, made its appearance. It was one of the things that led him to believe he was a creative person.

"He has a client who wants to go into dinettes and he wants my advice." He finished like a kid in school who has successfully listed all the islands in the Azores. Ma almost bought it except

[79]

that Poppy continued to look stricken the rest of the afternoon. She cornered him in the bathroom, where he was most vulnerable. "When are you going to the lawyer to talk about dinettes?"

"Tuesday, four o'clock."

"Good, I'm going with you."

The lawyer's office was furnished in red and brown Naugahyde with big poster prints on the wall. A wooden mallard decoy with a chipped beak sat on an end table. They didn't wait very long. That was the decision of the secretary, a pretty young woman with long thin legs that wrapped around each other like vines. She kept looking at Sanjo. The looking was obsessive, done against her will by some unknown force. Whenever she turned to face her IBM Selectric, the force swiveled her head around, causing her face to keep reappearing like a wooden dairymaid in a cuckoo clock.

Sanjo stared at a picture of a lion stretched out in the tall grasses. "That's a cat," said Poppy. Nervousness made him show off.

"No," said Sanjo.

"It's a cat," insisted Poppy.

"What are you telling her, Morry?"

"Didn't you know that lions and cats are in the same family?"

"No," said Sanjo. She couldn't be fooled. Poppy had no more to say. He looked straight ahead, not to the left, not to the right; like someone about to be guillotined, he had eyes only for the basket.

The lawyer was a tall thin man with a blond mustache that tickled the insides of his nose. He kept flaring his nostrils and twitching them away from the hairs.

"Now, Mr. Bernatsky and Mrs. Bernatsky, and—your daughter?"

"Sandra Joanne," said Ma, just in case. The secretary continued to swivel, even though she was alone in the outer office.

Sanjo smiled. The lawyer was pretty, like Sally and Joey Binko. "Hullo." She started to get up.

[80]

"Sit, Sanjo," said Ma. The words came through her teeth, plate and all. The force was amazing considering that they were clamped shut.

"As I stated in my letter, I'm handling the estate of the late Miss Runchel Bindlehouse, and I'm please to tell you that Miss Bindlehouse named you in her will with a bequest of ten thousand dollars. You might say that Miss Bindlehouse left you a bundle." No one laughed at his little joke. Morris turned to ice. "Of course, it will be some time before the estate is settled, but I thought you'd be pleased to know. I could have told you in the letter but I wanted to cushion the surprise." He was also looking for new clients, but that remained unsaid.

Ma turned. "Runchel Bindlehouse. Does he mean that old lady on Chester Street?"

The attorney checked his papers. "Yes, Miss Bindlehouse lived on thirty-three-oh-four Chester. May she rest in peace."

Morris was silent. Like Lot's wife, he had turned into a pillar.

"There has to be some mistake. We don't even know her," said Ma. "Not that we couldn't use the money. But right is right."

"Oh, no, there's no mistake. Miss Bindlehouse was quite clear about the bequest. In fact, only two people share in the estate, Mr. Bernatsky and a niece in Chicago." Poppy would have been glad to see the whole thing go to the niece. His speech was gone. Maybe it would come back.

"But why?" asked Ma. "It doesn't make sense. Why should she leave you so much money? You didn't even know her."

"Table," said Sanjo. No one paid her any attention. She said it to her chest.

The attorney, who was thirty and unable to conceive of any illicit goings-on among the elderly, especially his eighty-one-year-old, frail, partially paralyzed client who had a one-word vocabulary, suddenly realized the whole story. So did Ma. "Or did you?"

"I built her a dinette once."

"And for that she leaves you ten thousand dollars?"

[81]

"How do I know why an old lady does crazy things? Didn't your Aunt Mema feed pictures? It was disgusting. All the pictures of her family had crusts at the mouths. She used to prop them up at the dining table. She was old. Crazy. Like this woman. Can anyone say why?"

It was a good plea. Even the attorney was impressed, although he would have gladly given up his silver Audi for one month if he could have disappeared. He was not to be so lucky.

Sanjo knew the signs of trouble before he did. "No bad talk," she said. She stood up and patted Poppy's head with her stubby fingers, then kissed Ma's arm.

"How long did you know her, the old lady?"

Poppy wished Ma would stop calling Runi the old lady. "I told you I built her a dinette once."

That's it, thought the attorney, stick to your story. He had an idea of his own. "Lots of people leave money to perfect strangers."

"Not to us," said Ma.

The attorney lowered his voice to a deep muffle. "Maybe Miss Bindlehouse wanted to contribute to your burden." The burden was now clutching his arm. He shook it off like a horse rippling its back.

"What burden?" asked Ma.

"I got letter," said Sanjo to the lawyer.

"Sit," said Ma through her tetany.

The lawyer was sorry that he didn't state the whole thing in his letter as he should have done in the first place. There must be a better way to rout out new clients.

They rode back in silence. The only sound was the rattling of the fan belt. Sanjo sat in the back seat holding her head and rocking back and forth. Ma and Poppy had each insulated themselves in an air pocket and were as remote from one another as if each occupied a different pole. The commotion didn't start until they got home. It began with the fury of water rushing from a broken lock.

[82]

Ma turned to Poppy. "Why?"

"I don't know what you're talking about."

To help him, Ma turned up her decibel level. "Why? Just answer me that! And with an old lady!" she screamed.

"She wasn't always an old lady."

Ma started to cry. The screaming changed to keening. "When?"

Poppy shrugged.

"When? Does everyone know?"

"No one knows," he said.

"How do you know?"

"We were very careful."

Ma started screaming again.

"Flo, it was a long time ago."

"How long?"

"At least three years."

"Three years! Three years ago you were running around with an old lady should have been in a nursing home?"

Poppy sat with his head in his hands. He was trying to keep it from falling into the basket.

"When did you start?"

"A long time ago. Who remembers?" He remembered. Runi had comforted him when he told her about the child of fourteen months who had to be propped up with pillows. He remembered her tea that she made in a china pot and her bed with the down quilt. Once he fell asleep on it and awoke with a goose feather teasing his nose and Runi kissing his forehead.

"Why? Why? I wasn't a good wife?"

"Of course you were a good wife. It had nothing to do with that. I don't know why."

"I had chances myself, you know."

Poppy didn't take that remark seriously. The thought of Ma's infidelity was as remote as the rings of Saturn.

Ma started crying again. "You ran from here to Chester Street. From Chester Street back here. You were pretty busy."

[83]

Poppy couldn't remember why he went in the first place. "I made a mistake, Flo. I'm sorry."

"This doesn't count as a mistake. A mistake you make once. This was your other life."

"It wasn't another life. It was just a small part. Like a hobby." It was a bad analogy. Ma started screaming again.

Sanjo sat on the front porch and leaned against the railing. She covered her ears with her hands. The tears fell down her cheeks and mixed with the eddies that gushed from her nose and mouth, turning her face and neck into a delta. Her heart beat fast and hammered against her rib cage. She gagged once or twice. If she could have moved with any speed, she would have run away, but she had never learned how. Slow walking was the best she could do. The screaming continued. Mrs. Ryan's dog had gotten out and was barking. It paced back and forth on the sidewalk, railing against an unseen presence. Once it passed in front of Sanjo's porch and looked at the house.

Across the street Toby was having his own troubles with his ten-speed bicycle, which was now, for some reason, good for only two. He had to come downhill in second gear with pedals that spun too fast. He was trying to figure out what to do without success. He kicked at the wheels, struck at the chain, then flung the bike to the sidewalk. It didn't get up. He snarled at it, kicked it some more. Finally, he threw it into the Cervitanos' shrubbery. "You shit!" he screamed.

Sally Cervitano came rushing out of his mother's house. His mother was away, visiting her sister in New Jersey, and he had a woman inside. It was his first great opportunity in ten years. "What's the matter? What are you kicking your bike in our bushes for?"

The screaming from Sanjo's house and now the fuss over the bike had upset the woman, who was seated on Mrs. Cervitano's bed in her slip, refusing to take off another article of clothing.

"I'm sorry, Mr. Cervitano," said Toby. "I can't get this damned thing to work!"

"Take it easy, kid." Sally had kids and bikes of his own and knew what to do. His major goal at the moment was to send Toby on his way as fast as he could. A flutter at the window told him to hurry. He made a few adjustments, then handed the bike to Toby. "Hold it a minute, kid, I'll need a wrench. Don't kick it again."

Toby stood holding the bike. The screaming across the street continued and so did Sanjo's rocking. Now she was huddled in a ball at the edge of the porch, her shoulders slumped into her chest, her head buried in her lap. Skippy continued to pace the sidewalk, barking and snapping at ghosts. Penny came out of her house and stood in the middle of the walk. "Sanjo, you wanna see the peep show again?" she asked.

Sanjo continued to rock and sob. She didn't want to play. She just wanted the screaming to stop and Ma and Poppy to talk good again.

"All right, I'll play by myself. And I'm going to put something else in the peep show and I won't show you either!" Penny flounced away, her baby face already framing the look of spite.

Toby was nervous. Waiting made him edgy. He began to rub his fingers together and to step with the bicycle like a dancing partner all over the sidewalk. A few times he ruffled his hair. When he finally noticed Sanjo, he called to her. She looked up but didn't wave.

Sally Cervitano came out of his house with the wrench. Once he turned and waved to a figure that stood in the window. The figure disappeared. Sally made a few more adjustments. "Try it."

Toby was close to tears. He didn't know why. He unstrung easily these days.

The bike needed more work. "I have to get my pliers," said Sally, who looked as if he were close to tears himself. He was sorry that he started the whole thing rather than tell Toby to get lost, although that would have caused him more problems. Sally went inside. This time, when he returned, the figure accompanied him to the front door. It was a tall woman in a slip and a man's shirt with masses of red hair piled on her head.

"I'll be right back." The figure didn't believe him. "You think

[85]

I wanna do this?" The figure didn't answer. "Come on, for God's sake, gimme a break, go back in the house," he hissed.

"Who are you talking to, Mr. Cervitano?" Toby asked.

Sally's face became immobile. "No one."

"I saw you talking to someone."

"One thing a man learns, kid, is to keep his mouth shut, you understand?"

Toby understood and he didn't. He understood that if he wanted his bike fixed, he would say no more on the matter. He did not understand why Mr. Cervitano would not acknowledge the person standing in his doorway.

"Okay. That should do it."

"Thanks, Mr. Cervitano."

"No problem, kid, just don't kick it anymore into my bushes, okay?"

"Yes, sir."

Toby wheeled the bicycle away, thought better of his direction, and wheeled it across the street.

"Anybody at home with you, Sanjo?"

Sanjo cried. "Poppy and Ma talk bad."

"What did you say, Sanjo? Pull your head out."

Sanjo slowly lifted her head from the shelter of her huddled body. "Ma crying."

"Don't feel bad, Sanjo. My parents fight all the time. Mostly about me. Where are they?" Sanjo pointed behind her. He pulled his bike alongside her curb and sat on the steps with her. With a furtive look from side to side, he withdrew two pills from his pocket and popped them in his mouth. Sanjo didn't notice. Toby swallowed the pills. In a little while they took effect and began to cool him out. He relaxed. The need to rub his fingers together went away. So did the need to pace. He was content to sit.

Two other events happened at the same moment. The screaming stopped, and Mrs. Ryan, a thin little lady with knobby elbows and knees, came looking for Skippy, who continued to rage at nothing. "You bad boy." She kissed his silky ear. "What are you doing here? It's too hot outside." Skippy cast a malevolent glance over his shoulder. Like Cotton Mather, he knew evil even though he couldn't see it.

Toby didn't have a handkerchief, but he had a scarf that he used for a headband. "Here, use this." Sanjo tried to wrap it around her head. "No, Sanjo, wipe your nose."

Sanjo patted her nose and hiccuped.

"Let me do it, you missed everything." Toby finished the job gently and carefully. "Don't cry anymore."

"Sanjo cry."

"I know you were crying. Don't do it anymore. Everything's okay."

It was quiet again. "Bugs?" she asked.

"No Bugs today. I don't feel much like reading."

"Sanjo read." She opened her Snoopy purse and unfolded the letter, then began to speak. "Call Margaret, truly Mark."

"What is it?"

"Mine."

"Let's see." Toby read the letter. "Hey, that's all right. You got a club to go to." Sanjo nodded. "Who is this guy, who is Mark?"

Sanjo bobbed her head. "Mark in chair."

"Yeah? No kidding. And he wrote to you?" Sanjo nodded. "Did you understand the letter?" Sanjo didn't understand the question. "Are you going to go?" Sanjo looked puzzled. "You should call this guy. He'll talk to you on the telephone."

Sanjo didn't know how to call. She could speak on the telephone, she could twirl the dial, and once in a while she got a voice on the other end, but she could not get people to respond with consistency.

Toby became expansive. He began to speak slower. Once in a while he slurred his speech. "I'm going to get my own apartment." Sanjo snuffled. "With my own stereo. And you can come over any time you like."

The screaming started up again. Sanjo began to shiver.

"Gotta get out of here," said Toby. "Come on, Sanjo, we'll

[87]

go to my house. No one's home. And you can call that guy in the letter."

Sanjo made her way down the porch one step at a time. They walked together down the street, the boy with the coathanger arms wheeling his bike, and the wedge-shaped woman with her head hanging down, plodding alongside him. Every once in a while he stopped and waited for her to catch up.

Toby's house was empty as he said it would be. It was designed exactly like Sanjo's house but she was not able to make the comparison. Sanjo didn't touch anything. She waited in the middle of the living room while Toby wheeled his bike into the carport.

"Dark," she said when he came back.

"Don't be afraid. I'm going to put on the lights."

He tried to show her that the numbers on the letter and the numbers on the telephone matched, but it didn't mean anything to her. "You want me to dial?" Sanjo nodded. Toby dialed the number.

"Hello, my name is Toby and my friend here, she wants to talk to you, about the club, okay?" Toby got a response that pleased him. "You talk, Sanjo, he's waiting for you."

Sanjo picked up the telephone and banged it against her ear. "Hullo."

"Hello, who are you?" asked the voice.

"Sanjo."

"Okay, Sanjo, how can I help you?" Sanjo looked at Toby. "What is it you want to know?" Sanjo didn't speak. The voice on the other end had infinite patience. "Can you come to the club meeting?"

"Yes."

"Good. How are you going to get there?"

"Poppy drive."

"Would you like someone in the club to come and get you?"

"Yes."

"Okay. Where do you live?" No response. "Is there a number on your house? Let me talk to the guy with you."

Sanjo turned over the phone.

[88]

"What's her address?"

Toby thought for a minute, made a quick calculation, and said, "One-oh-two-oh Bergen. . . . He wants to talk to you again." Toby placed the phone against her ear. "Hold it like this," he said.

"Hullo," said Sanjo.

"Sanjo, we have your address. Do you know your telephone number?"

This time the question was properly framed and Sanjo responded. "Five-five-five-nine-eight-six-four."

"Could you say that again?" She repeated it. "I'm sorry. A little slower." She repeated it once more. "Okay, I think I got it. Now listen, we're going to call you on the telephone before we come to get you, okay?"

"Uh-huh." The speaker was silent. Sanjo was silent.

There was a full minute of silence before Toby took the telephone. "Hey, are you finished?" Toby listened, then hung up. Sanjo grabbed for the phone but Toby placed a hand on her arm. "Not again, Sanjo. That guy's finished and so am I." He was beginning to feel really loose.

While Sanjo was giving her phone number, Toby gave himself two more pills. The compound that was described in pharmaceutical textbooks in a hexagonal design of great beauty was slamming his neurons into insensibility. A sound brushed past his lips, less a whimper than a language shared by the wind.

There were no problems anywhere in the world. There were no hassles with his mother over his barbells, his grades, or his room. In fact, he forgot all about his mother. There was no supporting cartilage in his body. Toby folded onto the floor like an umbrella.

"Get up," said Sanjo. His eyes fluttered and closed. A tiny blue vein throbbed in one lid. Sanjo knelt on the floor beside him and shook his head. "Wake up." Then, with great difficulty, she flopped on her stomach and lay on the floor beside him, staring at the pattern in the carpet. "Toby tired." Pretty soon they were both asleep.

———

Toby's mother saw them first. "Oh, my God. Look at this. Jack, would you look at this! I can't believe it." Toby's father followed her into the living room, making the space between the front door and the center of the dinette in three strides. Sanjo had rolled onto her back and was snoring. Her arm was arched around Toby. The boy was nestled in her side, fitting into her spaces like a kitten. His face was softened by sleep, and faint perspiration glistened on the hairs of his upper lip. His mouth was slightly open and his breathing was deep.

"Who is she?" yelled Mr. Wright.

"You know who she is, the crazy one, down the street."

"What's going on here?"

Sanjo woke up. When Toby didn't, his father got his first major cue.

"He took something! What did you take, Toby? Wake up, dammit!"

"I can't believe it," said Mrs. Wright. She sat on a chair, still and shivering, like Jell-O just unmolded.

"It's your fault!" yelled Toby's father. "You're on his back all the time!"

"Why is it always my fault?"

He swung around to hit her. She drew back.

Toby opened his eyes. His father loomed over him, distorted and menacing. Toby began to cry and drive farther into Sanjo's side, trying to burrow beneath her. "Go away," he said.

"Get up!" His father drew him up by the neck and dangled him on his toes like a weed just pulled from the ground. "Stand up!"

Sanjo got to her feet. She stood with her head down and her eyes on the floor.

"Get her out of here!"

"I don't know what to do with her!" whimpered Mrs. Wright.

"Get her the hell out!"

Poppy and Ma were combing the neighborhood for Sanjo. They had reached a temporary truce due to the exigencies of

[90]

dinnertime and a lost retarded daughter. When they knocked on the Cervitano door, Sally's woman went flying into Mrs. Cervitano's closet, where she continued to cower despite Sally's reassurances that it was not her husband. Sally answered the front door holding up his trousers, which he forgot to belt. He was shirtless and his hair fell over his face like a veil.

"Is Sanjo here?"

"Nobody's here. Just me. I'm all alone. I'm taking a nap." They were too worried to wonder why Sally came to his mother's house to take a nap.

Their next stop was Penny's house. She answered the door but they didn't see her. She didn't reach their line of vision, even Poppy's, which was pretty low. Poppy yelled into the house. "Hello!"

"Where is Sanjo?" asked Penny. They looked down. It was amazing that she could talk. Like a begonia, she was put together in tiny pieces. Her mouth was the tiniest piece of all.

"What?" asked Poppy.

"Where is Sanjo?" asked Penny once more.

"She's not here?" asked Ma.

Penny's mother, recently into macramé, materialized out of the foyer carrying her strings. "What's the matter?"

Ma spoke. "We're looking for Sanjo."

"She was here this morning." Penny's mother made a knot.

"We have a peep show," said Penny.

"Let's go," said Poppy.

Their feverish search accelerated and they hammered and banged on every door on the block. They were walking to Toby's house when they saw Toby's mother under the lamp post leading Sanjo by her fingertips down the street. Sanjo's sandal was open and the buckle flopped on the sidewalk with each step.

"Sanjo, where were you?" screamed Ma.

"Please," said Mrs. Wright, "you should really keep her home." When she came up close they saw that she had a purple welt across her cheek and one eye that looked like a U.S.D.A. meat stamp.

[91]

"Where was she?" asked Ma.

Just then, a flashing ambulance rounded the corner and thudded over the potholes. Mrs. Wright grabbed at her throat. "You shouldn't let her out!" she screamed. She turned and followed the ambulance, awkward and disjointed, like a doll with "utility grade" stamped over one eye, in need of repair.

They stayed to watch. In less than a minute, two men had Toby on a stretcher and were loading him into the back of the ambulance, while his father gesticulated wildly and his mother sobbed.

"What were you doing at Toby's house?" asked Ma.

"I don't wanna know," said Poppy.

"Sanjo sleep," said Sanjo.

Sanjo was allowed up late because the visit to Toby's house was counted as a nap. She sat in the dining room cutting out cat pictures. Opposite her sat Poppy, spooning his favorite soup, split pea with carrot slices. Ma started yelling from the bathroom that her Fasteeth was gone. She came into the dining room to fix both her daughter and her husband with a stare. "It was right there," she said.

"You probably forgot, Flo, and put it somewhere else. We both don't remember so good."

"Oh, no, it was right there." Sanjo snipped off the cat's tail. "Sanjo, were you on the no-no shelf?"

"What's the difference?" said Poppy. "You don't need it until tomorrow morning anyway."

"Slurf lot fleith." Something happened to her tongue. It didn't respond. Ma tried it again. The sounds that came out had nothing to do with what she wanted to say. Poppy found another carrot slice wedged beneath a piece of parsley.

Ma put a finger in her mouth and pushed on her plate. Maybe it was loose, a distinct possibility since the adhesive had only so many hours' staying power. She felt a numbness in her hand, a pins-and-needles sensation in her fingertips where they touched the plate. She decided to go to bed.

[92]

5

News of Toby's overdose sifted into the neighborhood and filled the cracks and crevices of each house like grit in a sandstorm. It was unwelcome, especially to parents who regarded such things in the way parents once thought of polio or diphtheria. Most neighborhood parents swept it out of their minds with the grim determination of a Nevada housewife.

With the speed and efficiency of a stage manager releasing a new backdrop from the flies, they substituted scenes of their sunburned young making leather belts and ceramic ashtrays. Pushed from serious consideration was the possibility that, nestled in their child's camp as snugly as a chickadee in a rotted tree stump, was a dealer. Not a sinister adult wearing a pimp hat, seated behind the steering wheel of a chrome-fronted Continental parked in the forest, but someone with pimples who won the volleyball trophy and carried his store in a hollowed-out giant-economy-size toothpaste tube.

Mrs. Cervitano guided Ma and Sanjo about her lawn. She showed them each addition, as lovingly as a tour guide explains the beauties of Versailles. "The donkey is new," she said.

Sanjo was loyal to old favorites. She bent to pet the ducklings. "Nice boy," she said.

It was at the green glass ball that Ma confided what Mrs.

Ryan had confided to her: Toby had to have his stomach pumped.

"Ah, no." Mrs. Cervitano rolled her eyes the way one does when the topic under discussion is incest or cancer.

Sanjo tried it out. "Ah, no." She rolled her eyes into the shining green reflection. The glass ball, with the insensitivity of the inanimate, returned the image, but only after stretching it into preposterous proportions.

"Thank God we didn't have this. It's a terrible thing," said Mrs. Cervitano.

"What are you gonna do?" asked Ma. Her response was the rhetorical, if not philosophical, answer of someone who thinks of a pusher as a piece of bread used to help get peas on a fork.

"My son Sally says it's all his fault, that doctor whatzisname."

"Which one?" Ma was used to her contemporaries searching for names as younger people search for socks or keys. They were there someplace. You only had to keep looking. It was like trying to run an office without a filing system. Whereas the younger person still has an alphabetized code, older people sometimes lost the cabinet.

"You know the one, the baby doctor with the marchers," Mrs. Cervitano persevered.

"I don't know which one you mean."

"It'll come," promised Mrs. Cervitano, gently pulling Sanjo off a sheet. "The little grass underneath is coming up," she explained.

A mail truck jounced over the potholes, sending packages and letters flying out of their pouches. Great puffs of dust billowed like smoke from its wheels.

Skippy, who had heard the truck, flung himself against every window and door in the house, barking, yapping, snarling, slicking his ears back, and baring his teeth, a kamikaze pilot willing to die for his objective.

"What's the matter, baby?" asked Mrs. Ryan. She picked him up to kiss his silky ear. "Don't anyone open the door."

Mr. Niemeyer drove slowly by, waving a Hershey bar out of

the window. He stalled his truck and dangled the Hershey lower. The heat was beginning to mold it to the contour of his palm.

"Hello, Mr. Postman," said Mrs. Cervitano. "Eat it before it melts." He jerked the Hershey into the truck. Eyes narrowed to slits, Mr. Niemeyer had the crafty look of a big game hunter who has stalked his quarry into the preserve and now must lure it out into open country. Sanjo saw him. She smiled and waved her half wave. Mr. Niemeyer idled the truck forward in a slow creep, so imperceptible it was almost a glide. Sanjo followed for a few steps, then stopped. Penny was on the other side of the street chirping to her mother.

Like a compass needle swinging to magnetic north, Sanjo stepped up to the curb. "Cross me." She could be very imperious. Ma walked as fast as her grinding hip joints would allow. She placed a hand on Sanjo's arm. Sanjo turned to her and said, "Good girl," then laid her head on good girl's shoulder.

"Pick your head up, Sanjo. You have to look both ways."

Although Ma was smaller than Sanjo, she guided her with the mastery of a tractor pushing a 747 onto the runway. She felt a little weak in the other arm. It was the way she slept. Tonight she would remember to sleep on the other side. "You didn't look both ways," she said.

Safely on the other side, Ma released Sanjo. "Play nice."

"Spock!" yelled Mrs. Cervitano from across the street.

Sanjo plodded toward Penny, her broad flat feet splatting the sidewalk, her head down, a smile raising her cheeks to her eyes.

Penny and her mother were discussing girls and boys and the lack of difference between them. The subject came up when Penny began to whine for a doll. Penny's mother addressed the subject of a doll indirectly. She never said no. Instead, she rocked back on her Earthshoes and explained to Penny that in many ways girls were better than boys and, when they grew up into women, lived longer. Penny didn't much like boys. They pushed her down and liked to watch her cry. She still wanted a doll, the kind she saw on television that did everything, including, if one rocked it hard enough, getting car sick.

[95]

At Sanjo's approach, Penny's mother, who had heard that there might be more to Sanjo than met the eye, bent over for a piece of last-minute instruction. "Don't go into her house and don't bring her into our house. Stay outside to play." Then she vanished in a flurry of macramé strings to make another Chinese Crown.

"I changed the peep show," said Penny, twisting and dipping from side to side. "I don't know if I'll let you see it."

Sanjo stood mute, her head down, the smile receding like floodwater rushing into a sewer, her arms hanging limply at her sides, the defendant awaiting sentence. The judge took her time making a decision. She faced Sanjo at the level of her belly with her hands in little balls on her hips. She decided to show clemency and pronounced judgment to Sanjo's belly. "All right, you can see it, but you can't touch it."

Sanjo was happy again. She put her stubby fingers on Penny's head. "Nice," she said. They walked that way all the way to the peep show, Penny trying to twist her head free, and Sanjo, moved to an excess of affection, holding her hand as securely on Penny's skull as if she were screwing in a light bulb.

They bent to the earth. Penny brushed back the dried grass and twigs and blew dust off the plastic. The crayon was gone and so was the tube of Fasteeth. In their place were two dandelions and a pink ribbon. "That's not my best ribbon," said Penny. "My best one is blue."

"Pretty nice," said Sanjo.

A gust of wind like a whisper swept across the peep show. "Oh," Penny's mouth made a rose bud. "That bad wind. It spoiled our peep show."

There was nothing to replace the delicate veil of dried grass. Anything lightweight had been swept away. There was no grass. Sanjo found some rocks but Penny discarded them. They were all too large. "That's no good, silly." The difference in opinion centered on the ability to discriminate. They settled for dirt, now dried to the consistency of bread crumbs.

When they had covered the peep show, Penny brushed the

dirt from her hands onto her shorts. She wet her fingers and wiped off her knees, then wiped her fingers a second time on the shorts. She wasn't supposed to, but she was learning to trade expedience for absolute obedience. "You better clean up," she said to Sanjo. Sanjo wet her fingers and rubbed her knees.

Penny put her dimpled finger to her pursed lips and rolled her eyes up. It helped her to think. "I know," she said, through the tiny O. "We can jump rope. My daddy showed me how."

Sanjo knew jump rope. Jump rope was as much a part of her memory as rain. She had watched the children play jump rope for over thirty years, although she didn't reckon by the number, only the pervasiveness of the memory. She would sit on her step, arms curled around her knees, watching their expert feet in scrupulous precision dance and tease the rope that threatened to yank them to the ground. The little girls and an occasional boy would play by the hour, changing pattern, rhythm, speed, and players, increasing the complication and maneuvers of their skill, and chanting things like, "Blue bell, cockle shell, eevy, ivy, over." This went on until about the age of ten or eleven, when they would trade jumping rope for the dance steps the older children were doing, practicing elaborate routines on the sidewalk, in preparation for later expertise in lindy, twist, funky chicken, hustle, or whatever dance arrangement was current.

No one had ever asked Sanjo to play. She would watch from her step with all the devotion of a Green Bay Packer fan, chanting along with them—although under her breath, after one time when the children screamed at her to keep quiet. It seemed that there was a serious discrepancy in rhythm between Sanjo and one little girl who got tangled in the rope and fell to the ground, claiming that Sanjo's basso profundo monotone threw her off.

Penny was in and out of her house with a rope with wooden handles on either end. "You swing it like this." She made a few passes at the ground. Penny was no hotshot either, falling about three years short of true championship material. "Look, Sanjo, it's a snake."

Sanjo didn't understand *snake*. She had seen one once in the zoo, but neither Ma nor Poppy had bothered to name it for her because they couldn't look at it. Instead, Poppy had said "Feh," and they hustled her out of the reptile pavilion and into the aviary next door, a ground plan created by a diabolical zoo director who liked to drive the snakes crazy. The configuration and the subject never seemed to come up again.

It didn't matter that Sanjo didn't fully understand what Penny wanted. Frequently she didn't understand what Penny wanted. She was content to be with her and approximate the things she did in devoted, if not expert, mimicry.

"Jump over the snake, Sanjo." Sanjo stood immobile. Penny became exasperated. "Then you make it be a snake." She put the rope in Sanjo's hand. Sanjo waved it in the air. The handle on the other end hit her on the elbow. "No, no, on the ground, like this, okay?" Penny was close to tears. Her tolerance level was roughly equivalent to her attention span. They were both short.

Sanjo tried once more. The rope wiggled a little bit. For a while, that was enough for Penny. She jumped back and forth, first on one foot, then the other, and sometimes with both feet, never quite clearing the rope, but within inches of doing so. "Make it go faster." That was clearly too much to ask. Sanjo had, with great effort, mastered the stroke. Acceleration was another matter. Penny wrenched the rope out of Sanjo's hands. Her exquisite porcelain face set in pink and blue annoyance. "Oh, you don't know how to do anything!" She took a wooden handle in each hand and swung it over her head. It came to rest at the ground. She stepped over it, then swung again.

Sanjo felt it first, a sensation that she couldn't name. She was only aware of a difference. It had something to do with the weight on her skin, the feeling in her nose and chest, her sharpened senses of smell and sight, and her changing blood gases. Everything became quiet, as if a conductor had rapped a baton. A squawking mother robin with a hungry family screaming from their cup-shaped nest hurried in her hunt for food like a frenetic shopper who knows that the store is about to be closed.

Leaves hung limply from trees and bushes. The dandelions

closed up. Bees returned to their hives. A butterfly resting in the sun roused itself from its torpor and decided not to take any chances. Antennae vibrating, it went into hiding under a board, folding its wings daintily about its slender thorax like a fussy woman arranging her skirts.

The sky darkened and stroked itself in a wash of blacks, grays, and navy blues. Clouds gathered for the action, coming from all over, combining, multiplying, spreading, sometimes moving in two directions and on different levels at once, massing for the offensive with all the frantic activity of an army camp hoping to surprise the enemy.

The towering climbing mass became a majestic cumulonimbus, the top spread out in the shape of an anvil. The wind, which had whispered its presence earlier, now uttered hoarse cries and scoured the ground like Brillo, scraping leaves and twigs before it into the street. The temperature dropped swiftly. A new smell tickled the inside of Sanjo's nose. It was ozone, a result of the ionization of oxygen particles, now swirling down from its lofty origin.

The sky crackled as it released its pent-up friction in electrical warning fingers. Both Penny and Sanjo jumped at the first crackle. Over their heads somebody rattled an aluminum sheet. Sanjo began to tremble.

Penny scampered for her house, even before her mother stuck her head out of the window and said, "Come inside, it's going to rain."

Ma stuck her head out of her window and yelled the same thing, only she added, "And hurry up."

Sanjo reached the steps just as the first drops of water began their free fall to earth, striking the ground in a solid sheet and sending a steaming hiss skyward.

At first the water rolled over the surface of the parched earth. The dried earth molecules formed a barrier through which it could not pass. Ground that desperately needed water could not accept it. Instead, it rolled across yards, into streets, pulling out stakes from the lawns, tearing seedlings from under the sheets, exposing pebbles and rocks, and etching gullies. Gradually the top layer of earth was saturated enough for the water to percolate down and flood anthills, drown a family of chipmunks caught in an underground nest whose exit had been sealed with leaves, and fill storm sewers with topsoil, debris, and any tiny creature that did not have a chance to get to safety.

The mother robin, who was still shopping, tried to perch on a branch midway between the ground and her nest but was driven to the ground by the weight of the rain. It didn't matter. A dried branch, loosened by the force of the rain, broke the nest in half, dashing the baby robins from their elaborate grass, down, and spiderweb bed to the ground.

Ma ran around slamming windows with one hand. Poppy roused himself. "What's going on?"

"You could sleep through anything."

"I wasn't sleeping. I was only resting."

"You had your eyes closed."

"That's how I rest. Some rain, huh, Flo?"

The house got hot. Their window air conditioner could not cool fast enough to expel the vapor that hung suspended in the air. Ma began to worry about mildew. The telephone rang. "Don't answer it!" yelled Ma. "You'll get a shock!" After the sixth ring it stopped.

Sanjo watched the onslaught from the window. She saw the rain skim across the peep show, at first leaving the plastic intact but clearing away once and for all the debris which obscured and shielded it. The dandelions and the ribbon slowly floated to the top and began to press against the tiny window. Finally the water pressure forced it off the hole, causing it to lie on its side, just another piece of flotsam, and spilling the exhibits beside it.

"Peep," she yelled. "Ma, peep!"

"Please, I'm having my hands full." That was inaccurate. She was having only one hand full since the other hand was too weak to be operative.

A heavy feeling crushed Sanjo's chest, depressed her breathing, and slowed her movements to no movement at all, like a clock with a broken mainspring. She began to cry, softly at first, then matching the intensity of the rain, rubbing the knuckles of one hand across her eye while she used the fingers of her other hand to stem the flood tide coming from her nose.

"What's she crying about?" asked Poppy.

"Who knows? You ask her," said Ma, slamming another window.

"What's the matter, Sanjo?"

"Peep broke, Poppy." The pane of plastic was being edged toward the street. Deep agonizing sobs squeezed her like an accordion.

"What did she say?" asked Ma.

"Who knows."

Poppy was having his own problems. A midday nap always left him a little confused. Like an Indian who can track a deer by seeing how the twigs bend, Poppy read his life through its signs, only whereas the Indian reads forward to tell him where he's going, Poppy read backward to tell him where he had been. Right now he had to check out whether or not he brushed his teeth that morning. He went into the bathroom to see if his toothbrush was wet.

The rain stopped during the afternoon. Earthworms, threatened by suffocation from the sudden onrush of water, had fled to the surface of the ground and now lay paralyzed by the sun. To the mother robin, they were a bonanza. She picked them up in her beak, discarding one for another, successive choices increasing in succulence and size, and finally decided upon one. Once airborne, she couldn't find her nest. She darted from branch to branch, with the stunned worm dangling from her beak, and began to circle the tree like a plane which must keep a holding pattern. In her third spiral, she saw them from the air. When she reached them, two were dead and one was still alive, although badly mangled with a shattered wing and a crushed beak. The mother robin called to it. When it didn't respond, she flung the worm aside and flew away.

Sanjo was finally moved from her intransigent vigil at the window, where she had watched the hole fill up, the contents strewn across the lawn, and the plastic pane nudged along by the water into the gutter. She was led to the sofa to watch television and sat next to Ma, curled up against her arm and snuffling into her shoulder. Ma had on her favorite program. She leaned back and watched eight people in various combinations and recombinations in the space of one hour confess to a host of disasters, including infidelity, alcoholism, incest, a brain tumor that defied surgery, and one vague reference to being into leather. It really made the hour fly. When it was over, Ma switched channels.

"Look, Sanjo, 'Sesame Street.' " Like a cheerleader, Ma's function was to inspire optimism. " 'Sunny day, come and play, everything's A-okay,' " she sang, in her deep, estrogen-depleted voice, snapping the fingers of one hand and rubbing the fingers of the other.

Ma tried to get her sleeve unstuck from her shoulder, where it had been dampened by Sanjo's tears. Sanjo wouldn't pull her head out. She wouldn't even pull it out when Ma announced the arrival of Big Bird. Ma leaned over. There were other things to talk about.

"Look at you. Your hair is all over the place." Ma smoothed the bangs into place and pushed the sparse hair down over Sanjo's small turned-in ears. "You have to comb it."

"Sanjo combs." A subterranean growl.

"I know you comb, but not just in the morning. You have to look in the mirror to see what you look like. You were outside playing with Penny. Your hair is messy. You have to comb it again."

Mention of Penny triggered an association to the peep show. The two thoughts were connected to one another as tightly and as inextricably as Siamese twins joined through the chest. Sanjo's eyes filled and she began to cry once more, although with less conviction than before.

Ma's shoulder was now plastered with her tear-dampened sleeve. She didn't even try to move the fabric free. "Look at Big

Bird, look what's he going to do." Big Bird popped out of a garbage can.

"Peep," whimpered Sanjo.

Ma was good at cheering TV shows. She was somewhat of a pioneer. Her career began with the early days of television and Howdy Doody. She was still at it with "Sesame Street." Unlike a lioness, whose contract for motherhood comes up for renewal every two or three years, Ma was contracted in perpetuity.

Big Bird did a cakewalk. Sanjo turned to watch, the tears suspended in her hooded eyes. The bad feeling was gone. She hugged Ma, threw her head back, and thrust her throat to the television. The good feeling was back. It started low and worked its way up, like lava. Pretty soon she was smiling.

A bear fished in a stream. The bear swiped at the water with his paw and came up with a big fish which he grabbed in his mouth. "Don't drop it," warned Sanjo.

Kermit the Frog jerked his way across the screen. He began to dance and sing. Sanjo stood up and stepped about in a brisk waddle, the result of a pelvis that on X-ray looked like Mickey Mouse ears. Kermit sang to the accompaniment of a trio of flutes about the number six. "Six snails and six nails leaping over six pails." Ma clapped. Sanjo stepped about on her flat feet, laughing and turning with Kermit the Frog. Sanjo's shoulders were rotated inward so that she held her arms with the elbows out and the back of her hands facing her sides. It was an error in design that interfered with her early development of grasping and reaching but now lent to her dancing a certain style.

Poppy came in feeling pretty good after finding his tooth-brush wet and having a good solid bowel movement, the first of its kind in over a month. He decided to join Sanjo as Kermit continued to sing of six snails. Poppy stuck a finger in the air and twirled around, his bedroom slippers slapping the carpet, singing, "Diddle, diddle, di, di." Black-thatched puppets, a Greek chorus in green nylon fur, sprang up behind Kermit, adding their own comments on the number six, and everyone

[103]

danced and sang in a disjointed jerking and bumping, a sprightly cantata even Bach would have been proud of.

Kermit began counting the chorus: one, two, three, four, five, six; the chorus counted itself: one, two, three, four, five, six; Kermit counted the chorus backward: six, five, four, three, two, one; Poppy got dizzy and hit his big toe on the coffee table. "Oof," he said. Ma had on her serves-you-right look. He couldn't bend over to hold his big toe and comfort it. He had to sit down to do it.

Toby was waiting for the rain to stop before he ran away from home. Things looked good. Drops could now be seen in isolation where before they fell collectively and could not be separated. Pretty soon they would stop altogether.

The idea came to him at the hospital when he was waiting for his mother and father to take him home. He had had lunch and a visit from a resident from psychiatry he could relate to, an older chick who admitted to using some grass herself and once even taking mescaline. The resident asked him about his mother and father and his brother, Danny. She also asked him how he was doing in school. Toby told her he didn't care much for school and was into developing his muscles. He figured he'd be out of school in a few years, maybe sooner, but he would always have his body. When the resident left, Toby heard her tell the nurse that he was off suicide precautions.

The idea came to Toby that he would go home with his parents but he wouldn't stay there. He would go to a place where he could get a job, get his own apartment, have his own stereo, keep his dope openly in a sugar jar, and feel good. That such a place existed he did not doubt. Its details had yet to be worked out. He only knew that it was New York City first and then Los Angeles. The continent between, through which he must pass, he gave little thought to.

Toby had crossed over some kind of line in regard to his parents that allowed him to disassociate himself from them. He could look at them as if they were at the other end of a telescope, distanced and insignificant. All connection to the time they held him cuddled and powdered in the treetops of their arms was expelled from recollection. It was too far away and separated by too many actions that denied the cuddling and reaffirmed his parents as constant and relentless adversaries.

The drops assembled at the edge of the roof and puddled into the corners. The rain was slowing. It was time to make his move. Toby began to assemble his belongings. He had a carton of Bugs Bunny comic books for Sanjo. Most of these were from Danny's room, although they originally belonged to him. Danny, who was still at camp, had appropriated the comics from Toby piece by piece, whittling away at his older brother's collection with the sublety and ingenuity of a pack rat. There was no end to his hiding places, his deftness, or his derring-do.

When Toby complained to his mother, she told him to grow up. This was strange because when he tried to act like a grown-up she told him he was being smart. Danny wasn't a good reader and really didn't like Bugs anyway. What he really liked was the ability to cause a commotion, test and polish his appeal to his mother, and outfox his brother. Toby knelt and peered under the bed. Two more came out, along with a sock and a gum wrapper. A quick bathroom reconnaissance yielded one out of the hamper and four out of the toilet tank. Entirely missed was a Yosemite Sam anthology spindled into the faucet.

In a duffel bag, Toby crammed some underwear, a shirt, a sweater, three of his best tapes, including the Bee Gees doing "Nowhere Man," a picture of Judy Haskell, and some tooeys kept hidden in a vacuum cleaner bag that his parents somehow missed in their rampaging, mattress-slicing search for drugs. He wanted to take his barbells but they were too heavy.

Toby rode with the box balanced on his handlebars and the duffel bag tied onto the rack behind him. The puddles splashed against his sneakers and soaked his socks.

Poppy sat in the living room stroking his big toe and crooning to it. Sanjo stood behind him stroking his head. "Poppy dance."

[105]

Ma was standing before both of them. "Do you want to soak your foot?"

Poppy was angry. "Don't say one word."

"What word? What do you think I'm going to say?"

"Don't talk."

"Morry, stop being such a baby. Do you think I'm going to say that an old man who dances to a children's program and then stubs his toe gets what he deserves? Do you?"

"You said it! I knew you were going to say something!"

Sanjo tried to divert them. "Sunny day, come and play."

"Keep quiet," said Poppy.

Sanjo turned away and sang in secret to her chest, an always willing, available, and conspiratorial listener. "Thing's A-okay."

There was a knock on the door. Ma opened it, only missed a beat, and then asked him to come in. Toby had his arms full of the carton. Ma closed the door quickly. "Watch out for the air conditioning," she said.

"How's your stomach?" asked Poppy.

The Bernatskys had not seen him since he was taken away in the ambulance. They watched him in the same way the Pharisees watched Lazarus, waiting for him to fall over again.

"You wanna sit down?" asked Ma.

Toby dropped the carton on the floor. "Uh-uh, Mrs. Bernatsky, I came to bring these to Sanjo."

Poppy was distrustful. He watched Toby intently, waiting for signs of something, he was not sure what.

"Toby." Sanjo came over to give him a hug. Fortunately for Toby, he was so well developed that even when she brought his head down to her chest in a hammerlock he was not smothered. He had enough storage power to continue to breathe for at least another minute.

"These are for you," he said.

"Bugs?"

"Yup, all Bugs."

It was a treasure chest, and Sanjo spilled the jewels all over the floor, pitching them out of the box one after another. "Boy oh boy!" It was her major superlative.

"No, Sanjo, don't do that. You have to read them one at a time."

"One time."

"One at a time, see? You read it, like this, then you put it back. Otherwise they'll be all over the place. And don't give them to Danny, understand?"

"No Danny."

"Right, no Danny."

Poppy continued to stare. He had forgotten all about his big toe, whose throbbing had subsided to a dull ache. "You going to read to her?" he asked.

Toby looked at his Timex. "I don't think so. I gotta go." He knew that in fifteen minutes his mother would be home and in one hour after that his father. He had to get a head start. His plan was to get on his bike and go as far as he could take it. He was even prepared to ditch it if necessary.

Sanjo pulled his arm. "Read Bugs," she said.

Toby made a quick calculation. "All right, Sanjo. Just one page." They both dropped to the floor. Sanjo grabbed one of the comics and handed it to him, then sat next to him with her legs straight out in front of her and her arms at her sides, supporting her weight. Toby flipped over the cover and showed her the pictures. "See here, Sanjo, this guy is the Tasmanian Devil. You remember him." Sanjo nodded. "He likes to eat rabbits. But Bugs, he's too smart for him. Here he's making a fake rabbit. See how he pastes on rabbit ears?"

Ma was in the kitchen getting dinner ready. It was amazing that all the sun had to do was make its appearance for her arthritis to go away. She took a can of evaporated milk that Poppy liked with his decaffeinated coffee and slid it under the can opener. When she went to depress the lever, a funny thing happened. She missed it by a mile and lurched instead across the counter, bruising her cantilevered breast and sending the can flying into the sink.

Toby had finished describing how the Tasmanian Devil blew

up after eating four sticks of dynamite disguised as a rabbit. He closed the comic book. "I got to go now, Sanjo." He stood up and left Sanjo on the floor thumbing through her fortune. Suddenly he leaned over and kissed her on the cheek. "Take care of yourself, okay?" Sanjo grabbed his thighs in a whizzer hiplock, and he suffered imprisonment for almost a minute before he gently pulled away and walked to the door. With his hand on the knob, he turned. "Mr. Bernatsky, you should read to her. The stories are pretty good." He opened the door and left.

"Pisher," said Poppy. There were little puddles all over the floor, from Toby's socks and sneakers. Poppy groaned himself out of his chair and went to mop them up.

Toby hopped on his bike and wheeled away, past the dying baby robin, the scores of earthworms, the debris, the water shimmering on leaves and in puddles blinking its way skyward, the ants spreading eggs and pupae out to dry, and the bullfrogs croaking their two-sound song in monotonous repetition like a rock group with a limited vocabulary: "Grib it, grib it, grib it, baby, can you grib it?"

Mr. Ryan, having snuck out his own back door, ran by wearing a minimesh crew-neck shell, soft-skin running shorts, a yellow sweatband, and forty-dollar Nikes. The feat in itself was not remarkable except that at the same time he was belly breathing he was also taking his pulse. Mr. Ryan was an example of the effectiveness of training, passing in one summer from a man who experienced the wall after the eighth house to a serious contender in Fineschreiber Bakery's Mini-Marathon. He splashed past Toby.

Ma announced supper. The announcement was a simple two words, "All right." Poppy came to the table with one slipper. The other foot hurt too much to put a slipper on it. Sanjo shoved the box of comics across the floor and into her room. While the collection of Bugs Bunnies was not as important as her cat pictures, it was certainly a contender.

"What's for supper, Flo?"

"It's something you love."

Poppy was alert to the con. The smile gave it away. He looked up from lowered brows, waiting for the pigeon drop.

"Here, calves' liver, the way you like."

"There's no onions."

"You want your heart to attack you?"

"It's not the heart, it's the digestion."

"You're going to tell me they're not connected? One goes bad, they both go bad. The same as apples in a barrel."

Sanjo came in dripping water from her fingertips like Venus rising from the sea.

"You're supposed to dry your hands on the towel." Ma was having trouble bringing in the dish. She carried it cradled against her chest. "Wipe her, Morry."

Poppy took his napkin and began to dab. He had to hold her hands far away to see what he was doing. He patted the stubby fingers dry and went to work on the palm. It was amazing how much water attached to the skin and stayed there.

Venus sat down and tucked her napkin in her collar. Poppy skirted around his liver like a scuba diver getting ready to harpoon a ray. "Dadadadada," said Ma. No one noticed.

Ma stood up to cut Sanjo's liver and slid to the floor. Sanjo laughed. Poppy stared in disbelief. It had happened too fast for personal involvement. He was just an observer.

Ma lay partially under the table and partially between the pagoda doors of the cabinet and the kitchen door. Poppy speared his calves' liver. "Flo." It came out as a croak.

"Get up, Ma," said Sanjo.

Ma could not feel her right side. Her right arm and leg lay beside her like alien appendages, the property of someone else that banged into her. When she tried to move, all cooperation between body parts was gone and in its place a curious competition between forces, the right side against the left. She tried to get up but instead jerked about the floor like a fish flopping in the sand.

Poppy was on the floor beside her. "Oh, my God."

Ma wondered why her sister Tessie wouldn't help her up. She tried to yell at her but no sound came out. Her mouth felt as if it were full of spaghetti. Was it? she wondered. If she didn't get up, she would be late for school.

Poppy ran to the telephone, then ran to the bedroom to get his glasses. "Flo, my God." He put his glasses on and dialed a number. "It's my wife," he said.

"Your name, sir?" asked the operator.

"My name? What do you want my name for? It's my wife, Flo."

"I need your name, sir."

"Morris Bernatsky."

"Your address?" The operator was used to excited people hanging up before leaving such particulars. It was especially frustrating for emergency personnel, who knew that a serious problem existed but didn't know who had it or where it was. "Is this an emergency?"

Why else was he calling? Who leaves the table to make a call? "I don't know, she's laying on the floor, my wife, she can't get up."

The two young men riding the ambulance that turned into Bergen Street were actually firemen, now on volunteer duty as an emergency rescue team. Their faces were tanned and healthy, with perfect teeth that seemed to number in the hundreds and clear and steady eyes. They were spare and muscular, members of a well-nourished and well-exercised elite. One blond and the other brunette, they were color-coordinated by a dispatcher with an eye for aesthetics.

They had been additionally and specifically trained for their present assignment and, even if not able to leap tall buildings at a single bound, could scale sheer cliffs, scuttle down pipes after small children, untangle the still living from the wreckage of their smoking cars, manage burn victims, deliver babies, and in general give the upper echelon of medicine a run for its money.

Confident yet diffident, these crack troops now drove with red light flashing and siren muted to a low wail. They didn't career around corners or run red lights. Instead, they drove carefully and purposefully, intent on getting their vehicle safely to its destination. The driver was diverted for only a moment when he thought he recognized the kid on the bike as the o.d. they had picked up the other night.

Mrs. Cervitano heard the siren and peeked shyly from her picture window as reluctantly as a priest peeks from behind the curtain of the confessional. When she saw the ambulance stop in front of the Bernatskys, she sucked in a sigh, crossed herself, and ran across the street. Not a pushy woman, she waited silently on the sidewalk.

Mr. Ryan, making another lap around the block, although this time gasping, the glycogen already depleted in his legs, narrowly missed collision with the two men in navy-blue jumpsuits who sprinted from the back of the ambulance, pulling their rolling cot behind them.

Once inside, they sized up the scene. A gibbering, crying old man, a chubby woman who looked retarded—one of them recognized her as a Down's—yanking the victim by the arm, and the victim in the characteristic flexion of hemiplegia, her right leg rotated outward, right knee flexed, right arm held against her body in the way a shivering sparrow holds its wing.

The driver, wearing a small, blond, neatly trimmed mustache, brushed Sanjo aside, not harshly, just firmly. "Her face is lopsided," he confided to his taller partner. "It looks like a CVA."

Poppy grabbed the sleeve of the taller one. "My wife," he cried. "She can't get up!"

The taller one inclined his black-curled head. "Take it easy, old-timer, we're here to help her and we're going to do everything possible."

They knelt beside Ma. "Help is at your side, ma'am," said the driver. "Anything hurt?" The tall one felt below her rib cage, then put his ear to her nose and mouth. The driver took her wrist. Ma stared at them both. Who they were and what they

[111]

were doing was a puzzle lost somewhere in the bleeding in her head.

"Can you grab my hand?" asked the driver. Ma put out her left hand and clutched his like a lifeline. "That's fine," he said. "What happened to you?"

Ma moved her mouth. Spaghetti again. "Dadadadada."

"She fell," said Poppy. "We were sitting down to eat. She fell."

The driver elevated her head and shoulders with the roll of a blanket. The taller one dashed into the bathroom, found a washcloth, wet it, and returned in less than two seconds. He was just about to place it on her head when Ma started to vomit, disgorging chunks, cud, and gastric juices on the dining-room carpet, covering the roses and stems and leaves with her personal and private effluvium. The driver who had raised her head now quickly turned it to one side, tipping her chin up.

Sanjo gagged and wet her pants. Her heart began to pound against her chest. "Get up, Ma," she said. She stepped from side to side, rocking like a building in an earthquake.

Poppy sat in the chair with his golf cap on, ready for the ride to the hospital. He had his Medicare card and Ma's Medicare card in his pocket. He was somewhat bewildered. He remembered when firemen slid down poles. Now they acted like doctors. "You know what you're doing?" he asked.

"Don't worry, Pop, we're trained squad men."

"I thought you were going to take her to the hospital. She needs to get to the hospital."

"Don't worry. We'll get her there in no time."

Poppy ran to the bathroom. The two-hour leash his prostate kept him on had just been yanked. He decided to go while he still had the chance.

"Her pupils don't match," said the driver to the tall one.

"Let's go," said the tall one. They lifted her onto the stretcher as gently and reverently as a shopper holding a piece of Rose Medallion who sees the sign, *You drop it, you bought it.* They secured her with two straps and pulled her out of the house.

"You're going for a nice ride," said the driver, having been trained that even if the victim were out of it, like this one he pulled behind him, even comatose like the one he had yesterday, the sense of hearing was the last to go.

The crowd on the sidewalk had grown. Mrs. Ryan, alerted to the presence of the ambulance by her husband, who now lay collapsed on the living-room sofa measuring his recovery rate, stood with Skippy in her arms. She was giving him an ambulance lesson. "See the men. They're taking away Mrs. Bernatsky. See Mrs. Bernatsky, baby, she's sick."

"Woof," said Skippy.

Standing beside teacher and pupil was Penny's father, who thought it was Sanjo they were taking away. His wife had asked him to find out what was happening so they could prepare Penny. While he waited, he was planning how to resubmit his dissertation proposal to his committee. It was amazing to him that a group of people he had selected to be his mentors had turned against him.

"What happened?" he asked.

"See Mrs. Bernatsky," repeated Mrs. Ryan.

"Trouble," said Mrs. Cervitano.

The crewmen forgot all about Sanjo, and so did Poppy. He was being helped into the rear of the ambulance, after the tall one had set the golf cap firmly on his bald head, when he remembered. He clapped both hands to his head and knocked his cap crooked again. "Sanjo," he said. They had to help him down. Mrs. Cervitano was still standing on the sidewalk, keeping her patient vigil, her silhouette tiny and steadfast against the dusky evening sky.

"I'll take her, Mr. Bernatsky," she said.

They helped Poppy back in the ambulance. When he was settled on a leather bench across the aisle from Ma, they took off. The tall one repeated an action he did previously. He wrapped two fingers with gauze and inserted them into Ma's mouth to swab it clean. Then he took an oxygen mask and placed it over her nose and mouth, making sure that no air

[113]

escaped. "This is to help you breathe better." He slipped a cuff on her arm, pumped it tighter with a rubber bulb, put the earpieces of a stethoscope in his ears, and pressed the metal disk against the crease in her arm. He recorded her blood pressure on a piece of paper.

The driver called back. "I've got the e.r. What do you want me to tell them?"

"Her right side is crapped out, blood pressure one-seventy over ninety-six, pupils unequal, pulse seventy-four per minute and regular, respiration fourteen per minute and deep, sounded aphasic, systolic looks like it's rising, Babinski present."

The driver picked up his mouthpiece. "We have a seventy-year-old white female, looks like an evolving CVA. You got her on the gas, Joe?"

"Roger," said the tall one.

"Hemiplegic, assisted breathing, vomited, blood pressure one-seventy over ninety-six, pulse seventy-four per minute and regular, respiration fourteen per minute and deep, aphasic, rising systolic, Babinski present. . . . Hold it a minute." He turned his head to the side. "They want her mental status."

"She's out of it."

"Patient conscious but confused. We're bringing in her old man to give the history. Is Kathy with you? . . . Okay, man, don't get sore. Just asking. Be there in less than five."

Poppy knew a Bobinski once. He wondered if it were the same one. He began to cry. He leaned across the aisle and rubbed Ma's arm. "There was nothing wrong with the liver, Flo," he said.

The young man next to him continued to adjust the mask gently, never taking his eyes from his patient or the rising and falling inhalator bag. He regarded Poppy with a certain affection. He was very much like his own grandfather. The old ones got a little crazy. They couldn't help it. It was explained to him that it had something to do with arteries clogging up. He was thinking of a new trick with his fingers that he would try that night with Sue. His friend Eddy told him it drove women crazy.

His goal now was to get this CVA safely turned over to the hospital emergency crew and then go to Sue's apartment and make her crazy.

Sanjo stared after Poppy and Ma and the disappearing ambulance, even after it was out of sight, the way stargazers stare into the heavens, yearning for galaxies they cannot see. Mrs. Cervitano gently pulled on her arm. "Come, *poveridra.*" She took her into the house. "You have your supper?" Sanjo was too puzzled to cry. The events were too many and too fast. Like ice crystals in a snowstorm, the flurry was too great to be examined for individual merit. There was just the storm.

Mrs. Cervitano viewed the destruction in the dining room. She had decided to take Sanjo home with her but first she would clean up. She cleared the table, took the dishes into the kitchen, and washed them. Then she sponged up the dining-room carpet, exposing the roses and leaves and expunging the odor with vinegar. When she finished, the carpet smelled like a salad. No stranger to tragedy—her own mother went this way—she applied herself with stoic sadness.

Then she took Sanjo into her bedroom and helped her change her underpants. "We'll pack a bag. What do you want, sweetheart? Eh? Tell me, we'll take it." Sanjo didn't know. Mrs. Cervitano found a toothbrush. It didn't matter whose it was. "You want anything else?" she asked. Sanjo stood there without speaking. "You want the cats?" Sanjo didn't even look at her cat pictures, hanging by pushpins from her bulletin board. "Okay. You don't have to talk. It was a big shock."

The telephone rang. Mrs. Cervitano picked it up. "Who do you want?" They said something about citizens and asked to speak to Sanjo. It sounded like a trick. "We gave already," she said, and replaced the receiver. Then she took Sanjo's hand and led her across the street, past Mrs. Ryan, Skippy, Penny's father, and all the other people watching the show. Sanjo turned her head in the direction of the ambulance.

The first thing Mrs. Cervitano did was to visit her altar in the corner of the living room. It was a modest altar, a small table and two pictures on the wall, one of the Blessed Mother, robed and barefoot, and one of the Sacred Heart of Jesus, a picture of Christ with spokes radiating from his valentine heart. A small bouquet of yellow roses picked from her garden was placed beneath them. One of the roses was still a bud, and it revealed only a tiny bit of yellow, a stripteaser that promises to be gorgeous. A few petals had fallen from the older flowers, and they lay curled beside the vase. Two short round candles stuck in red glass containers were placed next to the vase. There was also a statue of Saint Jude. Like a bookie with too much action on one side of the point spread, Mrs. Cervitano like to cover her bets. If one Holy One couldn't handle a problem, surely the other two could.

Sanjo sat on the couch to wait. The plastic slipcover stuck to her legs.

Mrs. Cervitano lit the candles and crossed herself. "It's me again," she said. "But it's not for me I'm asking." Saint Jude, with all the patience in the world, looked out from his plaster eyes in benevolent understanding.

When her supplication was over, Mrs. Cervitano crossed herself and kissed her right thumb. Then she went to Sanjo, whose thighs by now had made a perfect bond with the polyethylene, and yanked her off the couch with a ripping, sucking sound.

Mrs. Cervitano gave Sanjo a bath. Modesty forced her to do the washing while turned away. Considering that she never once looked at Sanjo's naked body, she did a pretty thorough job, although once she poked Sanjo in the eye with the washcloth.

When Sanjo was tucked safely beneath her sheets, Mrs. Cervitano kissed her on the forehead, wished her a good night's sleep, closed the door, and went into her own room.

Sanjo was worried about Ma and Poppy. She made nice-nice. It helped the worrying. Pretty soon she fell asleep.

6

The hospital team, having been alerted, was waiting. As soon as the ambulance pulled into the semicircular drive of the emergency entrance, two burly attendants and a nurse ran out to greet it. Like relay runners, the hospital crew changed movements and duties with the emergency crew, taking over oxygen mask, papers, and Ma. Poppy trailed behind them, losing the struggle to keep up. They had to stand at attention before a triage officer who was sorting incoming patients as fast as a fruit shipper flipping oranges. "Number ten," she said, and they hurried into a cubicle, while the hospital crew transferred Ma carefully onto the emergency-room examining table.

Poppy staggered to the desk. The triage officer looked him over. "What's wrong?" she asked. He leaned against the desk to get his breath. The triage officer was already juggling a differential diagnosis of coronary insufficiency, emphysema, hyperventilation, and a piece of steak stuck in his throat.

"My wife," he gasped. "Just came in."

The triage officer dropped the balls. "She's in treatment. You'll have to go to the waiting room. They'll let you know."

"Where's Kathy?" asked the driver of the ambulance.

"She's on the day shift," said the nurse. The emergency crew left, pulling behind them their rolling cot, and in less than a minute the senior emergency-room resident appeared.

He gave Ma a hurried look and said in his most reassuring voice, "We're not going to do anything heroic, but we're going to do everything possible." Ma wondered who he was and gagged when he stuck his finger down her throat.

The resident gave her some water while holding her head up. "Can you sip this?" he asked. He turned to the white-jacketed medical student beside him. "I'm testing her swallow reflex." Ma sipped. The water went down somewhat but squirted out the corner of her mouth.

"Let's see you do a mental status," said the resident to the medical student.

The student tucked his stethoscope into his pocket and cleared his throat. "Where is San Francisco?" he asked. Ma turned to him. If she wasn't confused before, she surely was confused now. She was trying to think what a San Francisco was.

The resident turned to the nurse. "Start an I.V., five percent D and W. I'm going to see if I can get a history from the old man. We want to keep a vein open," he said to the medical student.

Another nurse gently loosened Ma's clothes and slipped her into a hospital gown that fanned away from her scapulae like a cutaway, giving easy access to her back, her front, or any other region they wanted to get into. Ma's pink hair, poufed by Mr. Tommy into a helmet, smeared her face like cotton candy. The nurse brushed it from her eyes.

All her life Ma had dressed for the hospital, choosing underwear with an eye to getting hit by a car and winding up being undressed by strangers. It finally paid off. Her underwear was clean and neat, freshly laundered with not a single tear.

The resident returned. "Well, it's better than a dump," he said. "At least I got the name of her doctor."

"Are you going to do a tap?" asked the medical student.

"Are you kidding? Did you see what's waiting out there? I've got my hands full. No, we're going to send this one up to the ICU. They'll do everything there. Her own doctor is on his way. Right now we just want to stabilize her. The next"—he bent to whisper this—"the next forty-eight hours are critical."

Poppy sat in the waiting room, his golf cap skewed. He checked each white-coated figure that went past, asking what had happened, what was happening, and what was going to happen. No one answered him. One nurse patted him on the head and set his cap straight. Finally a doctor came over and asked *him* what had happened. They were mixed up. They should be telling him.

Poppy continued to wait in the waiting room, the place reserved for family, friends, and those patients who were considered nonemergent, in the technical sense of not having a life-threatening medical problem. Anyone not suffering from a blocked airway, shock, a chest injury, a serious burn, a spurting knife or gun wound, poisoning, a virulent infection, or a crushed pelvis was not, at this moment, in the cubicles. Second-stringers, they would get into the game after the staff took care of the true emergencies.

A Puerto Rican family was waiting for a report on a little girl who had swallowed some pills by mistake. Clustered in the waiting room were twenty-eight of her relatives and friends who, armed with baskets of food, were prepared for a long siege. The smell of the food made Poppy sick.

A man sat holding his finger which had the base of its nail torn away. The woman who sat next to him whispered, "I'm sorry. What more do you want me to say?"

"Close your own door from now on," he said.

Attendants rushed a trolley carrying a black man with an open wound in his chest which spurted his blood in bubbling projectiles. Poppy was surprised. He didn't think people had so much blood in them. A woman ran beside him holding his hand and speaking softly to him in hushed, breathy tones of comfort.

A man in a leisure suit who had been treated for syphilis in the hospital outpatient clinic was waiting to learn if he had a negative serology. He smiled at Poppy to dispel his anxiety. He had a new girl friend and was considering his obligations if the report was positive.

A woman in an evening gown sat clearing her throat. Her

tuxedoed husband kept feeding her chunks of bread. Next to them sat two college girls in cut-off jeans, one with patches on both her eyes. The one with the patches kept saying, "Don't leave me."

A nurse was talking to her. "You're not going blind," she said. "You wore your contact lenses too long. You'll be better in twenty-four hours."

"But I can't see," the eye-patched student said.

"There's nothing more we can do for you. You have an antibiotic in your eyes. Leave the patches on till tomorrow and see our ophthalmologist before you put in your contact lenses."

"But I can't see. What am I going to do?" said the student.

"I'll take you to your mother," her friend suggested.

"No!" screamed the eye-patched student. "Take me back to the dorm. I'll lie in my bed. I won't bother you."

"All right, but remember I've got a date."

They walked away, the eye-patched girl holding onto her roommate's arms, her roommate, with the carelessness of the sighted, leading her into the wall.

A woman Pakistani resident, wearing a white coat over a long dress, came in to talk to the little girl's mother. "What kind of pills did she take?" she asked.

"They were jellow," said the mother softly.

"No, not what she ate, the pills, what kind were the pills?"

"Jellow pills. The pills were jellow," insisted the father. "Don't you understan' English?"

A drunk brought in earlier by two policemen had passed out. Personnel obviously was disgusted with him and left him strapped on a trolley to sleep it off, his head turned to one side so he wouldn't aspirate and choke on his own vile secretions.

Poppy wondered what was taking so long.

Spig Cervitano held two distinctions among his three brothers. He was the shortest and the only one in organized crime. Spig was a bagman. His mother thought he sold encyclopedias and worried about his going out in all kinds of weather. She used him as a reference source, asking him things like what the capital of Oregon was or how old Garibaldi was when he died. Spig always promised to look it up. It meant he had to spend a few hours in the library, but he didn't mind. Sometimes he would stop in the middle of a job and run into the library. "Where are you going?" he would be asked. "I have to find out the population of Sioux City."

Spig was a go-between. His job was to collect and deliver payment for his associates. Sometimes he carried the money in a bag, sometimes in a sack of groceries, on occasion in an attaché case, and sometimes in his inside coat pocket. Sometimes it wasn't money but some other negotiable that he delivered. Today he had diamonds hidden in the hollowed-out wooden heels of his three-inch platforms. The gems were part of an intricate deal involving a Lübevitche diamond cutter from New York, a Dutchman named Hans, and a Tupelo benevolent association.

He sat with his brother Richard in his mother's kitchen. Both had their jackets off. Mrs. Cervitano was hefting ravioli onto some plates. She didn't like to skimp. Her ravioli weighed more than other people's. Her sons loved to eat her cooking. She loved to cook for them. It was a wonderful symbiosis. Their wives could never measure up. They might try their whole lives long, trading recipes, scouring *Good Housekeeping,* lighting candles, but their cooking would always be second best.

Sanjo sat between Richard and Spig, cutting out cat pictures that Mrs. Cervitano had found in old magazines. Sanjo snipped carefully at the edges. Every so often, like a newborn kitten demanding to be fed, Sanjo would ask, "Where Ma?" and, less frequently, "Where Poppy?" It was a way of finding out indirectly what was going on. Mrs. Cervitano would reply, "At the hospital, like I told you," and Sanjo was content for a while.

Richard was feeling pretty good after having successfully settled the garbage dispute. His reputation as a labor lawyer was made. There was even talk that he was being seriously considered as the district nominee for the state assembly.

Spig had his brother's arm. "So what do you think?"

"I'm not going to launder it for you. Forget it," replied Richard.

Spig clutched tighter. "You gotta do this. You got the connections. This is your brother asking."

Richard shook his arm and his head. He wondered if Jimmy Carter had the same conversations.

"It's a little favor," said Spig.

Sanjo cleared the ear. She snipped off the tail instead.

"Look, I can't do it. That's all there is to it. And what's more, I don't wanna do it. Period. End."

"Where Ma?" asked Sanjo.

"Your ma is in the hospital," said Richard.

Spig fixed his brother with eyes that usually made other people do whatever he wanted. It was the intensity of the gaze and the way he narrowed his lids that gave the eyes their persuasive quality. "What do you mean, you don't want to?"

"I don't want to. Simple."

Spig loosened his grip. "I don't understand you, Dick. What are you afraid of? Since when were you afraid of anything?"

Richard dusted the front of his vest. "Drop it, will you?"

Spig tried another tack. He unknotted his eyes. "Look, you got a client, he wants to open a store, he doesn't have enough money. My associates have an interest, you get a piece, I get a piece, everyone's happy. What could be simpler?"

"Not doing it at all. I don't want to talk about this anymore. Enough."

"Where Poppy?"

Spig turned a wild-eyed face to his mother. "Ma, do something about her, will you? Why does she have to be in here?"

"Sanjo's not bothering anyone," said Mrs. Cervitano. "She sits there so nice and quiet."

"Who can talk here? It's crazy!" Spig jammed a ravioli in his mouth.

Mrs. Cervitano cupped his face lovingly in her hands, causing him to swallow the ravioli whole. He had scars on his chin and one at his throat. Spig always played harder than her other boys. "How's Gloria?" she asked.

"She's okay, Ma. Gloria's okay."

"And the baby?"

"The baby's got a little cold. Gloria took him to the doctor."

"Check your house for drafts."

"I did. We don't have any."

"You never know. You can't see them. Drafts could be any-where."

"Where Ma?" asked Sanjo.

"How long is she going to be here?" asked Richard.

"Who knows? When her poppa gets back. She's no trouble. As good as gold, eh, little sweetheart?"

Little sweetheart smiled. Cat pictures were stacked at her side like pancakes. Given enough supplies, she could cut out cat pictures all day long, trying to perfect the task of snipping around the outline with the zeal and persistence of the Cer-vitano wives trying to perfect their cooking.

"Is she all right with that scissor?" asked Spig. Spig was alert to potential weapons. He assessed his environment by the pres-ence or absence of threat.

"Sure she is. Sanjo, show Aldo how you cut."

"Forget it. I gotta get out of here." Spig put on his jacket and pulled his shirt collar over the collar of the jacket. He decided to open the shirt another button and expose some more chest hair. Then he swung his chain around so that the gold glinted right at the throat of the V. He pulled his shirt cuff down. "I like to show linen," he said. He kissed his mother good-bye.

"Aldo, what's the name of a rose, it's yellow and white in the middle?"

"I'll find out for you, Ma. If you change your mind, Dick, you know where to reach me." He gave his brother a jab to the shoulder and turned away on his diamond-filled heels.

After Richard gave Sanjo the whereabouts of her parents for the tenth time, he convinced his mother that she could go out by herself and take a walk around the block. Richard negotiated the settlement. She was to go around the block, not cross any streets, and not go to her own house, the door of which was locked. Sanjo agreed. Mrs. Cervitano wanted her to cross her heart, but Richard said not to bother. Mrs. Cervitano walked outside with her and watched from her step. "Don't talk to nobody and don't take candy from strangers in a car."

Sanjo stood on the sidewalk. It was like coming out of a cedar chest.

The sky had peeled itself clean, revealing an inner layer of drifting pale blues and whites, lazily skimming and brushing past one another. Green grass began to spread and multiply upon the lawns like mold. Rosebushes decked themselves feverishly in their lush blossoms, vying with each other for coverage and for vibrancy of color. The keen competition forced out new blossoms, some before they were even ready, and they burst on the bush in timid confusion, like understudies unused to the spotlight.

Everyone on the block who had roses was currying their favor, spraying them, dusting them, trimming them, cutting them, fertilizing them, propagating them, and tacking them to trellises. Most people called their roses by their color. They were either pink, red, yellow, white, or a combination. Mrs. Ryan, who preferred to call her roses by their catalog name, hustled six truncated Konrad Adenauers and four Lady Belpens, similarly dispatched, into a plastic bag and carried them into her house to grace her living room.

With it all, the roses were modest. Although they revealed their outer parts, the blossoms curled in upon themselves, lips upon lips, convoluted in secret recesses. They were also more sedate than the annuals. They knew they would come up again next year.

The annuals, which had only one shot, were rioting. Geraniums, petunias, phlox, hollyhocks, asters, zinnias, and pansies were having their last fling, putting on an exuberant display in the most flamboyant and defiant show of the summer. Even the milkweed in the empty lot was showing off, its pale pink and brown flowers and its silky seed tufts belying the treachery of an interior that captured insects by their feet.

Sanjo usually loved the flowers. She would talk to them, smell them, and caress their petals, and sometimes a neighbor would give her one. Today, she didn't care very much what they did.

The road crews were on the street patching the potholes. Five men stood behind wooden barriers, raking smooth hot tar that dripped from the truck, frosting the street like a cake. Two of the men were black and three were white. All had their shirts off. They cursed a little, took turns standing around on their shovels, made jokes, and discussed current events and women.

The subject of women was no accidental discussion. They treated it as serious research, sharing experiences, gathering data, and making a group evaluation of any woman that passed. The evaluation was composed of several variables such as age, body type, conformation, face, hair, walk, and an extra ingredient, an X quotient, that they couldn't name. Unlike judges in beauty contests who had to write these things down, they could keep all these factors in their heads. They always gave a woman a number on a scale from one to ten. When their appreciation was great, they liked to convey this to the woman in question, usually anyone over a seven, and they would call from their posts at the tar with such evaluations as, "Hey, baby, I'd like to ring your bells," "Ditch your old man and call me if you want some real loving," or, "Hey, bitch, you are a mean-looking fox." When Sanjo passed by, they didn't bother to rate her. In fact, they never even looked at her. When she stopped to watch, the only sign of recognition was from a black man, who said, "You don't want to touch that. It's very hot."

Sanjo's house had a heliotropic pull for her. She continued to face in its direction like a leaf drawn to the sun. The house was her biography. It brought to mind the events of the day before as well as her whole life. This was the first time in her experience that she had not awakened in it. It was also the first time in her experience that she had not been with at least one of her parents.

She sat on the curb to stare at her house, her heart pounding, her hands sweating, and her stomach turning. She had a strong need to go to the bathroom. The worried feeling was back. "Ma! Poppy! Come out!" There was no answer. She hugged her knees.

It was hard to be so worried when there were so few pieces she could use to figure the worry away. Other people have plenty of ways to handle worries. Some chew on pencils to help them think things through. Others drink, pop pills, smoke, take it out on someone else, or talk it over with a friend. Some people deny that they have a worry; some rationalize their worry away, creating elaborate internal dialectics; some lock it away so far they can't remember it. Some, like Scarlett O'Hara, say they will think about it tomorrow. Sanjo had access to none of these. It was like having a headache without being able to find an aspirin. There was no way out of the pain.

A few yards away, a swarming bee colony, carrying new queen cells with them, sequined a small tree, bending it over by their combined weight. Sanjo glanced at it, attracted by the shimmer, did not code it, and looked away.

Penny's mother was experiencing guilt. The kind that results from an overdeveloped superego, it stole up on her when she learned that the ambulance took away Ma and not Sanjo. Now she felt remorse for having had those feelings.

She felt that perhaps she had not done enough. When she looked outside her window and saw Sanjo sitting forlornly on the curb, she knew she had not done enough.

She turned back inside to think about getting Penny ready for school. Actually, Penny had been ready for school the day she was born. She was born for school: ready to learn, able to learn, delighted with learning, she would be a joy for any teacher, earn great report cards, and learn to test well, and teachers would write such things as "delightful child" and "outstanding student" on her cumulative record.

Penny's mother twisted her own long ash-blond hair in a single braid that lay straight down her back. While she was sealing the ends with a rubber band she decided to take Sanjo with them to shop for Penny's school clothes.

Sanjo didn't get up at the approach of Penny and her mother. She looked at them but didn't move. The swarming bees weren't too interested either. Although they had forced the tree into a backbend, they were not yet ready for their next move. Stinging was the last thing on their minds.

"Sanjo, how would you like to go to the store with us?" asked Penny's mother.

Not only was Sanjo not too interested, but a deal was a deal, and since she was told not to go with anyone, she would not. "Can't go," she said.

"Why not?" asked Penny's mother. The sentry in her mind that made her evaluate her own actions as either good or bad was causing her to persist where ordinarily she would not.

"Mrs. Cervy say no."

Penny's mother took Sanjo by the hand back to Mrs. Cervitano's house. Richard came to the door with his mother. Because of her size he felt very protective. After Penny's mother promised to return her safely, Mrs. Cervitano uttered the dispensation that would allow Sanjo to get into the car with Penny and grant peace to the conscience of Penny's mother. Richard decided this wouldn't be a bad-looking woman if she let her hair fluff out and wore clothes that showed off her body, which he imagined looked pretty good under that muu-muu.

Penny stood on the back seat of the Volkswagen and clapped her hands. Sanjo sat beside Penny's mother in the front seat. "Sit down and buckle yourself in," said Penny's mother.

"I can do it but Sanjo can't," said Penny, who had a full grasp of Sanjo's abilities. Penny's mother got out of the car to come around the other side and buckle Sanjo's seat belt.

As they pulled away, Richard Cervitano was rushing his mother into the house, shielding her with his arms from the swarm that shivered on the tree. They passed the road crew, all leaning on their shovels and having a spirited argument over whether or not a sniper who puts out people's eyes should get the electric chair. The truck continued to drop tar. It fell

[127]

unevenly, rippling the street like a mirage.

"Let's sing," said Penny. "Do you know any songs, Sanjo?"

Sanjo did but decided to deny it. It was easier than having to dredge one up on demand. Songs didn't come to her that way.

"Okay. I'll sing one. 'He's got the macho in his heart, he's got the macho in his heart. Macho, he's the real real one.' " She shook her head violently from side to side at the conclusion of each quatrain, a joyful and random discharge of muscle tension.

"Pretty good," said Sanjo.

The song triggered for Penny's mother an association of Penny's father. Ever since Penny was born and she had devoted herself full time to her house and child, she found herself more and more accountable for inventory, especially her husband's socks. "Where are my white ones?" he would ask, or "Where's the mate to the brown one?" She would always come up short, having to check hamper, washing machine, and the spaces around the bed. As she began to lose more and more socks—and her self-esteem—she came to the decision to go back to social work as soon as Penny was in school.

Penny continued to be onstage, acting silly, reveling in it, tossing her head about and singing "Macho Man" in a shrill little voice that trilled like glass to a swivel stick. Sanjo joined her best friend in the chorus. "Real real one."

Penny's mother was a wild driver. She especially enjoyed the expressway, where she could let the Bug out all the way, changing lanes, faking other drivers out, challenging eighteen-wheelers, all with cool, steely-eyed, grim-lipped determination. She was without peer for skill or courage. Other cars could go faster, but no one could sneak in and out of traffic as well as she could.

Instead, other cars swerved, pulled their brakes, or careened onto the shoulder. The warning spread quickly over the CB that a westbound beaver in a pregnant roller skate with both feet on the floor was smoking with the devil.

A driver in a flame-painted van with no appreciation for her skill gave her the finger. Penny, a quick study, gave him her finger back and taught Sanjo to do it, too, although Sanjo had to use her forefinger. The challenge was too much for the van. He came behind, waited for the opening, and made a move to the right to cut her off. This was duck soup for Penny's mother. She had plotted his move even before he made it. She was ready for it. She swerved into the right-hand lane, then swung back to the center, and cut him off instead. "Wave to the man again," she said.

The thrill ride, Penny's singing, and the new car wave made Sanjo forget her worry altogether. She was having too much fun. The good feeling was back.

At Swann's, Penny's mother decided not to pay attention to who stared at them. People had stared at her ten years ago when she wore army boots and frizzed her hair out to the width of her shoulders. She was somewhat used to it, even though in the meantime she had gone relatively straight.

The only one who stared openly at Sanjo was an old lady in a gray wig. The security officer was in disguise, one of many she used to appear each day as another shopper, all this in an effort to fool the professional boosters. Today she carried a shopping bag, wore glasses slipped down over her nose, and had penciled some lines on her face.

She had been watching for the red-haired booster, whose shoplifting technique still mystified her, when she saw Penny's mother, Penny, and Sanjo taking the escalator. Penny was on. Her mother followed. "Come on, Sanjo," said Penny's mother, rising like bread dough on the escalator. Sanjo stood firm. The steps that separated them increased. Penny's mother and Penny climbed higher and higher. "Oh, my God, come on, Sanjo." Sanjo held. Penny's mother had to make a return trip on the down escalator to get her.

After watching these maneuvers, the security officer spoke into her shopping bag. "Silver streak to base, we got a repeat, the lost and found retard is back, on her way with a woman and child to the second floor."

Penny chirped her way into the section, next to Toddlers, identified as 4–6X. She had been there before with her grandmother. Sanjo looked around for the pots and pans. They were there somewhere. "Sanjo's getting lost again." said Penny.

Penny's mother doubled back a second time to get Sanjo. "Don't you want to shop for Penny?" She turned her over to her daughter. "Hold Penny's hand and don't let go," she said.

The colors and the profusion delighted Penny. "Look, Mommy, look, Sanjo," she said, over and over again.

Sanjo plodded alongside, head down, smiling and clinging tightly to her hand. They finally went into the dressing room when the saleswoman, with clouds of colors heaped on her arm, said she couldn't carry any more.

At first they couldn't get the clothes over Penny's head. She figured out the problem. "Let go my hand," she said. Sanjo let go.

Penny's mother dressed and undressed her, tossing the clothes about the room as if she were peeling an artichoke. They decided on a blue dress, a yellow shirred jumper, two pairs of pants, some shirts, and a coat. Her grandmother made sweaters, so they decided they didn't need any. There was a scene over a blue velvet dress with lace at the collar and cuffs. Penny loved it. She touched it, fondled it, caressed it, begged to have it. "Mommy, it's so pretty."

Penny's mother hated the dress on principal. It represented everything that was oppressive. "You don't like that thing," she said. "It's not a dress, it's a sellout."

"I do like it. I do. Please, Mommy."

Penny's mother could be firm. "No. We don't want it," she said to the saleslady, who took her cue from the one with the money and withdrew the offending garment.

When Penny's mother went to pay, there was some problem, since Penny's mother was using her own mother's credit card and it had to be cleared. Penny and Sanjo decided to play Hide and Go Seek among the clothes in the next department. It was Penny's idea. The lieutenant barked the orders. The private was happy to carry them out. "You hide," said Penny, "Like this." She ran behind some dresses, then came squealing out. "Now it's your turn." Penny closed her eyes. "I'll count to ten."

Sanjo waddled and wiggled into a rack against the wall. If she parted the sleeves from time to time, she could breathe. She knew how to keep perfectly still.

"Where are you?" squealed Penny. No answer. "Come out, come out, wherever you are." No answer, only a sleeve waving on a rack.

Finally, Penny said, "Come out, Sanjo, I don't want to play anymore."

Penny's mother had been cleared. "Where is she?" she asked. The security officer who was lounging around the water fountain wanted to know the same thing.

Penny was getting thirsty. "Sanjo, if you don't come out, I'll never play with you again. You can't be my best friend."

The scream alerted them. A saleswoman had gone to get a dress for another customer. She grabbed for Sanjo and then saw the face attached, smiling at her from behind the clothes. "Oh, you startled me!" she gasped.

Sanjo was frightened by the scream. Penny's mother led Sanjo away. Penny was left to lug the bag, which was as big as she was. She managed to drag it about four feet before she rebelled. "Mommy, I can't carry this anymore!"

It was a serious conflict. Penny's mother couldn't manage Sanjo and the bag at the same time. It was decided that Swann's would deliver the clothes. That made Penny very sad. She pouted all the way home.

That afternoon, two yellow buses delivered to Bergen Street the neighborhood children back from camp. They pulled up to the curb and stopped, one behind the other. The sidewalks were lined with parents. Some of the parents had cried when the buses left. A few now cried at their return.

Some of the pets had come to the reunion. Dogs that had been outside were able to smell their own from as far away as two blocks and came barking and wagging their tails. A few cats were there, but more to instigate the dogs than to welcome anyone home. One mother was holding a hamster cage aloft for the grand moment. The hamsters, who had bred twice in the interim, didn't care very much about anything except spinning around on their treadmills, breeding some more, and sending pellets flying like missiles out of their cages.

One of the bus drivers, traumatized after ten hours of driving forty screaming passengers, leaned over his steering wheel and muttered to no one in particular, "Why me, God?" The other driver was in better shape. The bus he drove back had been as quiet as a hearse. What he had said was, "Whoever stays the quietest gets a joint."

The final week's dirty laundry made the buses smell like a condemned locker room. A few parents who had gotten too close stepped back. The doors flew open and the children erupted, tumbling and spilling over each other and their parents like Ping-Pong balls. Parents kissed the wrong child or each other. The dogs barked, wagged their tails, and yipped when they got stepped on. The hamsters spun themselves into a blur. Duffel bags, tennis rackets, trophies, and trunks came flying out of the bellies of the buses. It was like a bison herd which has just crossed the river and is trying to put together the right mother with the right calf, thunderous, haphazard, and generally successful. Noise and life returned to the neighborhood.

At the epicenter stood Judy Haskell, having spent the summer as a junior counselor, for which privilege her parents had to pay only half the fee. She was even more beautiful than when she left. The summer sun had given her a burnished look, gilding her skin and her hair. She had grown taller and more shapely, shedding adolescence like a carapace. Judy was looking for her parents and for Toby. She was going to tell him when she saw him that, if he still wanted to make it with her, she was willing.

She had been initiated into sex by a senior counselor, and it was really very nice. She couldn't see any point to waiting, as her parents requested, until she was married or at least engaged. Her parents were willing to settle. Marriage and engagement were light-years away, maybe never. Some of her friends told her that you didn't even have to like a boy to do it.

Mrs. Wright waited for Danny in the rear echelon. She wore dark glasses and a scarf to cover the multicolored bruise on her cheek and the egg-shaped lump on her forehead. Mr. Wright had decided to list Toby as a missing person. Before the police could put out an all-points bulletin on him, he had had to go to the station to give them a description. When he returned he did the only thing he could think of—he beat up his wife.

When Mrs. Wright saw her younger child return alive from Kee Wa Nee, she crouched on the sidewalk like a sprinter waiting for the gun. "Baby!" she cried from her crouch. Danny Wright rushed into the waiting arms of his mother.

The Lowen Volkswagen returning from Swann's picked its way carefully through the crowd of campers and parents. Penny saw Danny Wright and recognized him as the boy who came to play the first day she moved into her new house. "Boys have peepees," she said. Sanjo didn't answer. She wouldn't know a peepee if she fell over one.

"Penis," said Penny's mother.

After twenty-four hours, Poppy came back from the hospital. Jerry brought him home. They had told Poppy at the hospital that there was nothing he could do and the thing was now to wait. The next twenty-four hours would tell them everything. Then they would know something. There was no point to his hanging around. And anyway, visiting in the Intensive Care Unit was limited to only ten minutes every hour.

Poppy eased himself up his steps. It was harder for him to move. His hands seemed to have turned brown overnight.

"Should I come in with you, Morry?"

"No." Poppy waved a hand. "Go home."

The Fleetwood sped away.

Once inside the quiet, lonely house, he heard the refrigerator for the first time. He didn't know what to do. He wandered from one room to the next, turning over pillows, handling an eyeglass case, and rummaging through spoons in a drawer. He was killing

[133]

time until he woke up. He expected Flo to spring up: "Surprise, Morry, some joke, huh?" But Flo wasn't there. Her scent was there. Her hair was there in her brush. Her Supphose was there, hanging over the shower rod. But Flo was in a hospital in a bed in the Intensive Care Unit where she had been moved from the emergency room with something terrifying going on in her brain.

Poppy packed a small bag for tomorrow. In the excitement of the ambulance he had taken none of her personal things to the hospital. He put in her gown, her harlequin glasses on the cord, her robe, her slippers, a lipstick, and her avocado preparation. It would help her feel good. Then he cried.

He decided to get Sanjo. It was time to bring her home. She had been across the street—Poppy had to stop and think—over a day. It was time.

He walked across the street to Mrs. Cervitano's house. The children were out skateboarding under the streetlight, a shouting rookery on wheels, their barking dogs running after them, and a fully orchestrated band of crickets competing unsuccessfully. The children screamed in an esprit de corps of the victorious. The neighborhood was theirs once more.

The screen door was unlocked. When she didn't answer his ring, Poppy let himself in. Mrs. Cervitano was in the kitchen, stuffing Sanjo like a Strasbourg goose.

"No more," said Sanjo.

"How about cannoli? You love cannoli. Here comes the train, choo-choo, choo-choo."

"I've come to take her home," said Poppy.

Sanjo pushed away Mrs. Cervitano's hand. "Poppy!" She slid off her chair, waddled over to her father, bent over to kiss his arm, and remained thus attached to him.

"Where Ma?" she asked his arm.

"Ma is sick," he said. His face had fallen to his chin like a house that has lost its struts.

Mrs. Cervitano decided not to ask him about his wife. "Who's going to eat the cannoli?" she asked.

They walked across the street, Poppy clutching her suitcase in one hand, and Sanjo attached to his other arm with her head resting on his shoulder. They looked like a wide body with a single head at one end.

Some of the children turned to stare. "Here comes the retard," said one. Others never stopped and continued to skate, rolling on Simm's Pure Juice, spinning their 360s, hanging ten, and switching back and forth with neat precise tictacs, streaking in and out of the glow of the streetlight in a stroboscopic flash of faces, helmets, knee pads, elbow pads, bodies, and fiberglass.

Overhead the stars displayed their relationship proudly and openly in one of the few such revelations of the summer. Each cast its own light, clean and distinct, including one that had long since passed into oblivion, having exploded into bits thousands of years before.

In a water-filled footprint a female mosquito walked upon the surface tension of a thin film of molecules. The big-eyed mosquito was resting, on her way to suck blood with her long tubular proboscis. Hovering over the footprint lake was a glinting iridescent dragonfly, a super aerialist, better than any helicopter, zooming upward, diving, flying backward, covering his regular beat like a cop. The footprint was his turf. He followed the mosquito as it flew to a nearby leaf. A clawed underlip darted out from beneath his body, flicked back again between the forelegs, and the mosquito disappeared.

7

They lived for two days on Rice Krispies and pickled herring. The house smelled marinated and looked vandalized. Bedding was strewn on the floor, clothes lay where they had been dropped, newspapers were scattered through the house, and the bathroom was out of toilet paper.

The kitchen could have qualified for aid as a disaster area. Rice Krispies lay on the kitchen table and on the floor where Poppy couldn't see them to sweep up. Napkins, herring jars, boxes, paper cups, and broken eggshells covered the counter. A blackened frying pan with the remnants of scorched scrambled eggs lay soaking in Joy. The dishwasher was choked with glasses and dishes, washed as many as three and four times without being removed, a result of Poppy's throwing in a glass or a dish and running the whole load all over again.

Poppy still wandered from room to room like a sleepwalker. Sanjo never left his side. She followed him everywhere, crackling the Rice Krispies that stuck in her soles and seeding them throughout the house. She woke him up in the morning—"Get up, Poppy"—and banged on the bathroom door whenever he went in, saying, "Come out, Poppy." His fecal impaction seemed calcified; he was afraid they would have to use an air hammer to get it out.

Sanjo was happy. It was a relative condition. She was not as happy as she would have been if Ma had been home, but happier than she would have been without Poppy. Poppy was a good boy. He didn't ask her if she sprayed deodorant, he didn't turn off television at nine o'clock, and he didn't care if she combed her hair. He didn't ask her anything. He just made her stay in the house. "You can't go out," he said. "I got enough."

She stayed at the window, watching Penny play with the other children and waiting for Ma to come back. She was being weaned. She only asked for Ma a few times during the day rather than on the half hour.

A Camaro pulled up to their curb. Sanjo watched from the window. Ma? She pressed against the pane to get a better look. A young man in cut-off jeans ran around from the driver seat and sprinted to the front door. Sanjo recognized him immediately. He peeked through the screen. Poppy thought he was another Jehovah's Witness.

"We told you guys before, we don't want any."

"Don't you remember me, Mr. Bernatsky? I'm Eddie. I take care of Mark. We met at the Disabled Citizens' bash."

No wonder. Poppy had expunged the party and everyone connected with it from his memory as effectively as if he had rubbed clean with an eraser the convolutions of his brain in which it was stored. "What do you want?" asked Poppy.

"We'd like to talk to Sanjo, me and Mark."

"Who is Mark?" asked Poppy. Sanjo bobbed her head up and down. She knew who Mark was. She ran to get her Snoopy purse. "What do you want to talk to Sanjo about?"

"Look, Mr. Bernatsky, you're making this tough. We would just like to talk to her. Can't she talk to people?" Kids today were fresh. No wonder Manny couldn't understand his grandson, the one in the yellow gown. Who could talk to them?

Sanjo was back with the purse. "Truly Mark," she said.

Eddie opened the screen door. "Hi, Sanjo." He put out a hand and shook one of hers. "Listen, can you come to the car? We'd like to talk to you and it's hard to get Mark in and out."

Poppy looked at the car and its occupant. "Go to the car. It's easier." Sanjo went down the steps one at a time carrying her Snoopy purse. Poppy was right behind her. Mark Kinnon was strapped in a double seat belt in the front seat. He continued to bob and weave like a prizefighter who has heard the bell. His synapses were short-circuited so that the electrical messages, jumping across like frogs from one lily pad to the next, landed on the wrong pad. Like an enemy deliberately sending the wrong messages, his damaged cortex and basal ganglion continued to sabotage his muscles, his head, his tongue, his hands, and his torso. He was not still for a moment.

Sanjo came to the window. "I have letter," she said. Mark groaned and vaulted his tortured speech through his arching neck, his lolling tongue, and his only stable and cooperative part, his palate. Poppy rolled his eyes.

"Mark says how come we haven't been able to get you on the phone?" Sanjo stared blankly. Eddie was often a simultaneous translator, able to go back and forth in any direction. "Sanjo, you remember you talked to me on the phone and told me your phone number?" Sanjo remembered. Toby's house. She told him with her eyes. Eddie was good at reading eyes. "Well, we called you on the telephone. We wanted to give you a ride to the club meeting."

Poppy made his intervention. "She can't go with you to any club meeting."

Eddie looked up. "I'll take good care of her, Mr. Bernatsky. Tell him, Mark." Mark groaned and rolled.

"Some reference," said Poppy.

Sanjo put her hand on Mark's head and tried to hold it still. "Be quiet," she said. Mark groaned and flailed, more furiously than ever.

"What did he say?" asked Poppy.

Eddie was also a diplomat. "You don't want to know, Mr. B. I hope you change your mind about letting her go. It's a good experience. She'll grow."

"What do you mean, 'she'll grow'? She's grown already. Who

[138]

do you think you're talking to? Get out of here, both of you; leave us alone. We have enough trouble here."

Eddie thought Poppy was referring to Sanjo, which in part he was. He shook his head. "It's no use, Mark." He got in the driver's seat and ripped the Camaro over the asphalt mirage.

Poppy decided to take Sanjo to the hospital. It was actually Mrs. Cervitano's idea. "Excuse me," she said when he came home to pick up Sanjo, after his daily trip to the hospital. "It's not my business, but she should see her Mamma." At first Poppy thought it was a terrible idea. Driving with Sanjo to the hospital without Ma to run interference was looking for trouble. It was like praising someone you like without spitting for insurance. Then he thought that the sight of her child would cheer Ma up. Poppy decided to take her.

"You wanna see Ma?" he asked.

Does a florist look forward to Easter? Sanjo smiled and clapped her hands. "Boy oh boy!"

"Get dressed. Try not to make a mess."

Sanjo, who was in her pajamas when she got the good news, waddled into her room to get some outside clothes. Usually her daily clothing was laid out by Ma. This time she had to make the selection herself. She stared at the clothes hanging in her closet and chose a dress that buttoned down the front. She got most of the buttons. The problem was she was left with an extra hole. She grabbed a comb and slicked her hair down straight all around her head, her bangs in place, and the hair down over her ears. She found Poppy in the bathroom shaving.

"I 'prayed," she said, pointing to her armpits.

"That's a good idea," said Poppy. She looked uneven. He didn't know why. Maybe it was the way he was standing.

Poppy cut himself. He pressed a towel against the oozing scrape. When he took the towel away it was still bleeding. He pinched off a piece of toilet paper and stuck it to his chin. The skin thought the toilet paper was clotting fibrin and stopped bleeding.

[139]

At the last minute Sanjo decided to take her pocky. Ma liked it when she carried the pocky. "Where Ma?" she asked. They left the house attached.

Once in the car, it was hard for Poppy to manage the steering wheel with Sanjo clinging to his arm and shoulder. Moreover, it made it harder to rise up to see, which he had to do from time to time.

"Don't hang onto me in the car. I can't drive like that," said Poppy. He jerked the car out of the driveway. They passed the sapling that had been bent backward by the swarming bees. It was upright, its tenants having departed for a wonderful hollowed-out oak where at this moment, operating as a single idea, they were setting up shop.

Poppy and Sanjo approached the electronic doors of the hospital. "Don't start anything today," said Poppy. He nudged her through and they entered the hospital, the little old bald man with toilet paper stuck to his face, and his taller, wedge-shaped daughter carrying a purse with a picture of Snoopy.

The Intensive Care Unit was very strict about letting in visitors. At precisely on the hour, ten minutes were allotted for visitors, only two at a time to see each patient. The rest of the time, the waiting worried huddled together on two couches like Neanderthals watching the edge of the glacier.

Poppy sat with Sanjo on one of the couches. No one sat on her other side. She was given a wide berth.

"Where Ma?" she asked.

"In a minute," said Poppy.

Families whispered to each other, offering comforts like bonbons—he's looking good, she's looking better, his color has improved, she signaled with her toe—and, like hypoglycemics out of control who must have a belt of sugar, they gulped down the bonbons without questioning if they were hard or soft. Poppy had nothing to whisper to Sanjo.

The nurse appeared. "You can go in now," she said. Poppy stood up and sighed. He took Sanjo's arm and steered her in the direction of the Intensive Care Unit. Like a well-aligned car,

Sanjo didn't need to be steered. Her track was true.

The Intensive Care Unit was the Times Square of the hospital. Lights and action and noise were constant. The only thing missing were T-shirts, pickpockets, plastic ducks that drank water from a glass, and Belgian waffles. Even the advertising was the same. The vital signs of each patient were wired to a central control unit that maintained constant surveillance and posted each patient's EKG, heart rate, respirations, pulse rate, and heart rhythm. In addition, beeping monitors and flashing alarms at each bed advised staff of any malfunction.

All the patients were threaded to life with an intricate system of intubation and wires which pricked their veins and invaded their orifices. Those who were breathing with the help of a respirator and a black endotracheal tube jammed down their throats looked like scuba divers who had swallowed their gear.

Green curtains with clear plastic midsections, like store windows, skirted from the ceiling around each patient's bed. Now all the curtains were open except one. Poppy pulled Sanjo over to Ma's store. The sides of the bed were up. Ma's arms, covered with blue and yellow bruises in various stages of fading, were tied down.

One arm would have been enough, but the nurse didn't want to take chances. It was also cosmetic. Relatives of stroke victims were often frightened by the sight of worm-like movements that would cause an affected arm to bang against the bedframe in involuntary and irregular jerks.

Poppy cleared his throat. "Flo." He couldn't say any more. Nothing came out. His words lay stacked in his larynx like bodies trying to exit in a panic.

An intravenous needle was taped to the back of her hand; a tube that ran out from under her sheet was attached to a bag filling with urine; and an oxygen mask attached to her face had a rubber funnel, shaped like a golf tee, inserted in one nostril. Saliva lay at the corner of her mouth and dripped onto her chin.

Sanjo waddled from one side of the bed to the other. "Hullo, Ma," she said. She recognized the woman in the bed, of course, but there were strange new parts that she had never seen before. Ma's face was twisted as if she were trying to make Sanjo laugh. Sanjo accommodated her. Laughter in the ICU, especially a heavy vibrato, is rare. Everyone turned to check its source, then turned away when it confirmed their suspicions.

Ma looked at Sanjo a long time but didn't say anything and didn't laugh back. That worried Sanjo more than anything else. Sanjo primed the well, stretching her mouth all the way back, as far as it would go, but Ma did not smile back. Sanjo's worried feeling hit her in the solar plexus. It was hard to breathe. She went to the other side of the bed, her heart racing, afraid to touch the sides. "I got my pocky." She dangled the Snoopy purse overhead. Ma thought it was another tube that someone wanted to attach to her. She turned away.

Poppy got his voice back. "You're looking good, Flo." Poppy grabbed a passing nurse. "Doesn't she know me? She's got her eyes open. She should know me, I'm her husband."

The nurse smiled. "We can't tell, Mr. Bernatsky. We certainly hope so."

Sanjo began to back away. "Ma tired," she concluded.

Poppy wiped away the anguish from his eyes with the back of his hand. He gave it one more try. "Flo, if you can hear me, blink an eye." Ma blinked. Poppy was afraid to hope. Maybe he could work out a code. "If you blink twice, it means yes, okay?" Ma blinked. "It's not okay? Okay, one blink means no, okay?" Ma turned away again.

"Time's up," said the nurse. Family and friends were shooed out to wait for another hour and wonder when the nightmare would end and the strangers in the beds would take off their disguises.

Sanjo sat with Poppy, waiting patiently for the next hour when they could visit again. She opened and closed her Snoopy purse, pulling out the letter. She had forgotten most of it. She opened it up to read. "Truly Mark," she said. "Poppy, truly Mark." Poppy waved his hand as if chasing away a gnat. Sanjo peeked shyly at the woman next to her whose husband's pacemaker had been jammed by a leaky microwave oven. The woman was being rocked in the arms of a friend who was telling her that, when they fixed his pacemaker, his heart would be better than all the rest of their hearts put together.

Sanjo gave the woman her half wave, the tentative, just-in-case salute. The woman pulled back closer into the shelter of her friend's arms. "Really," said her friend. "As good as new. Better than new. Would I lie to you?"

The family that thought their old grandmother was signaling with her toe was listening to a resident who tried to explain that what they saw was not intentional signaling but a reflexive action, the result of hypoxia. The resident continued that because of this oxygen deprivation to the brain the toe movements they were seeing had nothing to do with conscious effort. The son, who had broken the code, did not believe him.

A nurse closed the door on the last visitor, and nurses, respiration technician, residents, nursing students, medical students, and an occasional attending physician rushed back to perform the functions of their fifty-minute hour. They clustered around each patient like atoms slammed together to form a treatment molecule, then broke their covalent bond to regroup at another bedside. A male nurse bolted from one group and sprinted to a bedside where an alarm beeped. He slowed his sprint when he realized that the alarm was triggered by the patient scratching his chest.

A cluster came to Ma's bed. "What's the story here?" asked the resident.

"Her diastolic went up during the night to one-sixteen. The BPs are being checked every fifteen minutes and she's on a nipride drip titrated to keep the diastolic down to ninety. She's making adequate urine and breathing on her own with forty percent oxygen by nose. She pulled on her tubes." The last was an afterthought.

"She should be on seizure precautions," said the resident. One of the nurses quickly taped a tongue blade and a syringe filled with Valium near her head, on her bedtable.

[143]

The resident shined his ophthalmoscope in Ma's eyes, piercing her pupils with the steady beam of light. He was looking at her eye grounds, scrutinizing the retinal blood vessels for signs of fresh hemorrhage, scanning optic disks for signs of papilledema. He didn't like what he saw. Neither did Ma. Everything was blurry.

"Stick out your tongue," he said. Ma stuck out her tongue. The resident released the restraints on her arms. "Close your eyes tight." Ma tried to close her eyes tight. "Smile," said the resident. Were these people taking her picture? Ma wondered. "Take my hand," said the resident. Ma didn't know which one to take. She decided to take neither. "Close your eyes again." The resident placed his stethoscope against her closed eyelids, listening to pulsations. He dragged a broken tongue depressor up the soles of her feet, heel to toe. The big toe on one foot went up, and the rest of the toes, with a mind of their own, fanned out. "Notice the Babinski," he said. Ma wondered what Joe Bobinski was doing there.

The nurses pulled the curtain around Ma to reinsert the catheter that had worked itself out. An attendant called from the other side of the curtain, "Where you been, fox?"

"We're fixing the Foley in here, attending to business, which is more than I can say for some people."

When Ma saw the curtain around her, she vaulted backward into time. She was twelve years old and lived over a candy store with her mother, father, cousin Milton, sister Tessie, brother Manny, and her mother's younger sister, Rifke, in two rooms, a tribute to the designing skills of her mother, who maintained modesty and discouraged incest by hanging sheet partitions that separated each person from the next as neatly as ice cubes in a tray. Everyone was always getting tangled, and in the summer it was hard to breathe.

"Open the sheets, Mama. I don't like it in here." No sounds came out. Instead, saliva bubbled at the corner of her mouth.

"I wonder if we should suction her?" asked one nurse.

At the bed next to Ma's, a medical student had just drawn

blood which he was transferring to several tubes. He was proud of his ability to juggle a handful of vials. He stuck the contaminated needle in the mattress as he always did on the other floors in the hospital. Unlike the mattresses on other floors, mattresses in the Intensive Care Unit were air-filled. The mattress did not deflate right away. It began as a slow leak. Staff was attracted to the hissing and thought it was oxygen escaping from one of the wall outlets. They checked around each outlet. "It's not here," said a doctor. "Try the one in the next bed."

The patient, who was slowly sinking, could have told them where the sound was coming from but, encumbered with an endotracheal tube, could only make it vibrate.

The resident made his way to the bed with the curtains pulled around it. "What's the holdup here?" he asked.

"We're waiting for you to pronounce him," said the nurse. The doctor disappeared behind the curtain.

Poppy and Sanjo left the waiting room. Both had to go to the bathroom. Since the Ladies' Room and the Men's Room were separated by a hallway, Poppy decided to take Sanjo, wait outside while she went to the toilet, then let her wait outside for him. He changed his mind en route. His prostate could be tyrannical. "Sanjo, can you hold it?"

"Okay," she said.

"That's good," said Poppy, "because I can't. Wait here." He was opening the door. "Don't talk to anyone." The door closed. "Don't go away" was shouted from inside.

"Okay, Poppy," said Sanjo.

Poppy couldn't hear her. He was already relieving himself, breathless against the urinal, wondering why, with all this rush-rush, it always started as a dribble.

A nurse and an orderly wheeled out a trolley with a patient who had died. They were taking the body downstairs to the morgue in the basement. The freight elevator was being repaired, and they had to use the visitors' elevator. Careful not to offend the sensibilities of people in the waiting room, they carried on a conversation with their dead passenger, something they often did in front of other patients. "Just a little way to go, Mr. Smith," said the nurse.

"Right," said the orderly, picking up his cue. "Down to X-ray in the basement."

"Hold on," said the nurse. "We're hanging a right."

"Thanks for telling me." The orderly was a bit of a ventriloquist.

Mickey and Jerry came to help Poppy with Sanjo. Jerry was afraid that his older brother's heart could not take the strain of caring for Sanjo and accepting the fact of a deteriorating wife at the same time.

The Fleetwood rippled over the street and into their driveway. Mickey and Jerry flashed out. Mickey walked holding all ten fingers in front of her like a baby who is learning to walk. Her new hobby was her nails. Each one was painstakingly wrapped with paper by her manicurist and coated with six coats of base, polish, and sealer. If she should break one, which she did often, the manicurist would glue it back with the same miracle glue that could suspend a truck from a wire. As a hobby, her nails were better than Bargello. They went everywhere she did and didn't require a carrying case. She didn't have to do anything herself—in fact, they prohibited her from doing anything, which was no problem since she had a maid. Looking at them didn't make her seasick, and she got compliments all the time, which is something she never got with the Bargello.

Jerry was a great dresser. When he was young, he used to wear ties that said *Kiss me in the dark, baby.* He had come a long way. Now he wore Cardin everything. He knew how to turn a shirt collar inside a jacket so that it stood up, knew how to stuff a handkerchief into his breast pocket with just the right insouciance, and wore high-ribbed socks that didn't show his calf when he crossed his legs.

Mickey dipped for her kiss. "Hello, Sanjo; Morry." Poppy pulled away from the tangerine smell. "Well, how did she take it? Did she understand?" Mickey didn't wait for an answer. "You're going to come with us, Sanjo."

Sanjo was puzzled. "Ma tired," she said. "She in hos'pal."

"Look how she knows," said Mickey.

"Of course she knows," said Jerry. "What do you think she is, an idiot?" He could have bitten his tongue.

Poppy didn't seem to care. "This is a very nice thing you're doing," he said.

"Morry, you're my brother. It's the least we can do."

Mickey helped Sanjo pack. "We're going for a ride in the car," she said. "What about her bathing suit? Maybe we could take her to the beach?"

"Let's not overdo this," whispered Jerry under his breath. Mickey packed the bathing suit anyway.

"Come on, Poppy," said Sanjo.

Mickey made a *chk*, a clicking of the tongue that is actually a word among South African Bushmen meaning "Leave my bongo alone." Jerry pursed his lips and looked away. Poppy rubbed his hand across his freckled scalp. "Your father's not coming," said Mickey. Sanjo seldom heard the word *father*. If she ever related it to Poppy, she chose not to do so now.

"Poppy go," she said. She found his baseball cap and put it on his head.

"I'm not going," said Poppy.

"We're going to have a wonderful time," said Mickey. "Close this thing, will you, Jerry?" Like a mandarin, she was helpless.

Sanjo had serious doubts. She was more in touch with the con than most and knew she was being bamboozled. She decided to sit it out. "No." She sat down.

"Come on, Sanjo. Uncle Jerry's ready."

Sanjo held.

Poppy recognized the signs. "Uh-oh," he said.

"Sanjo can't go," said Sanjo.

"Of course you can go. Why do you say you can't go? Get up," said Mickey.

Sanjo dug in, gritting her teeth so hard her gums bled and gripping the edges of the chair until her knuckles showed white. "No."

Jerry decided to try. Excellent at getting his prescription

[147]

customers to switch from brand to generic names, he said, "Sanjo, we're going to have a good time. You'll play with our dog, Oscar, and Aunt Mickey will take you to the beach."

Poppy hitched up his pants. Not only were they getting too long but they were baggy enough for him to dress in the middle. "Sanjo, you have to go with Uncle Jerry and Aunt Mickey. Ma said." The reading of the word, the tablet from the mountain. It worked every time. Sanjo got up.

"Okay," she said.

"Kiss your father," said Mickey. Sanjo already had Poppy in a hammerlock.

Mickey's and Jerry's apartment was decorated. That is, they had hired the services of someone who had not only a flair for balance, form, and color but a license to prove it. For this privilege, they paid through the nose. Everything in the apartment was color-coordinated in white, canary yellow, and apple green. Even the books on their shelves were wrapped to match these colors. Nothing was out of line. Everything balanced. Everything matched. While the essential style was contemporary—that is, straight lines, mylar, Lucite, and overstuffed pillows—the decorator managed to unload a piece left over from a previous job. He called the mixture eclectic. "It works," he said, pushing in an Early American corner cupboard painted apple green.

The first six hours were critical. They set the flavor for the rest of the visit. Jerry and Mickey never took their eyes from their niece for one minute. Mickey followed her everywhere, holding her fingers before her like the newly blind. Jerry behaved like the captain of a submarine who has discovered a destroyer overhead. "Where is she?" he would ask from time to time.

At first they put her to bed, although it was only five in the afternoon. Mickey dragged the dining-room chairs into the extra bedroom and stacked them around the bed so Sanjo wouldn't fall off. Sanjo watched her from the bed. Ma never put chairs around her. She blinked in mild interest.

When Mickey left, Sanjo lay on her back and stared at the ceiling. She wasn't tired. She really wanted to watch television. She thought about Ma. It was a brief picture of a familiar yet changed figure making faces at her and refusing to smile, one mystery among many. The picture changed to that of the dog, Oscar.

Mickey and Jerry sat in the kitchen planning an itinerary that would keep Sanjo busy every minute of a sixteen-hour day. By eight o'clock, Sanjo had had enough rest and was out of bed to join them. They were still in the kitchen, transferring the list to a complicated chart that Jerry drew up.

"Go back to sleep, Sanjo," said Mickey.

"I not tired," answered Sanjo. It was Mickey's first intimation —the first in her house, that is—that this was not going to be like taking care of Oscar. "Gimme drinka water."

Mickey got up to get water from the refrigerator spigot. "You want ice in it?"

"Uh-huh."

Mickey emptied the water and changed glasses, selecting one that was plastic. "Here," she said.

Sanjo sat with them in the kitchen. Oscar sat at the table too. He was an immense sluggish English bulldog with great folds hanging from his chops and a tiny bow taped on his head. Sanjo was afraid of Oscar. He snarled. She kept a safe distance, leaning all the way back in her chair.

"Don't touch his bow," said Mickey. That was the first of forty items that Sanjo was not allowed to touch, including a Lalique vase with angels on the outside. (For an extra precaution, Mickey rolled towels into sandbags and placed them around the base.) Sanjo, who had leaned as far away from Oscar as she could, fell over backward. Ice and water flew everywhere. Sanjo began to cry with the pain and the surprise. Jerry went into action immediately. He felt her head, checked for bleeding, asked her if she felt dizzy. She continued to cry.

By the third day of activities that changed as fast as a cruise ship, Mickey was bananas. She hissed at Jerry in bed one night. He thought at first it was a sign of passion and ran to lock the bedroom door. Back in bed he quickly learned that she was telling him something.

"This can't go on!" she hissed. "I'm too young of a woman to have such a terrible twitch in my cheek!" Jerry agreed to take them to the beach. After all, it was his brother, not hers. It would get everyone out of the house. Jerry hated to waste any effort. Since he had locked the bedroom door he had hopes. Mickey turned away to bury her twitching cheek muscle in the pillow.

"I won't look at your face," he said. "I can't even see it."

Sanjo no longer asked, "Where Ma?" She knew where Ma was. She had seen Ma rest before. Sooner or later she always got up. Now, in the car on the way to the beach, she asked, "Where Poppy?"

Jerry had a CB. His handle was Medicine Man. He first called himself PillPusher, but they were besieged on the highway by cars wanting to score a hit. It was amazing that Jerry, with a strong regional accent of the Northeast, sounded, once on the air, like a dirt farmer from Arkansas. He drawled and slurred, dropping his final g's and saying things like "good buddy," "lan' sakes," "glory be," and "ten-four we gone" until even Mickey couldn't understand him.

The beach was jammed with bodies in various stages of browning, a short-order rotisserie whose chickens had fallen off the spit. Some of the bodies were using suntan lotion and seawater to baste themselves into first-degree burns. The glinting silica, acting like tiny mirrors, reflected the brilliance of the sky and helped accelerate the process. Smells of baked dried clams, suntan oil, salt, and seaweed drying in the sun were baked by the heat into a steaming miasma that spread across the sand and seasoned the chickens.

Mickey, Jerry, and Sanjo picked their way through. Every blanket had a radio, and each blared a different station. The result was a furious competition of melody, beat, and voice which canceled each other out or harmonized in a cacophonous assertion of sound, despite the shushing of the waves.

Jerry brushed sand from his feet with each step. He hated it. Sanjo took off her sandals too soon. "Hot!" she yelled. The sand had burned her feet. Mickey and Jerry had to help her put the sandals on again.

"We're too far away," said Mickey. "Wait till we get closer to the water." If Oscar had sandals, she thought, he would have kept them on.

They decided to camp in a particular place. It was not an easy decision. It was based on proximity to water (it had to be close enough so that Sanjo could leave her shoes at the blanket and not burn her feet when she walked to the water) and relative freedom from debris and noisy parties drinking beer from cans. They spread their blanket elaborately and carefully. Jerry jumped on it, avoiding the edges and the sand that might contaminate him, and pulled himself into the middle, a fetus who preferred to float rather than bump against the uterine wall.

A young couple on a blanket next to them, under the guise of spreading suntan oil on each other, did everything except what could be strictly interpreted as sexual intercourse. They were amazingly single-purposed in their lubricious activity, especially since the legs of strangers continued to flash back and forth over them like high jumpers. Sanjo watched them poking into each other's suits. There was no connection between this and special delivery. Foreplay was out of her experience. The boy reminded her of Toby.

"Toby bring Bugs," she said.

"What did she say?" asked Mickey. Jerry didn't hear. He was brushing sand from his arm that someone had kicked on him when they tripped over the oiling couple.

Two men on their other side were also on a blanket. One sat with his back toward the other, his arms drawn around his knees. The one behind him was very beautiful. "It was a thing of the moment, Francis, a passing requirement, like grabbing a hot dog

[151]

off a stand. It doesn't affect us in any way."

The man with his arms around his knees kept his eyes firmly rooted to the horizon. "I thought we really had something. Obviously you don't know the meaning of trust."

The one behind him twisted the studded cock ring on his wrist. "Define trust," he said. Jerry pulled up tighter into the center of the blanket.

Mickey slipped off her beach coat. She had on an artfully designed bathing suit with a mesh front panel that canceled out her stretch marks. The bathing suit really did a very good job. Everything in it was sleek and trim. The only thing it could not correct, and that was because it was cut too high, were the BB shots in her thighs.

Sanjo wore a one-piece black suit which she had had for about fifteen years. It was designed before the maillot and was actually orthopedic design, strapped and crossed, puffing stiffened latex projectiles over her undeveloped chest.

She waddled down to the water. Refracted light rays covered it with diamonds. She loved the beach. "Boy oh boy!" People stood shoulder to shoulder. Even the Ganges didn't get a bigger draw. Although standing room was at a premium, people stepped aside when they saw her coming. Pilots who sprayed parathion got the same reaction. It was an instinctive response.

Sanjo sat at the water's edge with Mickey standing right behind her. The foaming wave, having absorbed its energy from the wind, pulsated on the beach, sending the water rippling over her feet, her legs, and her belly. What was a pulsation at the shoreline became a pounding farther out on the jetties, where barnacles, covering the wooden pilings, were closing their shells against the surf.

The water withdrew. "Come back here," said Sanjo, but she really wasn't angry. She knew the water was playing. The sand wiggled. Hundreds of little segmented bodies burrowed deeper, sticking two feathery eyestalks above them to see if they were being followed. "Oh, no," said Sanjo. It wasn't dismay, it was delight. "Hullo, cutie." She reached to grab a crab on its downward flight but it disappeared too fast. The eyestalks, topped with faceted eyes that broke Sanjo into prisms, advised the crabs to dig even deeper. A dozen sandpipers skittered across the sand to the bubbles that advertised the location of each crab and began to poke the wet sand.

The receding water always changed its mind and came back. The sandpipers managed to escape at the last possible moment and scurried up the beach ahead of the surf.

A wave came up so fast it knocked Sanjo on her side and she drank some of the salt water, choking and sputtering. "You see?" said Mickey, who hit her on the back.

Seated again in the water, although a bit more wary, Sanjo did what everyone does at the beach. She urinated in the water, casting her eyes down all the time so that no one could catch her at it.

Sanjo turned on her stomach in the foot-deep water and walked on her hands. She kicked her feet, splashing as hard as she could. She liked to swim. Mickey encouraged her. "Let's see you swim," she said.

Sanjo turned to pull away some seaweed that had wrapped itself around her foot so she could swim better. Alongside her were some shimmering jellyfishes. Also swimming with her, although so tiny they could not be seen, were diatoms, single-celled plants that would double their number in two days and within two weeks would turn the ocean brown. In fact, the diatoms weren't swimming. Swimming requires effort. The diatoms were wandering. Sanjo was trying to swim.

Nearby, at the water's edge, a little boy was making a drip castle with his father. The father dripped the sand carefully into turrets, bridges, courtyards—amazing structures, dizzying in their height and success. Sanjo stopped swimming. She edged sideways a little closer, not presuming to come too close but moving in their general direction.

The father looked up. He was an off-duty traffic cop, alert to objects that edged. He gave Sanjo a quick assessment, considering her in the way he did the general public; they all needed help. "You wanna play with us?" he asked.

Sanjo smiled down at her legs, now covered with the rushing suds.

"You can help if you want."

"Okay," said Sanjo. She rolled onto her knees and pushed herself up. Then she came over and sat down beside them. Mickey was right behind her, an alter ego.

The father continued to drip. "Like this," he said. The little boy grabbed a fistful of sand and sprinkled it on the castle. In the fistful were millions of protozoans, swimming through the water film between the grains. The drips contributed but didn't build. "You wanna do it, too?" asked the father. He put mud in Sanjo's hand.

"Don't knock it over," said Mickey. Sanjo's stubby fingers did not have the precision required to make a really good drip. One needed fine pincer action between the thumb and the index finger, and discretion and judgment to release the mud slowly enough, and in small enough mass to form a drip that dried almost as fast as it was placed. She plopped the wet sand on the turret. It knocked it down.

The little boy looked up at his father. "It's okay," he said. "We can fix it." The father did it himself, slowly, purposefully, and artfully constructing a castle as carefully as he controlled the flow of a heavily congested intersection—someone who had developed patience from hearing "Why is the red light longer on our side?"

Jerry volunteered to leave his woolen island and take Sanjo for ice cream. Sanjo huffed and puffed in her sandals. It was harder to walk in them, but cooler. She eroded a tiny zipperlike path made by a scavenger beetle, scuttling with a few footsteps the plans of a sea gull in a gray habit that was using the tracks to guide it to its lunch.

A little boy of ten who, like Sanjo, had an extra chromosome walked toward her with his mother. Sanjo and the boy passed one another. There was no hint of recognition from either one. The mother continued to stare after Sanjo, long after she had left them behind.

[154]

Sanjo was sleepy and happy when they left the beach, even though she had tar on her feet, Noxzema on the saddle of her nose and on her back, sand-flea bites, and sand in every secret recess and fold of her body. The sun and sea had had a soporific effect, lulling her like the plankton into relaxed and formless acquiescence. Her heart beat rhythmically and slowly, the way it was supposed to. The choking feeling in her throat was gone, and the chocolate ice cream, which dripped all over Jerry's Fleetwood, tasted wonderful.

On the way home, the traffic jam inched and jerked along. Jerry turned off the air conditioning and opened the windows so the engine wouldn't overheat, after seeing cars gasping on the side of the road with their hoods lifted up so they could breathe better.

A black Chevy with nine people and two yellow pillows on the rear shelf pulled alongside them. Two teenagers in the car called to Sanjo. "Hi, turkey," they screeched. Sanjo gave them the new car wave she had learned from Penny. Traffic moved unevenly and they pulled ahead of the Chevy. The ice cream was almost finished. Sanjo was down to the cone. In a few minutes, the Chevy pulled alongside them again, its occupants enraged, and now everyone, including an old grandmother, jabbed their middle fingers angrily at the Fleetwood, except one little boy who, like Sanjo, used his index finger.

"What's the matter with them?" asked Jerry. Sanjo waved back again. The car edged closer. "Did you see that? He almost ran into me!" said Jerry.

"Don't pay attention to them," said Mickey. She had already discounted the car and its occupants. "Talk to your friends," she advised.

"Breaker, one nine. Medicine Man here. . . ."

Mickey turned to take the cone away from Sanjo. "What are you doing? Don't do that. Look what they taught her," she said.

Sanjo wasn't as happy in the apartment as she had been on the beach. She began to worry again, about Ma and about Poppy. She wondered when she was going home. For one thing, she didn't like Oscar. He kept sniffing at her heels, and he snapped and snarled. She spent most of her time running from him. The other thing was that Mickey and Jerry were always whispering about Ma. They called her Flo, but the way they were talking was not a good way. Sanjo recognized the tone, even if she couldn't recognize all the words or the exact meaning they conveyed when strung together. She knew it was trouble.

Mickey was at the end of her rope. She began to swing from it when Sanjo, stumbling over Oscar, tripped and fell, knocking the Lalique vase from its washcloth barricade and dismembering two angels. Sanjo cried. She hurt her knee. Mickey also cried. Oscar jumped up on the chair to watch with heavily lidded eyes and dangling chops, Churchill after the signing.

Mickey decided not to wait for Jerry to come home. She called him at the drugstore. "The twitch is getting worse. We have to take her back before it becomes a permanent thing." Jerry was satisfied that he had done enough for his brother. He was getting tired of seeing Sanjo sitting in his living room whenever he came home, he was getting tired of "Sesame Street," and he was getting tired of hearing the deep-throated, "Where Poppy?" They took Sanjo home.

A week in August makes a big difference. It is a subtle change, primarily affecting the way sound is perceived. Noises become more distinct. The nights are cooler. The animals and the plants and trees know that fall is coming. They get ready, some to travel, some to turn down their thermostats, and some to brave out what is coming.

Sanjo ran up her walkway and hurried herself, one step at a time, up her steps. She carried her pocky. "Ma! Poppy!" Poppy came to the door. He let her strangle him for a moment, then disengaged her arms. "Ma's not home," he said.

"What's happening?" asked Jerry.

"Worse," said Poppy. "She won't open her eyes."

"Not won't, Morry, can't. She can't open her eyes."

"That's what I said."

"No, you said won't. That implies a willful decision."

[156]

Poppy shrugged his shoulders. He had not shaved in days, and a gray stubble covered his face.

"What are you going to do?" asked Jerry. He jerked his shoulder in the direction of Sanjo.

"I'll take her with me," said Poppy.

"How are you feeling?" asked Jerry.

"All right."

"Any pain?"

Poppy shook his head.

"Morry, it doesn't look good."

Poppy wasn't sure whom he was talking about or what. "What doesn't look good?" asked Poppy.

It looked worse than Jerry thought. "Flo."

"Don't say that. You don't know anything. You think you're a doctor? You're not a doctor. You're a druggist."

Jerry and Mickey left.

Sanjo went out to play. Poppy forgot to care if she went out. Sanjo had not played with Penny in over a week. Thoughts of Penny made her both happy and frantic. She was like a junkie who needed a fix. She decided to take the whistle that Uncle Jerry had bought for her on the beach from a concessionaire named Sharkey. She wanted to blow it for Penny. She went down her steps, one at a time, clutching the railing with one hand and the whistle with the other.

Skippy was sleeping on his front porch, deep in REM sleep, his legs twitching in chase. Mr. Ryan ran by on his tenth lap around the block. He had on a purple tank top and green shorts with a purple stripe down the legs. His chest was thrust forward. He knew he was looking good. He carried a plastic container of Gatorade, and he was planning to ask Mr. Wright, who was watering his lawn, to wet him as he ran by.

Sanjo knocked on Penny's door and stood with her head bent forward and her arms rotated outward. Penny's mother answered the knock. "Penny's not home, Sanjo. She's out playing. How's your mother?" Sanjo stood there smiling. She was beginning to like Penny's mother. Penny's mother raised her voice.

[157]

"Your mother is in the hospital. How is she feeling? Is she feeling any better?"

"Ma in hos'pal," said Sanjo. She shifted from one foot to the other. "I got whistle."

Penny's mother realized she had miscalculated the level of her voice and of her message. "That's nice. Maybe you can find Penny. She's that way." Penny's mother pointed down the street, then turned and went inside.

Sanjo went down Penny's steps one at a time and plodded down the street, her unbuckled sandals flapping on the pavement and the backs of her hands brushing her sides. She saw a little blond head and ran halfway down the block. The effort popped beads of sweat over her upper lip and plastered her bangs to her forehead. When she got close she saw that it wasn't Penny. Sanjo stopped, breathless. She looked around her, swiveling her head from side to side to check out the message of her peripheral vision. Penny was nowhere in sight.

A small band of children were playing at the end of the block. They were trading baseball cards and were too engrossed to notice Sanjo. All of them held cigar boxes in which they stored their cards, and they yelled offers at one another like traders bidding in a stock exchange.

Danny Wright, although only eight, was making the best trade, having gotten rid of the entire Baltimore Orioles for a Pete Rose and a Reggie Jackson. Baseball cards made Danny forget that his brother was gone and had taken most of the Bugs Bunny comics with him. His mother refused to buy him any more. The association was too painful, she said. Danny didn't understand why his brother ran away. Who would cook Toby's dinner, he wondered?

They didn't see Sanjo until she stood a few feet away. She stopped and they stopped. It was not a thing decided upon by anyone. It just happened.

The children began to draw into a circle and ringed Sanjo, closing their ranks tighter and tighter, like sheep dogs closing in on a stray lamb. None of them were higher than her chest. Sanjo

[158]

smiled, showing her pegged teeth. She liked children. "Hello, dopey," said one. Sanjo laughed. "Boy, is she stupid." Their faces combined a look peculiar to childhood, a feral combination of innocence and menace. They pressed together tighter, moving in a single intelligence.

"Do a dance," said a little girl. Sanjo began to be afraid. "Like this, jump like this." Sanjo didn't move.

Another little girl hit her on the leg with a stick. "Move your foot," she ordered.

Sanjo tried to avoid the stick but could not move fast enough. It hurt. Tears came to her eyes. "Stop it," she said. They continued. "Ma!" she cried. Sanjo made a move to leave the circle. The children pushed her back. The ring pressed in tighter. The whistle fell to the ground. A familiar little figure stood on the perimeter of the circle, hair haloed with light that shone behind it, face flushed with sun and running. Sanjo smiled in recognition of her best friend.

"Bad boys here," said Sanjo, shaking her head sadly. Although girls were included too, she gave to the ring a generic designation. Penny made a move to the circle, spinning her thistles.

"Let her in," said Danny Wright.

"Here, Penny, next to me," said a little girl. Penny moved into the circle, stood for a moment, stared at Sanjo, then took the hand of the child on either side.

There was no precedent for this in Sanjo's experience. She had no template against which to measure treachery. She looked about in sorrowful confusion, her eyes widened in the same frightened, puzzled look seen in any helpless creature at bay.

The children continued to torment Sanjo, hitting her on the legs and taunting her until Mrs. Renfrew called for Marjorie to come home that minute and practice her baton twirling. Marjorie, whose red hair was rolled into rags, was in the finals for Pert Little Miss. Her foot-stamping departure broke up the momentum and the circle. The children were getting bored anyway. They bent to pick up their cigar boxes, regrouped in twos and threes, and dispersed through the neighborhood.

[159]

Penny followed Danny Wright and a little girl. "If you're going to play, you have to keep up," said the little girl. Penny put all her effort into the run, her little legs pumping like pistons.

Sanjo picked up her whistle and ran after them, gasping and panting. "She's following us!" shrieked one.

"Oh, no!" shrieked the other. Laughing, they sped into the bushes, Penny right behind them. Sanjo lost them. She continued to follow in their general direction. She even called a few times into the giggling bushes. "Penny come out. I got whistle." She blew the whistle. The bushes giggled harder. She waited. When no one answered, she turned around and walked toward her house.

The mail truck came around the corner. Mr. Niemeyer's eyebrows flew up to his cap. All systems were go. Mrs. Cervitano's blinds were drawn, which meant she wasn't home, and Sanjo was right there on the front lawn petting the ducks. Mr. Niemeyer made a quick decision and parked in the driveway. Desperation calls for boldness.

"Sanjo," he called, "Special Delivery." Sanjo looked up in his direction.

"Good-bye," she said to the ducks. She wasn't feeling very good. Her legs hurt and so did her spirit. Mr. Niemeyer smiled. It was the first genuine welcome she had had from anyone in a long time. She walked over to the truck.

He didn't even have to hold out the chocolate bar. Mr. Niemeyer wiped the sweat from his round, perspiring face. "You little devil, you've been playing hard to get. Come on in. I've got a lot of letters." He pulled her in. "And lots of stamps." He pushed her in the rear of the truck. "And about five minutes."

Sanjo put her whistle on the floor, grabbed a stamp and a pad, and bent over to mark the packages. The heavily inked stamps, a result of Mr. Niemeyer's thoughtfulness, duplicated themselves with the precision of a cell in mitosis.

Impatience made him clumsy. He knocked her over three times before he had success. Orgasm made him blind and deaf. He never heard the car pull up beside him in the driveway.

Mrs. Cervitano got to the truck first. When she peeked inside, she tried to bite her thumb off at the knuckle. Then she yelled, "Murder!" She couldn't yell rape.

Sally and Spig were out of their car in an instant and into the truck. The truck began to rattle. Sounds of Sally yelling "Pree-vert!" and Spig yelling "You goddam dirty pree-vert!" and Mr. Niemeyer yelling "It's a mistake!" emanated from within. Sanjo escaped, clutching a stamp, and Mrs. Cervitano hustled her into the house.

Skippy roused himself from his slumber and his dream of cats. He wrinkled his forehead, erected his ears, sniffed, and skinned back his lips, exposing his teeth. He looked in the direction of the mail truck. He pitched a terrible whine, which escalated to a snarl, which in turn was followed by a growl. Skippy sped across the street, barking and snapping.

"Where are you going, baby?" asked Mrs. Ryan.

Baby didn't answer. Like anyone on a seek-and-destroy mission, he was maintaining radio silence. Skippy didn't even need to jump on the step. He bounded into the truck with one leap.

Sally and Spig, with all the rage of the avengers of the innocent, proceeded to beat their mailman to a pulp. The rattling truck attracted Mr. Wright, who had been outside watering his lawn. He jumped in the truck, not fully knowing the story but understanding the action.

Mr. Ryan was too exhausted to do anything but lean against the jouncing mail truck and yell, "Give it to him!" which is precisely what they did. They kicked Mr. Niemeyer in the kidneys, in the groin, broke several ribs, gave him a subdural hematoma, and ruptured his spleen. Spig broke his glasses.

The noise brought Poppy to the picture window. He looked outside and saw the mail truck jerking in the Cervitanos' driveway with Mr. Ryan leaning on it. He couldn't figure out where all the racket was coming from. He went back to his wandering throughout his house.

When they couldn't rouse the mailman, they all began to get worried. Mr. Wright went home to water his lawn, and Mr.

[161]

Ryan crossed the street, carrying Skippy in the crook of his arm. Spig and Sally were stuck with the task of calling the ambulance. Spig wrote a note saying "We did it," (signed) United Parcel Service," and pinned it on the mailman's pocket.

When the ambulance came, they found the mailman still unconscious and a note pinned to him. After they hauled him away and called the police to come and get the truck, the driver remarked that for a quiet neighborhood they sure got a lot of action.

It was decided not to tell Poppy. You don't tell a man whose wife has had a stroke that his daughter has just been sexually assaulted by the mailman. Instead, Mrs. Cervitano gave Sanjo another blind bath, this time with brown soap. Of its ability to kill anything, including spermatozoa, Mrs. Cervitano was certain. She also lit a candle to the Holy Mother. This was a matter for women. "Don't let her get a belly. She's not married, no disrespect, but with you it was a holy thing."

8

A coma can bring out the best in friends and relatives. When Ma's eyes were open, the only ones who came to see her, besides Poppy and Sanjo, were Jerry, Mickey, and Mrs. Cervitano. As soon as the word was out that Ma was comatose, hovering somewhere in the twilight between sleep and death, they came out of the woodwork.

Like Camille, who got most of her action when the coughing got worse, Ma had visitors she hadn't seen in years. They came by train, by bus, and by car. Some came by subway, and one, Ma's younger sister, Tessie, who preferred to be called Tina, came by plane from Chicago.

A coma is also very serious business. The word itself is the toll of a bell, a mystical incantation, a sounding, both prayer and warning. Witnessing one is like running with the bulls, a little scary but thrilling too, a skirt with death so close the spectators can smell its breath. Friends and relatives, caught up in the drama, become grandiose and entertain the notion that they alone will be able, with their voice, their touch, their kiss, to bring the comatose person back to life and living. Didn't the prince do it, after all?

They came tentatively at first, peeking around the corner of the waiting room, murmuring in the corridors, bumping into each other, and speaking in sepulchral tones, sounds to be made around granite and moss. No one smiled or laughed. Everyone was keenly aware of the gravity of the situation.

They kissed Poppy, shook his hand, and patted Sanjo on her head. A few, reluctant to touch her, wriggled their fingers at her, flipping them down, one after another, like ducks in a shooting gallery.

There are stock questions that help anyone to interact with the children of friends. These range in ascending or descending order, depending upon one's point of view, from "Where's your nose?" or "What's your name?" or "How's school?" to "How's the job/spouse/children?" Everyone was thrown off with Sanjo. To ask the first and second would be insulting to Ma and Poppy; to ask the third and fourth would be irrelevant. People shuffled around her, most not saying anything at all. If they did, it was usually a question they answered themselves, something like, "Remember me? Aunt Dora. You remember me." Sanjo would say "Hullo" and smile shyly, mostly at her chest, and that would end the conversation. They would stand around, uncomfortable for a few seconds, then move on, which in the case of the waiting room was only a few feet. When she was in their line of vision, they created a visual blind spot, a conversion hysteria of sorts that blocked her from view.

They lined the hallway, identifying themselves and their relationships to Ma in the way a sports announcer at a ball game gives the names and positions of the players.

At first there was great confusion. People recognized the wrong person and embraced strangers. Ma's brother, Manny, confided to Poppy that he would never have recognized Kitty Cucinsky. Poppy told him Kitty Cucinsky wasn't there. People thought they were related to one another only to learn that the relationship to Ma was sometimes just a nominal sanguinity. "Oh, you said *practically* cousins. I thought you said cousin." There wasn't a person in that hallway who didn't claim intimacy to Ma of one kind or another.

The major problem was logistics. Naturally, almost everyone

wanted to see Ma. The question was, with twenty people and only ten minutes every hour, who and in what order? Jerry was making up a list. Jerry could ring up facts as fast as a cashier rings up money in a register. *Bing.* Manny did not want to go in with Tina, with whom he was not speaking. *Bing.* Neither Sally nor Spig wanted to go in at all. *Bing.* Mrs. Cervitano said to pay no attention to them. *Bing.* Ma's cousin Jean Rosemond had to leave at two o'clock.

They crowded around the cashier to make their complaints. "I got to you first, why is my name all the way down here?" "I'm her sister, why am I after Jean, who's only a second cousin?"

Through all this, Poppy sat with his baseball cap in his hand, trying to stretch his feet to the floor, his face poxed with tiny blood-dried bits of toilet paper.

He had seen the doctor earlier that morning. The doctor had told him it didn't look good, especially since Ma had passed from stupor, a point at which they were at least able to get her to open her eyes, to coma. The transition at her age, he said, was significant. The doctor also told him that they didn't know how much brain damage she was having. They were going to do some tests to find out. Poppy's felt as if his brain were filled with ice cubes. He couldn't think straight.

With it all, Poppy had the responsibility of Sanjo nonstop. Everyone that he could have left her with was at the hospital, and even if anyone remained at home, she had already worn out her welcome. The only one who would have taken her for a few hours was Mrs. Cervitano, but Richard advised her that because of what happened to Mr. Niemeyer it would be better not to do so.

It wasn't that Sanjo didn't behave. She sat beside Poppy wearing the same dress she wore the first time she went to the hospital, only this time the leftover buttonhole was on the top. She had her pocky. She even remembered to put on white socks under her sandals, something that Ma had campaigned for vigorously. At first she was pretty good about sitting and waiting. Even if once in a while she got up and walked around, it was mostly just from one side of the hall to the other. But having her with him was like trying to cross a heavily trafficked street with no stoplights. There was no letup.

Poppy was getting a headache. It struck like a jackhammer. "Anyone got an aspirin?" he asked. Tina produced a tin out of her capacious purse. Poppy couldn't get it open. He pulled, he squinted, he twisted, he squeezed. It was not only child-proof, it was Poppy-proof. "What happens to people with arthritis?" he asked.

"You have to press in the red dots," said Tina, on her way back with a paper cup of water to wash it down. Poppy grunted his gratitude and swallowed the aspirin.

Mrs. Cervitano sat flanked by Sally and Spig. They were maintaining a low profile according to instructions of their lawyer brother after the United States Post Office brought charges of felonious assault against them. Richard, who had posted bond for their release, was now in court making a motion to quash charges.

When the police came, the first thing they did was discount the note pinned to Mr. Niemeyer, since it contained the word *signed.* They traced the whistle to a concessionaire on the beach named Sharkey, but reached a dead end when Sharkey told them he had sold hundreds of such whistles in the past week alone.

A resourceful detective checking around the neighborhood got a statement from Mr. Ryan, who said there had been a fight in the truck. Mr. Ryan implicated Mr. Wright and the Cervitano brothers. He neglected to mention the complicity of his dog. The Post Office ruled that until this was settled, the Cervitanos and Mr. Wright would have to pick up their mail. For some reason, the Post Office extended this edict not only to Ma and all four of her sons but to anyone in the city named Cervitano.

Mrs. Cervitano stood up to brush back Sanjo's bangs. "So you can see," she said. Then, because she did not wish to presume, she sat down again between Sally and Spig. Spig was planning revenge on Mr. Ryan. Sally told him they didn't need more trouble.

[166]

"Not to him. Maybe something to his car."

"Forget it."

Sanjo squeezed in next to Sally, her old childhood friend. She put her head on his chest. "Sally pretty," she said. Sally didn't mind. He stroked the back of her head, surprised, as he always was, to find that it was so flat.

Mrs. Cervitano prayed her rosary. Her wooden beads were in her dress pocket, and she told them with one hand, over and over again. Even though there were fifty-nine, she made it around the track in twenty minutes, spinning through the mysteries with the earnestness of the truly devout. Her friend was lying in there with something awful. She had seen this before and she wasn't too optimistic. The tears rolled down her heart-shaped madonna face, right through the tiny mustache that quivered over her whispering lips.

Minnie Hightower appeared with Georgio, a forty-year-old Italian she had found on the Riviera, who didn't think a seventy-year-old woman was old, particularly if she had some bucks. Georgio was actually a Bulgarian but found it didn't sell as well as other nationalities.

Since he was easily mistaken for a citizen of any country in which the males are likely to have raven-wing black hair and dark eyebrows, he could be Greek for women who were a little kinky, French for those who didn't know any better, or Arabic for those who liked falofal.

When he asked Minnie Hightower what kind of men she liked, she replied, "Italian, like you." He did not disabuse her. It was easy to change Gregorius to Georgio.

Georgio was as polished as the chrome trim of a Rolls-Royce. He gleamed and shone. He was first-class merchandise, although a little shopworn. Minnie's children, who were older than Georgio, hated him.

"That's not what we sent you on the cruise for. We sent you to meet people your own age."

"I don't like people my own age," replied Minnie. "They're too old."

"What do you know about him?" they asked.

She knew he was capable of multiple acts of intercourse within a single afternoon, but how do you tell this to your own children? "I know he's a very nice person," she said.

"What's wrong with Mr. Pfeffer? We thought you liked him."

Mr. Pfeffer urinated in the bed. That's not something you can tell your children either.

At first she was worried that the thinning walls of her vagina would cave in, but no such thing. The nonstop sexual activity had a salutory effect on Minnie. She began to gleam almost as much as Georgio.

Minnie went in first to see Ma with Poppy. That caused a minor riot among the others, all of whom claimed seniority on the list. Poppy waved them away as if dismissing a gnat. "She's Flo's best friend. She's coming in." Minnie followed him into the ICU.

Ma had been moved to another bed. Her eyes were closed. Her breathing was quick and shallow. One cheek puffed out and fluttered with each exhalation. Her skin was flushed. She made little noises from time to time that sounded like the mewing of a kitten.

Ma was in a state of insensibility. She did not respond to anything in her environment. She didn't feel the prick of tiny pins inserted into her scalp early that morning when they performed an electroencephalogram, a test to study her brain waves. She didn't respond when nurses inserted a tube through her nose to suction her secretions. She could not be roused even when her doctor pressed his fingers deep into the sockets above her eyes.

She was not dreaming, so engrossed in unconscious unravelings that she could not attend to the external events around her. Rather, she was like an insect in chrysalis, whose state cannot be forcibly changed even with the most invasive prodding.

Minnie and Ma went way back. Having both passed their

[168]

seventieth year, they had the special regard of mutual survivors, like the redwoods in Muir Forest. At first when Minnie approached Ma's bed, she was not distressed. Who among her friends would look good lying on her back in a hospital gown without makeup, without a good bra, with her hair plastered on the pillow in strings, and with tubes coming out of her nose?

"Flo, can you hear me? I brought you back some things from Europe. A scarf, it's gorgeous, some cologne, and some pills made from"—she bent over to whisper this—"the testicles of goats. It keeps you young." Ma mewed. "I know, who likes to get old? Nobody, right?"

Poppy stood twisting his baseball cap. "I don't think she hears you, Minnie."

"Who knows what she hears? I'm going to talk to her anyway," and Minnie Hightower proceeded to whisper to Ma all the events of her trip around the world financed by her children, including her first meeting with Georgio and the details of their first night together. Poppy rolled his eyes. Whom else could she tell? Her own middle-aged children got hysterical at the mention of his name. Things were so tense that even a reference to the state of Georgia, which admittedly did not come up too often, was likely to start a commotion.

Sanjo sat beside Georgio in the waiting room. Georgio wore his jacket over his shoulders. He elevated his eyebrows, swept his eyes about the waiting room, and retracted his nostrils, snuffling them in like straws. Nothing worth his attention. He buffed his nails.

Sanjo turned to watch him making the same motions that Ma made on the ironing board, back and forth, back and forth, gliding the buffer across each nail. She imitated him. Georgio didn't care. "Ma sleeping," she said.

Georgio looked up for a moment. "Yes."

"She tired."

"Assuredly," he said. His nails began to gleam as much as the rest of him. He reached in his pocket. Georgio always had something for somebody. "You like it?" It was a compact he

kept to spruce up the raven's wings. Sanjo took the compact and
turned it over in her hand. It felt cool in her palm. Georgio
opened it for her. She peeked into the mirror. Narcissus could
not have been more pleased.

"Pretty nice," she said.

"Keep it. It's yours." Georgio smiled and flashed a lateral
incisor of fourteen-karat gold.

Minnie Hightower returned with Poppy. She was crying, her
tears running like tributaries through the Firmo-lift Rachel No.
2 cream base that covered her face.

Georgio stood up. He took her hand and pressed it to his
chest. "Too much, sweetheart, too much. We'll go and find a
way to cheer you up, no?" Minnie Hightower's tears dried on
the way to the river. She kissed Poppy and Sanjo good-bye and
left on the arm of Georgio.

The ICU went back to its fifty-minute hour. Ma was getting
another neurological check, this time by the medical student.
He tapped her ankle with his hammer, which he held at its
fulcrum, making his thump with the neat snapping wrist action
of a carpenter.

Since his deflation of the air mattress, he was known as Dr.
Prick. He knew staff was watching him, and he was very carefully
evaluating the performances of reflexes, pupils, muscles, mind,
and nerves. He moved to the next bed. A priest came in and
traded places with him.

"Are you sorry for any sins that have separated you from
Christ?" Ma mewed. Her eyes weren't open, but the priest's
latitude was great. "Very well. I forgive you in the name of the
Father, the Son, and the Holy Spirit."

The medical student held up his patient's leg under the knee.
"Father, I don't think that woman is Catholic."

"Oh?" The priest was puzzled. He had been here at the same
bed the day before. "What happened to Mrs. Flannery?"

"She died this morning. We took the body down to the
morgue."

"That's too bad." The priest folded his white silk stole. "To

[170]

save me a trip," he said, "are there any Catholics in here?"

"I don't know. Ask the ward clerk."

The student continued to shine a pen light into the eye of the patient. He was puzzled by the fixed pupil of one eye. He had seen unequal pupils but never anything like this. He switched the light to the other eye and back again: the same thing. The left eye was totally unresponsive, fixed and staring. A nurse walked over.

"Any problems, Dr. P.?"

The student flipped his name plate with his free hand. "The name is Fogelman. I was wondering where the lesion is."

The nurse convulsed against the wall, triggering a like convulsion of all the staff at the central control, who clutched at their stomachs and doubled over in contorted jackknifes, as if they were poisoned. Then she pulled herself together, leaned over the patient, and with elegant panache plucked out his left eye. It was glass. The student reminded himself that his service in the ICU was finite. It would only go on for another two weeks.

Jerry and Poppy decided to break up the ten-minute visiting allowance in this way: five minutes to Poppy and another person of his choice, which usually fell by default to Sanjo, and the last five minutes to be spread two persons every minute. It seemed a fair and equitable way to handle the discontented and rebellious mob in the waiting room. Jerry would stand in the doorway to keep the traffic moving.

It was Poppy's turn. He started in with Sanjo but stopped at the doorway to talk to Jerry.

A few feet away, in another bed, was Mr. Niemeyer. He had more wrappings than a mummy. The only things that showed were his rounded cheeks, his eyes, and one hand. Everything else was bandaged, casted, intubated, or wired shut. His wife stood on one side of his bed, and his son, an intense young man in an army uniform, wearing a crew cut that showed patches of oyster-white scalp, stood at the other side.

Mr. Niemeyer saw Sanjo walk by. He gave no sign of recognition, but his sympathetic nervous system did. It changed the rhythm of his heart from a steady beat to an arrhythmia, something that was quickly picked up on the monitor and changed the beat from a fairly steady bloop to one that was syncopated.

"See what's going on with number four," said one nurse to another. The arrhythmia passed when Sanjo walked away. Nursing did not connect the two events.

Sanjo stood at Ma's bedside and shuffled from one foot to another. She was feeling pettish. She waited for Ma to wake up but Ma wouldn't do it. She was getting tired of waiting. She banged a fist against her side. It was something she rarely did. It meant she was really annoyed. Sanjo shook Ma's arm. "Get up, Ma," she said. "Come on." No response. "Ma-a-a-a!" Ma mewed. "Wake up!"

Poppy, who was still talking to Jerry, didn't see her pull on the I.V. tubing and jerk it out of Ma's arm. The back of Ma's hand bled. The tubing snaked across the bed, leaking fluid over the top sheet. Sanjo tried to untie the restraints but had trouble with the knot. She bent down to yank on the tube of the catheter.

Two nurses were already on their way to the bed. "I don't believe this," said one. "What the hell are you doing, lady?" She gave the other nurse a hasty look, a sweep of the eye like a sparrow looking for a place to land. "She's . . . you know."

Reinforcements ran in. Ma mewed again. Two hustled Sanjo away while another two remained to repair the damage, which was a simple matter of changing Ma's top sheet, getting a new I.V. outfit, and reinserting the tip of the catheter. It was all accomplished in less time than it took Poppy to get Sanjo settled in the waiting room. At the doorway, Poppy was instructed that, if he brought her in again, he had to watch her very closely. They would not be responsible if he did not..

Sanjo was very confused. She had done something wrong but she didn't know what. She felt it in their hands when they grabbed her and heard it in their voices. "Bad girl," she said to her chest.

"What's the matter with you?" asked Poppy. For the mo-

ment, he forgot the answer. He led her to the couch. "Sit."
Everyone made room for them.

Sanjo kept her chin on her chest.

"What do you want to hurt your mother for?" Sanjo didn't
know. Poppy lowered his voice to a hiss. "Don't touch anything
in there. Nothing! You understand?"

Sanjo moved as far back on the couch as she could go and put
her hands over her ears. "No bad talk, Poppy."

Jerry indicated to the Cervitanos that it was their turn. "It's
okay, Mom," said Sally. "We'll wait out here for you." While
they recognized their duty to their mother and sat with her
willingly in the waiting room, which also fulfilled Richard's
demand that they lie low and not talk to anyone, neither one was
anxious to see the inside of the ICU, which years later was still
vividly associated with their father's death.

"You go," said Spig. "We'll be right here."

"Rispetto!" hissed Mrs. Cervitano. The waiting room was
beginning to sound like a snake pit. They both stood up and
allowed their mother to hustle them in. Mrs. Cervitano rushed
ahead to the bedside of her friend.

Sally and Spig dawdled on the way, walking as slowly as one
could walk and still be walking. They stopped near Mr.
Niemeyer, midway between Ma and the door, but did not recognize him. He was just another muffled, wired, bandaged, and
intubated body.

"Dick is sure he won't testify anyway."

"How can he be so sure? Ryan already fingered us."

"Because it was a sick thing he did. What man would admit
to a thing like that?"

Mr. Niemeyer's bloops became syncopated again. His computer, programmed to respond to certain combinations of rate,
irregularity, and frequency, remembered that his heart showed
a strange rhythm only minutes before and activated a flashing
red light that said, "Somebody go and do something." The
nurses shooed away his wife and son, whose crew cut at this
moment could be seen growing, and stabilized Mr. Niemeyer

[173]

with a direct hit of fifty milligrams of Xylocaine, followed by an I.V. that was calculated to drop in fifteen microdrips per minute.

It's terrible to wait, and even more terrible to wait surrounded by people who tell you not to worry. Inherent in that message is just the opposite. Poppy was getting more nervous by the minute. They kept coming all day long, bringing candy, flowers, fruit, and hope. They all knew someone just like Ma who was rescued at the last moment by some marvel of medicine and who now was playing "B" tennis.

By the late afternoon, Jerry went back to his drugstore and Mickey went to have her nails wrapped. There was, after all, nothing any of them could do. Life goes on. So do nails and pharmacies.

Poppy was getting stiffened by the inactivity. It became harder for him to get on and off the couch. "I'm getting nudgey," he said. Sanjo was not talking to anyone. She was mad at herself for being a bad girl, mad at the nurses who talked bad to her, and mad at Ma, who was also a bad girl and wouldn't get up. She didn't know what Ma was doing in there, but it really made her angry. She banged her fist against her leg. When that didn't help, she stamped her feet like a rowdy spectator at a stadium.

"Go home, Poppy," she said. "Go home!"

The final straw for Poppy was Ma's brother, Manny, who said that Flo always looked like that when she slept. How did he know? He hadn't seen her sleep in over fifty years and then only when he peeked under the sheet curtain. Poppy alone knew what Flo looked like when she slept. He had slept with her for almost half a century. She may have been a little disheveled from time to time, but she never, in her worst night, looked anything like that woman on the bed.

"Go make up with Tina," Poppy said to Manny.

"You sure?"

"I'm sure."

The doctor entered the hallway. Poppy jumped on him as on a life raft, clutching his collar with both hands. "What's going on?" he asked.

"Mr. Bernatsky, we don't know any more this afternoon than we did this morning. She's holding her own. That's about all we can say. There's some activity, we know that."

"What activity?"

"Brain activity."

Poppy was confused. "What's her brain doing?" he asked.

"It's working. How much, we don't know, but it is working."

"Can you do anything to help it along?"

"I wish there was something. We're doing all we can. I can tell you, though, it's very, very critical."

Poppy twisted his baseball cap. By now the visor had been rubbed raw at the edges by his fingers. "When is she going to be able to come home?" It wasn't that Poppy was stupid. Who wants to take a tornado head on? The threat was too terrible. Poppy did what most people do when faced with disaster. He turned away from it.

The doctor sighed. This was going to be tough. "Look, you'll have to accept the fact that she maybe won't be coming home. I hope that's not the case, and there's always reason to hope. She may come out of it, we don't know, and that's the truth of it."

Who knew the truth of it? The truth of it to Poppy was that his joints ached, his head ached, and he was hungry. Poppy knew he had to get out of there. He decided to check with the nurses first. Maybe they had a different story.

One of them cleaned his face, cupping his chin in her hand and removing the bits of toilet paper, while he talked. She assured him that he should take a few hours and get some dinner.

"What if things change?" he asked.

The nurse turned his face in her hands and wiped away the last piece of paper. "Things don't change that fast," she said.

"Come on, Sanjo," he said. "We'll get a little bite."

The visitors who remained clucked their tongues and whispered to each other. "That's trouble," they said.

On the ground floor next to the lobby was a combination gift shop and snack bar which had a counter, three tables, two customers, and a waitress. Poppy pulled a reluctant Sanjo past an island with a display of cigars, boxed candy, stationery, tulle caps, beaded flowers, and cups that said *Get Well Soon.*

There is a need in a crisis to tell everyone, even in casual encounters, of the situation. Poppy wanted to announce, "My wife is very sick. She's critical," and get the attention he deserved, like, "Yes, sir, right this way; sorry, sir, would a cup of chicken soup make you feel better?" Instead, he brushed off the crumbs from a seat at one of the tables, sat down with Sanjo, and tried to act like an ordinary person whose life was not up in the air like a juggler's balls.

The waitress brought them two menus and went back to the counter, where she rearranged the doughnuts on a glass-topped lazy susan. Poppy couldn't read the menu. It had nothing to do with his eyesight. It had to do with his concentration.

"What do you want?" he asked Sanjo.

"Go home."

"We can't go home. What do you want to eat? You want a hamburger?"

Sanjo had been eating fruit and candy all day long. She wasn't hungry. She was cranky. She turned to stare at the waitress behind the counter.

"Yes or no, do you want a hamburger? How about a hot dog?" Poppy asked.

Sanjo shook her head from side to side.

"All right. Don't do me any favors. Don't eat. I'm going to eat." He waved at the waitress, who was still rearranging her doughnuts. "You coming over or what?"

"Take it easy, pops."

That did it. "Come on," Poppy said and led Sanjo out of the snack shop. The other customers turned to stare.

A security guard in the lobby told him they could get hot and cold sandwiches from the vending machines in the basement. There was only one minor problem. The coin-exchange machine was broken. Poppy put his hands in his pockets and came up with two nickels. "Let's go home," he said to Sanjo.

Late that afternoon, the doorbell rang. Poppy thought it was the telephone. He shuffled into the living room, saw Judy Haskell through the screen door, and reached for the telephone. His reflex arcs were mired. Once an action was begun it was hard to get a recall going. He held the telephone up to his ear, heard the dead buzzing on the line, and then called through the screen door, "What is it?"

Judy was uncertain about her mission and stood on the front step, swinging her head to clear her long hair from her eyes. "I'd like to see Sanjo."

Poppy didn't respond. He was as nonplused as a hard-rock DJ getting a request for Frankie Avalon.

"Can I?"

"Okay. Come in."

Sanjo recognized Judy right away. "Toby bring Bugs," she said. She wanted to establish a connection.

Poppy waited to see what possible kind of interaction this might be.

"Don't you know that Toby's gone, Sanjo?"

"Where Toby?" asked Sanjo.

"He sent me a letter. It's from Boston. There's a part in it for you." Judy shifted her weight from one foot to the other, an actor who doesn't know how the director has blocked out the scene. She swished her hair. Sanjo stood before her, waiting.

"Sit down," said Poppy. He was learning to be a stage manager.

They went to sit on the couch. "Well, most of this is for me, but here is the part for you. Do you understand what I'm saying?"

"Uh-huh."

[177]

"Okay. I'd hate to be doing this for nothing. 'Dear Sanjo, I'm okay. In case you're wondering, I'm on my own. I picked up a couple of rides and they were all going north. So here I am all the way in Boston. It's nice here. You can sleep on the grass and no one cares. Sanjo, I hope you are okay. Some day maybe I'll send for you when I get my own place. I'm out of money so I am going to look for a job. You probably don't understand all this. Ask Judy to explain it to you. Judy will also read you Bugs. Your friend, Toby.' Do you understand?"

"Where Toby?"

"I knew it was going to be like this." Judy swung her hair to the left.

Sanjo pushed herself off the couch and waddled into the bedroom. She came out dragging a box which scraped across the floor where there was no carpet. "Read Bugs," she said.

Judy pulled out a comic. "All right. Here's one. Did Toby ever read you the one about Yosemite Sam?" Sanjo nodded her head. "Well, you don't mind hearing about him again, do you?"

No, Sanjo didn't mind.

" 'That durn rabbit. He thinks he got the best of me. Well, Mr. Bugs, you got another thing—no, think—coming.' "

Judy twirled her hair as she read. It was a comforting gesture. Sanjo twirled her hair too. Judy didn't read like Toby. She did it straight. There was no editorializing and no commentary, but it was better than nothing. The story was soon over.

"Does that do you?" asked Judy.

Sanjo smiled. "Uh-huh." She was feeling better.

"Well, I gotta get going. See you, Sanjo." Judy unwound herself, standing up with the natural grace of any young well-formed creature whose coltish buckling is over. She went out the door, switching her hair out of her face and sending it flying behind her.

On the side of the house, covering their giggles with their hands, like Trojans inside the horse, were Danny Wright, Penny, and Pert Little Miss. They had followed Judy to the house. That, and some other damning information which Penny gave Danny, led him to conclude that Toby's Bugs Bunny comics were inside the Bernatsky house.

When Judy came down the steps, they ran from the side of the house to the sidewalk. "Hi, Judy," said Danny. He smiled his brightest smile. Already, as a result of having had much practice on his mother, he had a way with women.

Judy glanced at him. She was impervious. Toby used to complain about him all the time. She wasn't fooled. "Hullo," she said, with the noblesse oblige of one who is six years older. Penny stood behind him, her lustrous little face framed by her wispy golden hair.

"Who's this little girl?"

"That's Penny," said Danny. "She's new."

"She's a kindergarten baby," said Pert Little Miss, making practice twirls with her wrists.

"I'm not a baby," said Penny. "I'm going to school next week. I have pencils and a book."

"Silly, you don't write in kindergarten."

"Yes, you do. My mommy said you can do anything you want in kindergarten."

"How's Sanjo?" asked Danny. He knew when to switch from the general to the specific.

"She's okay."

"What were you doing in her house?"

"I was reading to her."

"What?"

"Comics." A first down.

"What kind?"

"Superman," she lied. Second and twenty.

Sanjo had heard Penny's voice and opened the door. She offered her beaming face like an Eskimo who has suffered through a long winter and feels the first rays of the sun. "Bring red," she said.

"I don't want to color," said Penny.

Danny and Pert Little Miss turned to leave. Penny followed after them, running with her fists at her sides. Danny turned back. "So long, Chinko." Pert Little Miss giggled.

"Chinko," said Penny.

Sanjo's tears coated her eyeballs and shimmered there.

"Don't listen to them," said Judy. "They don't know anything." But they did. That was the trouble.

The next day Poppy came to the hospital to find that Ma's breathing had stopped during the night and staff had put her on a respirator. Her breathing had changed to a Cheyne-Stokes pattern, a dramatic event that starts off slowly, builds to a crescendo, then diminishes to zero, sometimes for as long as a minute. The effect is that of an obscene caller who keeps backing away from the phone. The staff didn't wait. They threaded an endotracheal tube into the vault of her throat and attached her and the tube to a respirator.

When Poppy took Sanjo in to see Ma, she looked different from the day before. She lay on her back, her limbs straight out, her color yellow and waxy, the result of tissues that were only a passive participant in the act of diffusion. The only thing that was strong was her rhythmic breathing. She breathed with the help of a square-shaped affair with a round cylinder on top. Her breathing was even and heavy, transporting blood gases where they were supposed to go.

Poppy was grieving. The woman in the bed was not Flo. When did they make the substitution? He was also getting angry at the doctors for not giving her the right thing to pull her out, a shot, an electric shock, anything to melt the yellow wax and wake her up.

Sanjo was uninterested in speaking to Ma, a bad girl who did not want to get up. She continued to enter the ICU with Poppy throughout the day, but she did not make a move to touch the intubation or the body into which it led. Neither would she look in its direction. Instead, she listened to the gasping respirator and watched the robotlike arm that moved the sleeve up and down on the volume control.

The waiting room had now dwindled down to Jerry, Mickey,

Manny, and Tina. Everyone who wasn't family decided to stay away. If they came, it was only for a minute and then only for the briefest of visits to Poppy. At this point, they were not interested in seeing Flo. Tina asked Poppy what he was going to do with Ma's jewelry.

The doctor went to look for Poppy. He put his arm around him. Trouble. "This is a hard thing for me to tell you, Mr. Bernatsky." Poppy looked up sideways to better dodge the blow. "Your wife is very, very bad."

"I know that," croaked Poppy.

"Mr. Bernatsky, it's like this. We did another EEG on her and it's flat."

"That doesn't mean anything. She's laying down. Of course it's going to show flat."

"No, I don't mean that. I mean it shows no brain activity."

"It'll show tomorrow."

"I don't think so."

"How can you tell?"

"We can tell. We know that when it shows flat like this—and we've done other tests, too, to see what her reflexes are like; they're practically all gone—we know that when it shows flat, she has, in fact, died. The brain has died. The only thing that keeps her going is the respirator. Without it, she'd be dead, without question."

Poppy looked up at him. What did he want from him?

"We're going to have to make a decision."

"Okay, make it."

"No, it's not that easy. It's a decision you're going to have to make with us. It's our opinion that she is clinically dead. That to continue her on life support is wasteful—for us, for the hospital, for you, and for the community." What did the community have to do with this? "So we'd like your permission to discontinue."

"You what?"

"We would like to discontinue the life support."

"What do you mean?"

[181]

"Discontinue life support. Stop the intravenous. Disengage the respirator."

Jerry and Mickey were at his side. "It's the best thing, Morry," said Jerry. Tina began to cry.

"What happens if she gets better? She could get better. It happens all the time," insisted Poppy.

"Not like this. If she gets better, as you say, she would be a vegetable, not a person as you know her. In all probability she's not going to get better, under anyone's definition."

"That's all you need, another vegetable," said Mickey.

Poppy seemed to have shrunk. The doctor put his arm around him. "I know the decision to unplug life-supporting equipment is a hard one."

"That's not a toaster in there. It's my Flo."

The doctor turned to Jerry. "Maybe you can talk to him," he suggested.

Jerry sat with Poppy and explained all about life and death, the implications of leaving her on the machine, and the unlikelihood of her recovery. Poppy went in once more for another look. The woman on the bed now had her neck arched back to better receive the endotracheal tube. Her skin had a new translucence and was even more waxlike than before, something like the fake fruit Flo kept in a bowl on the kitchen table.

Poppy heaved up his shoulders for a massive sigh, a respiration that released his carbon dioxide and his despair into the Intensive Care Unit.

He shuffled back into the waiting room. Jerry and the doctor were talking. Manny had his arms around Tina. Everyone stopped what they were doing. Sanjo sat on the bench and banged her knuckles together. "All right," he said, "but don't let her suffer."

The doctor was relentless. "Look, there is one more thing we have to ask. We'd like your permission to do an autopsy."

Poppy looked for a way to escape. This was a crazy man. "You mean cut her up?"

"An autopsy is not what you think. Actually . . ."

"What for?"

The doctor had the answer for that one in his pocket, along with his stethoscope. "To help us understand what happened to her." He wouldn't give him the real answer, that the committee which reviewed hospital deaths preferred to have all loose ends tied up, and one of those loose ends was a tissue confirmation of the cause of death.

Poppy screwed up his face, displacing his nose. "No. I don't want any trouble from the cemetery."

"What trouble?" asked Jerry.

"They won't bury her without everything the way it's supposed to be. Forget it."

"It's not like that anymore," said Jerry.

"I'm not taking any chances. And you wouldn't either if it was your wife." Mickey said a quick "God forbid," and Poppy signed a paper for the doctor.

Then Manny, Jerry, Mickey, and Tina walked Poppy and Sanjo to his car. Manny was crying. Jerry patted his older brother on the shoulder. Mickey kissed him. Tina told him she wasn't mad that he allowed them to pull the plug on her only living sister.

"Are you all right?" asked Jerry.

"Sure."

"Can you drive by yourself?"

"Yeah, yeah."

"All right, we'll see you in the morning."

They left for their cars. Poppy turned for another look at the hospital. Whatever they did, they were doing it now. It's one thing when someone you love dies. It's another thing when you're the one who signed the paper to do it.

Poppy turned away from the hospital. At first there were no tears. He stood there choking, gasping, the sobs racking his body, making him twist, bend over, and rock forward as if he were praying. His baseball cap fell off and lay in the dirt of the parking lot. The noises he made were terrible. "Oh, no. Poppy crying." Sanjo tried to hug him, but he jerked away to lean against his fender, choking on spasms that began to steam-clean his throat, eyes, and nose with tears.

In the Intensive Care Unit, the doctor walked in with the paper. "All right," he said, "flip it off."

Their movements were coordinated and efficient. It wasn't that they were callous. It was that efficiency was the only way to deal with death and dying on a daily basis. A nursing student cried. She wasn't as efficient yet as she was going to be.

9

Even though it was still warm, the early morning September air had crispened like the edges of a pie. Leaves had yellowed and a few had turned the color of brandy. Some of them, already desiccated and withered, refused to let go, and swung on their tenuous attachment like hanging men from a gibbet.

Skippy was a new dog. He lay on his front porch with the sated look of one who has been to the big city and gotten all the action he wanted, as limp and inert as if his neck had been broken, his legs twitching without conviction, disregarding the growing commotion on his front lawn.

It was the first day of school and children began to gather on the sidewalk in front of the Ryans' house to wait for the buses. All the pets who were present for most events were there, as were a few parents, including Danny Wright's mother, who carried his lunch box, and Pert Little Miss's mother, who stood behind her pulling out the rags from her hair. Penny's parents weren't there, although their eyes were. They had decided to encourage her independence and just watch from their window; the only evidence of their observation and their concern was the occasional movement of the new macramé window hangings.

At first the sidewalk was spotted, a child here, a child there, like the first sign of measles, but then the gathering began to pick up momentum, the isolated figures turned into a cluster, and the cluster combined with other clusters to form a full-scale rash of children.

Penny stood on the edges of the crowd, but she was already part of it. Most of the other children knew her name, and one of the older girls, with the largesse of a seven-year-old, said, "Don't get too near the curb, honey, that's where the bus comes."

There were movement and sound overhead, cries, chatterings, and the rustling of the beating wings of the airborne who had decided to call it a day and head south. Actually, it wasn't their decision at all but the judgment of their pituitary glands, triggered by light changes and by their own rhythms which set the timer on their biological clocks.

Young black-beaked golden plovers, destined for the pampas of Argentina, traveled in advance of their parents, even choosing, like adolescents in other species, a different route. A flock of large, brown, orphaned Monarch butterflies, on their first solo and their first migration, whisked their way to Florida. The ex-mother robin with a few of her friends was also on her way south, but she did not aspire to the distances of the other travelers and would settle for Virginia.

Not everyone who could fly was heading south. A pug-nosed bat, one of a cluster of émigrés from an abandoned New Jersey iron pit, hung suspended from one foot in the rafter of the Stebbinses' vacant attic. His plan for the coming winter was to stoke up and lower his thermostat. He had just spent the night laying down fat. Now, with his beady eyes hidden in the folds of his wrinkled, hairless skin, he was sponging himself down with his long red tongue, using one foot to clean and brush where he couldn't reach the debris from his eating binge.

The children began to get restless. Slicked, washed, starched, trimmed, and polished—and excited, although most of them wouldn't admit it—they started to chant "The bus, the bus, the b-u-s," the incantation that would speed them on their way. When it didn't work, they grabbed the lunch boxes of the

[186]

unwitting and threw them about. One opened and spilled its contents on the lawn, and one of the dogs began to eat it. The lunch-box owner, a little boy, went crying to retrieve an orange, the only thing the dog didn't want. The children continued to knock one another all over Mrs. Ryan's lawn, smashing into her rosebushes and generally carrying on in a kind of reckless abandon that would make Mrs. Ryan that very morning call the school board to demand that they change the bus stop. The handwriting was on her wall and it said, *Mary Jo Sweeney sucks.*

Danny Wright ducked a flying lunch box and, on his rise, caught a movement on the Bernatskys' porch. He squinted to see better. The shapes were vague and undistinguishable. When he shaded his eyes, he could make out Sanjo sitting in the shadows on a chair against the wall. He darted from the cluster.

Danny had to stand on the top step before he could see her in detail. Sanjo sat against the wall in her pajamas, her hair uncombed, her face unwashed, and her pegged teeth filmed over.

"Hi, Sanjo," he said.

"Go 'way."

"You mad at me?"

Sanjo looked at her chest.

"Don't be mad at me, Sanjo. You wanna see a giant pencil?"

Sanjo looked up. Danny took out a large object from his pocket. It was not a pencil at all, but a case shaped to look like one. Inside went other pencils. Danny opened the case, took out the pencils, and stuffed them in his back pocket. He held out the case.

"You want the pencil? Look, you can have it."

Sanjo took it but didn't look at it.

"Danny, come back here," called his mother. Danny paid no attention.

"Does Judy read to you?"

"Uh-huh."

"What about?"

"Judy read Bugs."

[187]

"Whose Bugs?"

"Mine."

"You got a lot of Bugs?"

The question of amount was a quantification Sanjo was not prepared to confirm. She didn't respond.

"How many Bugs you got?"

Sanjo curved her arms out wide. Danny was trying to estimate the size of their enclosure when the yellow bus turned around the corner of Bergen Street.

"Do I have to come and get you?" his mother yelled.

Danny turned for one last query. "Where are they? The Bugs?" Sanjo remembered that Toby had told her not to give the Bugs to Danny. That was a specific instruction. It included no general proscription against the release of information that would lead to the same end.

"Bugs in box."

"Thanks, Sanjo, see ya."

Danny sprinted up the sidewalk and scrambled on the bus, a new third-grader who had already made a big score on his first morning of school.

Sanjo watched him go. Over her head, a drab comb-footed spider, on her way to make repairs, skittered across a guy wire which anchored the central maze of her web to the eaves of the front porch. She was not as graceful as she used to be. Two legs, shorter than the other six, had been regenerated to replace the originals, sacrificed in her escape from the beak of a bird.

Poppy came to the screen door, his face unshaven and his eyes obscured by puffy and swollen lids. He beckoned with his finger. Sanjo got off the chair and followed him to the kitchen table.

"Eat your Rice Krispies."

Sanjo heaped sugar into a small mound that covered the cereal like a snowcap on a mountain.

"Coffee too," she said.

Ma used to make her coffee. It was composed of one part coffee, one part milk, and an ice cube to cool it off.

Poppy didn't know the recipe. He simply poured coffee into

a cup and set it in front of her. Sanjo didn't know the recipe either. She sipped the coffee and was surprised when it burned her lips and tongue.

"Hot!" She put the cup down, spilling the coffee. Sanjo waited. No one wiped it up. Now it lay spattered onto the Rice Krispies and puddled on the table. Sanjo stared at her shimmering reflection.

Poppy finally noticed it when he leaned his arm on the table and it came away wet. "Oh, for God's sake." He got a towel from the bathroom and mopped up the puddle, then threw the towel in the kitchen sink.

He looked her over for the first time since the previous night.

"You have to get dressed," he said.

"Where Ma?" Sanjo was willing to forgive.

"Ma went away."

"Beauty parlor?"

"No, she went away. She's sleeping."

Sanjo remembered that Ma would not get up.

"Bad girl," she said. She banged her fist into her side.

Poppy sighed. "Go and get dressed." He started to cry again. Sanjo stood bewildered.

"Get dressed, get dressed."

She waddled into the bathroom, where she took a shower, brushed her teeth, and washed her face. She put on the same rumpled dress she had worn the day before, a pair of white sox, and her brown sandals. She forgot to comb her hair.

Poppy walked out the front door and Sanjo followed. They crossed the porch and passed underneath the quietly waiting spider, who in less than an hour had repaired the structural damage to her intricate suspension bridge, the lines of which rivaled steel for tensile strength.

Jerry, Mickey, Manny, and Tina met them at the undertaker's. They were ushered into an office in which the floors, walls, and ceiling were covered with wood. Placed at strategic locations, like ashtrays, were boxes of Kleenex. The funeral direc-

[189]

tor sat behind a wooden desk, immutable and stiff, looking as if he mainlined his own embalming fluid.

"Who is the bereaved?" he asked, his scalp shifting on the word bereaved.

For a moment no one moved or spoke. The actors had forgotten their lines. The funeral director's scalp shifted back, like a shot-putter preparing his next shot.

"Who is the principal mourner?"

Jerry pushed Poppy forward. There were a lot of decisions to be made. Open or closed casket? Three votes in favor of closing, two opposed, and one abstention. How many thank-you cards were needed? Poppy said twenty, Tina said two hundred, and Jerry said fifty. The funeral director said he would split it down the middle and give them one hundred.

When it came to a concrete vault to protect the casket from bacteria, slugs, earthworms, and other agents of decay, the vote was unanimous in favor because Sanjo, who wanted to do what everyone else was doing, had her hand up too. The question of pallbearers presented a problem. Jerry's back, Manny's back, and Poppy's back were too far gone to lift anything, much less a casket, and Poppy wasn't really being considered since he was the principal mourner. Even the sons of Poppy's generation were having back problems. They decided that Manny's grandson, Steve, the three younger Cervitano brothers, with their consent, and two aides from the funeral parlor would make up the complement of pallbearers.

All the major decisions had been made except two. Before they got to them, the funeral director asked for a recent picture of Ma to help the makeup man. Mickey asked what difference did it make if they were going to close the casket. The director said they wanted to be prepared since the family sometimes changed their mind. Poppy said he would bring in a picture.

They were in the middle of deciding how many limousines they would need when a short red-faced man broke into the office.

"What did you do to my father?" he yelled.

[190]

"What do you mean?" asked the director.

"I don't recognize him. How could you have distorted his face like that?"

"Calm yourself," said the director. "What chapel were you in?"

"There, the one on the end." The mortuary, designed like an indoor mall, had little chapels lining each corridor.

"That explains it. Mr. Greenspan is in that chapel. Chapel Fourteen is where your father reposes. You saw Mr. Greenspan."

"I think one limousine is all we need," said Jerry.

The last decision was the coffin itself. The funeral director led them out of the office, down the stairs, and into a room filled with dozens of coffins, some metal, some wood, each with a different ornamentation, interior, and price tag. They were all lined with shiny satin, the kind of fabric transvestites insist on when they buy their first gown. Sanjo put out her hand to feel the lining on one of the coffins. It was smooth and slick like nice-nice.

"Please don't let her handle anything," said the director.

"Don't do that, honey," said Tina.

Sanjo caught one of her own hands with the other, then shyly poked out one finger like Michaelangelo's Adam and touched the satin. Tina took her hand away.

"Oh yes, oh yes." Sanjo stamped one foot and then the other.

"You can't, the man said so."

Poppy had the helpless look of a man caught in a downpour without a place to duck into. He pulled his head into his shoulders and kept moving.

Sanjo began to cry, stamping one foot and then the other. The only thing that moved on the funeral director was his scalp.

"Oh, oh," said Manny. "We have to call the policeman."

The funeral service was held in the chapel the next day. Mrs. Cervitano, wearing a black crepe dress and black netting pinned to the top of her head, was there with all four sons and their wives. Bruno's wife was pregnant. She had already "dropped," and her husband watched her like a time bomb. Minnie Hightower sat in the back row with Georgio so he could keep his hand on her thigh. It was very comforting. Her children, whom she had invited, had given her an ultimatum: It was either them or Georgio. Minnie made her pick. Mrs. Wright came with Mrs. Ryan. They both wore hats. Mrs. Ryan's was the same floppy hat she wore when she took care of her roses. A few aphids, which had escaped into the curl of the brim, hung there, waiting for deliverance. Manny's son, Phil, and his wife, June, were there, in addition to Lou Green and some of the other men who played chess in the park.

One of the nicest things that happened was that Steve, Manny's nineteen-year-old grandson, came wearing a suit. It was his Bar Mitzvah suit and his arms and legs stuck out, but at least it wasn't the saffron-colored robe he usually wore. His scalp lock dangled over his shiny shaved head. Everyone was so relieved he came wearing regular clothes that they decided, in the tacitly polite manner of someone who will not look at an amputee, not to notice.

Poppy and Sanjo were ushered to the front row along with Manny, Tina, Mickey, and Jerry. The rabbi waited for them to get comfortable while he looked over the assemblage. It wasn't a bad house. It wasn't packed, but it wasn't a showing anybody had to be ashamed of, either. His hair turbaned his forehead and swung in a low curve to his eyebrows. He began to speak in generalities, his tone orotund and somber, pitching out his words like wet blankets.

He directed his attention to the front row in order to spell out the meaning of the current event in personal terms.

"Florence Eisman Bernatsky is gone. What does this mean? For Jerry and Mickey, the loss of a beloved sister-in-law. For Manny and Tina, the loss of a beloved younger sister."

"Older," said Tina, under her breath.

"For you, Morris, the tragic loss of a wife, a companion, a devoted life partner."

There was only one person left. The rabbi hesitated, then put in his big toe. "And for you, Sandra Joanne . . ."

Sanjo smiled at the mention of her other name.

The rabbi dived into the lake. "Mother's not coming home anymore."

Sanjo threw out a grappling hook for that one. It was close but she couldn't get it. She made no response.

The rabbi was ready. "You'll never never see her again." The grappling hook missed its mark and clattered against the cliff. The rabbi smoothed his turban across his forehead. He could have strung out a thousand "nevers" like Chinese lanterns; their combined strength would not have shed any more illumination. Death and its permanence had no meaning for Sanjo and, at that point, little meaning for most of the mourners in the chapel.

Sanjo wasn't sad. The rabbi had reminded her to be angry at Ma for not getting up. She banged her fist against her leg and then turned her attention to something that didn't make her mad, the flowers that covered the coffin. One of them was still a bud. It beckoned to her with the old promise, a winking of petals that says, I'm going to be a pink one.

Sanjo got up to smell the bud but Mickey pulled her back. "Sit," she hissed.

At the cemetery they sat under a canopy. They had to wait while a flock of wild geese in a V formation, a flight pattern that allowed each bird a chance to see where it was going, flew overhead, impatiently honking their way south. The rabbi waited for the honking to pass, then asked Poppy and Sanjo to stand up.

Poppy spoke some words that Sanjo had heard before on rare occasions, but had never coded for meaning and therefore never registered.

> *Yis gadal*
> *V'yis kadash*

Shmey rabbo
Be'olmo divro.

People began to cry; Sanjo turned to look at them. Tina yelled, "Take me instead!"

No one considered it a serious offer. The rabbi, who hated these grandstand plays, gave her a censoring look, a stare under lowered brows that said, Cut it out. Poppy began to cry and his hat fell off. Jerry put it back on.

It was a bim-bam-bum affair, over in less than ten minutes. Sanjo and Poppy got separated. Jerry and Mickey took Poppy to their car, and Sanjo was hustled out by Manny, Manny's son, Phil, his daughter-in-law, June, and his grandson, Steve.

They rode back to the house in the big black limousine. Sanjo sat in the back seat between Phil and Manny. She liked the way the leather smelled but couldn't get her nose close to it. Instead she gave her cousin Phil a tentative smile.

"She doesn't understand any of this," said Phil to his father.

Steve sat quietly trying to free his elbows from his six-year-old Bar Mitzvah suit. His mother watched him out of the corner of her eye. If only somebody would tell her what had gone wrong with a boy who was in the National Honor Society, scored 1450 on his SATs, got accepted by Brandeis, and never, in all the years he was getting one, asked for an increase in his allowance.

Sanjo had her eyes on Steve's scalp lock. She put out a timid finger to touch it. Although he had shaved his head scrupulously, Steve had overlooked the hairs on the back of his neck. They erected. Steve swung his scalp lock out of reach.

The house began to fill with people who settled into every available seat. Although Sanjo liked parties, she wasn't much up to this one. She was feeling empty, something like hungry but not really hungry. She watched each arrival from the couch where she sat with Poppy, especially the women. She continued to wait for Ma, even though she was mad at her, even though a lot of people had told her Ma was not coming home anymore. Poppy sat beside her dazed.

Strange women took over the kitchen like Visigoths taking over a Roman basilica. They threw things out and brought things in. They slung salad, cold cuts, bread, and cakes onto platters, ripped cellophane from fruit baskets, searched for cups, found them, and set everything on the dining-room table.

At first conversation was limited. The whole business seemed to come as a surprise, and people said things like, "I can't believe she's gone," "I saw her last month," or, more philosophically, "What can you do? That's life."

As they picked up steam, conversation became more animated and they spoke of ordinary things like ball scores, the new postman who mixed up everybody's mail, what was going to be with the President's cabinet, and if any European wine could rival Tipo Red.

Someone, on occasion, even laughed, a discreet laugh, of course, not a real fall-down-on-the-floor-and-kick-your-heels laugh, but a chuckle that came out like a hiccup.

Mrs. Cervitano came, followed by Richard, Sally, and Spig, who was transporting negotiables again in the heels of his shoes, and their wives. Bruno's wife had gone into labor between the chapel service and the burial and was taken to the hospital by her husband.

Mrs. Cervitano made her way first to Poppy. "It's a terrible loss," she said. Then she bent to kiss Sanjo's forehead. "Ai, multissima poveridra." Poppy acknowledged her condolence as he did the condolence of everyone else, like a man who humors a crazy guest.

Penny's parents, both looking a little embarrassed and self-conscious, like children who have shoplifted a package of chewing gum, came pulling Penny behind them.

"We're very sorry, Mr. Bernatsky," said Penny's mother. She shook Sanjo's fingertips. "Sorry about your mother, Sanjo."

Penny's father shook Poppy's hand. "Very sorry to hear your wife died, sir."

It was a jarring note. Everyone turned. They couldn't have been more startled if he had come in on roller skates. He was the only one who used the correct verb for what had happened

[195]

to Ma. Everyone else used the word *lost*, as if Poppy had misplaced her, or the phrase *passed away*, a euphemism so innocuous all it did was suggest a slow drift.

Poppy looked at Penny's father and mother and tried to remember who they were. Penny peeked out from behind their legs and darted behind them again when she saw Sanjo. Sanjo put out a hand to touch her, but Penny, like a subliminal image, was too fast.

Penny's parents, having said what they came to say, turned on their heels and moved into the crowd. They were replaced by a continual procession of someone or other who also had something to say. No numbers runner got more action than Poppy got that afternoon.

Sanjo was restless. "Go toilet," she said to Poppy. He thought it was a good idea too. They both got up. Their place on the couch was not vacant long. Like water seeking a level, the Cervitano wives rushed in to fill the space. They settled their skirts and continued a discussion of recipes.

Richard's wife, Seraphina, the heiress-apparent to grande dame of the Cervitano family, was adamant. "No, no. The point is, when you add the bay leaf, you only put it in for a minute. You have to fish it out right away."

"How do you find it?" asked Spig's wife.

"You keep it in a little bag on a string you make out of some old mesh, like a pantyhose toe."

Sally's wife, beginning to resent Seraphina's high-handedness, sat back and did not enter into the discussion.

Seraphina turned to her. "Isn't that right, Terry? The secret is in the hint of bay leaf."

"I don't think bay leaf is Italian," said Terry, who was Irish.

They called in the expert. "Help us, Mom. We are talking about Risibisi. Who is right? I say you dip the bay leaf for a second, then yank it out. That's the secret to a good pork stew."

All eyes except Terry's hung on Mrs. Cervitano. She sat on the edge of the sofa. "Myself, I don't use bay leaf."

When Sanjo returned, there was no place for her to sit. There was no place to stand either. She was passed farther and farther back into the room like a log being carried in a flume. She wound up next to the dining-room table and began to circle it like an Indian circling a wagon train.

Mrs. Wright came with Danny. Her bruises had healed. With her face unmarked and unpuffed she was a pretty woman.

"I don't know why you want to come," she had said on their way up the steps. "A funeral is a very sad thing. You remember when Tino went to sleep?"

Danny had his doubts. "Is Mrs. Bernatsky sleeping?"

"It's the same thing."

The discrepancy between what he knew his parents thought and what they said they thought was amazing. He was the first kid on the block his age to know that Santa Claus was a lie. He had only to listen to their voices to know they were trying to put one over on him. His mother was doing it again. Danny knew dead from alive.

Mrs. Wright found Poppy, offered her condolences, and mingled with the other neighbors. No one asked her where Toby was. It was a painful issue everyone preferred to avoid. Most of them knew he was responsible for the utmost catastrophe a child can create for his parents: He had run away. Not overnight, to be found the next morning at a friend's house or to creep home on his own, ashamed and contrite, but away, *Adresse unbekannt,* with no farewell, no word, no nothing. Everyone concluded one of two things: Either Mr. and Mrs. Wright were terrible parents or Toby was a terrible child.

Danny jumped up and down. It was the only way he could see over the crowd. He couldn't find Sanjo and he couldn't find Penny. He brushed against a very old lady propped up on the sofa. Her entire circulatory system was visible. It reminded Danny of the ant tunnels he could see through the glass shield of his ant farm.

Tante Sophie was Mickey's mother, and she was over ninety. She came out of the nursing home for the special event. Her skin had the look of parchment. She was very tiny and very thin.

Everyone just stood around to watch her breathe. Danny stayed to watch her blood circulate. Tante Sophie couldn't hear, although her eyes were razor sharp. She was also a little demented, not too much, just enough so that no one left her alone for more than an hour at a time. They didn't have to worry. She wasn't going anywhere so fast. "Look at that," they said. What they meant was, She's still alive. Everyone came to pay homage.

"Hello, Tante Sophie, I'm Manny, Flo's brother."

"Who?"

"Flo's brother," Manny yelled.

"Who's Flo? Where's Miriam?"

"I'm here, Ma," said Mickey. "What is it?"

"Where's the groom? I want to give him some money."

Danny watched as Tante Sophie's corpuscles flowed evenly and without incident into her capillaries.

Richard took Sally and Spig aside and told them the U.S. Attorney's office, upon reconsidering the United States Post Office versus Cervitanos and Wright, which they referred to as the Unfortunate Incident, was dropping charges of felonious assault.

"You settled out of court?" asked Sally.

"There was nothing to settle. The prosecutor entered a plea of *nolle prosequi*, which means he wants to forget the whole thing. Now all they want to do is keep a lid on it."

"He had it coming, the creep," said Spig.

Mr. and Mrs. Ryan changed their faces at the door, trading in expressions that were relatively neutral for those more suitably somber, kicked over a pitcher of water, and walked in.

"It's him." Spig hit his brother in the elbow.

Richard clutched his elbow to steady his buzzing nerve. "Forget it."

"Are you kidding? He was the one put the finger on us."

Richard's elbow was still ringing like a stuck doorbell. "It doesn't matter. We got the Post Office to drop it, so you drop it too. The guy's in the hospital, for God's sake. Don't blow it."

The crush was so great, Mr. and Mrs. Ryan had to walk in sideways. They brushed past the Cervitano brothers back to back, like flamenco dancers.

Spig turned and came face to face with Mr. Ryan. *Ole!* He fixed him with his look. Mr. Ryan's mustache lifted like a bird about to take flight.

Spig decided to spiff up his usual look with the Evil Eye. He pulled down a bottom lid with his index finger. Ryan's insides began to liquefy.

"What do you say, Ryan?"

"Sad day, sad day."

Spig stepped closer. "It could be a lot sadder."

Sally, who thought of himself as a lover, went to talk to Mrs. Wright, a little mileage on her but not bad looking.

"I fixed your kid's bike," he said.

Mrs. Wright was busy stuffing a slice of turkey—one of the few things she recognized—into a roll.

"So how is it, the bike?" Sally asked.

Mrs. Wright began to cry.

Sally wished he could have asked his standard "Come here often?" It was much less trouble and closer to the point. "Look, I'll fix it over."

Sanjo, on her sixth foray around the table, appeared around the turkey platter. "Sally," she said. She stood in front of him, to lay her head on his chest.

Imperial Rome pushed her away. "Not now, Sanjo." Get away, Germanicus, we have enough goat tallow in the coffers.

Sanjo moved on to the Danish.

Nearby Penny's parents were having a heavy discussion over which one of them was inner-directed and which one was outer-directed. Penny's mother said that anyone who relies upon the judgment of a committee to tell them if they're any good can't be inner-directed. Penny's father said she didn't know what she was talking about and that she was hostile since she wasn't the one seeking the doctorate. Their discussion escalated and disintegrated. By the time Sanjo got to them, they were speaking

[199]

through their teeth, which was harder for them than most of the others present since their gums were still in good shape. Penny's mother called her husband a chauvinist bullshitter and he countered with the lowest blow he could deliver, a slam into her nether parts. He said she was just like her mother.

Sanjo recognized bad talk. She reversed her direction in mid-revolution and wound up next to Sally again, who was saying, "So what kind of work does your husband do? I mean, does he go to an office or what?"

Steve was in the basement. He had his jacket off. The saffron robe was underneath and he was tugging it out of his pants. He looked like a butterfly coming out of a cocoon. The feeling was back in his arms again. Steve flashed his scalp lock over his head and went back upstairs.

He began to talk about Krishna, Jiva, and Shiva to the people on the closed porch. They thought he was talking about what they were doing. Steve was talking about how Ma's *preta* was awaiting its new fate. Pretty soon everyone on the porch was mesmerized by Steve and his eloquent proposals. He could have led them, like lemmings, into the washing machine.

He began to chant. At first he sounded like an old-time vegetable man. Manny did not pay attention to it. "Hare Krishna, hare Krishna." Phil heard it and so did his wife, June.

"He's starting again," whispered June to Phil.

"Who?" asked Phil with the marvelous ability of one who can flip trouble from his mind as easily as a light switch.

Tina found Manny shouting to Tante Sophie.

"Your grandson is acting crazy," she said.

"What do you mean?" he yelled.

"Don't shout. I can hear. Listen to him."

"Krishna, Krishna."

Manny went to the closed porch. Steve was really rocking. He had discarded his shoes and socks, and he moved back and forth, barefooted, little bells in his hand, eyes closed, swaying as he moved, and singing the glories of Krishna.

"What are you doing? This is a shiva."

"Hare, hare."

"Stop it, will you?"

"Hare Rama."

"Phil, come and get your kid."

Phil was in the kitchen with his fingers in his ears singing "The Star-Spangled Banner." His switch was no longer working.

"Hare Rama."

Manny stared at his grandson, his little Stevela, dancing from side to side in a yellow gown chanting something crazy that had transformed his face into an expression both beatific and pained, like someone having an orgasm or an enema. It was too much. He slammed into Steve's shoulder, catching him off guard and knocking him into the front row of spectators.

"Get out of here and go back to the airport where you belong!"

Steve picked himself up. He looked very hurt. "You should be worried about her getting into a good new body," he said.

"You need a good new head," said Manny, already feeling terrible that he had hit his only grandson.

Danny found Penny by accident. He was tired of jumping up and down to look over the grown-ups for Sanjo and tired of watching Tante Sophie's blood circulate. He sat down on the floor to rest. When he moved aside to make room for a guy in a yellow skirt, he saw her shoes in a space between all the legs, the only shoes under six inches long in the room.

Conferring between the legs of the grown-ups was like speaking through tree branches. Danny and Penny finally managed to reach one another after twisting and crawling through the forest of adults. United, they continued to push their way through the crush of bodies, making people spill their coffee, knocking plates off laps, and sending Tina sprawling into the rabbi's lap, which confirmed the rabbi's diagnosis that the woman was an actress. They came to a clearing.

"Look at this blondie. What's your name, honey?"

"Penny Lowen."

"Whose little girl are you?"

Penny couldn't find her parents. All she could see were the trunks of bodies. She pointed in the general direction of the pagodas.

"She's so cute. Do you know you're cute?"

Danny yanked on her arm. Grown-ups could be so dumb.

"Come on," he said. He led her through the legs. Unbroken walls told them they were finally in the hallway. The search began. They ran from room to room.

"Which one is hers?"

"This one," said Benedict Arnold in ringlets.

They found the comics easily. They were next to Sanjo's bed in a big box.

Mrs. Ryan ran from window to window. She was worried about Skippy, whom she had left all alone. Mr. Ryan worried that she had left her husband all alone, trapped in a weird conversation with Spig, who stood with his thumbs hooked into his belt, growled in a scary voice, and made mysterious reference to secret things.

"My brother says you run," said Spig.

"That's right," said Mr. Ryan.

"You pretty good?"

"Well, it's not a question of good or bad, it's conditioning and training." He was surprised and relieved that Mr. Cervitano was not angry that he had had to tell the police who was in the truck.

"What I want to know is, can you run or can't you run?"

"Yes, I can run."

Some people when pushed against the wall for a yes or no will provide it if given the proper impetus.

"Start."

"Start what?"

"Start running, Ryan. We know you fingered us."

Mr. Ryan's face drained of all color. Richard saw it. He was over in a shot.

"Aldo, go and talk to Mom."

The color had not returned to Mr. Ryan's face. His autonomic nervous system, which automatically equipped him to run away or to stay and fight in a situation of danger, had broken down. It was now preparing him to stay and pass out.

"We're still discussing," Spig said to his brother.

"What are you discussing?"

"I don't see Skippy," said Mrs. Ryan from the window.

Sanjo got tired of circling the dining-room table and set up camp near the Danish. She could see most of the party from that vantage point. It wasn't exactly a bird's-eye view, but it was the next closest thing. Mrs. Cervitano found her at her post, nibbling a prune Danish, and kissed her forehead.

"Don't get sick, little sweetheart, you ate enough."

Sanjo had seen the flash of legs as Danny and Penny disappeared into her bedroom. The vigilant portion of her brain had taken over like Mighty Mouse. She didn't have to do a thing. Programmed to associate danger between Danny and the comics, the subcortical alert mobilized her body into a galvanic response, setting her in motion like a tank, while Mrs. Cervitano continued to hang on to her forehead.

In a few minutes, Danny and Penny came out, dragging the box across the floor, banging into the shins of grown-ups who considered them a minor inconvenience like mosquitoes.

"Bugs!" yelled Sanjo. She pulled free of Mrs. Cervitano and pushed through the crowd like a salmon swimming up a waterfall, threshing, backpedaling, getting up the greatest forward thrust she could muster.

Danny and Penny moved faster, pulling the crate out the front door. Mrs. Ryan even held the door open for them.

"Bugs!" It was the sound of an anguished foghorn. She began to rock. "Come back here!"

"What's the matter with her?" Mrs. Ryan asked.

Everyone stopped. Sanjo balled her fists and stamped her feet. The wailing was awful.

"She finally realized what happened," someone whispered.

"What is it?" asked another.

"She's grieving for her mother," said a third.

[203]

"Bring Bugs!" screamed Sanjo, drowning out everyone around her. "Bring Bugs!"

Poppy came beside her. Even though his mind was glazed over, he recognized the serious character of her rage.

"What is it? What do you want?"

It was hard to get her to hold still.

Jerry said they should get her into the bedroom and give her a tranquilizer. Poppy, who forgot that he had close to 2,000 pills, asked, "Who has a tranquilizer?"

"I do," said Jerry.

They corralled her in the bedroom.

"Take this, Sanjo."

Sanjo turned her head away. She wasn't taking anything, especially since she was full of prune Danish.

She continued to rage, like a tornado that hasn't spun itself out yet. Surrounding her at a discreet distance were Jerry, holding the tranquilizer, Mickey, holding a glass of water, and Tina, shredding her Kleenex into confetti.

"Bring Bugs! Bugs!"

"She's talking about bugs. Look around. Do you see any?"

Tina distributed bits of Kleenex about the room. "I don't see anything."

Mrs. Cervitano came to see what the problem was. "What'sa matter?" she called from the door.

"We're trying to give her a tranquilizer," said Mickey.

"A pill?"

Jerry nodded.

"You're doing it all wrong. You have to mush it up, good, like this. Then," she whispered, "you hide it in a piece of chocolate."

Tina went back to the living room. "Anyone have a piece of chocolate? A candy bar?"

"No, but there's plenty of stuff on the dining-room table. Try a Danish, the prune ones are all gone, but the cherry cheese are good."

Mrs. Ryan said she had some chocolate. She had to go home

to get it. Mr. Ryan said he would go home with her to help her find it. She came back. He didn't.

Jerry opened the capsule, spilled the contents into a declivity he had made in the softened candy and folded it over.

"It's cooking chocolate," said Mrs. Ryan.

"It'll be fine," said Jerry.

"Sanjo, you want some chocolate?"

Sanjo's rage had spun itself out. The fight was over. They won by a TKO. Sanjo took the chocolate and ate it, not noticing that it was semi-sweet.

The duration of the mourning period known as the shiva, although dictated by custom, is dealer's choice. Most people determine how long their own shiva will run.

The first and last shiva session for the Bernatskys was over that night. Poppy slept like a baby, exhausted beyond belief, dreaming of taking Flo on a bike ride through Central Park, several moltings back when he was young and strong and could make a bike rear like a horse.

Sanjo slept a drugged, more leaden sleep. Her dreams were pieces and flashes, mostly of Ma making her forehead nice.

Tina, Mickey, and Tante Sophie were in the kitchen. Tina and Mickey were washing dishes and putting them in the wrong places.

Manny and Jerry sat at the dinette table, a chrome and Naugahyde fantasy of Poppy's own creation. They searched the paper for the obituary column. Jerry found it and read it aloud and Manny and Tina cried all over again. They didn't know that there was something else in the paper related to Ma. They wouldn't have recognized it anyhow even if they saw it, since it wasn't signed with her name. It was on the editorial page.

The young people today have no respect for property. One of the worst things they do is throw their beer cans out their car windows. Every Sunday morning I have to pick up beer cans. They are all over my lawn. I'm not the only one. The beer cans are all over the neighborhood. This is the problem. It is getting hard for me to bend over. Maybe there could be a wire basket at the corner of Bergen Street and they could throw their cans in it. Maybe an incentive plan, so many points for each can that makes the basket. If you don't print this, I will understand, since you have already printed six of my letters. If you print it, thank you.

Tired of Stooping Over

After the kitchen was cleaned up they talked about the "problem." The problem, of course, was Sanjo and what was going to happen to her or, more specifically, who could or would take care of her.

"It was a wonderful affair," said Tante Sophie.

10

Three weeks after the funeral Sanjo was still alternating between storming and snuffling. Just about the time of the autumnal equinox, when the sun's rays strike the equator directly, creating an equal amount of daylight and darkness, the storming took a back seat to the snuffling and was almost extinguished. Except for brief flareups, the snuffling took over. Sanjo's face looked as if it were leaking.

She went into a depression that coated her tongue and made her breath foul. Loss is a visceral feeling. A significant piece was missing from her and, like a double negative, it attained positive status, a mathematical paradox, the presence of an absence.

Sanjo didn't do much talking or much of anything. She cried on occasion for Ma, no full-scale, all-out bouts, just intermittent whimperings, like a radio station that is losing its signal. She spent most of the time sitting by herself and curling inward, until she seemed to grow smaller, shriveling like the autumn leaves on the sidewalk.

The first two weeks there was an endless supply of food. Gradually, as other people returned to their own lives, the supplies began to dwindle. When Poppy realized the enormity of what had happened, he began to grieve in earnest. The insult was twofold. His wife of almost fifty years was gone, and he was left with a calamity bigger than an earthquake, bigger than a flood, bigger than a plague of locusts: He was left to deal with the house and with Sanjo. His calamity was irreversible.

Sometimes he didn't put the lights on when it first got dark but waited until he couldn't see anything at all, not even the switch he had to push.

Jerry and Mickey made the sacrifice of offering their Ida Lou for two days a week until things got straightened out. They brought her over in the Fleetwood, saying how she was one of the family, while Ida Lou, who had her own family and these folks were not it, kept her counsel. Ida Lou stayed for a week. She left saying it would take years to get that house straightened out, forget the folks in it, what about all those spiders on the front porch? If that wasn't enough to do anybody in, she didn't know what.

Mrs. Cervitano suggested her widowed sister in New Jersey. That sounded like a good idea. Poppy agreed to try it for a while. The deal was she would cook, keep house, and help take care of Sanjo for a nominal fee and an opportunity to spend some time with her sister.

She was a lovely woman. She looked just like Mrs. Cervitano, was the same height, and even had the same little mustache. The only difference was she was much plumper, as if Mrs. Cervitano had been put to an air pump and blown up like a balloon for the Thanksgiving parade.

She didn't work out either. She was always across the street talking to her sister. When she wasn't doing that she was cutting noodles on every available surface in the house. She also couldn't make it with Sanjo. She kept saying things like, "Come on, kid, cheer up." Sanjo stayed away from her. Mrs. Cervitano's sister didn't approve of Poppy either, especially the way he slept every afternoon. She felt uncomfortable around a man who "didn't do nothing." She too lasted for one week and then left to go back to New Jersey.

While people are attracted to sudden disaster like fire or accident, prolonged sorrow is too great to witness, especially in a friend. Mrs. Cervitano, aware of the disintegration across the street, couldn't watch it. After her sister didn't work out, she began to inquire less frequently how they were doing, and now when she saw Poppy and Sanjo, even when they had to evacuate their house from time to time to wait for the smoke-filled kitchen to clear, she went quickly into her own house or hid behind the donkey.

Besides, Mrs. Cervitano had a new grandchild. She spent most of her afternoons visiting at Bruno's home, showing his wife what to do with her baby.

One day not long after Mrs. Cervitano's sister left, Poppy pushed himself up from a chair in which he had sat for six hours straight, not counting the three times out he took to go to the bathroom, and said to himself, "Okay, Morris, it's now or never." He decided to urinate first, since the pressure on his bladder was making it hard to think; then he opened the medicine chest. On the top shelf was his collection, not all of it, but the best stuff. There were pills in all colors, sizes, and shapes. The variety of their manufacture was infinite. Poppy emptied a few bottles. The contents spilled over his hand and onto the sink.

Poppy filled a glass with water. He didn't like the way the glass looked, swished out the water, and filled it again. He took a deep breath, leaned against the sink, and looked at himself in the mirror. He wondered if they would be able to bury him. He wasn't sure about the policy on suicides. Maybe they recognized extenuating circumstances. If this wasn't an extenuating circumstance, he never saw one.

The doorbell rang. A man couldn't even kill himself in peace. Poppy threw the pills in the wastebasket.

Judy Haskell had come to read Sanjo a letter. The front door was closed but it wasn't locked. Judy let herself in after ringing the bell and calling through the screen. She knew they were in the house. Everyone on the block knew it.

It took a minute for Judy's eyes to get used to the darkened living room. Sanjo was sitting in a chair. She looked up when the screen door creaked, shifted her weight, and looked down again at her chest.

"There you are. How come you didn't answer me? Boy, it's dark in here."

Poppy came in from the bathroom. "Who's there?"

"It's me, Mr. Bernatsky. Judy."

"Oh." Poppy went to sit on the couch. He switched on a lamp.

"I have a letter from Toby."

"Fix me," Sanjo said.

"Fix what?"

Sanjo pointed to her face.

"Don't you have a Kleenex?" Sanjo didn't answer.

"They're in the bathroom," said Poppy. "Over the toilet."

Judy brought back a Kleenex and wiped Sanjo's face gingerly but thoroughly.

"Where can I throw this?"

Poppy pointed to a wastebasket filled with trash hanging precariously over the edges.

"The letter, Sanjo. Do you want me to read it?"

Sanjo looked at Judy's feet and then away, out the window, over the tops of the trees, even past the roof on Toby's house.

Judy turned to Poppy, who sat on the couch with his chin against his chest to hold fast a sock. He was sorting them, taking two at a time from a pile in his lap, rolling his ribbed, elasticized, size-ten cotton socks up by the toes and twisting both into one.

"What should I do?" Judy asked him.

Poppy waved his hand to chase away a fly. The house was full of them despite the efforts of the comb-footed spider and her friends.

"Boy," said Judy. She stood in the middle of the floor, a favorite spot of the perplexed.

Sanjo turned in her direction. "Where Toby?"

"Oh, wow. I thought you were getting flaky." Judy switched her hair away from her eyes and read:

" 'Dear Sanjo, Judy told me your mother died. She was pretty old so don't feel too bad. I'm in this house. It's really a neat place. This guy, Shep, he used to be a priest, he runs it. There are lots of other kids here. Shep talks to me about a lot of things. We never talk about running away. We talk about life. Shep doesn't talk to me like a kid. My job is to rake the leaves. How are the comics? You should be through the whole box by now. Your friend, Toby.' "

Judy was sorry the minute she read the last line. Danny's recapture of the comics had been broadcast over the whole neighborhood. His exploit had even been heard about six blocks away. As soon as the first word escaped from her mouth, she tried to retrieve it with her tongue but wasn't fast enough. It tumbled over her lips, pulling those that followed after it, like mountain climbers on a rope.

Sanjo sat looking at Judy like a cashier who has just closed her window. Then she started to bang her head.

"What are you doing?" Judy switched her hair.

Sanjo slammed her head into the back of the chair. *Smack! Bang!*

"Stop it, Sanjo." *Bang! Whap!* "Sanjo, you could hurt yourself!" *Crack. Whap.* "Mr. Bernatsky!"

"What are you doing?" Poppy asked Sanjo.

Bang! Thwack!

"See, she's banging her head. Make her stop." Judy was on her feet.

Once he caught on to what was happening, Poppy moved fast. He grabbed a pillow and put it behind her head.

"If you're gonna hit something, hit this."

Whup. Whup.

Judy crumpled her letter, switched her hair in the other direction, and ran out the door, buttoning her sweater on the way. She continued to run under the blazing maples and beeches that lined the street, a conflagration kindled by a failing supply of chlorophyll that enveloped the whole neighborhood.

As she ran past the hollow oak tree, the nursemaid bees in their new hive looked in disgust at the remaining eggs doing

[211]

nothing in their cells. Knowing there wasn't time for them to hatch with the cold coming on, they carried them out of the hive and left them, like Spartans, to die.

A cab rippled into the street. Judy turned to see where it was going. The cab stopped in front of the Stebbins house. A few minutes later, Mr. and Mrs. Stebbins and all their bags emerged from the cab. They had come home after visiting their son in California for three months. Their return trip was paid for by many small contributions arranged for by their son, who cadged, begged, and scrounged from every source he knew, including a good friend at the checkout counter in the A&P.

The Stebbinses stood on the sidewalk holding their bags. Their lawn was grown over and waved back and forth like hay except where it had been trampled and matted by the children. They began to trudge through the high grasses, picking their way toward the front door. Field mice, who were finding the lawn a pretty good place to live, ran out the edges of their savannah.

Most of the children were outside, taking advantage of the remaining daylight of their shrinking afternoons. Pert Little Miss, with her baton tucked snugly under her arm, was on Penny's porch teaching her to play jacks. Penny's hand wasn't big enough to get past twosies.

"You can't do it at all," said Pert Little Miss. "I can twirl and everything. Even behind my back. Wanna see me?"

She didn't need any encouragement. She went right into her act, smiling her sunniest, sweetest smile, bringing her lower lip down to expose her bottom teeth, and moving to remembered rhythms of "Strike Up the Band."

Judy hurried by.

"Hey, Judy, watch this."

Judy kept going.

Penny turned to look at the Stebbinses struggling with their suitcases. "Who's that?" she asked.

"The Stebbinses." Pert Little Miss tossed the baton over her head, caught it, passed it back between her legs, and triple-twirled for a grand finale. Then she went back to try to stretch Penny's inadequate hand around three jacks.

The Stebbinses found the bats when they went up to the attic to put the suitcases away. Mrs. Stebbins ran out of the house screaming.

Mr. Stebbins was yelling in the attic, committing mayhem, hitting the bats with a broom. Those bats who weren't stunned or injured fluttered out of the broken attic window, emitting high-pitched squeaks, flying with the membranes of their naked wings, which flexed above them like a parachute. One bat, deafened from a blow to the head, blundered into a tree, even though his eyes were wide open.

Penny noticed the bats. "Look," she said. "Halloween."

"It's not for three weeks, silly," said Pert Little Miss.

"They're all gone," yelled Mr. Stebbins from the attic window.

"How can you be sure?" Mrs. Stebbins was backed up all the way to Penny's front door.

"Because I can see and I tell you they're all gone. Just bring up a plastic bag."

Sanjo and Poppy heard the shrieks and squeaks. It was hard not to hear the commotion even with both doors and most of the windows closed. Poppy continued to sort his socks. He came up one short and tossed the odd sock in the wastebasket. The basket shivered and fell on its side. Sanjo watched it fall, saw the torn envelopes, newspapers, Kleenex, and the single sock spill on the floor, and gave it no more attention than she did the fly perched on her sleeve.

Things went from bad to worse. Sanjo forgot many things she knew. She seemed to be spun backward into her own time, like a running back who has made it to the fifty-yard line and is returned to the twenty. She didn't eat very much, didn't talk very much, didn't seem to want to dress herself. Poppy had to dress her every morning, wash her face, and comb her hair. By nine o'clock he had to lie down again.

It wasn't too bad when she wet her pants on occasion. The final straw came when she defecated in a pair of pants that said Wednesday and sat in it all day long. Poppy finally smelled it. At first he thought Ryan was raking his compost again and went to shut the window in the living room. He came into the darkened room and smelled her before he saw her. Sanjo was one of the shadows. As Poppy became accustomed to the dim light, her outline began to develop like paper in a darkroom tray. Poppy didn't know what to do. His first impulse was to close up the house and run away.

"How can you sit like that?"

Sanjo didn't know. She shook her head.

"Come on." Sanjo followed him. He wasn't sure where they were going. Somehow, gagging all the while, which made Sanjo gag too, he got Sanjo's pants off, threw them in the garbage, and got her into the tub.

After she dried herself he brought her a box of talcum powder.

"Shake this on. It will help you feel good."

Sanjo shook the powder into her hand and patted it on her stomach.

"No, down there." Poppy pointed, jabbing his finger in the air while turning away his head, like a hummingbird darting blind. Sanjo topcoated her pudenda.

"Did you get your tushy?"

"Uh-huh."

Poppy called Jerry on the telephone. Jerry and Mickey came over that night.

"You finally came to your senses," said Mickey.

"You're doing the right thing," said Jerry. "Just know that, Morry. Flo would have wanted it this way."

Poppy doubted that.

"First of all," said Jerry, "we're going to see how much the whole thing will cost. I think you can qualify for public assistance. You're not earning a living and you're over sixty-five."

"I don't want welfare."

"It's not welfare. Forget that part. Let me worry about it. The main thing is the place. I'll start checking around. What was the name of the place you went to before?"

"Who knows? It was over thirty years ago."

"It doesn't matter. Let me line up a few. You can inspect them while Mickey stays with Sanjo."

Opening to their fullest extension, Mickey's eyes flashed every bit of white they had.

Jerry continued. "Mickey, whose senile mother I *schlep* all over the place and who I contribute three hundred a month for, will be happy to do it."

Mickey got the message. Received. Checked. Understood. Ten-four we gone.

"I don't know," said Poppy.

"I do," said Jerry. "It's the only way. You can't be a nursemaid to her anymore. You spent enough of your life. Give your old age a chance."

"A chance for what?"

"Don't take every word I say literally."

"How do I know they'll treat her right?"

"We'll get a place that's licensed. And you can visit her."

"It's like I keep my rings in the vault," said Mickey. "I'm there practically every week."

"Believe me," said Jerry, "it's the only way."

One life-and-death decision a year is enough for anybody. This was Poppy's second in the space of a month. Poppy put his head on the table and cried. Jerry took off his glasses, rubbed his eyes, and kissed his brother's freckled pate.

Sanjo lay in her darkened bedroom. The covers were up to her chin. Her pillow was wet.

"Hurts me," she said to no one in particular.

The first place Poppy checked was a Georgian mansion tucked away on thirty well-tended acres called The Range. They wanted too much money. The fee for residential care for one year was $25,000. While they accepted a handful of public assistance cases, The Range said their quota was full. Poppy was staggered by the fee. The only good thing was that rich people, with all their money, had problems too.

The second place, called Cowslip, an arrangement of three row houses with a common entrance, was appalling. Even Poppy, among the worst housekeepers in the world, appreciated the depths of its destitution. It wasn't that Cowskip was cluttered. Clutter is sometimes a good sign, usually an indication of activity and an attitude of institutional flexibility. Cowslip was dirty, plain and simple. Accumulated filth coated the furnishings and the residents with a kind of moldy husk that was apparent to anyone with eyes to see. The smell, strong enough to leap even Poppy's high threshold of nasal sensitivity, sent him flying out the door before he even gave his name.

The third place was called Heaven Sent. It was run by a Reverend Thackery. There was a general air of despondency, as if no one expected things to get any better. Everyone sat on rows and rows of long benches that lined the walls. It looked like a bus terminal. Reverend Thackery kept talking about Gifts and Blessings, but Poppy never got his point. He just knew that the place made him more depressed than he already was.

Larkspur was the fourth place Poppy visited. It was laid out like an African village. A few round stucco buildings, looking as if they had been patted into shape overnight, stood in a compound behind a fence. Residents walked back and forth between one round house and another. Most had on sweaters or jackets. A few who forgot, or who had managed to escape the notice of others more responsible, shivered.

Poppy sat in the main office. It was furnished in hand-me-down painted-walnut Danish-style sofas with tweedy upholstered cushions placed face down so no one would be offended by the yellow stuffing poking through. Sheet linoleum in a pebble design covered most of the floor and rolled up at the corners. The supervisor who entered the office didn't see him at first.

"Where'd he go?" she asked.

"He was here a minute ago," said the woman who tripled as clerk, nurse, and cafeteria monitor.

Poppy stood up.

"There he is."

"Can we help you?"

Poppy faced a woman well into her fifties with the look of one who's been there and back.

"I came about my daughter."

"Yes, I know. Your brother called. I'm Claire Finney."

Poppy waited.

"Come in."

Poppy squeezed behind Miss Finney into a tiny office that was the size of a walk-in closet. It had a desk and two chairs. Miss Finney went to clear things off the second chair—charts, letters, coats, a much-used checkers set, and a lampshade.

"It's okay, I'll stand," said Poppy.

Somehow Miss Finney found a place for everything, including the lampshade, which she stacked on another lamp. "Now it has a hat," she said.

Poppy looked at her sideways and sat down.

"Okay. Tell me about her."

"She's retarded. She has Down's syndrome."

"I love a Down's," said Miss Finney.

"She's thirty-four years old."

"She did very well, didn't she? What's her name?"

"Sandra Joanne, but we call her Sanjo."

"Who's we?"

"My wife and I. My wife died last month. That's why I'm here."

"I figured that."

"I can't take care of her anymore."

"What kind of care does Sanjo need?"

Poppy was afraid to tell her everything. He planned to start with the easy stuff first. "She can tie her shoes, but she can't buckle, sometimes."

"Go on."

"She can comb her hair if you remind her."

"Uh-huh."

"She used to dress herself."

"What do you mean, used to?"

"Before my wife died she dressed herself. She doesn't do that anymore."

"It's not unusual to go backward a little in bad times. We all do. What else doesn't she do that she used to do?"

Poppy looked at his shoes. He picked his head up and twirled his baseball cap. "Go to the toilet." Miss Finney made some notations on a piece of paper. "But that's not all the time. She goes by herself plenty too."

The clerk/nurse/cafeteria monitor came and stood in the doorway.

"Billy Lawrence is lost. The gym sent him to the Arts House but he hasn't shown up yet."

"Tell them to look in the showers. Billy likes to turn on the faucets."

The clerk/nurse/cafeteria monitor left.

"What are you looking for, for Sanjo?"

Poppy thought that was obvious. The question threw him. "I don't know. A place where she'll get fed, dressed, stay clean."

"I'd be looking for more than that if I were you."

"Like what?"

"Sanjo should be encouraged to be independent again."

Poppy twirled his cap. He didn't want to get into that. She would understand the situation better when she saw it. What he wanted to know was yes or no. She assured him that they did have a place for Sanjo. There were just a few requirements. Sanjo would have to have a medical examination and a psychological evaluation.

Even before they reached the top of the hospital's granite steps, Sanjo began to hang back. By the time they got to the glass doors, she had calcified. Poppy was not impatient this time.

"It won't hurt you."

Sanjo didn't believe him.

"Look, I'll do it first."

Poppy went in and out of the doors, which sprang to let him through like an announcement.

"See, nothing happened to me."

Sanjo didn't move.

"Okay. You want me to give it to the door?" Poppy stormed up to the doors and shook his fist. "If you start anything, I'll give you such a smack, you'll be sorry!" He turned to Sanjo. "How's that?"

She took his arm and clung to him until they were safely through.

"Didn't I tell you?"

Sanjo remembered that Ma was sleeping in the hospital. She pulled Poppy to the elevators. "See Ma upstairs."

"Ma's not here."

"Ma here."

"No she isn't." He took her arm and propelled her to another corridor leading to the elevator that serviced the outpatient clinics.

The physical examination was nothing. Her heart, lungs, and blood pressure were fine. She came away with a clean bill of health except for rhinitis, conjunctivitis, and vaginitis. The doctor could do little for the first. The second and third he put under treatment and expected to have cleared up within weeks.

At the end of the examination the doctor called in Poppy and said, "I'm surprised you haven't had her sterilized. I don't see anything written on her chart about it. I still feel a uterus. Has she had a tubal ligation elsewhere?"

"A what?"

"Has she had her tubes tied?"

"No."

"It's recommended in situations like this. She's still fertile. I'd think about it seriously, if I were you."

By the time Poppy got the appointment with the psychologist, it was the middle of October. His office was in a clinic. His name was Dr. Joe Hunt, and he was small, thin, black, and looked as if he were fifteen. When he first came out Poppy thought he was going to hit him up for a quarter.

"Hi, Sanjo."

Sanjo bit her thumb. It already had a small callus. She moved away.

"You have to go with him," said Poppy.

Sanjo turned around, her back as eloquent as a service station sign that has just been turned off.

"Let me handle it, Mr. Bernatsky. Come on, Sanjo."

Dr. Hunt took her shoulders, spun her around, then put his hand on her back and pushed her forward. "We're going for a walk."

"No."

"Sure we are." Hunt was tougher than he looked. Although he came from an upper-middle-class background, Hunt had street experience. His previous job was as a youth coordinator. That meant he got street gangs to make precise decisions on which territory was which, not only by street but by number, and to agree on a DMZ, a neutral turf where no one would get hurt.

Not only did he mediate agreement, he enforced it. Sanjo, in comparison, was a cakewalk, although he didn't know what a cakewalk was.

"Right in there." He closed the door after her.

Sanjo was given pictures and asked to name them. She didn't name a single picture. She flipped them casually on the table, only stopping briefly to look at a cat. Dr. Hunt gave her some things to do.

She didn't do them. She was given colored one-inch wooden cubes, a paper and a pencil, objects of all shapes to fit on a board with depressions of all shapes, dolls, toys, pellets, holes to drop them in, sticks, and coins. Nothing interested her. She looked out the window, her mouth sagging, her eyes downcast.

Dr. Hunt took a mint, touched it to her tongue, put it on the table in front of her and waited for her to pick it up. She didn't touch it. He made a sudden deliberate noise behind her. Everything sprang to action like an orchestra making a false start. Her eyes squeezed shut, her mouth opened, the muscles in her neck tensed, her shoulders hunched, and her knees bent. In the space of a second all her parts undid themselves and she returned to her original disinterest.

Hunt talked to her softly, simply, crooning a persuasive melody, the kind of things one says to someone very sick, very young, or very old. Sanjo looked away. He watched her quietly for another half hour. At the end of the session he questioned Poppy and then wrote on a chart while Poppy and Sanjo waited.

He placed the chart in a manila folder and handed it to Poppy. "I'm going to mail this, but you're entitled to see it. Would you like to look at it?"

"Okay." Poppy looked inside. He saw the letters TMR and the number 30±. "That's wrong," he said. "Sanjo is thirty-four."

"That's not her age, Mr. Bernatsky, it's her I.Q. But it's not accurate. It's really not possible to evaluate her developmental state while she's depressed. Actually I spotted her a few points."

Everything was set. The paper work, expedited by Jerry, was finished. Larkspur was ready for Sanjo. Sanjo was as ready as she was going to be for Larkspur.

They left two days before Halloween.

They told her she was going for a ride, a common euphemism that in other circumstances often winds up as a trip to the New Jersey marshes.

Jerry helped Poppy pack. Mickey said she couldn't bear it and stayed home. Poppy filled the tub and told her to take a bath. While Sanjo splashed halfheartedly, they packed her clothes in two large suitcases.

She came out in her underwear.

"Do you want the cat pictures?" asked Poppy.

Sanjo didn't know she was changing her address permanently. "No."

She pulled his hand from the bulletin board. Poppy waited for her to leave the room and packed them anyway. He had been told to bring personal things that she liked, and they were the only things he could think of.

The slanting light of afternoon cast monstrous shadows, dimming Bergen Street in giant and melancholic images. Somehow the neighborhood found out, as they found out everything. Mrs. Ryan was at her rosebushes, cutting them back for the winter. She had changed her floppy hat for a knitted navy watch cap that covered her ears.

Mrs. Cervitano heard they were sending Sanjo away. She came over to say good-bye. She slipped a medal over Sanjo's neck when Poppy wasn't looking, broke into tears, stumbled back across the street, and went to have an incoherent discussion with Saint Jude.

Penny's mother was outside, frankly watching. She was worried about Halloween. It was the first time that Penny, no longer in a city apartment, would follow the other children through suburban streets, knocking on the doors of strangers for treats. She worried about things like razor blades in apples. She shivered in the cold, wanted to say something to Sanjo, who stood waiting on the walkway, thought better of it, and went back into her house.

Pert Little Miss's mother, preparing for Halloween, watched from behind her front window where she stuffed candy corn into one hundred and fifty little bags. As soon as she was finished, she was going to put the yellow satin collar on her daughter's orchid tulle costume and wrap a baton to match. Mrs. Wright, also preparing for Halloween, was bringing everything into her house that could be marked, scored, graffitied, stolen, defiled, or otherwise vandalized. The mailbox could wait until her husband came home.

"You have everything?" asked Jerry.

Poppy checked Sanjo's bedroom. All her clothes were packed. Her dresser drawers were emptied. One lay on the bed upside down. Hangers were left swinging in her closet. The cat pictures were gone, leaving the bulletin board with bits of paper and pushpins.

Poppy came down the steps, took Sanjo's arm, and led her to the car. Everyone stopped what they were doing, even a squirrel who paused in his frantic search for nuts. No one said a word. Jerry drove up Bergen Street past Penny's mother, past Mrs. Cervitano, past Mrs. Ryan and Pert Little Miss's mother, who was winding a baton with yellow silk.

Poppy and Sanjo sat in the back seat. Poppy thought he should tell her good-bye, then changed his mind.

"Did you comb your hair?"

"No."

She was right. It stuck out over her ears and spiked her forehead. Poppy smoothed it with his hand.

"It's getting cold outside. Wear a sweater," he said.

Sanjo had no idea where they were going. It took almost forty minutes to get there. They turned in Larkspur Drive and made the circle around the compound.

Poppy's lips started to tremble.

"The faster the better," said Jerry.

Miss Finney came running out.

"Hello, Sanjo."

They all walked into the office. Jerry and Poppy each brought a bag. Poppy stopped and put his bag down.

"I can't do it." He began to cry.

"You have to," said Jerry, "for your own sake, for her sake. Morry, you can't take care of her."

No mention at all was made of the two-thousand-dollar non-refundable deposit.

Miss Finney put her arm around Sanjo. "Hello, Sanjo. I'm glad to see you," she said.

Sanjo looked her over and pulled away.

Poppy signed some papers.

"Everything is set except her canteen money."

"How much is it?" asked Poppy.

"A dollar a week is pretty standard. Some get more, some get less."

Poppy fished out a few bills. He only had three dollars in his pocket. Jerry added another dollar.

"Tell her good-bye," said Miss Finney.

Poppy sighed. "Good-bye, Sanjo. Be a good girl. Do what they tell you. I'll come to visit you." He took her head in his hands and kissed her neck.

"Poppy." Sanjo recognized the sound and feel of trouble. She also had no trouble in recognizing this as a strange place with strange people.

Poppy bolted, for him a slow trot, with Jerry right behind him, shooting out his arm like a battering ram to open the door for him.

"Next Sunday!" Poppy yelled.

"Come back!" yelled Sanjo. Miss Finney held her fast.

"Poppe-e-e-e! Wait!" Sanjo bit her thumb. The callus began to bleed. She looked around her, thrashed wildly, kicked, quieted, then screamed again hoarsely, finally broke free, and ran to the window to watch them drive away, her heart hammering against her chest like something caged.

Miss Finney and the nurse/clerk/cafeteria monitor stood behind her, exchanged a look, and each took one of her arms.

11

Their timing was perfect. They waited until the car rounded the driveway and Jerry and Poppy disappeared from view.

"Now!"

They dragged her away from the window. Miss Finney gave Sanjo's suitcases to a big-jawed man she called Harold. Harold hefted the suitcases as easily as if they were newspapers and followed after them.

"Do you think we ought to get Dr. Olsen to give her something?" asked the clerk/nurse/cafeteria monitor, whose name was Irene.

"Let's see what happens," said Miss Finney.

"She's not cooperating at all. Come on, Sanjo, walk."

Sanjo hung between them like long winter underwear that has been frozen solid on the wash line. No matter which way they tugged her, she was stiff and unyielding.

"Sanjo, we're taking you to your house. Don't you want to meet Fay and John? They want to meet you."

"Maybe if I push and you pull," suggested Irene.

She stepped behind Sanjo and pushed with her knee in Sanjo's back. Miss Finney pulled from the front.

"Stop that!"

"Then walk by yourself, we don't have all day," said Irene.

[225]

"At least she'll talk to us," said Miss Finney.

Pulling, tugging, pushing, with Harold right behind them, they got Sanjo out of the administration building and onto the gravel walkway.

The phone rang. "Oh, damn, get that, will you?"

Irene ran inside, her bobby socks coming down over her space shoes.

"It's the laundry. They can't deliver until Tuesday."

"Ask them about the liners. We were supposed to have them in the last delivery."

"Miss Finney wants to know about the liners."

Like a turtle, Sanjo slowly pulled her head out to look around. A few onlookers stood nearby to watch, as silent and noncommittal as birds on a power line.

"They said they'll send them with the towels."

"We need more washing machines. Then we wouldn't have to worry about deliveries. Tell them we better have the liners by Tuesday."

They started over. Sanjo pulled in her head again. It was tougher going. Sanjo learned to lock her knees and went hydroplaning on her heels, sending up a rooster spray of gravel. The burden of mobilization fell on Irene.

They got about five yards before Miss Finney realized she no longer heard Harold's footsteps crunch on the gravel. She turned to see what was going on. Harold had stopped to pick his nose.

"Cut that out! You're supposed to do that with tissue paper or a handkerchief. Ask John to give you something when we get to Redbird."

Harold wiped his finger on the suitcase.

They passed a young girl with a red football helmet on her head. The girl turned back and ran beside them.

"Who's her?" she asked.

"This is Sanjo. She's come to live with us."

"Where does her sleep?"

"With Fay and John in Redbird."

"Them in the dumb house."

"It's not the dumb house, Peggy. There are no dumb houses here."

"Oh, yes, there are. Her goes there."

"What's the matter?" Miss Finney asked Irene.

"She's stalled. I can't get her moving."

Harold dropped the bags again.

"Don't do that!" said Miss Finney. She turned to the girl with the red football helmet.

"Peggy, go to Fay and John and tell one of them to come out, will you?"

"Sure." Peggy ran with her coat flopping on her ankles and her football helmet glinting in the fading sunlight. She disappeared into a round stucco dwelling and came out with a woman wearing a big sweater over a long cotton skirt. The woman's blond hair was twisted and knotted on the top of her head. Some of it wisped down over her neck.

"Here she is, Fay. This is Sanjo."

Fay was tall, blond, and stalwart. She had a way of staring into the distance, the result of myopia that made her strain to focus. She looked like a Valkyrie.

Fay smoothed Sanjo's bangs over her forehead. "There, now you can see us."

Like afterthoughts, a few stragglers followed out of the building called Redbird. One woman walked with the jerking motions of a puppet in the hands of an amateur. She flailed after Fay, caught up with her, and clung to her skirt. Another woman, who looked something like Sanjo, hesitated, turned back, and stood in the safety of the doorway. A man with gray stubble on his face approached Sanjo slowly, inching forward until they stood toe to toe and nose to nose.

"Take over," said Miss Finney. "We have to get back. Don't put down the bags until they're in Redbird, Harold." Harold held them aloft like a duck hunter bringing in a brace of birds. Miss Finney and Irene walked briskly away, crunching their way back over the gravel.

"Come on, Sanjo." Fay turned and strode back to Valhalla.

[227]

Sanjo didn't move. Neither did the man with the gray stubble, who looked as if he were trying to find a way into her pupils.

"We're going to leave you there." Fay continued to walk away, with the bobbing puppet woman attached to her skirt and Harold tagging after them holding the bags in the air. Sanjo stood fixed on the gravel.

"Oh, Christ." Fay disengaged the puppet woman from her skirt and returned to uproot Sanjo. "Don't give me a hard time." She slipped her hand into the slack of the Snoopy purse strap and pulled her toward Redbird.

The man with the gray stubble stood where he was, staring after the space that had contained Sanjo like someone watching the dot disappear on the TV.

"Come on, Roger," called Fay. "John wants you."

Sanjo was led to the women's hemisphere of Redbird. Several women were sitting on their beds. Two sat tied in wheelchairs. One of the wheelchair occupants had great bushy eyebrows that met over the bridge of her nose. Her face and arms were hairy and her skin was the color of linen stained in tea.

"We'll have to move you a little, Nancy," said Fay to the bushy-browed woman. She put her to one side of the narrow aisle like a chest of drawers, while Harold brought through Sanjo's suitcases. They left Nancy facing nowhere. She didn't seem to mind.

Fay led Sanjo to the third bed from one end. A little gray nightstand stood beside it.

"This is where you'll sleep," said Fay. "And this is where you'll put your toothbrush and your comb, and things like that. Let me help you."

Fay's offer was gratuitous. She was planning to do it anyway. She opened a suitcase and began to poke through Sanjo's clothing. Sanjo tried to close the case but Fay pushed her hand away. Sanjo waddled to the window, looked outside, and called through the glass. "Poppy!" It was not a sustained yell, rather a declarative statement.

Fay grabbed a handful of dresses and slacks and hung them

in a two-foot-wide partition in the communal closet opposite the beds. She found the cat pictures under a sweater and held them up.

"Where shall I put these?"

"Mine!"

"I know they're yours. Where would you like them? Here?"

A woman with a birdlike face smacked a woman with a large head who carried a potholder.

"Don't do that, Alice," said Fay, "You'll mess up her shunt. Vera, give Alice back her potholder. She made it, not you."

That wasn't true. The arts and crafts teacher was the one who made it.

Another woman stuck her hand in the suitcase and dragged out Sanjo's cheongsam. The fabric was luminous, even in the autumn light. Sanjo bellowed. Fay put the cat pictures on the bed to rescue the blue silk. Vera took the cat pictures. Sanjo's belongings flew about like ejected matter from a cosmic explosion. The Snoopy purse lofted, spun around, and disappeared. Sanjo bellowed again.

Fay tried to bellow, but without Sanjo's vibrato her despair stuck in her throat like a chicken bone. "John!"

A voice came through from the bathroom on the other side of the closet wall. "I can't come now. I'm cleaning up Marty."

Despite the velocity and the drift of Sanjo's personal effects, Fay finally managed to put everything away after making everyone sit on their beds. The cat pictures were rescued from Vera and put in Sanjo's drawer, and the cheongsam, a little soiled, was jammed into Sanjo's allotted two feet of closet. The Snoopy purse was found in Nancy's lap, dangled over her knees.

Showers and toilets, whose use for men and women was regulated by schedule, stood in an elliptical common room in the center of the building. No one in Redbird showered alone because of the danger of turning on a hot-water tap.

Sanjo showered that night with eleven other women of Redbird in two oversized stalls. The shower was more like a wetting down. Sanjo, whose strong suit was baths, didn't know how to play the hand. She ran in and out only long enough to get sprinkled.

"Come on, Sanjo," said Fay, whose hair was now down around her ears and who was hustling Nancy from her wheel-chair onto a stool under the shower. "You can dry yourself." She threw Sanjo a towel.

"Need any help in there?" called a voice.

"No, thanks, John, I think I got it knocked."

"How's the new one doing?"

"Having a tug-of-war with Vera over her towel."

Sanjo put her pajamas on but didn't button all the buttons. The bottoms fell and hovered around her hips like low-flying clouds on a mountain range.

Her new bed was smaller than the one she was used to. When she turned, her arm fell over the side and touched the floor. She brought her hand up to tuck it under her neck when she saw Nancy staring at her from her pillow, her eyes under their bushy brows glinting with reflected light from the small lamp that glowed in the dormitory.

Sanjo woke up the next morning confused. There was a bed on either side of her. She looked around for Poppy and saw instead a lot of strangers in their underwear. Then she remembered and ran to the window. All she could see was a gravel walk and a field beyond.

Fay hustled them outside and lined them up, then poked them in and out of their places, putting Sanjo between Lenore and Nancy, separating Vera and Alice, as easily as if she were playing a marimba. The men filed out soon after. They had two things in common with the waiting women. Their dentition was poor, and they had little to say.

John came out of the round stucco building last. He had a beard. It covered his face so successfully that all Sanjo could see was his forehead, nose, and eyes.

The beard wiggled. "Hi, Sanjo."

Sanjo waited for the beard to move again.

"I'm John."

She put her chin on her chest.

"Hey, I know I'm not Redford, but I can't be that bad."

"Rumplestiltskin would be closer," said Fay.

The beard wiggled in Fay's direction.

"Up yours," she said.

"Okay, troops, move 'em on out."

Redbird was going to breakfast, the first group in Larkspur to go because they took the longest time to eat. Another building took longer, but since they didn't eat in the cafeteria, they didn't count.

"You want to push Nancy?" Fay asked Sanjo.

Sanjo shook her head and clamped her lips tight.

"Okay, Lenore, you push her, but go slow."

The troops followed behind John, the battle of 1776 without a drummer boy, jerking, flailing, scuffling, shuffling, rolling, and plain walking into the cafeteria.

Irene had on a big white chef's apron. She was a quick-change artist. As soon as breakfast was over, she would whip off her apron and put on her nursing cap. Now she pushed a trolley loaded with trays.

"How's she doing?" she asked.

"So-so," said Fay. "Slept through okay, still a little punchy." Fay put a piece of toast in Nancy's hand and led it to her mouth, saying, "You know how to do it. You do it."

Nancy dropped the toast.

"Come on. You did it yesterday." Fay put the toast back in Nancy's hand and led it once more to her mouth. The toast fell again.

"Here's breakfast," said Irene, slinging trays faster than a stewardess in economy.

Sanjo stared at the yellow plastic tray in front of her. It held a plate with scrambled eggs, a box of Cheerios, toast, and a glass of milk. Sanjo was hungry. She picked up the spoon and fed herself the eggs. The fact that most of them fell back on her plate was not her fault. The eggs were very slippery.

Irene came to pat Sanjo's mouth with a communal napkin.

[231]

Sanjo let her. Irene moved down the line, folding and refolding the napkin until every square inch was used.

Even though the men of Redbird weighed more, were taller, and were somewhat more muscular than the women, they were no harder to manage, even for John, who was by any standards a little man. Most of his responsibilities had to do with cleaning up. John had several cleanups that breakfast. The most spectacular was when a fellow with bulging eyes spilled his milk. Before John could mop it up, the man with the bulging eyes put his hands in the milk and splashed, getting milk on everyone within range, including Sanjo. The milk dripped down her neck and soaked her collar.

"Fix me," she said to John, but he didn't hear her. The milk was not the only thing to get on Sanjo. By the end of the meal she looked like a Jackson Pollock painting.

After breakfast it was back to the bathroom. Sanjo had to sit on the toilet even though she didn't have to and didn't want to. She sat with five others who had the same assignment, "Sit there until you do something." Larkspur was too shorthanded to do it any other way. Like an essay test, any answer was acceptable.

When Sanjo was allowed to leave the bathroom, she checked the window and then her cat pictures. She tapped out on both. Poppy wasn't coming and the cat pictures were gone. In their place was a potholder. Sanjo bit her callus. Fay and John turned the place upside down. They found the pictures in Vera's nightstand.

"These aren't yours. They belong to Sanjo," said John.

Vera smiled. She wasn't the least bit contrite.

"Bad girl," said Sanjo.

"Yes," said Fay. "She's a bad girl." She sniffed at Sanjo's milk-dried dress. "Boy, do you smell sour."

At nine o'clock all the Redbirds were herded into the gymnasium and turned over to Mr. Frank. They were put into a circle while Mr. Frank, wearing warm-ups and a whistle around his neck, threw a ball to each one in turn as he called their name. The object was to catch the ball and return it. Half of them didn't try. They stood still while the ball struck them on the legs and in the stomach, and echoes of their names rumbled from the walls and ceiling.

"Come on, you guys," yelled their coach, "catch it, like this. It's easy, you can do it."

A quarter of them tried to catch the ball but couldn't do it; the ball fell through the hoop of their arms and bounced at their feet. The remaining quarter caught it, and a few of these not only caught it but returned it. Sanjo was in the first half who didn't try—period. The ball smashed against her knee. It came again and hit her in the arm.

"Catch it, Sambo," yelled Mr. Frank. "Put your arms up."

Sanjo didn't know what he wanted. "Stop that," she said.

Mr. Frank continued to blow his whistle and throw the ball. The figures who circled him, with the exception of two or three, were as silent as the monoliths at Stonehenge. "Come on," he said. "This is fun!"

On Sanjo's third day, Larkspur had a Halloween party. The Lions Club and their ladies set up the whole thing. They decorated the cafeteria in orange and black crepe paper, put up witches and cats, and cut out pumpkins. They put sheets on two of the long tables and covered them with cupcakes, cookies, pretzels, and paper cups filled with punch. They brought a tub for an apple-bobbing contest, but Miss Finney was afraid someone might drown and made them take the tub away.

When the Redbirds were summoned to the cafeteria, the men of the Lions Club and their wives were waiting with cats and witches pasted on the windows and smiles pasted on their faces. Sanjo went to touch one of the paper cats. A lady in a blue-dotted apron told her to leave it alone. One of the Lions put on a pumpkin mask and scared everyone, including Harold, who started to cry. Then the lady in the blue-dotted apron went to the piano and played her own adaptation of "Santa Claus Is Coming to Town." She substituted "Halloween" for "Santa Claus" and leaned back from the piano, smiling around her like

[233]

Liberace. It was clear she was having a wonderful time.

Alice dragged a sheet off one of the tables and put it over her head. "Look at that, will you?" said one of the Lions. "She's being a ghost."

"I don't think so," said Fay. "She always does that when strangers are around."

When the party was over, Sanjo had learned the refrain of a new song. Everyone was stained with punch, and cake was all over the cafeteria floor. Harold sat huddled in the corner, and Lenore, who had eaten a whole plate of cupcakes, threw up. Irene gave the Lions a certificate and hustled them out so they could clean up the cafeteria and the revelers.

Sanjo was awakened every morning at six thirty. She washed with the other Redbirds, toileted with them, and dressed with them, while Fay masterminded the entire schedule, barking orders, running around, buttoning buttons, zipping zippers, tying wraparounds, and tucking up her hair. Every minute of the day was accounted for. Sanjo wasn't always doing something, but someone always knew where she could be found even when she was doing nothing. By seven o'clock she was showered and put into bed, and by eight all lights were out except the night-light glowing in the hall. It was a regimentation endured in common by the military, the convicted felon, the orphan, the nursing-home resident, the overnight camper, and the seminarian.

Fay and John had Sunday off. Their replacement was a married couple by the name of Kane. Sanjo woke up Sunday morning to a new voice shouting, "Get up! Come on, move it!"

The voice belonged to a woman standing over her bed. Sanjo didn't recognize her. Mrs. Kane had dyed red hair and pores so big that, if other systems had cooperated, she could have done all her breathing through her face.

Mrs. Kane leaned over and squinted, as if she were peering at the contents of a Petrie dish. Her eyes, what little could be seen of them, were as red as her hair.

"You're the new one. What's your name?"

Sanjo rubbed the accumulation of the night from her eyes. "Sanjo."

"How old are you? Do you know? Probably not. Okay, Sanjo, get up. It's time to get washed." Mrs. Kane went to the next bed and routed out Lenore, who couldn't get mobilized. Mrs. Kane yanked off her covers, dragged her legs to the side of the bed, and placed her feet on the floor.

"When I say up, I mean up. Don't make me nervous."

Sanjo put on a pair of elasticized slacks. Unlike many Redbirds, who had to wear a wraparound, she was allowed to wear her own clothes. She had trouble pulling on the second leg, tottered, and fell against Alice's bed. Alice was in it. Alice started screaming.

Mrs. Kane, who was putting Nancy into her chair, drew back her lips. "Take those slacks off." To Alice she said, "You stay there until I can get to you."

Mrs. Kane grabbed everyone indiscriminately, pulled the remaining pant leg off Sanjo, made her wear a wraparound that belonged to Alice, and left fingermarks on her arm.

Sanjo was dressed before most of the others and wandered into the bathroom where the men were getting shaved. They were all naked. Sanjo looked. It was the first time she had had a full, frontal, in-person view of the male genitalia. It was a mild fascination.

Mr. Kane, a big beefy man with a towel slung over his shoulder, was shaving Roger and didn't see her right away.

"Go like this. No, like this. Make your face like this!" He wound up pulling Roger's nose in one direction and his chin in the other, rearranging his face as easily as Silly Putty.

"Look," said Harold.

Mr. Kane looked up. Roger's face sprang back. Sanjo stood in the doorway, Linnaeus with a question. Mr. Kane slung the towel over his other shoulder.

"Get out of here. Paula!"

Mrs. Kane came running. "What is it? What are you doing here?" Elbow straight, she raised a hand for a forehand volley

[235]

and smacked Sanjo on the buttocks. Harold laughed. "Get out and wait in the lounge!" yelled Mrs. Kane. "Aren't they something?" she said to her husband.

Sanjo had never been smacked by anybody in her whole life. It stung. More than that, her feelings were hurt. She waddled out, her chin to her chest, tears filling her eyes.

"Bad girl," she muttered.

The visitors began to arrive after breakfast. They came all day long, most of them leaning backward while walking forward, in the old approach-avoidance conflict of someone who doesn't want to do what they want to do. Poppy was not among them.

Sanjo didn't know to look for him anyway, even though he had yelled "Sunday," since the names of the days in the week were not in her repertoire. Even if they were, a particular place in time, distinguished by another particular place in time, was a difficult concept.

The visitors kept their coats on. They brought candy, cake, and cookies, which was frowned upon by Miss Finney, who preferred fruit and vegetables. Try telling visitors, feeling guilty anyway, that they should bring carrot sticks to someone they have institutionalized. Some of the visitors took a Redbird out for a walk. When they did, they were usually back in ten minutes.

By nightfall all the visitors were gone. Mrs. Kane hustled everyone back into bed, put out the lights, including the nightlight, at six thirty, and waited for Fay and John to return.

The first and only thing Fay said to Mrs. Kane was, "Why the hell is it so dark in here?"

Sanjo asked for Poppy from time to time and continued to watch for his car. She stopped asking for Ma. Fay told her Poppy was busy and would come to see her soon. Privately she told John she was going to write him a letter and tell him what a bastard he was. John said to stay out of it.

Miss Finney came to check on her. "How's she getting along?"

"She's doing all right. Better than most in some things, not so good in others," said Fay.

"An antidepressant was suggested. Should we put her on the list for Dr. Olsen?"

"Like Mellaril?"

"Probably."

"I hate to see her doped up."

"I don't think Dr. Olsen would keep her doped up."

"She doesn't need it."

"Let me know." Miss Finney ran off. She had one hundred and eight others to keep tabs on.

John took them for walks. Fay stayed behind with those in wheelchairs, or those who couldn't keep up, and sat with them outside the Redbird house in the lengthening, sunlight-speckled shadows.

Going for a walk was a major project since no Redbird could be trusted to make the ultimate decision of what constituted appropriate outdoor dress. While Fay and John could entertain freewill in September and October, November was too cold for such egalitarian consideration. For instance, the question of gloves. Only a few Redbirds could find their own. Those who couldn't had to be reminded not to take the gloves of others and to keep their hands in their pockets. Sanjo was one of the latter.

Before they left for their walk, Fay brought a jar of cold cream to Sanjo.

"You have to put this on your face when you go out in the cold," she said. She took Sanjo's fingers and dipped them into the cold cream, then dabbed it gently on her face.

"Here, you do it."

Sanjo got it on her face and on her bangs. Her skin glistened like a newborn colt.

The day was raw, windy, and cold. It seemed to be waiting for something. Dull colorless skies bleached into grays and whites, and an edging of ice coated the fields like frail crochet. Unruly white-tipped starlings combed the ground like mine-

[237]

sweepers, cracking the filaments of frost as they ran and screeching at each other like Mrs. Kane.

It was hard to keep up with John. His pace was as brisk as the day. He pointed out things and named them.

"That's a rock. The rock is round. That's a stick. The stick is brown."

The cold nipped at Sanjo's nose. She put her hand on it to cover it. Her fingers, out of the shelter of her pocket, grew cold and then numb, while John named the world of Larkspur.

"This is ice. It's very cold."

Alice didn't want to walk anymore. "I'm going to leave you here," said John.

Alice, who was forty-six, didn't care. She was tired.

"I'm not kidding. I can't stand here with you. Do you want Harold to take you back?"

Harold was at the ready, his arms like levers in a lift position. Alice took one look at him and moved.

Sanjo struggled not to fall behind. Her breath came out in puffs of smoke. When they came back, her cheeks tingled and her fingers burned.

"Rock is round," she said.

Fay had her hands full with Nancy and didn't hear her.

Sanjo was mobilized. Being kept so busy in the general business of staying alive and caring for herself, dressing, toileting, eating, and moving about did something to her biochemistry, which in turn did something to her. It was a circular event. Her depression began to lift. It was no longer a dull ache but an occasional twinge like a root that needs a new canal.

"Where Poppy?" she asked Fay.

Fay shook her head.

In Sanjo's third week at Larkspur, the Redbirds went on a field trip to the zoo, in particular the petting zoo. Those who went were handpicked. Sanjo was one of them. This time John stayed behind.

The bus driver was named Al, a big rangy man who wore a tan sweater over fatigues. Al and his clothes were the same color. He did a last-minute check on the bus, lying on his back to scrutinize its metal underworkings, while the Redbirds waited in line with Fay. He pulled himself up, brushed off his hands, and nodded. Fay led them into the bus.

Al poked his head in while they picked their seats. "Don't you be fooling around in there," he said. He ran a tight bus.

Alice knocked over Lenore's hat. "Sit down and stop that," said Fay, "or you can't go."

Lenore got up to leave.

"No, not you, her."

Lenore was leaving anyway.

"You don't want to go?" Lenore was already out of the bus and on her way back to Redbird. "Okay, go find John. Make sure you let him see you when you get back."

Roger sat in the front seat right behind the driver. Gray stubble covered his chin. Most of his teeth were missing, and he sucked in his mouth.

"Oh, boy," said Fay. "Didn't John shave you this morning?" Roger smiled. "Where are your dentures?" Roger looked out the window. "Don't turn away. You know you're supposed to have your teeth in. Otherwise how can you eat?"

Roger looked down in his lap. Al turned around. "Ain't nothing wrong with gumming."

Fay sighed and turned to face the occupants of the bus. "Listen, everybody, we're going to the zoo. We're going to see animals, and you can pet them."

"Got any other news?" asked Al.

"That's about it."

"Sit down then, we gonna move this sucker."

Al doubled as a security guard. Once at their destination, he brought up the rear, helped with lunch, drinking fountains, and toilets, and discouraged unfeeling bystanders from snickering. Now he walked behind them, catching stragglers and putting them back in line.

[239]

The zoo in November is a lonely place. Most of the animals are in their shelters. The ground is bare and has begun to harden like stale bread. Leaves have blown away; not even candy wrappers break the monotony of the gray earth. The only visitors are illicit lovers looking for a place to meet and people like the residents of Larkspur, who make use of free passes restricted to off-season months.

The Redbirds filed past an elephant covered with ticks, some dispirited lions, and a bear with bald spots. Fay named the animals for them and even told them what they ate. A few pointed and stared and said a word or two, but most of the Redbirds passed without making any response. The reason was that large animals at a great distance had little relevance. The Redbirds lacked critical information about the roaming shapes that gave them their ultimate meaning and lent them their inspiration for awe. Their goal was the tangible, palpable experience of the petting zoo. Redbirds needed to know what things felt like and smelled like, besides what they looked like.

Fay led them around a stone wall and down a bank of cracked stone steps covered with doilies of gray-green lichen, to a small enclosure in which chickens, ducks, goats, a descented skunk, rabbits, sheep, and some turtles were available for handling. The animals waited for their massage. None of them had an inclination to bite, although they did not get the same guarantee from their visitors.

After some coaxing and demonstrations by Fay and Al, the Redbirds began to pet and fondle the animals of the petting zoo. The animals tolerated the experience with amazing forbearance, including some rough though well-intentioned pawing by hands less coordinated than most.

One of the Redbirds, anxious to get at what he saw, banged a turtle on a rock ledge. The zookeeper grabbed it away. He was very upset.

"You have to watch them better than this," he said to Al.

Al's eyes were grim. He locked them to those of the zookeeper, suspending all blinking and narrowing his lids for the encounter.

The zookeeper spoke into the hole where the turtle's head was disappearing as if it were a microphone. "We don't like people who don't know which end's up, do we, honey?"

"That dude better watch hisself," said Al.

The turtle didn't wait to find out what was going on. After the first bang sent shock waves throughout its body, it withdrew into its shell until its personal all-clear said everything was okay, which would be in about two days. Its keeper wished he could do the same thing.

Sanjo liked the sheep. There were young lambs and some older seasoned ewes who didn't mind getting stroked. The sheep were supposed to be the color of oatmeal, but constant exposure to polluted city air made them look like the inside of a fireplace.

Their thick woolly coats were damp, the result of foggy mornings and the lack of sufficient sun to dry them out. Sanjo got close enough to smell one. She wrinkled up her nose and made a judgment. "Sweaterboy." She did not mean that the wool would become a sweater. That was too circuitous. She meant it smelled like a sweater.

"Touch it," said Fay.

Sanjo put her hands on the sheep's back and felt the curled, soft, springy wool. The fibers, accommodating and resilient, clung together and tickled her hand.

Al had a rabbit in the cradle of his arms. "Give something else a chance. Don't play favorites," he said.

Sanjo banged her knuckles together and deserted the sheep. Al handed her the rabbit.

"Hullo, cutie," she said.

"Why don't you sit down with it?"

The rabbit felt different from the sheep. It was soft and warm. It twitched its nose like someone getting ready to sneeze and sat stoically in her lap while Sanjo glided her hand back and forth over its powder-puff back. She made no connection between this

[241]

silky creature and any comic-book hero who might have adopted its costume.

It started like a tickle. The good feeling woke up, stretched itself, and lazily started to work its way up. It wiggled her toes, prickled her skin, and expanded her chest. When it got to her throat, Sanjo thrust her neck to the sky and smiled.

It was time to go. Fay started to flap her hands like the chickens that were running away from Roger, pushing and shushing everyone into line.

Roger wanted to keep one of the chickens. Al finally got it away from him. "You don't want that ol' chicken. Man, don't you know chickens bite you, right through your hand and everything?"

They filed past the lichen, an alliance of fungus and alga that grew where nothing else could survive. Alice brushed her hand over the white threadlike net spread over the rock, releasing spores to form a new colony.

When everyone was back in the bus, Fay did a head count. It tallied. Al called back over his shoulder, "Let's see you appreciate this fine afternoon. Act right as you can be." They left for Larkspur.

The zookeeper tried to coax out the turtle. "You can come out now, they're gone." The turtle, who wasn't taking any chances, stayed under the shelter of its carapace.

Sanjo woke up to the glowing night-light. The afternoon's excursion had made her thirsty. She got out of bed. Everyone was sleeping except Nancy, who lay on her side and watched her go, her big eyes wide and staring.

"Fay." No answer. Sanjo heard sounds, rustling and murmurings that led her to the part of the house designated as the lounge. John and Fay were on the couch. They had resolved the substantial difference in their height.

Sanjo stood behind Fay's head while John probed Fay's hard and soft palate and almost made it to her epiglottis with his tongue. It was hard to tell which one had the beard. He had his hand inside her shirt under her sweater. Fay was leaning back, her eyes open, her eyeballs rolling to the back of her head like lemons in a slot machine.

"Fay."

The lemons rolled forward and stopped. *Chunk. Chunk.*

"Go back to bed," said John.

"I want water."

"You know how to work the sink," said John.

"No, I'll get it." Fay unraveled herself from the couch, went into the bathroom, and poured water into a glass. "Here you go."

Sanjo threw her head back and chug-a-lugged; most of the water went down. The rest dripped onto her chin and chest. Some splashed on Fay.

"Thanks."

"What did you say?"

Sanjo didn't repeat it. She was on her way back to bed.

"Wait a minute, you." Fay threw her arms around Sanjo. She smelled like John. "You're welcome," she said.

Passion for the uninhibited and healthy is an easy commodity to come by. Fay went back to John on the couch, molded herself to him once more, and without missing a beat went back to where she was. Sanjo went to sleep, just as fast.

The decision to force-feed Nancy was force-fed to Fay. She didn't want to do it. Nancy hadn't eaten in a week. Not only would she not finger-feed herself but she would not accept food from anyone else. Since she was malnourished to start with, everyone was concerned with weight loss.

Miss Finney and Irene came to discuss the matter with Fay and John. If they did not get solid food one way or another into Nancy's stomach, she would have to go to the hospital and be given intravenous feeding.

"It has to be done," said Miss Finney. "There are some things in this business that nobody likes, and this is one of them. The alternative is worse, so let's get to it."

Irene offered some biochemical information. "She's already

ketotic; her metabolites could get messed up."

"I don't want her starving to death, and neither do you. You've been coaxing her for weeks. It's time. Irene will help you," Miss Finney added.

"Jesus God," said Fay.

John put his hands in his pockets. "I've done it before. It's not so bad."

The Redbirds were shushed out, but most of them came back to the doorway to watch. Nancy was laid on her bed. Her arms were the only limbs they had to contend with. It was easy to tie them down. She offered little resistance, just watched them, scarcely blinking with her staring brown eyes. The only thing that came close to resistance was when she choked, snorted, and twisted her head away while Irene threaded a long tube into a nostril and worked it down into her stomach.

Fay and John mixed the contents of a jar into pap that they shoveled into a funnel.

"It's not wet enough," said Irene.

They added water.

"Okay, that's good."

Gravity sent the pap down the tube. The food bypassed Nancy's unwilling mouth and puddled into her stomach.

"We eliminate the middleman," said Irene.

"How much?" asked Fay.

"About two cupfuls," said Irene. She bent to pick up her sagging socks.

Nancy continued to stare, although more wildly than before, her eye movements quick and nervous, darting about the room like frightened birds hopping from one branch to another. She thrashed her head once, was steadied, and did not do it again.

Sanjo made no sense out of what she saw. They were doing something to Nancy. It was just like the elephant at the zoo. If she had touched it and felt it, she would have known more about it, although not the whole story. She lost interest in watching them put cereal in Nancy's nose and turned away to watch the wind outside whip branches and garbage cans all over Larkspur, tearing up the set of the landscape.

That night Fay said to John in the lounge, "I can't hack it anymore. I just can't."

A few days later, when John brought them back from gym, they found Fay packing. Sanjo ran to the window. "Poppy!"

"You're not going, Sanjo, I am. I've been knocking around here too long. I'm going to Colorado. I got some friends out there."

Fay had no illusions that Sanjo understood what she was talking about. She boiled it down and offered her the distillate.

"I'm going away."

Mrs. Kane came as a temporary replacement until they could get someone else. She screamed and smacked and yelled, "Don't make me nervous," all day long. She wasn't as fast as Fay, and some of the Redbirds didn't get showered or get their teeth brushed every day or finish every meal. Whoever she could catch or bully did. John poked his head around from time to time to see what was going on, but Mrs. Kane scared him too.

Sanjo saved her requests for John.

"Go out," she said one afternoon.

"Come on, buddy, gimme a break, it's cold out there."

"Walk, John."

"Sanjo, you don't want to go out."

Sanjo nodded her head. Yes, she did. She smiled.

John threw on his mackinaw. "Who else wants to go?"

No takers.

Mrs. Kane heard the whole thing. "You're not leaving me in here with all the rest!" she said.

John went into negotiations. "How many do I have to take for it to be all right?"

"Eight."

"Four."

They split it at seven. John mobilized six other protesting Redbirds and hustled them into their coats. Sanjo went for the cold cream.

"What are you doing? Put that away," said Mrs. Kane.

"She's supposed to, her skin is dry."

"So is mine. I don't run for cold cream every time I go out."

They went out. Sanjo walked beside John. For the first few yards, John had to push the others like wind-up toys with a broken spring until they gathered their own momentum.

"Do you know what this is?"

Sanjo didn't answer.

"It's goldenrod. It's going to stay like this until spring."

Sanjo held the weed.

"Don't get too close to it in case you have allergies or something."

Sanjo rested her head on his mackinawed arm. "Nice."

"Pay attention." He clapped his hand. "One."

Sanjo's head jerked with his arm.

"I can't do this if you rest on me. You have to watch. Now watch." Clap. "One. You do it."

Sanjo clapped.

"Say one."

"One."

John repeated the clap. "One."

At the end of the walk, Sanjo could clap and say one together.

"Way to go, Sanjo."

The test. John clapped his hands. "How many is that?"

Many she didn't know. John rephrased the question.

"What's that called?"

"One."

That night Mrs. Kane screamed everyone into the showers. The hot water wasn't working. There was no latitude with Mrs. Kane. They all had to be bathed, or as many as she could get her hands on. She put them under anyway. Sanjo shivered, balked, but in the end did as everyone else. She had learned not to fool around with Mrs. Kane.

It was getting harder to go to the cafeteria. They had to walk to meals three times a day, and sometimes the cold wind pushed them backwards. No sooner did they get their coats off than they had to put them on again.

They were in the cafeteria having lunch in their coats. Mrs.

Kane discovered it was easier that way. She also discovered that she could force Nancy's mouth open if she pinched her nose. Irene came by with the communal napkin. She made a brush at Sanjo's mouth. Sanjo pushed her hand away.

"Sanjo does that," she said.

Irene moved on. There was a *woosh,* a sucking rush of air, as if a vacuum had just been unsealed. Sanjo turned around. Across the aisle, Peggy, one of the Yellowbirds, was on the ground, her body contracting spasmodically, the red football helmet that covered her head banging on the cement floor. Her expression was that of someone biting on a lemon. Irene and two counselors rushed over and kneeled on the ground beside her. The counselors held Peggy down while Irene jammed a spoon into her mouth. Peggy's body jerked under their hands as if an electric current were going through it. Then someone pulled the *off* switch and it was over.

Mrs. Kane hustled them out. "See what happens when you're bad," she said.

Despite the cloud cover of Mrs. Kane, the sun came up in Sanjo's head. It irradiated a piece here and a piece there. She stopped soiling and wetting; she began to comb her hair and brush her teeth without being reminded. She only asked for Poppy once in a while, although she continued to watch each car that entered the grounds.

Mrs. Kane didn't notice it. John did. He went to speak to Miss Finney. Next week, Sanjo was transferred to the Bluebirds. John helped her move.

"You're going to live in Bluebird. You'll like it there."

"John too?"

"No, I'm staying back with the Redbirds. You can see me when you like, but you'll be too busy to want to."

The Redbirds watched her go. Nancy stared from her wheelchair. Roger pulled on Sanjo's hand and made a noise like a siren when Mrs. Kane made him let go. John carried her suitcases. Halfway between Redbird and Bluebird he put them down.

"Do you remember this?" He clapped his hands.

[247]

Sanjo did the same. "One," she said.

"That's right. One. How many suitcases is this?" He answered himself. "This is one suitcase."

Sanjo watched.

"But look, now we have two." John clapped twice. "How many suitcases? We have two. Two suitcases. How many suitcases, Sanjo?"

Sanjo clapped once. "No, two," said John. "Now there are two." He clapped twice; then he picked up the suitcases and took her to Bluebird. It was too cold to continue the lesson.

Mrs. Brewster, a black woman with a bosom like a pillow, met them at the door. She hugged Sanjo into the pillow, led her inside, and said, "This is your drawer space, and this is your closet. Put your things away. You know how to do a hanger?"

Sanjo looked puzzled.

"Nothing to it." Mrs. Brewster took her hand and showed her. After a few minutes, when she was confident Sanjo had learned the maneuver, she said, "You do it. When you're finished, put your suitcases under the bed, here." She went out. Somehow, Sanjo got her clothes on hangers, most of them lopsided, hanging by sleeves or collars, some of them falling on the floor; threw her things in the drawer, including the dog-eared cat pictures, the glossy parts of which were coming off the cardboard backing; then got down on her knees to put her suitcases under the bed. "Two," she said to the box springs.

Bluebirds dressed themselves. Mrs. Brewster's functions were jammed zippers, inspiration, reinforcement, and conscience. She told them they looked good, yelled at them when they gave her a headache, and hugged them when they did well. Her counterpart in the men's half of Bluebird was Mr. Fred, who was deaf but read lips. Mr. Fred was very scrupulous about attending to his responsibilities. He faced everyone squarely when they indicated, usually by pulling his sleeve, that they had something to say to him. He spoke in a low-pitched, inflectionless monotone, like a voice being raked over gravel.

After the first snowfall frosted the grounds of Larkspur in a frothy glitter, Mrs. Brewster and Mr. Fred decided that Sanjo was ready for shop. Sanjo had to trudge through loosely packed snow up to her shins to get there. She fell in line behind Billy Lawrence, who smiled at her and then bolted, when Mr. Fred wasn't looking, to stumble his way to the gym. Hexagonal snowflakes continued to whirl about her, thickening her sparse eyelashes and melting on her tongue. By the time they reached shop, everyone's feet were soaking wet.

Mr. Leo, the man who ran the shop, was so tall he reached the lintel of the doorway. He had to stoop to get in and out. "Where's Billy Lawrence?" he asked. He had to shake Mr. Fred's shirt. "Where's Billy?"

Mr. Fred ran outside to the gym.

The shop was run on a subcontractual basis. Larkspur was paid for the services it performed and used this money to offset some of the operating costs. Participants in the program were given occupation and credit on their monthly bills; the contracting concern got something for their money and the feeling that they were doing some good in the world. Everyone was happy.

There were several large tables in the shop. Everyone took a seat and went to work. They wound ribbon on bobbins and made bows for gift wrap, cut foam into pieces, stuffed pillows with the foam, and decorated hangers with pieces of wool. Some, more able, were trained to proof a printed page for ink marks. To do this, they had to be able to distinguish random spots from formed letters, although they could not read.

"Do you know how to cut?"

Sanjo nodded.

"Let's see you," said Mr. Leo.

Sanjo took the scissors and cut a piece of paper. Mr. Leo was satisfied. He gave her a paper carton and a piece of foam and showed her where to sit. After she was seated he gave her a pair of scissors and showed her how to cut the foam into the box. By four o'clock Sanjo had decimated the foam into tiny shreds. Mr. Leo told her she did good work.

When she returned to Bluebird, the wind had shattered the delicate rays and spikes of the snowflakes, rounding them and fitting them more tightly together until they compacted into an icy crust. Sanjo had to crunch down for each step.

After one week, Mr. Leo decided that Sanjo could learn something else besides cutting foam into shreds. He had two reasons. First, cutting was a former skill. He had the obligation to try to teach her a new one. Second, bow-making was an important subcontract, especially with Christmas coming up.

It wasn't an easy transition. Mr. Leo had to take Sanjo's hand and guide the ribbon on the bobbin, back and forth, back and forth, back and forth, back and forth, stop, twist, tie off, and cut. It took Sanjo four hours and eighty-two trials to get it. No dancer worked harder on a routine than Sanjo did to master the sequence of actions that made a perfect bow. She finally got it by herself. Sweating over her upper lip, surrounded on all sides by eighty red rejects aborted into scraggly haphazard approximations and one green bow, made from a ribbon from someone else's pile, she held up the perfect red bow.

Mr. Leo pronounced her a bowmaker, not the elite of the workshop, but certainly a step up from shredders and stuffers. Sanjo made bows all afternoon, five days a week.

On Saturday afternoon there was no shop. Sanjo stood outside Bluebird watching Mr. Fred knock down icicles that hung over the doorway. Some Bluebirds were putting the icicles in their mouths.

"Ice cream," said Billy.

"Danger," said Mrs. Brewster, who made them throw the icicles away. She pulled Mr. Fred's arm and faced him squarely. "Don't let them do that."

"Okay," said Mr. Fred, and he threw the icicles across the field like javelins.

Later in the afternoon the icicles were all knocked down. Sanjo stayed inside and traced her fingers over the crystalline patterns of the frosted window. It was close to five o'clock, and the dusk gathered up the day in a quick swoop. Sanjo cleared a hole and discovered that she could see out through the small, circular, frosty lens. She made out a shape. It came closer, moving through the foot-high snow of the field. Even though it moved closer, it was difficult to see because the pane frosted over and the day got darker at the same time. It looked like a coat hanger.

The coat-hanger figure looked around, appeared puzzled, then decided on the Bluebird house.

He didn't see her at first. "Hello!" he called from the doorway.

Shivers rippled down her arms. She banged her knuckles together and hustled flat-footed toward the coat hanger, her shoulders rotated in toward her chest, the backs of her hands brushing her sides.

"Toby."

"Hey, I didn't see you there."

They had trouble accommodating to each other. Sanjo tried to get his head in a hammerlock but couldn't reach. He had gotten taller. Toby tried to hug her but she had somehow turned around, and he wound up mugging her. They finally straightened themselves out, as would any embracing twosome of mutual regard and reasonable intent, and achieved the proper alignment.

"They said I could come even though visiting day isn't till tomorrow. I hitched out here. I would have come sooner but I had to wait a long time for my third ride."

Mrs. Brewster suggested that Sanjo sit in the lounge with her guest.

"So how do you like it here?" he asked.

Sanjo smiled her broadest, toothiest, gummiest smile. The good feeling, once in full swing, makes it tough to talk.

"Do they treat you good?"

"We treat her very good," called Mrs. Brewster through the quarter-inch Sheetrock.

They sat side by side. Sanjo pasted him to her eyes.

"I'm living home again," he said. Sanjo smiled. "You know

[251]

who told me you were here?" Sanjo waited. "Judy told me. How long you been here? Whoops, I forgot."

Sanjo hugged his arm tighter. "Sanjo make bows."

"Yeah? You make bows? That's pretty good."

"Read Bugs." So much for gingerbread. Back to basics.

"That's why I like you so much, Sanjo. All you want me to do is read Bugs. Everyone else bugs me."

Toby liked his joke. He leaned back in his chair and put his hands behind his head.

Sanjo wasn't interested in credo. She drummed her feet, flung her head from side to side, and smiled. "Read."

Toby rocked forward and laughed. "How did you know I brought you a comic?" He took a comic book out of his back pocket. It was rolled so tightly he had to pin back the pages with both hands to read. "I hope you like Road Runner." Now it was dark and Mrs. Brewster put on a light. A few other Bluebirds came to listen. Toby read. "This story is called "Fast and Furryous." See this guy with the black feathers and the chicken feet? His name is Road Runner and he goes *beep-beep, beep-beep.*"

"*Beep-beep,*" said Billy.

"This guy with the field glasses, he's a coyote. He wants to catch Road Runner. See how he's got a knife and fork? He wants to eat him up."

Toby read the whole book. The last page finished with the coyote slamming himself senseless into a brick wall.

"What time is it?"

"It's six thirty," said Mrs. Brewster.

"Oh, boy. I gotta get home. Shep and me made a deal with my parents. They're gonna be pissed." He put on his jacket. "So long, Sanjo, I'll see you when I can."

"Say good-bye to your friend."

"Good-bye," said Sanjo.

Toby left, crunching through the snow, a taller, thinner coat hanger, stringing out like a bean, his elongating body reaching for the man he would become.

12

Toby's last ride, in a van whose interior, including the steering wheel, was upholstered in synthetic zebra hide, put him close to Bergen Street by eight o'clock.

He walked the remaining blocks in the dark, frigid night. Even the few stars looked cold and glistened with a frosty sheen that would stick to any finger bold enough to touch it. Snow blanketed everything, supplying nitrates, sulfate, calcium, and potassium to the soil and treachery to the street. Since Bergen Street was a tertiary road, it was assigned low priority and given only the most cursory plowing. The plows left a slick of snow that iced over, turning the street into a rink upon which the Saturday-night traffic skidded, some of the cars sliding sideways like skaters. Most cars had to back up to the top of Bergen Street to get the running start they needed to catapult them over the corner. Those that didn't spun crazily over the ice, squealing like stuck pigs, for traction.

Across the street, Mr. Ryan, with a woolen scarf wrapped up to his nose, pulled Skippy around the block on his new leash. Skippy didn't want to walk and dug his claws in like a sphinx, but the sidewalk was slicked over too, and Skippy slid along like the cars.

Toby passed the hollow oak whose occupants clustered together for warmth, the head of one under the abdomen of the next like well organized, if not biased, group sex. The bees shaped themselves into a hollow sphere, with an outer crust, the insulating shell, shifting continuously inward, so that those on the outside, which were getting cold, could move within the sphere to shimmy their abdomens like belly dancers.

Toby passed the Bernatsky house and glanced in its direction. It wasn't the same without Sanjo. It had changed character, the way houses do when the composition of their occupants changes. With one room dark, the house was lit like a wink. Toby hurried home.

Inside, Poppy was kicking the washing machine, yelling "Nah!" with each kick, the way a karate expert accompanies his chops with "Heeyah!" He had learned that, if he gave it a good kick on the bottom near the leg, it wouldn't walk all over the basement floor. Good kicking also stopped it from shrieking.

Poppy had learned other essentials of his own survival in the past several weeks. He learned to buy frozen foods, to open cans, and to cook a little, nothing fancy, but no smoke-filled kitchens either. He learned that if he picked up after himself, he didn't have to punt his way through mounds of clothes and newspapers. He learned that if he hung up his towel and smoothed it out, it lasted for days. From Lou Green, he learned about a service for senior citizens, sponsored by the city, called Hostess on Wheels. For a nominal weekly fee, a truck painted to look like a chuck wagon delivered a hot bland evening meal in a disposable plastic tray. Although Poppy made his selections from a menu with ten choices, everything tasted alike. Poppy didn't fault the service. He thought it was his taste buds, declining at the same rate as other systems, that made Salisbury steak indistinguishable from fillet of haddock.

The same outfit offered a homemaker service. Once every two weeks, a woman came in to overhaul the house. No washing windows or moving furniture, only essentials like toilets, tub, sink, and refrigerator made sterile—or almost so—with a disinfectant spray and, when she had time, running a vacuum cleaner over the living room.

Poppy was still grieving for Ma, although with less anguish. He had reached the stage where he knew that he could live without her, and he was even able to think of some of the things she used to do that annoyed him. He only cried occasionally. Whether one has to make so many revolutions around the sun in order to feel better; whether the interval itself is effective, a period to think things over, like the time out given to a hockey player in the penalty box; whether it is the rest, a space to regenerate a part like the comb-footed spider, or an opportunity to marshal one's own resources, there are healing properties in time.

More painful than his present state of grief was the guilt about Sanjo that clutched him in the night, waking him from his sleep and causing him to lie and stare at the ceiling, agonizing over what he had done. When he did go back to sleep he had dreams of losing things.

Jerry persuaded him to stay away from Larkspur for at least a month in order to give Sanjo time to get adjusted. It was not hard to follow Jerry's advice during the day, since Poppy was so busy learning to take care of himself. It was at three o'clock in the morning that he would have gone rushing to Larkspur except that it was so dark and he was so tired.

Poppy had achieved a limited degree of competence. His socks still didn't come out even, but he chalked it up to one of those unexplained mysteries of life, like red moons, why cole slaw gives you gas, or women.

Who would believe that the telephone of a seventy-one-year-old man would never stop ringing? Somehow the women found out that Poppy was available. They offered to cook, to clean, to wash, to go to bed with him, and to take modified disco lessons (no backbends or dips) at the community center or any studio of his choice. Their object was not pity or consolation. It was commitment. Poppy was a statistical rarity among his age-mates, whose wives usually outlived them. He was an available, relatively intact, unattached male.

The women were relentless. They called and introduced themselves. Friends of friends called. Relatives called. Someone had someone in mind—if not themselves, then a friend. Sometimes they called, introduced themselves, and then introduced a third person, to whom they turned over the phone.

Poppy wasn't looking for anyone. They all made him nervous. They didn't seem to know they were in the position of supplicant and behaved like pool hustlers, calling their shots and his as well.

Some came clear across town through ice storms, sliding their cars onto his front lawn and saying that they were just passing through, which in one instance was almost the case.

A few were marvelously considerate and well informed. One widow, after preparing him a big dinner of his favorite foods, including kasha varnishkes, finished off with Courvoisier which she set in a brandy glass.

"Let it breathe," she said; then, "Sit. Digest. There can't be nothing doing for three hours yet on account of your heart, if you get my meaning." He did.

It was a new day.

They didn't all want to get married. One woman told him that they could live together. That way she wouldn't lose her Social Security check.

Poppy rearranged the wash around the agitator, after pulling free an undershirt that was stuck beneath the blades. The telephone rang. It is interesting that even though one would rather stay in the basement and talk to the washing machine, a ringing telephone has the authority of a summons. Poppy ran upstairs to answer it, stopping at the top step to lean against the doorframe and catch his breath. He had plenty of time. Sometimes the telephone rang for as many as thirty rings.

It was Minnie Hightower. It wasn't for herself she was asking. It was for her friend, Edna Salter. Edna was a wonderful woman, a marvelous conversationalist and an intellectual; she read hardcover books. Poppy said he didn't know. Minnie said Columbus took a chance. Poppy said he would think about it. Minnie

Hightower started to giggle and said she had to get off. When Poppy hung up, he seriously considered getting an unlisted number.

A new feeling began to emerge. Despite the attention he was getting, Poppy was lonely. He missed Sanjo. He wanted to know if she dressed warmly and if she was eating. Mainly he wanted to see her face. He told Jerry that he was going to Larkspur. Jerry asked if he wanted company. Poppy said no, he would go by himself.

A car came into Larkspur looking as if it were driving itself. It was a source of some wonder to Irene, who watched from the office window. As it got closer, she could see the rounded bald head of a man in the driver's seat.

"He's here," she said.

"Who?" asked Miss Finney.

"Sanjo's father."

Poppy stamped the snow off his feet. He went to the desk carrying a paper bag.

"I came to see her."

"Sanjo's in shop now," said Irene. "You may have to wait until they come out."

Poppy wondered where she was shopping and what she was buying.

Miss Finney leaned out of her closet office. "Mr. Bernatsky can go now if he likes. Show him where it is." She disappeared into her closet.

Irene took out a piece of paper and drew a series of circles.

"We're here, Mr. Bernatsky, and this"—she indicated a circle —"is shop. You're better off leaving your car where it is and walking."

Poppy took the paper with the circles and walked outside. He looked at the round stucco buildings. He turned the paper upside down to make the design conform to the buildings before him, decided he was holding it wrong, turned the paper around again, and set off in the direction of one of the circles. He went to the gym by mistake. He could tell it was the gym

[257]

because of the guy in the sweat suit.

Mr. Frank blew his whistle when he saw Poppy and threw the ball to him. "Catch it!"

"What? Oof!"

The ball caught him right under the sternum, the place where the sandbag lodged on occasion.

"Sorry, sir. I thought you'd want to participate."

It took a few seconds for Poppy to catch his breath. Mr. Frank came over.

"I'm really sorry. I thought you saw me."

Poppy made a sound like a harmonica. Mr. Frank looked worried.

"Shop." Poppy wheezed.

"What?"

"Where's the shop?"

"Oh, shop. Well, let's see. We're here." Mr. Frank traced circles on the floor with his whistle.

"Never mind the map, show me."

Mr. Frank pointed and blew his whistle. Poppy ran hunched and wary, his arms across his chest, his eyes on the ball until he reached the safety of the door.

Poppy finally came to the building designated as shop. He hoped this was it. He was getting tired of walking through the snow. The door was unlocked. He went in and saw the tallest man in the world. The man bent down.

"Can I help you?"

"I came to see Sanjo Bernatsky."

"Sanjo? She's right over there. Are you her grandfather?"

"Her father."

Mr. Leo led him past the front two tables, around which dozens of people sat making things. Billy Lawrence looked up from his cutting, his eyes peeping over the top of his cardboard box. A woman handed Poppy a dress hanger covered with woolen strings.

"See?"

Poppy inspected the hanger.

[258]

"We sell those," said Mr. Leo.

Poppy was wondering who bought them, when he saw her. She was sitting at a bobbin. She took a length of ribbon, locked it in place, moved it back and forth, back and forth, back and forth, snap, twist, close, tie off, and cut, then put the bow at her side.

"What is she doing?" asked Poppy.

"She's making bows for gift wrap," said Mr. Leo. "She's really very good at it."

Poppy stood quietly for a minute. He didn't want to interrupt the bow in progress. It was fascinating anyhow, since he always wondered how they did it. He waited for her to put it at her side.

"Hello, Sanjo."

Sanjo looked up. Her face cracked into a smile like an ice jam suddenly broken, wide, wide, lifting the tops of her cheeks until her eyes were almost shut, showing her reddened gums, her pegged teeth, and her furrowed tongue.

"Poppy!"

Poppy creaked down to the bench and hugged her. He was surprised to see that he was crying. Sanjo wasn't crying. She got his head in a hammerlock, smothered him against her chest, and crooned to it.

"Poppy come."

It was the second time in less than fifteen minutes that he had trouble breathing.

"Let go," he said. "Lemme see you."

"I'll make room for you," said Mr. Leo. He moved aside some green ribbons that belonged to the woman sitting next to Sanjo. The woman started to protest.

"Don't worry," said Mr. Leo, "I'm putting them right here."

Poppy sat down next to Sanjo.

"I got you something." He handed Sanjo the dripping paper bag. "It's chocolate-swirl ice cream, the kind you like."

"Boy oh boy!"

Mr. Leo came rushing over. He kept a very clean shop.

"Use this." It was his own coffee cup and spoon. "You're

getting it all over everything." He rushed the carton outside the door to harden again in the snow.

Sanjo ate the chocolate-swirl ice cream, lovingly folding the spoon into the plumpings of her mouth. "Pretty good," she said.

"I'm glad you like it. So what have you been doing?"

Poppy forgot himself for a minute. He was attempting to have a regular conversation.

"Uh-oh. Billy going," she said.

Sanjo was Mr. Leo's early warning system. Billy was on his way out the door.

"Oh, no, you don't!" yelled Mr. Leo.

"Sanjo make bows," said Sanjo.

"I saw."

Sanjo gave him one. It was red. He held it up.

"Mmmm. That's a pretty good bow." He wondered how she got it so neat. He put it in his pocket. "You ready for more ice cream?"

"Yes."

Poppy went outside. Mr. Leo was dragging in Billy Lawrence.

"I would appreciate it if you scooped that stuff outside. Don't bring it back in here."

"Okay," said Poppy. He returned with the coffee cup full of ice cream and sat while Sanjo ate it. He couldn't think of anything more to say. When she finished he said, "I got to go now."

Sanjo didn't scream this time, bite her finger, kick, or anything. The only thing she said was, "Stay, Poppy."

"I can't. You got work to do and I got to get home. Wear a coat outside. It's freezing."

Poppy left with the bow in his pocket. He kicked some snow over the ice-cream carton until it was covered over. By spring, who would care?

The community center was less crowded in the winter. Some of the regulars stayed home, afraid of falling and breaking a hip. Today only a handful came to watch the match.

[260]

Lou Green held out both fists.

Poppy pointed over the chessboard. "That one."

Lou Green opened his hand and exposed the black pawn.

"How come you always get white?" asked Poppy.

"What are you blaming me for? You picked."

They set up the board.

Lou Green was feeling pretty expansive. He leaned back in his chair. "You know my son, the doctor in Boston?"

They all knew which one.

"He got a new car. Drove down to see us. It's a beauty."

"You don't say," said Mike D'Angelo.

"The price of cars today," said Phil Donovan. "They're going crazy."

Poppy waited for a break in the accolades. He found one. "My daughter makes bows."

"What?" It was a polite response, the kind one would get if one were to say, "I think Alpha Centauri is sending us a delegation."

"She makes bows. Look." Poppy pulled out the red plastic ribbon, in the multiple convolutions that are integral to gift wrapping. There was silence.

Lou Green picked up the ball. "That's wonderful. You think it's easy?" he asked the others. They didn't know the question was going to be on the test. "You have to make like this, like this, then like this, somehow; I don't know myself, it's very hard to do."

"That's a nice bow," conceded Mike D'Angelo.

Poppy caught the pass. "A new car, huh?" he said. "Tell me, Lou, what kind is it?"

Poppy turned on the television. He was lonely and liked the company of voices. The television, unlike the women, didn't want an answer. Sometimes he left the television on after he went to sleep.

"Sunny day, come and play, everything's A-okay," sang a chorus of children's voices. How come the children on Bergen

[261]

Street never sounded like that? Poppy went to change the channel. He was crying again. He wondered if his mind was going. Why would a grown man cry at "Sesame Street"?

He went back into the kitchen, where he was encouraging his frozen hamburger meat to defrost by leaving it under the hotwater tap. "A-okay," he sang to the hamburger, as it began to soften and turn gray.

The children were outside sledding. Poppy saw them through the kitchen window. Like space engineers, they plotted their angle very carefully. They decided their best pitch was down the Wrights' lawn, across the street, and down the Bernatskys' driveway.

Poppy heard them shrieking, saw them shoot across the street, come to a stop where his driveway leveled off, tumble into the snow, pick themselves up, and begin all over again, carrying and dragging their sleds to the top of Mrs. Wright's lawn.

The littlest one was Penny. The only way he could recognize her was her size and the pale blond hair that wisped around her face. She had more trouble than the rest. The snow was deeper, relative to her body, and harder to trudge through. She was also bundled so thoroughly she had to hold her arms out, which made it difficult to maneuver the sled.

Every now and then some parent would come to yell about their trajectory across the open street. The children stopped, listened, bobbed their heads, and, when the parents went inside, resumed their original course, which by anyone's calculation was clearly the best.

A decision, even of the moment, is seldom as momentary as it seems. It usually has been cooking somewhere on a back burner. Poppy woke up one morning in the second week of January and turned off his back burner. It was the time of year people start to worry that maybe the seasons have changed their minds, that spring will never come back, and that they are living in a new ice age. It was also the time of year that gave primitive magic men their best trick and allowed them to say to a frightened populace, "If you want it to get warm again, fill my hut with your best furs, provide my family with grain for the rest of their lives, slaughter a pig, bury it feet up in the ground, and spring will return."

Poppy backed the car to the top of Bergen Street, got a running start, and, squealing and skidding, made the curve into the cross street.

The snow that covered Larkspur had dappled and dimpled like Mickey's thighs, the pockings filled with city dirt and country dust. Poppy pulled into the driveway, drew in his stomach, and walked into the office.

"What did you say?" asked Irene, who still had on her morning nursing cap.

"You heard me. I'm taking her out."

"For a visit, you mean."

"For good. She's coming home."

"Well, I don't know if you can do that."

"What is she, a savings certificate, I have to leave her for six months before I can make a withdrawal? She's my daughter. I can do anything I like."

"Miss Finney!"

Miss Finney came out of her closet. She was on her way anyway, having heard the whole story from where she sat. "Mr. Bernatsky, the deposit which you made at the time of Sanjo's registration, and which is considerable, is not refundable."

Poppy didn't think of the money being his in the first place. It was Runi's. "I don't care."

"Have you thought this over very carefully?"

"There's nothing to think over."

"Maybe you ought to try for a weekend."

"No, I need her home with me now—period."

"She's not a potted plant, you know. You can't just move her around like this."

"I know."

"I don't know," said Miss Finney.

[263]

"I do," said Poppy. "Get her ready."

Miss Finney told him to wait. She went into her office, dialed a number, and called him inside. "Someone wants to talk to you."

Poppy took the phone. It was Jerry. He was screaming so hard Poppy couldn't make out what he was saying.

"Take it easy, you'll live longer. . . . Yeh, I know what I'm doing. . . . Uh-huh, I know that. I don't care. . . . I know two thousand dollars is a lot of money. . . . No, I'm not feeling dizzy. Listen, I'm doing it and that's that. . . . You saying I'm incompetent? Is that what you're saying? Tell me if that's what you're saying. . . . Well, it sounds like it. . . . Now. I'm doing it now. That's that. I don't have time to talk." Poppy hung up the phone. Sanjo came by her stubbornness naturally.

Poppy walked to Bluebird with Miss Finney, who said, "It would be a terrible thing to take her home and change your mind again."

"It's not going to happen."

"How can you be so sure? Why is it you think you can take care of her now when you couldn't two months ago?"

"I miss her."

Sanjo was helping Mrs. Brewster clean up. The Bluebirds made their beds and hung their towels out so they would stay fresh longer. Some vacuumed and swept. Sanjo liked to dust. She had a cloth that she ran over any surface she could find.

Sanjo took the rag out to shake it the way Mrs. Brewster showed her, waving it like a signal flag. She saw him coming with Miss Finney.

"Poppy." Her smile cracking the rind of ice again, she hung her head down and smiled into her chest.

"Come on, *tatela*, we're going home."

Mrs. Brewster helped them pack the cat pictures, her clothing, and a potholder that her arts and crafts teacher had made. After they double-checked the closet, all the nightstands, and under the bed, Mrs. Brewster, Miss Finney, and some Bluebirds hugged her good-bye. Mr. Fred said, "I'm very happy for you," in his metallic voice, signing, at the same time, a series of delicate fingerings to his eye, face, and chest, where he made tiny feathery strokings.

Sanjo brushed out from her chest in the same way and said to Mr. Fred, "Happy."

John came running over from Redbird when he heard the news from Billy Lawrence, who ran around like Paul Revere, telling everyone that Sanjo was going home.

John helped carry the suitcases to Poppy's car and put them in the trunk for him. "Mr. Bernatsky, Sanjo is used to a lot of people."

"Okay."

"What I mean is, she needs company, you know?"

"I know."

John hugged Sanjo. "'Bye, buddy."

Sanjo stroked his beard. "John pretty."

"No one ever hung that one on me before."

Then Sanjo attached her head to Poppy's shoulder and walked with him to the car. Everyone waved from the windows. It was too cold to go outside. They drove out of Larkspur.

Poppy was feeling wonderful. The good feeling made him as buoyant as if he had air bags in his armpits. Sometimes when good feeling gets going, it can lift someone off the ground and make him do crazy things.

"You want a cat?" asked Poppy.

"Bigboy."

"No, it won't be Bigboy. It'll be another cat. Want one?"

Sanjo banged her knuckles together and sang to her chest, "Halloween coming to town."

They drove to the animal shelter. A little boy, crying on a cat flopped listlessly in his arms, went ahead of them. His mother followed after him with a worried look. She knew this was a funeral and hadn't told him yet. Poppy and Sanjo had to wait.

Soon a woman called them to the desk. "You're looking for a pet to adopt?"

Poppy nodded.

[265]

"A dog or a cat?"

"We want a cat," said Poppy.

"Bigboy," said Sanjo.

"I can't guarantee we'll have the size you want," said the lady, "but follow me and I'll see what I can do."

She led them past a large room full of barking dogs to the section reserved for cats. Cages and cages of cats, stacked three deep, faced them on all sides. The cats were mewing, yowling, purring, yawning, and scrutinizing them.

"Two cats," said Sanjo.

"What do you mean two? There are fifty thousand cats in here."

They were both wrong. The actual count was one hundred and forty-seven, with eight destined for the Big Sleep—nine, actually, after the cat brought in by the little boy was evaluated.

"Take your time," said the lady. "Look around. We want you to be sure and not sorry."

"What about this one?" asked Poppy. He had his eye on a gray cat with soft fur.

"That's a nice one, folks," said the lady. "It's part Persian." She put her hand in the cage. "See how the fur fluffs out on my finger?"

Sanjo didn't see it.

There was a cat in a middle cage. Danny Wright would have described it as dumb-looking. Certainly it had no redeeming features. It was ribboned in grays and browns. It had yellow eyes. The fur was short and in one place seemed to be growing out. One ear drooped. On closer inspection, a piece of it was gone. It came close to the mesh of the cage.

"*Prrt,*" said the cat.

"This is a nice-looking cat. Look, Sanjo."

Sanjo was already transfixed.

"What about this one?" Poppy was seduced by a sleek little black cat with a white blaze on its nose.

"This one is still a kitten, aren't you, baby?" said the lady. It yawned and flexed a pink tongue the size of a zinnia petal.

Sanjo and the gray-brown cat were nose to nose through the mesh.

"It looks like your wife has made her choice."

"No, she hasn't," said Poppy. "We don't want that one. It's damaged."

"He's not damaged," said the lady. "A little the worse for wear, but a fine healthy cat."

"Is he all right? He doesn't look all right."

"What's the matter with him?"

"His ear is funny."

"He was in a fight. That's because he's a tom, isn't that so, fella? All our animals are checked. Outside of the fact that he's a little plain and has a pinched ear, he's a perfect, healthy pet."

Sanjo was in love.

"Get away from that cage," said Poppy. "That's a bad-looking cat. We'll get one of the other ones."

"There's a definite advantage to the one she likes. He's had all his shots. You just have to come in once a year for a booster."

"I want him," said Sanjo.

The air bags had him too high to get into an argument. It's hard to fight with your feet off the ground. If that was what she wanted, that was what she would have.

"Are you sure?" asked Poppy, with a fond and lingering eye still on the gray part-Persian and the sleek black kitten with the white blaze, a might-have-been, still-could-be look, the kind one gives over the head of one's date to a dynamite someone else on the next bar stool.

Sanjo and the cat were already in conversation.

"*Mirreee,*" said the cat.

The lady took the cat out of the cage. It was the worst-looking cat Poppy had ever seen.

"Come and meet your new mommy and daddy."

Sanjo smiled and took Poppy's hand. "Boy oh boy!"

"If you take one of our cats, you have to sign a paper promising to get it neutered."

"What do you mean?"

"Sterilized."

Her too. It was everybody's business.

They put the cat in a cardboard box with holes in it.

Sanjo wanted to sit next to the cat, but Poppy wouldn't let her. He put the box in the back seat. "You sit in front with me."

The cat yowled all the way home, an eerie noise, developed deep in the recesses of its larynx, resonated in its thorax, catapulted past its throat, and emerging as a spine-cracking, bone-ringing, skin-lifting wail. Poppy's air bags began to deflate when his scalp shifted.

"Talk to it. Maybe it'll shut up."

"Hullo, cutie."

"Yawrowrer."

Poppy brought in Sanjo's suitcases one at a time while Sanjo walked in and out of every room in the house with the cat in her arms, checking everything to see if it was still where it was when she left. When she was assured of the relative permanence of her home, Poppy said, "Let him down. Maybe he needs to go to his litter box."

She put the cat down. It sniffed its way around the house, with Sanjo close behind, sometimes darting, sometimes creeping, sneaking under the sofa, and once jumping straight up in the air in an amazing action that lifted it horizontally in a split second, the distance of two feet, as if it were attached to sky wires.

When it scrambled up a drape, Poppy began to lose his patience. They stood trying to coax it down while it clung to the valance. "Get down from there, you animal!" yelled Poppy, shaking the bottom of the drape.

The cat dug in and hung by its claws like a mountain climber clinging by his pitons. "Don't make me nervous," said Sanjo to the cat.

Poppy went into the kitchen. "Oh, boy, wait'll you see what I got for you." He clattered the dish on the floor, and made four revolutions around the can with the electric opener. "Ps-s-s-s-s. Ps-s-s-s-s. Ps-s-s-s-s. Call him, Sanjo."

[268]

Sanjo did better than that. When the cat jumped down, she grabbed him in a massive scoop the way she learned to catch a ball from Mr. Frank, brought him into the kitchen, and put him down next to his dish.

The cat hesitated. Sanjo put his face into his pulverized fish heads.

"Eat," she advised.

The cat sputtered, looked offended, backed away from the dish, and fastidiously began to clean his face.

"He has to have a name," said Poppy.

"Bugs."

"We can't call him that. He's a cat. That's a rabbit's name."

"Bugs."

The cat made a test with a paw. When it came away unsoiled and he was confident that his face was clean, he went back to his dish and polished off its contents.

"How about Browney?"

Sanjo stared into her chest.

"Okay, what about Bigboy, like your old cat?"

Sanjo was silent.

"Or Van Gogh? His ear was off too."

Sanjo shook her head.

"You really want it to be called Bugs?"

"Uh-huh."

Poppy sighed and went to spoon out another blob of cat food. This one looked like an eater.

The word was out. Bergen Street knew that Sanjo was home. From their mailboxes, their newspapers frozen solid on the sidewalk, their cars, and their windows, they all stared in the direction of the Bernatsky house, like the faithful in Saint Peter's Square waiting for the puff of smoke.

The doorbell rang. It was Mrs. Cervitano with Bruno's wife carrying a bundle. Poppy answered the door.

Mrs. Cervitano came in and kissed him. "You're a good person, a saint. Where is she?"

[269]

Sanjo stood in the dining room while Bugs sanded her ankles with his fur.

Immigrants who steamed into New York Harbor looked at the Statue of Liberty the way Mrs. Cervitano looked at Sanjo.

"Sanjo." She smothered her in her tears. "How are you?"

"Mrs. Cervy."

"She calls me Cervy," she said to Bruno's wife. "So what's new, eh? Look what we brought to show you. Take his clothes off, he's going to catch a cold. You like him? His name is Paul."

Bruno's wife began to peel her baby. It was an embarrassment of riches. Sanjo didn't know where to look first. The cat ran, leaped in the air in a grand jété, and continued on his way.

"What's that?" asked Mrs. Cervitano.

"Sanjo's cat," said Poppy. He rubbed his scalp. He couldn't bring himself to say Bugs.

"Watch he doesn't sit on Paulie's face and smother him," she said to Bruno's wife.

Sanjo stared at the unveiling of Paulie. Raphael made his cherubs like that, chunks of fat folding over creases, dimpled, golden-toned pink skin, with dark brown eyes and red-brown ringlets coiled upon his head. He was already so complicated, so beautiful, it was hard to imagine that a little over a year ago he was a blastocyst, a tiny collection of a few cells shaped like a basketball. He was brand new, as crisp as a shirt still folded with tissue paper, sized, clean, and unmarked.

"Little baby," said Sanjo.

Mrs. Cervitano sat on the couch with Bruno's wife beside her. The baby, held against his mother's chest, kicked his legs, leaned back, and wriggled his body like a tadpole.

"Put him against the pillow. Show how he sits," his grandmother said.

"Is he wearing rubber pants?" Poppy didn't know that rubber pants had long since been replaced by other, more efficient water-repellent materials.

"He's all right," said Mrs. Cervitano.

Bruno's wife leaned her baby against the pillow.

The baby steadied, swayed, tipped to one side, and slid over, like Sanjo's old Toby Tippy toy. Bruno's wife righted her baby. He stayed for a minute, then tipped to the other side.

Sanjo stood in front of Mrs. Cervitano, watching the baby with her chin resting on her chest.

"You wanna hold him?" asked Mrs. Cervitano.

Bruno's wife held her breath.

"Here. Sit down. You can hold him."

Sanjo banged her knuckles together. Some days, as any astrologer will tell you, are perfect. All the planets spin together in harmony, the sun is in its right house, and everything is fine. She sat on the couch. Mrs. Cervitano put the baby in her arms, placing the baby and Sanjo as carefully as an artist arranging a still-life. The baby stared at Sanjo, looked for its mother, was satisfied she was still there, turned back to look at Sanjo, arched his back, swung out a fist in a random swipe, caught some of her hair, and pulled.

"Oh, no," said Sanjo. She was smiling.

"Oh, you're such a bad boy. Pulling on Sanjo. Don't pull on Sanjo. She's our friend." Mrs. Cervitano disengaged the tiny fingers from their prize. The baby made an explosive sound, an important precursor to speech. The baby said, "Ba."

The baby's mother, gasping like a fish out of water, made movements to retrieve her child. "He said mama," she claimed.

But Mrs. Cervitano, who was blocking her at every turn, said, "No, he didn't. He said, I wanna stay with Sanjo."

Sanjo put her face in the baby's neck and inhaled a deep draft of the powder that had mixed with the baby's chemistry, creating an idiosyncratic scent, a private blend of soap, talc, sodium chloride, potassium chloride, and urea. The baby made rapid high-pitched exhalations, squeals that would later become laughter.

"Okay. We gotta go now. Dress him."

Bruno's wife laid the baby on his back and began to layer him for the return trip across Bergen Street.

[271]

The cat jumped on the couch and stopped within inches of the baby's face. The baby stopped kicking and froze. He eyed the cat intently while his stomach began to rise and fall. His mother recognized the signs immediately. She picked the baby up on his first cry and held him away from the cat.

"Paulie. Paulie."

The cry was stopped in mid-expression.

"I made some manicotti," said Mrs. Cervitano to Poppy. "I'll bring you a nice dish."

"We got Hostess on Wheels."

"So what? You can put it in the icebox and have it for lunch."

Bruno's wife held her baby up to inspect him for damage. Sanjo stood in front of them and clapped her hands.

"One," she said.

The baby smiled and swung out a fist again, like a crane sending out a wrecking ball against a building. It went in a general, but not a specific, direction. Sanjo put her head against his hand to help it. The baby's fist closed upon her hair.

"Look at him!" said Mrs. Cervitano. "Oh, you little devil. He's something, this one."

"Did you see this?" Poppy pulled the bow out of his pocket.

"What's that?"

"Sanjo made it."

"No. You made this? This beautiful bow?"

"Uh-huh."

Mrs. Cervitano crossed herself. "Can I have it, little sweetheart? We'll put it on the carriage."

Mrs. Cervitano and Bruno's wife left with their bundle and the bow.

It was an exhausting day. At least the telephone didn't ring. Toby came over in the late afternoon with Judy. They stood in the living room in their coats, their glove-encased hands at their sides, their eyes shining, their skin glowing from the cold which flecked promontories like cheeks, chins, and noses with blush. They leaned in toward each other, not touching, just pulsing in each other's direction, like interlocking puzzle pieces about to snap together.

The cat arched its back to meet Sanjo's hand. "That's a neat cat," said Toby.

"Him Bugs."

Toby turned to Poppy. He didn't hear her. "Is she home for good?"

"You think the cat's for me?"

Toby was already beginning to translate the veiled statements of adults. "Oh, wow! That's great!"

Judy was detached from the conversation. Her thoughts had leaped ahead to the Stebbinses' unlocked heated garage.

Toby pulled a comic book out of his pocket.

"Read Bugs," said Sanjo.

"I can't, Sanjo, me and Judy gotta go to the store before it gets dark. Maybe you could read to her, Mr. Bernatsky." He handed Poppy the comic book.

Poppy turned it over in his hand like a chimpanzee with the Rosetta Stone.

"The stories are good," said Toby. "Well, we'll see you later."

They hesitated for a moment, then turned in tandem and left.

"Good-bye," said Sanjo. She waved to them through the window while the cat on the sill continued to arch and bob under her other hand, demonstrating its pleasure in ecstatic excesses.

"Sit down. I'll read," said Poppy. Sanjo sat next to him on the couch. The cat stayed close to her knees, brushing against her and revving up its purr.

Poppy started off slow; then, as he became more confident with the material, picked up speed. " 'The snares of the trapster. You guessed it! Cap is in one of the special workout rooms which were constructed for his training by Tony Stark, weapons director of Shield. The indefatigable avenger devotes every spare minute to these dangerous devastating exercises.' You like this?"

"Read."

The cat jumped into Sanjo's lap, turned around once with its haunches elevated, settled like a beanbag, closed its eyes, and vibrated itself to sleep.

[273]

Poppy continued. A few times he was diverted by advertisements for switchblade combs, a mini-skull flashlight, and a special offer asking if he wanted to be a skilled locksmith.

"'Captain America, helpless? Don't ever count on it.'"

As stories went, it wasn't too bad. Once or twice he forgot and read ahead silently to himself, but Sanjo never let him get too far. She always reminded him. "Read."

Outside, stirring under the snow, was a purple crocus, surrounded by its leaves like a ballerina with her arms folded over her head. It worked its way upward, after having broken free of the outer shell of the corm, its starchy storage bin. The crocus, with a minimum of chromosomes, only eight, was metabolically inexpensive, yet, with nothing to spare, could not afford error. It was getting ready for its spring appearance and rustled through the snow to push aside a pebble in its way.